GIVE  MERCY

GIVE *me* MERCY

C.B. O'MALLEY

Copyright © 2024 C. B. O'Malley. All rights reserved.

No part of this publication may be reproduced, stored in a retrieval system or transmitted in any form or by any means, electronic, mechanical, photocopying, recording or otherwise, without prior permission of Halo Publishing International.

The views and opinions expressed in this book are those of the author and do not necessarily reflect the official policy or position of Halo Publishing International. Any content provided by our authors are of their opinion and are not intended to malign any religion, ethnic group, club, organization, company, individual or anyone or anything.

No generative artificial intelligence (AI) was used in the writing of this work. The author expressly prohibits any entity from using this publication to train AI technologies to generate text, including, without limitation, technologies capable of generating works in the same style or genre as this publication.

For permission requests, write to the publisher, addressed "Attention: Permissions Coordinator," at the address below.

Halo Publishing International
7550 W IH-10 #800, PMB 2069,
San Antonio, TX 78229

First Edition, November 2024
ISBN: 978-1-63765-684-6
Library of Congress Control Number: 2024919023

The information contained within this book is strictly for informational purposes. Unless otherwise indicated, all the names, characters, businesses, places, events and incidents in this book are either the product of the author's imagination or used in a fictitious manner. Any resemblance to actual persons, living or dead, or actual events is purely coincidental.

Halo Publishing International is a self-publishing company that publishes adult fiction and non-fiction, children's literature, self-help, spiritual, and faith-based books. We continually strive to help authors reach their publishing goals and provide many different services that help them do so. We do not publish books that are deemed to be politically, religiously, or socially disrespectful, or books that are sexually provocative, including erotica. Halo reserves the right to refuse publication of any manuscript if it is deemed not to be in line with our principles. Do you have a book idea you would like us to consider publishing? Please visit www.halopublishing.com for more information.

IN DEDICATION...

TO THOSE WHO ARE HOPELESS, LOST, AND BROKEN.
I SEE YOUR BROKEN PIECES AMONGST THE RUBBLE OF MY OWN.
YOU MAY BE LOST AND HOPELESS—JUST KNOW YOU'RE NOT ALONE.

TO THOSE WHO FIND THEMSELVES AT THE END OF THEIR OWN ROPE.
I KNOW YOUR JOINTS ACHE, MUSCLES SHAKE, AND EXHAUSTION
SETTLES DEEP INTO THE BONE.
I KNOW THIS BECAUSE I FEEL IT WHILE I HANG THERE, TOO—
NOT QUITE READY TO LET GO.

TO THOSE WHO'VE FOUND ROCK BOTTOM AND ARE TEMPTED TO CALL IT HOME.
I PUT THE KEYS UNDER THE WELCOME MAT.
YES, I TOO HAVE BEEN THERE BEFORE.

TO THOSE WHO NEED REASSURANCE OR JUST A HAND TO HOLD,
THE HOPE OF THIS STORY IS TO REMIND YOU THAT YOU ARE NOT ALONE.

STAY STRONG.
BE STUBBORN.
DON'T. LET. GO.
KNOW IT CAN GET BETTER...
I PROMISE.

TAKE THIS AS MY WAY OF OFFERING A HAND FOR YOU TO HOLD.

CONTENTS

PROLOGUE — 15
  PART I: PIECES AMONGST THE ASHES — 19
    CHAPTER 1 — 21
    CHAPTER 2 — 30
    CHAPTER 3 — 38
    CHAPTER 4 — 47
    CHAPTER 5 — 55
    CHAPTER 6 — 67
    AIDEN

    CHAPTER 7 — 81
    MERCY

    CHAPTER 8 — 85
    MERCY

    CHAPTER 9 — 99
    AIDEN

    CHAPTER 10 — 107
    MERCY

    CHAPTER 11 — 112
    MERCY

    CHAPTER 12 — 124
    AIDEN

    CHAPTER 13 — 131
    MERCY

CHAPTER 14 MERCY	141
CHAPTER 15 MERCY	153
CHAPTER 16 AIDEN	157
CHAPTER 17 MERCY	163
CHAPTER 18 MERCY	177
CHAPTER 19 AIDEN	185
CHAPTER 20 MERCY	191
CHAPTER 21 AIDEN	194
CHAPTER 22 MERCY	196
PART II: PIECES AMONGST THE ASHES	207
CHAPTER 23 AIDEN	208
CHAPTER 24 MERCY	215
CHAPTER 25 MERCY	232

CHAPTER 26   251
AIDEN

CHAPTER 27   252
MERCY

CHAPTER 28   262
AIDEN

CHAPTER 29   276
MERCY

CHAPTER 30   276
AIDEN

CHAPTER 31   296
MERCY

CHAPTER 32   299
MERCY

CHAPTER 33   303
MERCY

CHAPTER 34   307
AIDEN

CHAPTER 35   313
MERCY

CHAPTER 36   317
AIDEN

CHAPTER 37   324
MERCY

CHAPTER 38   329
MERCY

CHAPTER 39 MERCY	336
CHAPTER 40 MERCY	342
CHAPTER 41 AIDEN	350
CHAPTER 42 MERCY	359
CHAPTER 43 MERCY	367
CHAPTER 44 AIDEN	372
CHAPTER 45 MERCY	387
CHAPTER 46 AIDEN	394
CHAPTER 47 MERCY	398
CHAPTER 48 MERCY	404
CHAPTER 49 AIDEN	408
CHAPTER 50 MERCY	417
STAY CONNECTED	423

We are a way for the universe to know itself. Some part of our being knows this is where we came from. We long to return. And we can, because the cosmos is also within us. We're made of star stuff.

—*Carl Sagan*

PROLOGUE

Do you remember the first time you realized that life ends? I do. I was around the age of five when the realization struck, robbing me of any blissful and naive view of life I had. Despite its having been at least twenty-five years since this core memory was formed, every detail remains clear in my mind. I would even argue that it heavily influenced the person I've become.

The core memory started innocently with my five-year-old self scrubbing my scalp with more shampoo than I needed. I remember tapping my toes in the water, suds pooling around my pruning toes, and belting out the lyrics to my favorite song at the time, "Hakuna Matata."

I held the last note proudly, only to have it abruptly cut off by a hiss that escaped from my mouth as some of the extra shampoo found its way into my eyes. With my vibrantly blue eyes squeezed shut, I reached from behind the shower curtain, grasping for a towel to bury my face in to alleviate the burning sensation that was building. Proud of myself at the time for not calling Mom for help, I carried on with the task at hand, circling back to the beginning of another rendition of "Hakuna Matata."

In this moment of little me feeling strong and independent, my imagination took control, and I wondered about the ultimate goal of growing up. Having recently graduated from baths to showers, I knew adulthood was only right around the corner for me, right? I began to go through a mental checklist of other things I had recently accomplished, further supporting my self-appointed change in status from child to adult.

I had already started losing some of my baby teeth. I was about to start kindergarten in the fall. Plus, I'd finally mastered the craft of drawing lions and—in my opinion—creating some of the finest Lite-Brite displays. I was making progress with my art every day, which gave me the confidence to feel that I could be a rising star in the art world. Pride beamed from my little body as I continued to daydream of my "near" future under the warmth of the running shower.

This got me thinking about all the cool things adults can do. There were no limits that I could think of once a certain level of adulthood was reached. Bedtime? Not necessary. School? Completed. Ice cream for dinner? Who's going to tell me no? This stream of innocent and illogical thoughts any five-year-old might have continued on until my mind took a sudden and unintended hard-right turn. Originally thinking I had eternity to live out this incredible future I had planned, a disturbing thought shook me back to reality.

See, my mother had me at a young age. At the age of five, I was not only lucky enough to have family who lived close by, but also young enough to have been babysat by my great-grandmother. At this point in my life, I had yet to experience even the death of a pet. So can you imagine my little five-year-old mind thinking of all the things I would be able to do as I grew older, only to have the awful realization strike that, no matter what, time does run out. There was no such thing as eternity for me…or for anyone.

As the water flowing from the showerhead started to turn cold, I could feel hot tears roll down my cheeks. The thoughts in my head started to suffocate me, sending me into a panic. I tried to soothe myself with answers I wanted to be true. *If I never get in a car, I won't ever get in a crash, and then I won't die. Right? If I never get sick and have to go to the hospital, I won't die. Right? People only die when bad things happen to them…right?*

My breathing became labored, and that burst of confidence and pride I felt only minutes ago began to wash down the drain with the last of the soap washed from my body. I knew the answers to those questions. I just didn't want to accept them. And so, I did what any five-year-old would do when faced with the hard, scary truth of life. With blue lips from the now-freezing water, I briefly snapped out of my downward spiral just long enough to leap out of the shower, wrap a towel around my shaking body, and run straight for Mom.

Gasping for air, through sobs and snot, I found my mother vacuuming in the living room. Mother senses tingling, she proceeded to whip around to face her waterworks, snotty mess of a child. Kneeling down and wrapping her arms around me, she asked with concern in her voice, "What happened?"

Looking up at my mother through bloodshot eyes, I wiped my nose using the corner of my towel and through sobs asked my question I already knew the answer to, "Does everyone really die?"

Just like that, I had gone from thinking myself a hopeful and enthusiastic self-proclaimed young adult singing about having no worries for the rest of my days, to a trembling child having nothing *but* worries for the rest of my self-actualized, time-limited life.

PART I

PIECES AMONGST THE ASHES

CHAPTER 1

BEEP! BEEP! BEEP! BEEP!

I feel around for my phone, attempting to hit Snooze one more time before facing whatever sweet hell the day has in store for me. One hand pressed to my forehead, the other finally finding the source of that godforsaken abrasive sound, I silence my phone and stumble out of bed. Still feeling the lingering sensation of a hangover resulting from a forced night out two days before, I groan as I drag my sorry ass out of bed. Will I ever learn that my body simply can't tolerate the amount of alcohol it takes to relax my restless mind or ease my social anxiety? Eh, probably never.

I pop three Advil, wash them down with a swig of water that has been sitting on my bedside table for a few days and nights now, and let out an exasperated, *"Fuuuck* this." Both hands now pressed against my eye sockets, I rub the sleep out of my eyes and stagger my way to the bathroom. *This is what happens when an introvert has extroverts for friends. I should have just stayed home where I belong.*

I flick the light on and wince at the woman staring back at me. Dull blonde hair sits like a rat's nest on the top of my head in a tangle of knots, instead of the perfectly crafted, messy bun I had assembled two nights before. Dark circles accentuate the multiple bags under each half-opened, bleary eye. And it doesn't take twenty-twenty vision to know that my skin is splotchy and oily. I don't even want to know what my breath smells like. I suppose an entire Sunday nursing a hangover in bed and a night of self-loathing, watching trash TV until Mr. Sandman came around to knock me out of my misery, will do that to one's appearance.

Shower. I need a very, very hot shower to burn off the remnants of this past weekend. A quick twenty-second final rinse of biting-cold water to shock the system might help, too. Standing under the showerhead, my teeth chatter as I wait for the heat of the water to rise. Once the water reaches a scalding temperature, I attempt to wash away the sins of the weekend, allowing the water to burn and wash away the soap I've aggressively scrubbed into my skin. *Clean.* I keep scrubbing in an attempt to rid myself of an invisible layer of ick I so desperately need to cleanse myself of.

I watch the soapy water collect around my toes as it rinses off my body and circles the drain. Knowing I'm already running behind schedule, I flip the handle of the shower to Cold and sharply inhale as icy water strikes my bare skin. I begin to count down from twenty, increasing the tempo with each number, "Five…fourthreetwoone," the last four seconds coming out in one quick breath. Blindly reaching for the towel, I hold my face directly under the last bit of cold water before turning the shower off completely.

This time, the woman staring back at me in the mirror doesn't look close to death, as she did pre-shower. Don't get me wrong; I still look rough, but not nearly as bad as when I woke up. Good enough for a Monday. Definitely good enough for my type of clients.

I slap some makeup on, trying to conceal the bags under my eyes and to bring a bit of life back to my face. Instead of fighting my hair, I quickly throw it into a loose braid that dangles down between my shoulder blades, after which I exchange my towel for scrubs.

A quick peek at my phone lets me know that I have about ten minutes before I need to run out the door. Not enough time to make myself breakfast, but definitely enough time to throw some coffee on and look for my favorite travel mug.

With heavy feet, I trudge my way to the kitchen, my mind begging me to go back to bed. Once down the stairs, I meander first to the TV. I turn the news on to fill the looming silence, then continue my morning's quest for much-needed coffee.

I can't handle silence—especially in this current state of self-inflicted suffering—even if it's for a brief moment of time. Silence gives the voice in my head an excuse to start spiraling out of control. So I do everything I possibly can to stay busy and keep the voice distracted. Because of that voice, I've become skilled at running my body ragged by working too much, drinking too much, or hyper-fixating on something until I inevitably lose interest. I guess that's what happens when you've had about two decades to try and figure out this invisible, unwanted illness I've been burdened by since I was young.

This is why at the age of thirty, while most of my friends are settling down and getting all their ducks in a row, I'm out being a train wreck of a human being still trying to figure shit out. My version of getting ducks in a row is more akin to a constant battle of corralling a flock of chickens—all of whom have had their heads lobbed off and are frantically running around a busy highway. Fun, I know.

Whatever fills the silent and empty spaces in my life, I grab on to with teeth and nails; otherwise, I'd be subject to the unforgiving chaos that is my mind. Whether it be good for me or bad, I will sink my claws into it. So long as whatever *it* is distracts my mind from wandering and forces the voice in my head to shut up, it's good enough for me.

"Shit, I need to go." I grab the keys to my truck, fill my mug with coffee and cream, take a cursory look around the open-layout cottage I call home, and head on out the door.

The veterinary clinic I'm currently working at is only a fifteen-minute drive from home. Fifteen minutes I have to myself to enjoy my coffee and blast the latest audiobook or podcast I'm listening to through the speakers of my truck—one of the few nice pieces of property I have left to my name. Occasionally, I throw on some music, but that is only on my good days. The days when I know my mind is at peace enough to enjoy the music, instead of disregard it completely or use it as the soundtrack to whatever anxiety-riddled mess my mind would like to come up with or remind me of next.

This being the start of a new week, and because I'm still recovering from the weekend, a podcast is queued up and ready to play. I start down the road, on my way to work, when the story of a brutal murder is interrupted by an incoming call.

Before I'm able to say hello, I'm greeted with, *"Finally! Proof you are alive!"* Tess is on the other end, and I can hear the slightest twinge of concern mixed into the usual chipper cadence of her voice.

"Ha. Very funny. You knew the consequences I would face after you dragged me out to the bar the other night. I have no guilt about my absence or lack of texting you all Sunday," I say to her, knowing that I'm lying just a bit. I do, of course, feel guilty for not reaching out to Tess. I know she would have preferred that I at least check in with her the day after our night out. Unfortunately, everything hurt in that moment, and the only thing I could stand to do was bury myself in my blankets and self-pity.

Ever since the divorce, Tess has been trying her best to get me out of the house, as if I were her puppy that needed a lesson in socializing. I know she means well, and I love her so much for all that she does for me, but I'm the last person in her life she needs to worry about. The last person in her life *worth* worrying about.

"Well, just be happy I didn't come kicking down your door to make sure you weren't dead!" Tess huffs.

I snort at her purposefully dramatic claim and hear the soft chuckle she's let escape. If only she knew what the voice in my head spewed that entire night out and following day. *She might be joking now, but it's not like my death is out of the realm of possibilities...*

"But seriously, Mercy. You pulled an Irish goodbye on us, and all I get from you is a text at midnight saying 'home' and thanking me for a 'grape night out.' Really?"

"Okay, you knew what I meant—"

"Yes, yes. I know. I know. Anywho, that's not why I'm calling."

Tess is always good like that. Never one to hold a grudge or let petty things get in the way of our friendship. I always worry how my actions, words, or even tone of voice affect others—a perk of my nagging anxiety. I can say a simple hello to someone and end up overthinking and overanalyzing how that person may now feel about me. It is exhausting, to say the least. Not with Tess, though. Tess is what I refer to as my comfort person.

"Sooooooo, what did you think about Bert?" She drags out the "so" in a way that makes me know she's expecting a rave review.

"His name is Bert," I put it simply.

"*Oh! Come. On!* He was TOTALLY into you!" Tess exclaims in a show of both support and disbelief at my lack of enthusiasm on the matter.

"He wanted to know what my five-year goals were after watching me throw back two shots of whiskey. Talk about not knowing how to read a person." I turn onto the main road, now only seven minutes away from work. "I didn't know you were forcing me out on a job interview, and not a 'much-needed girls' night out' you claimed it was going to be," I bite back while internally contemplating if I have enough time to stop for a breakfast sandwich. My stomach has decided that now is the time for it to remind me it's been fueled only by liquor, followed by water, saltine crackers, and Advil.

"Someone woke up and chose crankiness today." I can hear Tess's amusement behind her sarcasm.

"Look, I'm sorry. My morning definitely didn't start bright and early with birds chirping, a gentle breeze waking me, and sun salutations," I say, my voice a bit brash. *Food.* I definitely need food.

"Namaste, Snow White," Tess responds in a comically serious tone.

"I'm sorry, Tess. You know how I get when I'm hungry." I chuckle through a smirk, trying to lighten my own mood.

"Not only are you hungry and obviously still tired, but you're apparently blind and not thinking clearly, too. Not only does Bert have his shit together, but did you…did you actually *look* at the man?" Tess follows her question up with an awestruck sigh.

"All right, all right, calm your tits, Tess. Why don't you go for him, then?" I joke.

A brief moment of silence makes me think the call dropped, but then I hear Tess clear her throat before responding, "I'm not exactly on the market anymore…" Her voice trails off as if she is contemplating whether or not to tell me something. "Doesn't mean I can't appreciate a good view when I see one!" she continues, her voice chipper again.

I can't see her, but I can picture the wink I know she just gave to accentuate the statement. Not quite ready to open the can of worms I believe Tess to be hiding from me, I avoid inquiring about why she isn't "exactly on the market anymore."

I pull through the drive-through at the local coffee shop and order my usual. The warm smell of a freshly baked croissant stuffed with bacon, egg, and cheese wafts through the cab of my truck.

In a voice a bit more sincere, Tess continues, "On a slightly serious note though…"

"Oh boy. Lay it on me."

"Honestly, Mercy. I'm just…I'm just a concerned friend, is all. I just miss you." I can hear the worry in her voice.

"We just saw each other! And what about our Feast and Be Feral Fridays?" I try to defend myself even though there is no reason to be defensive.

"You know what I mean."

"I do." My response is barely above a whisper.

"One day, you will have to forgive yourself, Mercy. You can't keep on living this way. You've buried yourself in work and whatever introverted-type hobby you are currently obsessing over. I can see it, you know. I know you think you're brilliant at masking it, but you're not. I expected the sadness. I expected the grief. I even expected the drastic changes you made..." Tess's uninterrupted speech begins to drift off, and silence follows. I can hear the apprehension in her silence. "I just...I expected anger, too. Frustration. Absolute rage! Maybe even reckless abandonment I would have to reel you back in from." Tess emphasizes each emotion as she says them out loud. "I just...I just didn't expect you to fade away."

I'm now parked outside the clinic, forehead on my steering wheel and phone cradled to my ear. "I'm sorry, Tess."

After a brief pause, as if she needed a moment to collect her thoughts, Tess responds in one full breath, "No. Do not be sorry. Never be sorry for how you feel. You, especially, never need to apologize to me. I just wish there was something I could do. All I know is that"—she pauses to inhale before continuing—"I love you. I want what's best for you, and I want to see you smile again. I'm sorry for trying to force something on you when it's probably the last thing you need right now. I was just trying to...oh, I don't know... ignite that spark in you again! Remember all the fun we had in college together?"

I'm definitely late for my shift by now, but I can't leave Tess hanging there, as she always is, hand outstretched and there for me to hold on to for support. "We aren't twenty anymore, Tess."

"No, we are not...but we are still *alive*, and we deserve to have fun and be happy. *You* deserve to be happy." I know she wants to finish that statement with "just as much as he," but she refrains from doing that.

There is so much I want to say, so much I want to argue, but I don't have the time or energy to get into it with her.

That's a conversation for another day, or maybe never at all. It's hard to communicate to anyone how the voice convinces me otherwise. How the voice says with almost-indisputable conviction that I am where I am because that's just simply how it's meant to be. *I don't deserve happiness. I haven't earned it.*

I don't deserve Tess. Just as I didn't deserve him.

I answer the only way I know how in the moment, "I love you, Tess."

"Call me tomorrow? We need to plan what we are going to regret gorging ourselves on Friday night. I'm thinking ice cream and fries."

I know this is her attempt to lighten the mood and bring an end to the increasingly depressing conversation. Hoping she can hear the forced smile in my voice, I respond, "Sounds good to me."

"I love you, too."

The line drops, and I look up to see Henry staring at me through the large, street-facing window of the clinic. He's tapping the glass face of his watch, staring at me with a mildly irritated frown, most likely for having to assist with opening the clinic—typically my job—with our insufferably imperious coworker, Megan. Something I promised I wouldn't let happen again.

Today is going to be fucking fantastic.

CHAPTER 2

"Late… Again?"

I use all the willpower I can muster to keep myself from rolling my eyes at Megan's icy greeting. "I'm sorry, Meg. You can leave five minutes early today if that helps." I force a smile and do my best to fake a sympathetic expression. God forbid I'm five minutes late to a shift that gives us more than enough prep time before the first client walks through the doors.

"It's not about the time. It's the principle," she snarks.

My blood starts to boil, and I attempt to control my sanity through deep breaths. It's too early for this shit.

"Just be happy Henry and I were here early enough to open up before Doc arrived," she adds with a pretentious smile.

"Well, thank God for that." I allow the sarcasm to hang on each word as I make my way to the back room to check on our overnight patients and to avoid any more criticism from Megan.

The lights flicker on as I walk past the motion detector, and I'm greeted with a melody of excited barks, meows, and a few annoyed hisses. "Good morning, my people,"

I announce to the room while placing my belongings on the far table. "What are we thinking for the morning? A trip outside to use the bathroom and then breakfast?"

Not expecting a response, I grab two leashes from the hooks by the door and make my way to the two Labrador retrievers that are certainly more excited to see me than Megan was moments ago. They paw at the kennel door, and I have to be quick with each dog's collar and leash. As I'm being dragged towards the back door, I make sure to swipe my breakfast sandwich from the table.

With one leash in each hand, I hold my sandwich between my teeth and guide the dogs over to the fenced-in yard just a few feet away from the building. I catch movement with my peripheral vision and am grateful when Henry comes into view as he reaches to open the gate after seeing my hands and mouth are full.

"You must not be too annoyed by my lateness this morning if you were willing to get the gate for me instead of watching me struggle." I nudge Henry with my elbow as we both lean on the fence while the dogs take care of their business.

"I was tempted." Henry flashes a wide, bright-white smile that pops in contrast to his rich dark-chocolate complexion. The same smile that caught my attention in high school when he transferred late junior year from a few states over. I remember the first time I introduced him to Tess at lunch and almost had to wipe the drool from her chin.

"Oh, come on...you would *never* think about him that way?" she had asked when trying to convince me to invite him to prom so we could double-date with her and her current fling. High School Tess could be insufferable, especially when it came to boys. She never could quite wrap her head around the fact that I never sought Henry as more than a friend.

To be fair, of course it had crossed my mind for a brief moment when he first struck me with that smile, and even more so when I discovered we shared similar interests ranging from a love for animals to the unexplained mysteries of space. How could I not be interested in this boy with a humble personality that only helped to emphasize his boyish charm? Tall runner's body, strong jawline he'd eventually grow into, and eyes that held both compassion and sharp intellect in their brown and amber coloring—anyone back then could see Henry was a catch. The same can be said especially now in adulthood.

But my teenage hormones were not to be outdone by my imbalanced levels of serotonin and dopamine. That voice of self-doubt truly blossomed with puberty. Beyond telling me he was out of my league, the voice convinced me that with time, he would never see me as enough for him anyway. So I settled on the fact that we would be friends. Since then, Henry, Tess, and I have been inseparable. And I wouldn't have it any other way.

"So? How was your weekend?" Henry asks in a way that leads me to believe he knows more about my weekend than I care to admit.

"I'm going to go out on a limb and say you've spoken to Tess since Saturday?" I say, still working on the bite of sandwich I had just shoved into my mouth and side-eyeing him.

"She tried to pull a fast one on you, didn't she?" he asks rhetorically through a soft laugh.

"His name is Bert," I state as if it's a good enough excuse to have written him off.

"Yeah, short for Robert? Come on, Mercy, you're in no position to judge someone based on their name," he teases, nudging me with an elbow.

"First off, my name is the result of someone who gave birth to me right before she turned twenty. No one makes good choices at that age." I think back to my first two years in college and cringe. "Second, why not Rob? Or Robbie? Hell, even Bobbie! But Bert? Now that was a choice. A *bad* choice. Enough said." I emphasize my claim by popping the final bite of my sandwich into my mouth.

"Tess just wants to see you happy, Mercy, and…unfortunately for you…the only way she thinks she knows how to do that is by playing matchmaker," Henry tells me as he starts to make his way over to the German shepherd he brought out earlier.

I grab the leashes for my two and follow behind Henry through the gate. Both dogs come barreling towards me as if it's been hours since they've seen my face, and I brace myself for impact as their furry bodies collide with my legs. Tongues lolling and drool dripping, both dogs patiently wait for me to attach their leashes. I scratch under their chins and respond to Henry's comment before standing back up, "I am happy, though," the lie almost getting caught in my throat. It's almost become my own personal inside joke with myself.

Back inside the clinic, I stand beside Henry as we prepare breakfast for each of the animals. I'm happy Henry chooses to change the topic of discussion as we start to dish out each animal's prepped meal. That is another trait I love about Henry—he always knows how to read the room.

As we monitor each animal, making sure they eat everything we've given them, including the prescribed medications we have so masterfully hidden, Henry animatedly recounts his weekend.

"I honestly was so proud of them; they put in the work this season, and it really showed," he proudly boasts about the high school track-and-field team he coaches when he isn't working his shifts at the clinic. "I have two girls who I'm confident will be considered for a scholarship to their top school of choice, and one girl who is so close to breaking our school's record in the eight-hundred meter."

"I'm sure their need to impress you does wonders for their motivation. Although I'm happy that they are running faster for you…not tripping head over heels for you," I joke. "Maybe I would have joined the track team if I had a hot coach to swoon over." I can't help but tease the guy.

"That reminds me." Henry takes a deep breath and rolls his eyes. "You would have been laughing your ass off at my expense during this incredibly awkward encounter with one of the girls and her mother after practice the other day." He groans.

I smirk and lift my brow at him in encouragement to continue.

"Let's just say I had a very single mother practically throwing herself at me in front of her daughter, telling me how amazing a coach I am."

"Oh, how horrible. How dare she compliment you like that!" I mock him, unable to hold back a shameless smile.

"Oh, it didn't stop there. She kept finding every excuse to gently smack my shoulder flirtatiously or touch my arm." He cringes at the memory. "I smiled and tried to stay calm about it, but that took a turn when I noticed her daughter—my athlete—start looking jealous of our interaction! Thankfully, I was rescued by someone needing my help with taking the gear back into the equipment shed."

Now I'm laughing.

"See! I knew you would laugh at my expense!" He makes a face before flashing me a toothy smile.

"Oh, I needed that laugh today, Henry. Thank you." I begin to walk away while humming the tune to "Stacy's Mom."

"Ha. Very funny. While you continue to relish in my discomfort, can you check with Meg up front to see what we need to prep for Doc for today's appointments?"

I groan at the thought of having to interact with Megan again. Then I give him my best impersonation of high school teenager's peppy "Yes, Coach!"

The rest of the day flies by, thankfully. It helped that Doc was in a good mood, which was the result of an overall routine and uneventful day—the preferred type of day for a veterinary clinic.

I clock out five minutes after Meg gathered her things to go home and assist Henry with closing up for the day. With no patients needing to stay the night this time, we luck out and are able to leave earlier than expected.

"Any plans for the night?" Henry asks as he turns the key to lock the door behind us.

"Other than a date with myself in my garden that I've neglected all summer?" I suck in a breath and huff. "Probably just sleeping off the lingering aftermath of this past weekend," I tell him. "You?"

He's silent.

I furrow my brow at him, confused as to why he is hesitating. I can see the gears churning in his head as he contemplates how to say whatever it is he's about to tell me. I watch as he brings his hand to the back of his neck and drops his gaze to the ground. Well, this apprehensive silence certainly isn't the response I was expecting. I can't stop the panic that starts to build inside me.

"Okay, Mr. Mysterious, what the hell is going on?"

"We didn't know how to tell you..." Henry's words drift off as he stands uncomfortably in front of me.

I impatiently watch him contemplate how to tell me whatever the hell it is he needs to tell me. He tries to start, but seems unable to get the words out exactly. *Whatever it is, it can't be good.*

"What the fuck, Henry? You're leaving me hanging here. Just spit it out," I snap at him.

"TESS AND I ARE GOING ON A DATE!" His words rush out as if they had been begging for release. I see his shoulders drop as relief seems to wash over him now that the cat is out of the bag.

Fuck.

"That's great! That's really, really...*great!*" My response is far from convincing, and my face is flushed. My reaction is not out of jealousy about their new-to-me relationship, but out of anxiety over what might happen to our friendship because of it. *I am officially a third wheel to my two closest friends. How long will it take before I'm just a cog in their relationship, one they need to dispose of?*

Never having had a problem with being a third wheel before, it is the fact that two of my best friends are trying to start something together. Don't get me wrong—I am and always will be rooting for them, BUT—

There's always a but. *What happens if they don't work out. Will I have to choose? I can't lose either of them. What happens if they do work out, and I just become an afterthought or forced company to them? Our group hangouts will be obsolete; they'll become date nights for them and a night at home alone with a pint of ice cream for me. Forever alone. Forever undeserving. Forever a burden.*

I'm spiraling internally when Henry's hand gently rests atop my shoulder. I can feel his warmth through my scrubs as I meet his gaze.

"This changes nothing between us. Between any of us. We are all still best friends, and no matter what, Mercy, you know Tess and I will make sure that doesn't change. Our friendship will never change. No matter what happens," he says as he brings me into what is supposed to be a comforting embrace.

I hug him back and force a smile as we let each other go. His response makes it evident that my reaction was a concern of theirs. A concern that should never have felt warranted by them, but is understandable when they have my unstable ass they feel the need to worry about as a friend. *Burden. I am a burden.*

Feeling selfish over my reaction, I break the silence. "I really am happy for you. For both of you. I'm both shocked that this is happening, but also shocked that it hasn't happened sooner," I tell him, hoping he sees past my selfish state of worry over our friendship. "You both deserve to be happy. This is definitely a *good* thing." I meet his eyes and will myself to put on a convincing face.

What I don't say out loud—but think to myself as we say our goodbyes and I tell him to be ready to give me all the juicy details tomorrow—is *I just don't want you guys to forget about me. I'm still here. Well...for now, at least.*

CHAPTER 3

The front door of my little house creaks open as I shove my way through, tossing my keys and purse onto the entryway table. A glance at the wall clock hanging in the living room lets me know I have another hour or so left before the sun sets, which leaves me plenty of time to attempt some sort of resurrection of my garden. It might be a bit of a lost cause at this point in the year, but I need something to keep my mind busy; otherwise, the paranoia and twinge of jealousy will set in.

Only a few steps into the kitchen, my inner voice is as loud and chaotic as the town's only local bar on a Friday night when the drinks are cheap and the place has reached max capacity. Were I to speak what I am thinking out loud, I would be thought to be possessed, as the dooming thoughts are infinite and fleeting, most starting before others are finished. Shame and anger flush my face red as the thoughts that race are too selfish for me to even be thinking and make me question my worth as a friend.

Without any luck, I shake my head in an attempt to rattle the chaos into some sort of control. The only thing that does is make the chaos louder and more suffocating until I want to crawl out of my skin. The best I can do, without going all Buffalo Bill on myself, is change out of my work attire. So in the laundry room off the kitchen, I rummage through the dryer for something that feels less constricting—baggy sweatpants and an oversized sweatshirt.

How long before Tess and Henry don't want to deal with a third wheel imposing on their time together? the voice chimes in, not even trying to be background noise as I strip down and throw my dirty clothes into the wash basket.

Best friend turned cockblocker, I'll be spending more days alone, finding myself fixated on some new "promising" project I'll never have the motivation to finish. The voice continues as I shove one leg at a time into a pair of the many black sweatpants I own, *I'll have no one to pull me out of the isolation I wrongly find comfort in, convincing myself there's no reason to leave my own trap.*

My sweatshirt is now pulled over my head, but no relief of the invisible constriction I feel tightening around me is found. *Why am I making myself their burden to worry over, though? This is ridiculous. I am ridiculous. A ridiculous fucking burden.*

My absurd paranoia over something meant to be celebrated sparks a note of anger within that's only directed at myself. I cannot possibly let something as small as a date between friends unravel me in such a drastic way. Yet here I am. Clearly, the outfit change didn't help much, but I know two other things that will. I shift my focus to the unopened wine bottle and pre-rolled joint sitting on the counter and smile. This should help quiet the irrational voice, as well as make gardening a bit more fun.

I struggle with the bottle opener, unable to get the cork out fast enough, in desperate need to muffle the voice in my head. *They are my best friends, my found family, my emotional support system...that I'm about to lose to each other.* A few curses slip from under my breath before I'm finally able to uncork one of the toxic solutions to my problem. As much as I want to just drink straight from the bottle at this point, I reach for a wineglass, keeping an eye out for the lighter I know to be floating around somewhere.

The search for my lighter, though quick, gives the voice plenty of time to hit home and address the deep-seated root of fear my friends' budding relationship has revealed.

It will be another harsh reality slapped in my face. The reality where I'll be left stuck behind. Alone. Becoming the unhinged "aunt" to their future children, the aunt who comes around only when invited on special occasions like birthdays. An example of someone they can point to as who not *to be when grown up. An example of someone who tried once for that life of happiness and completely failed.*

The unwarranted concern in regards to the self-determined downfall of our friendship leads me to picture the life I know they'll have, the one that once I tried so desperately to make work for me. A life I know Henry and Tess will have no trouble achieving. My mental grip slips and loses control to selfish jealousy for what they found together. Their newfound love threatens to force the pain of my own failed attempt to resurface.

There's no life like that for someone so broken. For someone like me. It just doesn't work.

"Fucking hell." I pour myself a generous glass of pinot noir, grab the joint, and start to make my way to the door that leads out to the garden. As the fingers of my outstretched hand reach the knob, I pause and backpedal to grab the wine bottle. *Numb. I need to feel numb.*

In my mind, the unstable wall used to block out memories of my failures begins to crumble, threatening to collapse in on itself if I fail to mute the negative voice within. My fragile mental state still triggered by Henry's revelation becomes the voice's excuse to revisit any unresolved trauma from my most recent failures. The voice, influenced and strengthened by my demons, weakens the infrastructure of that wall by agitating all the anxiety and depression I've fought so hard to brick up. The voice, further invigorated by my shattering willpower, is now free to remind me of all I've lost, all I've done wrong, and how I will never be enough.

Following the worn path to my garden, I try to take deep breaths—in through my nose…out through my mouth. My heart stops racing, but my mind keeps stirring. I grip the neck of the wine bottle in one hand, while the other carries my glass of wine with fingers pinched around the stem. Each step closer to my garden brings with it vivid imagery of recent haunts that only confirm the negative opinions of me the voice in my head continues to conjure.

The voice finally decides to put aside the sought-after trigger that is Henry and Tess's new relationship for something more satiating. Something it has been truly after all this time, waiting for the final drive of life's hammer to assault my mental wall and cause its collapse. As the voice strikes with a few more final thoughts of disappointment, the wall gives, and my demons are freed to do with me as they will. Using my insecurities, doubts, depression, anxieties, trauma, guilt, anger, and reminding me of all my flaws to break me further. To end me.

One step, then one swig of wine, and that pesky internal voice reminds me of the art degree I failed to use after graduating college, unable to find work that would allow me to support myself.

Wasted degree on hyped-up, mediocre talent.

Another step, another swig, and I'm reminded of the failed marriage I jumped into at too young an age. A marriage that ended because of my inability to simply make him happy, my refusal to deliver his dream of a family, and my inability to get over the feeling of never being enough.

Too broken, too selfish, too much, but not enough to make things work. I caused the divorce all on my own.

A few more steps, another swig, and I'm reminded of the strain I put on my parents after the inevitable divorce forced me, a grown adult in my late twenties, to lean on them for financial support. Never did they say anything but words of support and love, but I know deep down I was an unnecessary worry for them.

Financial burden. Disappointment of a daughter. Too needy.

Final steps to my garden, the last drop of wine, and the mental wall I have built in my head over the years disappears for good. I'm drowned by the thoughts of everything I wanted but failed to accomplish in life…the potential others saw that I couldn't live up to…the promises to get better that I can't seem to keep…and the demons inside I can't seem to leash.

Finally at its entrance, I stare out at my shit excuse of a garden. The sight of it conjures up a self-directed anger that twists within my sadness and fear. The emotional whiplash causes my head to spin. Placing my wineglass and bottle on the stump at the border of my garden, I pluck the joint tucked behind my ear, stick it between my lips, and light it. The skunky smell of my second-choice toxic solution to my problems permeates my senses as I take a long drag. A few moments later, I start to feel sweet relief finally dulling the toxic voice inside my head. I ignore that it's only a temporary escape.

After one last toke and a few swigs of wine, I step through the entrance of my garden in hopes of further distracting my mind from continuing down the dangerous path of self-destruction, fearful of what will happen at that path's end. The sight before me is a bit defeating and intimidating, forcing a rush of breath made heavy with dejection. I've neglected my garden for so long that it has become more of a jungle of weeds and withering flowers.

The drug and alcohol start to flood my system, and I can't help but pause and acknowledge that this once-thriving garden is a perfect reflection of me. From a distance, my garden might look like controlled chaos, perhaps as if it is just giving way to summer's end. Occasional pops of color from flowers still holding strong are slightly visible, despite the weeds and vines that tangle and twist over the garden's edges. The sight at first holds promise and opportunity; next year it will come back even stronger.

Up close, however, the appearance of the garden becomes clearer and gives off a totally different energy. Instead of the untapped potential I originally thought it had, I now see the unruly chaos for what it truly is—invasive weeds that need to be ripped out from the roots in order to stop the suffocation of all that I had originally planted there. The vines that grow beyond the garden's perimeter aren't simply flirting with their surroundings, as they appeared to be from a few feet away. Instead, I realize they are reaching out for much-needed space, expending energy as if the vines themselves were fingernails or claws grappling at the earth's soil. They beg for an escape from the environment in which they've been housed, but that release is far from imminent, thanks to the untouched weeds that grow stronger by the day, strangling anything they touch and holding hostage whatever wants out.

Sporadic pops of color throughout the mess are dulled by the decay of most of the plants that are wilting or dead. The soil is dry as the desert, everything within it having given up on desperate pleas for water due to my lack of nurturing and reliance on rain from Mother Nature. And when Mother Nature did come and complete the responsibility meant to be my own, she didn't simply quench the thirst of the vegetation. No. Instead, she drowned it, washing away any nutrients or support that the earth had to give—an unfortunate punishment that was truly intended to solely punish me for my lack of care and unreliable efforts.

What once was vibrant, healthy, and bold now takes up unnecessary space and has become more muted and lifeless as each day passes. What this garden once had to give, it has lost. What this garden once was, is no more. What this garden has become is an eyesore for all to see what should be stripped from the earth. What this garden has become is the result of neglect. *What I have allowed myself to become is my garden.*

Feeling overwhelmed, I throw myself onto my hands and knees, head spinning from the mix of alcohol and drugs, and drive my fingernails into the dirt. Each weed ripped from the soil is replaced by a tear that breaks free from my burning waterline. I dig at the earth under me, tearing it to shreds. My breathing becoming labored and catching in my throat, I tumble into the fetal position on a bed of dead lavender and rock myself while gasping for air. I've gone beyond spiraling at this point and anticipate the looming threat of inevitably hitting the deepest imaginable pit of rock bottom.

I can't control the flow of tears or the anxiety-induced, full-body convulsions as I shake and wallow in the decay surrounding me—both internally and externally. I rock myself, my knees tucked into my chest, lamenting the woman I know I could have been had it not been for the voice that grew stronger with age, amplifying my demons who continue to work against me. I make a feeble attempt to self-soothe and repeat a mantra over and over again to drown out the self-deprecating voice that has been with me my whole life.

"I am here."

One breath in through my nose, out through my mouth.

"I am here."

Again, one breath in through my nose, out through my mouth.

"I am here."

I continue the pattern of words and breath work to bring myself back to my body, in desperate hopes of quieting the nefarious voice that holds my mind hostage.

Time passes while I lie curled up on the ground. With the voice finally becoming just a whisper, my eyes remain transfixed on nothing but the now-darkening tree line. My heart starts to slow, my breathing becomes more regular, and my eyes begin to dry. With one hand, I shove myself up from the earth and look around once more at my garden. Taking in my surroundings, I look to the flattened lavender, the few fistfuls of shredded weeds, and then look down at myself. Face covered in tears and dirt, hands black as the soil I now kneel in, I hang my head and allow my shoulders to drop forward in defeat.

Growing up, I thought myself a fixer and a doer, capable of anything I set my mind to. Through bloodshot eyes, I now look at what I've done and think back to the past couple of years. I am far from the girl I once was, full of promise and excitement for the world. Instead of being that fixer, that doer and overachiever, I became destructive and a detriment to myself, overwhelmed by the unnecessary pressure only I was responsible for manifesting. My expectations and constant reach for perfection turned into an unhealthy battle that I would never admit can't be won.

A battle based on societal and self-made expectations—mostly self-made, if I'm being honest—took an inevitable toll on me, and instead of building my life up, it allowed the voice to tear me down; nothing I did was good enough. And when the pressure I put on myself became too much, I could not stop myself from setting my whole life ablaze, becoming a destructive wildfire and taking down anything in my path, myself included.

I am not enough in this world. Everything I touch falls apart, withers, and dies. I want to create, yet all I do is destroy. I am unworthy of love. Unworthy of good. Unworthy of life. I am nothing but a waste of a human being.

My cries are soon replaced by contemptible laughter at myself. I knock my glass of wine over as I fumble around reaching for it and instead make contact with the bottle. *Fuck it.* Taking the bottle by its neck, I bring the opening to my lips and begin to down its dregs. I choke after a few seconds as I funnel what's left down my throat. Pissed, I chuck the bottle into the turned-up mess of weeds and dirt and slowly stand.

I give up. I can't do this anymore.

CHAPTER 4

The next morning, I find myself splayed out on the couch in my living room. How I managed to get myself into my house last night is beyond me. Blinking to try and clear the fog that has its hold on me, I feel around for my phone, hoping that I didn't lose it somewhere after last night's breakdown.

My heart gets stuck in my throat when I eventually do find my phone…and the twenty missed calls and texts left unread from Henry and my boss. The time on my phone reads 12:00 p.m., and I know for a fact I've fucked up. *Again.*

No.

No.

No.

No.

I can smell the wine seeping from my pores as I leap off the couch. My head spins, and I'm forced to catch myself on the coffee table before falling over completely. I focus on putting one foot in front of the other and stumble towards the upstairs bathroom. Using the railing for support, I drag myself as quickly as possible up the stairs. Head pounding, heart racing, stomach churning, I brace myself on the landing and take a second to collect myself before staggering into the bathroom.

I make my way to the sink, only to be diverted to the toilet by my nauseated stomach. Slamming the toilet lid up, I white-knuckle the rim of the toilet seat as I retch the contents of my stomach. Red bile gushes out from my mouth, burning my throat and nasal passages. I do this until I'm dry heaving and finally able to catch my breath. I fall away from the toilet, lean my body against the cool porcelain of the claw-foot tub, knees tucked into my chest, and try to stop myself from hyperventilating.

Slowly, I stand and climb into the tub. I reach up to turn the showerhead on and don't even bother with closing the shower curtain. I do my best to wash myself as quickly and thoroughly as possible. Dirt, sweat, and filth flow from my body and circle the drain. After one final rinse, I wrap a towel around my violently shaking body.

As I stand in the tub, still dripping, and take off the towel to use it on my hair, I catch a glimpse of myself in the mirror. The eyes staring back at me are lifeless; I see nothing inside them. Clavicle and hip bones jut out from my body, dark circles cup the bottom of my eyes, and my ribs have started to become more prominent than before. Slowly, I climb out of the tub and reach for the drawer I know holds my Xanax. I pop a pill under my tongue and stare into the void that is my reflection in the mirror. I see nothing but a vision of all that my life's decisions, trials, and errors add up to. I see a body with no spirit left inside.

I can't do this anymore.

My phone screen lights up, and I look at the preview of the latest unread message sent to me.

Megan: Don't bother coming in.

A few second later, another text pops up.

Megan: I overheard Doc telling Henry that he's over it. I'm more than positive you're fired.

As if to confirm Megan's assumption, one final message pops up.

Doc: Call me. Now.

I walk to my bedroom, leaving wet footprints behind, and collapse onto my bed. I wrap myself once again in the towel, grab my pillow, and bury my face in it as I let out a muffled, guttural scream.

Once I'm able to somewhat collect myself, I scroll through my contacts list until I find Doc. I tap his name, and the phone begins to ring. It only gets through three rings before I hang up. At this point, what's done is done. There is no way I'm not fired, and I'm not exactly in the greatest mindset to have a conversation regarding that.

Naked and shivering, I tuck myself into bed, hug my knees to my chest, and let sleep take over. Just as I'm about to lose myself to the safety of darkness, I mutter a plea in the form of a prayer—having given up on God years ago—for the universe to let the darkness consume me in hopes of not waking up.

I don't want to do this anymore.

Late-afternoon sun seeps through my curtains, causing my eyes to flutter open. My plea to not wake was granted for all of only three hours, when what I had in mind was more indefinite. Begrudgingly, I sweep my lower body across the mess of blankets and damp towel and place both feet on the floor. My body now upright, sitting at the edge of the bed, I feel that some of the effects from last night's coping mechanisms remain. The headache still lingers, but the nausea is finally tolerable. I need coffee, water, Advil, and food…in that order.

I try to stand, but the room starts spinning, and I know it has little to do with the hangover and everything to do with what's going on in my head. I've been lying to myself, for too long, thinking I had a handle on my depression and anxiety. The therapy, the medications, the self-help books—all just Band-Aids for my fucked-up mind that's unwilling to accept any help. Everything I have been shoving down finally bursts out, no longer able to be contained. The irrational worry over Henry and Tess's relationship is weightless, yet too heavy on top of all that's accumulated over a not-so-long lifetime.

Wearing only a towel, I lean bare thighs against the side of my bed for support. My shoulders hunch forward, and my chin tilts down while the palms of each hand find the sides of my head. I put as much pressure behind each touch as I can and squeeze my eyes tight as if it's going to help hold me together. Tears force their way through tight eyelids, and I whisper no over and over again until the voice takes control.

So this *is rock bottom? Maybe worse. Who the fuck am I anymore? A drunk? An addict? Definitely unreliable. Certainly pathetic. A burden to anyone in my life. What happened to me? What am I going to do? I'm too much. All the time. Too much. Too much and not enough. Not enough.*

"I am here."

Not enough.

"I am here."

Waste of space.

"I am here."

Pathetic.

"I am HERE."

Ugly inside and out.

"I AM HERE!"

Give up.

I'm shaking, can't catch my breath. I want to run but can't manage more than a quick shuffle from one end of my room to the other. The voice is louder than it's ever been. And now I feel as if I were drowning on the very oxygen meant to keep me alive.

Panic wraps itself around me like a cold, wet blanket, and I'm at an absolute loss on how to take it off. Pacing the room, my eyes dart from one direction to the next as if I'm looking for a lifeline. The edge of my thumbnail is torn and dripping blood because of my anxious habit of picking, and the skin that isn't covered by the towel I'm still wearing is splotchy and tingling.

With shaking hands, I pull clothes out from my closet and try to focus on the familiar routine of dressing. At this point, I'm talking out loud to myself, hoping by speaking what the voice is saying to me, I can somehow release myself from its choke hold. With that tactic not working, but being finally dressed, I grab a pair of sneakers, continue talking to myself out loud, and make my way down the stairs and out the front door. "Fresh air and movement. I need fresh air"— I choke down a sob that is stuck in my throat—"and movement."

I start down the driveway and take a turn onto the back road dappled by the late-afternoon sun filtering through the trees. My staggered shuffle turns into a brisk walk, which turns into a light jog. Running used to help quiet the voice when I was in my teens and early twenties, and it's currently the only option I have left in my arsenal of tricks to ease my mind. So I run.

Staring straight ahead, down the long, winding road, I hit the pavement one foot at a time. Each footfall leads me farther from my home, farther from myself. I discovered a long time ago that for a brief moment, it is possible to run from one's self—that explains why I have run myself ragged ever since. I'm not quite where my mind needs me to be—lost in the rhythm of quick feet hitting pavement—so I start to speed up, chasing another form of high than the one I found last night. *Breathless. I need to feel breathless.*

My chest rattles as my breathing becomes heavier, and I can feel the sweat starting to bead around my brow line. My lungs begin to burn, my legs start to feel heavy, and I know I'm almost there. I push myself to continue past the point of exhaustion, past the point of caring how my body is screaming at me to stop, and past the point of my mind's negotiating when I'm allowed to slow down. Just as I'm about to reach that desired point in my run, I'm interrupted by the sight of a large black figure emerging from the tree line up ahead.

Startled and decreasing my pace, the whole world seems to slow down as I take in all that is about to happen. On the opposite side of the road is a large raven picking at what must have been roadkill. Barreling down that same road is a cherry-red Corvette being driven by a person I've never seen in the area before. And in front of me is what I've come to realize is an enormous jet-black dog eyeing the bird, oblivious to the quickly approaching death omen on wheels. For once, my mind isn't spiraling, and the voice actually encourages me instead of taking on its usual cynical tone.

Run.

And so I do just that.

The easy run I had settled into breaks into an all-out sprint. My feet pound the pavement as I race towards the now-lunging dog.

"NO!" I scream as I hurl my body towards the black mass, unaware of an echo of the word that follows my plea.

A piercing yelp deafens my ears as my body makes contact first with fur and then with pavement. A gust of wind whooshes past in a blur of candy-apple red before the sound of a car horn is directed angrily at me.

Asshole!

The raven takes flight with frazzled caws adding to the cacophony of chaos. Now tumbling on the ground from the momentum, my body fully envelops the warm, furry body against me.

The adrenaline that fueled my reaction completely drains from my system at the last moment of my save, heedless of the hazards to my body. I can feel the flesh of my shoulder, back, and hip rip apart as each part of me makes contact with the ground. The impact is made more painful due to the weight of the black dog cradled to my front and the friction of the rough pavement under my skidding body. Once my body has come to a stop, the last part of me to make contact with the ground is my head.

My vision starts to blur, and I feel the dog come loose from my arms as it uses my body as a launchpad to flee the scene. *Of course, this is how I will die. Saving an ungrateful animal from death and in return suffering from an internal brain bleed...alone. Fitting.*

Finding a new level of rock bottom, a hysterical smile creeps across my face. The edges of my vision start to blacken, and I feel as if I were floating. The blackness consumes me, and I'm left to wonder who is carrying me and to where. *Has an angel come to take me? Perhaps a demon. Am I being taken to heaven? Hell? Eh, who am I kidding? I'll probably end up in purgatory.*

I go limp and allow whoever or whatever to take me away. No longer awake. No longer afraid.

CHAPTER 5

"Oh my God," I grumble when I finally start to come to.

"Which one you looking for? Depending on who you're calling, you're most likely shit out of luck."

A man's voice startles me, and I launch my body up to a seated position.

"Actually, I'm pretty sure all of them are *busy* at the moment." He makes air quotes to emphasize his sarcasm while using the word "busy."

My head is spinning from the upright position, and I immediately plant the heels of my hands to my eyes as I sharply inhale.

"Mmmm. Yup. You probably don't want to do that," the man chimes in.

"Excuse me?" I turn and look at him with one eye open, head still spinning.

"Move quickly. You probably don't want to make sudden movements. You hit your head pretty hard." His tone is far from concerned, which is the exact opposite of how I'm feeling. "I was surprised your head didn't bounce when it made contact with the road. I was waiting for it to happen, but nope."

I am now staring incredulously at the man sitting in a chair on the opposite side of the room. My eyes take a second to focus, and I gently work my jaw side to side, trying to assess the damage. Aside from the pounding headache, nothing seems broken.

My fuzzy vision begins to clear, and I can finally see to whom the voice belongs.

Well, aren't you a fucking cliche.

Starting from head to toe, I examine the specimen who casually lounges in the leather chair cozied up to an empty fireplace. Dressed in what looks to be tailored-to-perfection black dress pants and a white button-down, it is easy to see he takes care of himself. His clothing fits comfortably snug around his muscular body and leaves little to the imagination. A tie drapes loosely around his neck, undone and framing his pectorals, which peek out of his unbuttoned shirt. A hint of what appears to be ink threatens to reveal itself from beneath the silky white fabric.

At first glance, the shadows in the room cause the angles of his face to appear sharp and menacing. As he rolls up his sleeves, I can see the veins in his forearms and hands protrude as he leans the weight of his upper body forward onto his knees. Face now painted by the warm light emanating from the floor lamp, his features, though still sharp, soften just a bit. A crown of loose, dark curls sits ruffled atop his head. The occasional tendril drifts down, drawing attention to the vibrant green eyes staring back at me.

Yeah, I must be dead. Purgatory does seem to have some good-looking residents. So I won't complain.

My hope for relief from the life I have been living is cut short when I come to my senses and realize I am, in fact, very much still alive. Still alive…and in some random man's bed. Becoming more aware of the new danger I may have found myself in, I start to pull myself out of the bed I had no memory of getting into. The sheets stick to my skin as I make my way to the edge, and I can feel them pull at my sticky, fresh wounds as I start to stand.

"Jesus Christ," I groan as the searing pain of my torn skin shoots throughout my damaged body.

Through blackening and starry vision, I catch the sight of hands flying up defensively. "Not me, and I'd rather He not get involved. He still owes me money from our last bet a couple millennia ago." The man brings his forearms back to his knees, rolls his eyes, and frowns.

I ignore his strange comment and stand, but not as steadily as I would have hoped. *I may not be dead yet, but there's a chance I'm definitely about to be.* I go to make a move, and a dizzying sensation grabs hold of me. Before I hit the ground…*again*…I'm caught under the arms by those same hands I notice to be dotted by what must be ink stains.

"Again, how about we *avoid* sudden movement?" I can hear a twinge of concern mixed into his sarcasm as I'm being scooped up effortlessly and placed back in bed.

I try to wiggle myself out of his hold, but it's no use. My body is weak, and I am so fatigued. On top of the pounding headache, my stomach growls in distress from lack of food and from the hangover I was trying to take care of earlier that afternoon. *Just put an end to my misery already.*

I'm being gently placed back under the covers when I snap back up to a sitting position, almost nailing the man in the head, refusing to be placed in a vulnerable position. I'm exhausted and in pain, but there's no need for me to give this stranger a reason to believe I'm not willing to put up a fight, if needed. He's been helpful, it seems, so far, but for what purpose? Until I'm certain of no ill intent, I force myself to stay alert and on guard. *I can at least admit to myself that if I'm to be put out of my misery, I want it to be quick...not...whatever this could morbidly turn into.*

"Wait!" I try to think of any way to get more information from this stranger, to suss out his intentions, but my questioning quickly gets straight to the point. "I have so many questions. Where's the dog? Is the dog okay? Where am I? Who even are you? Did you...did you...ABDUCT ME?" My head is spinning, and my sanity—what's left of it—starts to slip.

"Ah! Watch yourself." My captor swiftly dodges my head by pulling his back. He places both hands on my shoulders and pushes me back down to rest my upper body and head against the stacked pillows surrounding me.

My eyes are wide in both fright and curiosity. As the warmth of the comforter soothes my chilled body, I feel pressure moving along my side, followed by an aggressive thump on the bed. I turn and am greeted by a large black mass of fur rolling around beside me. A feathered tail wags erratically while two different-colored eyes stare into mine. Tongue hanging out and pointy ears pressed against the bedspread, I recognize the ginormous beast as the dog I risked my life for. *Not that I had anything to risk. Better me than the dog.*

"You're okay." My breath catches as I whisper the words, and a small smile spreads across my face as I lose any sense of self-preservation I just had. The dog rolls onto its back; I bury my fingers in the soft fur behind its ears and am thanked with a soft sneeze and gentle lick on my hand.

"Orthus has selective hearing apparently and refused to come when I called. Had you not interfered...I don't know what would have happened." The man's voice sounds genuine and sincere, which makes me feel a bit more at ease.

The gentle expression of gratitude he gives me further encourages me to relax; I want to believe his intentions are good—his hospitality is gratitude for my actions that knocked me unconscious, battered, and bruise in an effort to save his friend.

"Orthus, huh? That's a name." Feeling more at ease in the situation in which I find myself, I let my pounding head rest against the pillows piled high behind me. My eyelids feel heavy as they close softly. I keep one hand on Orthus's massive paw and crack one eye open. "Speaking of names, I never got yours."

The man clears his throat as if he's about to announce something of importance. "My apologies. I'm horrible with introductions. The name is Aiden."

Aiden stands at the edge of the bed, flashing me a sly smile of pearly-white teeth, and two subtle dimples become more apparent. Slight stubble frames his jawline and emphasizes the angles of his face. Were it not for his tousled dark hair that brings softness and warmth to his look, he would appear both hauntingly beautiful and menacing—far from approachable, but hard not to stare at.

"Uh, though I am flattered, I would appreciate it if you could share your name with me…once you've stopped eye-fucking me, of course." His subtly arrogant smile reaches from ear to ear, and he lets loose a soft chuckle.

His audacity in calling me out on what I now realize I was shamelessly doing drains whatever color is left from my face and snaps me to attention. "Mercy. My name is Mercy."

"And you were making fun of Orthus for his name?" he asks rhetorically with arms crossed and one brow lifted.

I roll my eyes at him and am about to make a snarky remark when I'm stopped by a brief coughing fit. As I am looking around for something to drink, a glass of water is shoved in front of my face. Struggling with the dryness that has settled in my throat, I grab the water from Aiden's hand and swallow large gulps of the cold liquid. After finding a bit of relief, I settle back into the mass of pillows and blankets. I'm exhausted and in pain, but alive...*for now.*

With my head against the pillows, Orthus curled up by my side, and Aiden searching for something in the dresser drawers next to me, I take the moment to map out my surroundings. I clearly have a concussion, so occupying myself with bouts of curiosity, trying to make sense of the situation and environment I'm in, helps to keep me awake.

Shades of deep navy, rich maroons, forest greens, and pops of gold are scattered throughout the room. Had the fireplace been blazing, the room would have felt cozier than the chilled, dark atmosphere it is now. Floating shelves occupy one corner that overflows with books, what appears to be rolled-up parchment papers, bottles of ink in a variety of colors, odd and ancient-looking sculptures, and the occasional empty glass. Maps of a country I do not recognize are pinned to the wall without shelving, and a small sitting area is made up of one oversized leather chair and a square coffee table adorned with partially melted pillar candles. Heavy curtains cover the three windows from floor to ceiling, and with a quick glance down, I notice a plush rug offering bare feet relief from the cold wooden floor beneath. I take it all in before looking back to Aiden still shuffling around in his dresser drawers.

"This should work." He tosses a light pair of sweatpants and an oversized T-shirt into my lap. "Bathroom is down the hall and to the right. I'll make a pot of coffee and see what I have for you to eat—don't expect anything fancy."

"Oh, you don't have to do that. I'm fine with a glass of water, and I'll just be on my way." Suddenly, I'm a bit self-conscious about the situation I'm in, instead of the discomfort and wariness I should have felt upon waking up in a stranger's bedroom.

"I think you have established already, or I'm hoping you have, that I don't plan on killing you or abducting you. I'm just trying to help." His tone once again starts off snarky, but then fades into something more genuine.

I look at the clothes he has thrown into my lap, the glass of water on the bedside table he has given me, and then at the puppy-eyed stare of Orthus before saying, "Oh, fuck it. I'll meet you in the kitchen."

"That's the spirit." He smirks and runs a hand through his unruly hair. "Just follow the smell of coffee once you're done…fixing yourself." He waves his hand at me and shoots me a bit of a grimace.

Fuck, how bad do I look…or smell?

I twitch my lip and let out an annoyed "thanks."

I am indeed able to follow the aroma of coffee, which leads me farther down the hallway after I do my best at cleaning myself up. Turning the corner, I'm greeted by Aiden sitting at the kitchen counter, which holds a plate of buttered toast and coffee, and Orthus drooling at his feet.

"Oh, look. You've come back from the brink of death." Aiden lifts his coffee mug in mock celebration.

I scoff at him and plop down on the empty seat in front of the toast and steaming coffee. I take a tentative sip and am surprised that it has been made exactly how I usually make it. My brief expression of delighted surprise grabs Aiden's attention.

"Is it all right?" he asks earnestly.

"You used honey to sweeten this, didn't you?" I question him and get a gentle nod in response. "You knew how I take my coffee?"

"Lucky guess, I suppose." He shrugs and returns to drinking from his own mug.

"Mm-hmm." I give him an inquisitive look and begin to pick away at the toast at the request of my grumbling stomach.

"In truth, it was the only thing I had to use as a sweetener. I don't picture you as a black-coffee kind of person," he unnecessarily relays as if he's trying to cover up the coincidence.

Awkward silence fills the room as I continue to sip my coffee and snack on my plate of toast. Light pours in through the large open windows, bringing warmth to the open kitchen and surrounding living room.

Still feeling like garbage and desperate for the comfort of familiar surroundings, I take another sip of coffee and clear my throat. "Thank you for your help. I appreciate it."

Aiden looks at me, green eyes softer than they've been since I first saw him, and gives me a closed-lips smile. "Of course. And I must thank you for saving Orthus." He ruffles the dog's fur between the ears while smiling down at him.

"Maybe look into a leash." I can't keep myself from making a quick, lighthearted jab.

"*You* can take that idea up with Orthus," Aiden responds, one eyebrow raised towards the furry black beast.

I laugh and go to grab my things, but then realize I have nothing to grab. Remembering I went for a run mid panic attack, I stop my search and push myself back from the counter to stand. Unsure of how to properly excuse myself, I shove my hand towards Aiden. "I should be heading out now, but thank you again for the hospitality."

Leaning back against the wall, still sitting on the stool, he looks at me through thick lashes I would probably murder someone for and raises both a corner of his mouth and an eyebrow. He lets out a dry, subtle laugh as if he is amused and takes my hand in his. "Anytime."

He holds my hand a little longer than necessary, my gaze with it. There's a familiarity in his look that I can't seem to place, and if I'm not mistaken, I swear he's thinking the same when looking at me. I shake it off.

He rises to his full height and gestures for me to walk down another hallway that leads to the front entrance. "Let me grab my keys, and I'll take you home."

"That won't be necessary. I can walk a bit and have a friend of mine pick me up along the way."

"Mm-hmm. And how would you contact this friend of yours?"

He's reaching for his keys with a smug look on his face when I realize I have no phone on me and no knowledge even of where I am. I sigh in defeat.

Independent woman, my ass.

Ahhh, there's that voice of support. For a hopeful moment, I thought it might have been knocked out of me.

Continuing on to the front door, we pass a set of stairs leading down to what I assume to be a finished basement. At the bottom, however, I'm surprised by the sight of a ginormous and daunting door. Black in color and solid in appearance, it is stamped with what appears to be a gold-plated slab in lieu of a doorknob. My interest is immediately piqued.

"What the actual fuck are you keeping locked up down there? Dead bodies?"

He snaps his head back around and catches the direction of my gaze. His face drains a bit of color, and he lets out a light but devious chuckle. He tries to make a joke of it. "Not exactly."

My face blanches as I trip over my own feet and catch myself by pressing a hand to the wall.

His facial features relax, and he tries to tell me that the old house had many interesting characteristics, explaining it was those oddities that drove him to buy the place.

I nod and force myself to accept that as a reasonable explanation for the off-putting vibe I all of a sudden begin to feel.

"You'll need this." He throws me a leather jacket, distracting me from asking any more questions about the door.

"It's the end of summer, early fall. It's still warm out." I take the jacket and give him an inquisitive look.

"For safety precautions. No need to add any more road rash to that body of yours."

He ushers me out the door, and I see in the driveway why I was handed the jacket. "You would own a crotch rocket."

Clinging to Aiden for dear life, I try to keep the little bit of toast down while he whips around the tight turns of our town's backroads. My fingernails dig into my arms, which are wrapped tightly around his torso. Wind whips through the hair that flows from beneath the skullcap I was forced to wear, and my watery eyes are squeezed tightly shut.

"You're perfectly safe so long as you loosen your grip a little so I can breathe!" Aiden yells over the roar of the bike's engine.

"I might feel safer if I wasn't on the back of a bike with a guy I *just* met, who rides like a fucking psycho with a death wish!" I holler back at him, slightly confused by my outburst, seeing as I've recently been the one with the death wish.

I could technically just let go.

"Let go!" Aiden yells back at me.

"Excuse me?" I'm startled by his reaction. *Did he just read my mind? And if so…thanks for the fucked-up sense of support, I guess.*

"Trust me! Just"—he pauses as we take a sharp turn that leads to a long straightaway—"LET GO!"

With that, my mind loses control of my body, and I do just that—I let go. I let go and spread my arms wide, forcing myself to peel away from the safety blanket Aiden's torso has become. Shaky at first, I begin to let my fingers splay, allowing the wind to cascade around each one. A tight-lipped smile starts to spread across my face, and I start to sit up taller.

"How does it feel?" Aiden asks.

"Like a moment of much-needed freedom!" I yell to the back of his head. I can't see him, but I know he's grinning.

"Now that you've let go, let it out!" he demands.

Swept up in this moment of pure adrenaline, I throw my head back and let out a primal howl. And for the first time in a long time, the voice isn't clouding my thoughts, an invisible weight is lifted off my chest and shoulders, and I feel alive.

In front of me, I can feel Aiden's body vibrate with pure joy and laughter. Laughter not *at* me, but *with* me. And in this brief moment, I'm overwhelmed with a taste of happiness. A few tears escape as my smile spreads farther across my face, teeth showing in a genuine smile.

Not too long after this rare experience of joy, I'm struck by reality when we reach the stop sign at the end of the road. We are now only a few minutes away from my home, from my reality, and from the consequences of my actions. *It will never be that easy to just let go and live. But it was nice for the minute or so that it lasted.*

Aiden guides his bike into my driveway and comes to a stop. With both feet planted on the ground, he turns off the engine and engages the kickstand. When I hop off the bike and turn to hand him his helmet, he looks at me, at my front door, at the two cars parked haphazardly in my driveway, and then back at me with a questioning look.

I'm too dumbfounded by his obnoxiously attractive face to acknowledge his silent question.

"I'm guessing one of those vehicles is yours, and the other hopefully belongs to someone that you know?" he asks with slight apprehension.

I snap out of my daze, pray that I'm not drooling, and shake my head.

"No?" His eyes go straight to the door, and he squints.

"Sorry, I mean yes. Yes, I know who the other car belongs to," I answer. Slight shame contorts my voice because I know Henry and Tess are in my house and probably wondering where the hell I am and if I'm okay. *I really don't deserve them.*

Green eyes stare, challenging me.

I'm once again overwhelmed with a feeling of self-consciousness. At a loss for what to say, and knowing I'm going to have to face my friends at some point, I thank Aiden for the ride home and the hospitality.

"Thank you for saving Orthus."

His statement, though heartfelt, leaves me wondering if there is something more he wants to tell me. Or ask me. Being the epitome of grace, I stumble backward while saluting him and force an awkward grin. "Anytime."

Unsure of what to do after completely embarrassing myself in more ways than one, I offer him a shy wave and scurry off to what awaits me inside.

CHAPTER 6
AIDEN

My newly named "crotch rocket" kicks up gravel when I drift into my driveway. Feelings of unease and confusion overrode my senses as I made my way home from Mercy's. Those same feelings now still linger in the back of my mind. I have the odd sense that I'm supposed to know something, or I've forgotten something very important, and it can't help but eat away at me. Normally, I would just assume that if I can't remember it, it's clearly not that important, but…this time, it's different.

I toss my keys onto the table in the entranceway and pause in the foyer, just in the middle of the witch's knot—one of many protection symbols scattered around the house—that's inlaid in the wooden floor. I rake my hand through my hair, fingers snagging in wavy tendrils mussed by wind during the ride home. Pacing back and forth, I'm bothered by a mental block I can't figure my way around. Something about the woman I just met has triggered a suppressed memory

I was unaware I had until now. It's almost as if we were meant to have crossed paths.

Had Orthus not bounded through the door upon my arrival home from meeting with the art gallery's manager, I would not have chased him through the woods. Had I not chased him through the woods, he would not have seen Mercy running...or the car that I could tell was aiming for her, not Orthus. Had she not had the heart to save the dog by trying to shield him from a direct hit, I would have been taking her to the hospital and grieving my friend.

Having heard me come home and the sound of my boots pacing against the hardwood floor, Orthus trots over to me and positions himself a few feet in front of where I stand with hands on hips. He tilts his head, pointed ears reaching diagonally out, and blinks his two-toned eyes as if offering to be a sounding board for the questions crowding my mind.

"Why?" I lean forward, bracing my hands just above my knees, and make eye contact with the oversized wolf I've somehow managed to convince people is a rare breed of domestic dog.

Intelligent eyes stare back at me hopelessly, but they seem to indicate a willingness to communicate the answers to my questions. He seems to be blazing with frustration over his inability to speak and my inability to understand. All he can manage is a huff and two stomps of his front paws.

"How did *you* know she was in trouble? And why would you risk yourself for a stranger?"

My only answer is a low growl as the word "stranger" leaves my lips, as if the word is an insult or offensive to him. So I lean in even closer to his eye level and tease him out of a force of habit. "It's because you thought she looked pretty, you dog." I wink. "Have you been sneaking out, trying to find another lap to curl up on? Prefer the company of a beautiful woman over my own? I wouldn't blame you..." I pause as my thoughts begin to drift; I think back to the eyes of the bloodied and bruised woman I carried home.

She was a stranger then, and just barely no longer one now. But there was something in those eyes of hers that looked familiar. It was only for a brief moment, just before she fell into an unconscious sleep after I scooped her lithe body into my arms; a light that caught my attention flickered in her eyes. As quickly as that light appeared, it vanished, her gaze receding to a dull, vacant stare before she finally succumbed to the consequences of a blow to the head. Even before her eyes went dull, the hope that shined briefly left me feeling both empty and sad.

Orthus smacks me in the leg with his paw, grabbing my attention and pulling me back to the present.

Narrowing my eyes at Orthus, I continue my questioning. "Who *is* this woman to you?" I lift my eyebrows in interrogation, a teasing smirk lifting the corner of my mouth.

Orthus's response is that of pinned ears and a snap of his maw, which causes me to instantly jerk back. With massive paws, he steps closer to me and points towards my chest with his nose while maintaining eye contact.

Had it been anyone else in my position, they would be shitting their pants. Having known Orthus for so many lifetimes, however, I am sure he won't hurt me; he's just agitated that I'm not understanding whatever it is he wishes me to know. And honestly? *Same, bud. Same.*

"Calm down. I'm sorry for teasing you. Trust me, I wish you could talk to me, too." I pause before adding, "However, I think you being able to talk would end up backfiring on me."

Orthus squints his eyes at me before turning and stomping away to brood in front of the fireplace.

Perhaps there is something I can do to trigger my memories. And if anyone knows how to do that, it is good old dad.

Pricking my finger with a pocketknife, I carefully draw in blood three runes on top of the gold slab crafted into the oversized door made of nuummite. First is Eihwaz, then Perthro, and I finish with Algiz, the three runes stacked vertically one after the other. Palm pressed flat to the runes, smearing them into the gold slab where a doorknob should be, the metal starts to warm, and the heavy door begins to creak open.

"I should probably oil those hinges," I mumble under my breath.

I'm greeted by the scent of incense and coffee as I step through the doorway and feel an electrifying shift in energy that pulses through my blood. The brightly lit sconces illuminate the stone walls of the underground hallway connecting my house to the underground bomb shelter that has since been transformed into my father's realm.

Leave it to doomsday preppers to create the perfect accommodations for a buyer in need of a home that provides both privacy and secrecy against the outside world. So long as my father and I have possession of this particular door, the only other thing we need is the right space. The door is created of nuummite; it bridges our spiritual and physical realms, and the space behind it exists completely on another plane—hence the need for a lot of space and, most importantly, secured privacy.

One hand in my pocket, I let the other hang down by my side, fingers reaching out just enough to lightly drag across the engraved runes covering the entirety of the hall's stone walls. I've only ever tried to decipher bits and pieces of the history the runes weave, reading enough to know they attempt to describe the story of creation—life, death, rebirth, and how everything came to be. Each lifetime, I take another stab at translating another portion of the hall, and I become more enlightened than I was in the preceding lifetime; that's the reason I'm more aware of myself and my past lives than the average person is. Another reason for my awareness is my father, as he is the overseer of Helheim.

The hall eventually opens into a central space resembling a grand, open-layout dwelling. Polished concrete floors run throughout the entire space, the expanse broken up by light-colored fur rugs that I've tried time and time again to explain to my father would be considered poor taste nowadays. The matte-black painted walls reach cathedral-high to an ivory ceiling decorated with intricate embossments of ancient patterns and symbols, a large dome light in its center. The light reflecting off the scattered accents of silver throughout the decor and furniture, as well as the bone-white sculptures depicting gods and goddesses from an assortment of religions, helps to lighten the otherwise-dark atmosphere.

To the far left, tan-leather furniture claims one section as a space akin to that of a great room, boasting a fireplace made of stone the same ivory color as the ceiling and large enough for a cow to occupy. Framed and hanging on either side of the fireplace are some of the first star maps I ever created for my father, inked with blood on stretched and tanned animal skin. Below the maps are iron-framed, wooden shelves filled with tomes dating back thousands of centuries—some even bound in human flesh. I can't help but occasionally laugh at the thought of the horrified look on some vegan's face if one ever found themselves in this space.

To the far right is a fully functional chef's kitchen. Botanical specimens used for tinctures, rituals, and food prep wrap around the kitchen and dangle from hanging shelves centered over a large island covered in used and unused glass bottles, beakers, and flasks. Pestles and their mortars of varying sizes are scattered across the butcher-block countertop situated under the fully stocked apothecary cabinets spanning the length of the wall behind a large dining table.

At the center of it all, under the light of the dome fixture, and the first thing to be seen upon reaching the end of the rune-engraved hall, sits a gargantuan mahogany desk atop an ornamental rug. Behind the desk, in a high-back chair, sits my father sipping his tea and fooling around with his intricately detailed model of this solar system. His backdrop is a floor-to-ceiling window that offers a view of the cosmos more impressive than any telescope known to man—one of the perks of magic-infused ancient glass.

Because my father is obviously entranced by his current project, I clear my throat to announce my presence. I watch as he is startled by the noise and fumbles with the tools in his hands, knocking off its base the planet he is working on. The glass ball rolls across his desk, and he snatches it just before it can crash to the ground, shatter, and release the gases of the planet it represents. With the glass ball cupped in his outstretched hand, he turns his head to make eye contact with me.

"You know better than to startle me when I'm working with such delicate pieces," he says, his voice reprimanding but calm.

"My apologies, sir. Although, you have to admit that it's not a bad thing to have your reflexes checked every so often at your age." I saunter farther into the room with my hands in my pockets and plop down in one of the two chairs he has in front of his desk for the visitors he rarely receives.

"I take it you didn't come down here to check on my reflexes out of concern for my—your beloved father's, might I add—health?" He leans back in his chair with a hand placed over his heart, his glasses slipping to the end of his nose and his eyes peering over the lenses satirically.

"You're basically immortal, so of course that's not the reason I came down." My eyes follow him as, despite his body's age, he gracefully stands from his chair and walks over to the kitchen area. I can't help but notice the bit of bounce in his step, increasing my curiosity, which was already piqued when he actually tried to joke with me just seconds ago. I continue to observe the sprightly old man as he returns from the kitchen with a mug in each hand.

"Tea?" Without waiting for my response, a mug of steaming-hot tea is shoved into my hands.

"You're awfully chipper this morning," I grumble, placing my mug on the large desk in front of the window. I start to poke one of the planets dangling from his model, only to have my hand slapped away before touching it. Subtly rolling my eyes, I wait as my father begins to clear his throat, apparently readying himself to start rattling on about some newfound solar system, star formation, or planet I know I'm going to have to map out for him.

"How can I not be excited when I believe I have uncovered some new findings amongst the stars?" he questions, his dark-brown eyes sparkling as if they hold their own galaxy, as he raises his bushy white brows enthusiastically.

The question would have sounded poetic to an average person, but for me, it just means more work, mapping the stars for whatever cosmic question my father is trying to find answers to. At least they make for exhibit-worthy art pieces when he finds them to be of no use. Turns out my artistic talent is more lucrative than I could have imagined.

I reach for my tea and breathe in heavily through my nose. Feeling the need to parent my own father, I take a second to collect myself. My fingers pinch the bridge of my nose as I let out a deep exhale. "While you were making these discoveries, did you happen to check in on the souls, especially the newest members? Or have you been solely focusing on your latest…fixation?"

"BAH!"

He startles me with his outburst as he flicks his hand at me to indicate I do not appreciate his work…well, hobby. I appreciate his work when he—oh, I don't know—does any. Instead, he spends all his time tinkering with the maps he has me create and the solar-system models he cherishes dearly.

"It's not like the souls are in a rush to go anywhere. They've reached their destination, so to speak. They'll manage until I have time to visit."

"All you have is time, Dad. The souls should be your priority, not"—I throw out my hands to gesture at the mess of research, graphs, and maps that is scattered around his desk—"whatever this is."

"You don't see the bigger picture yet, Aiden. You must see the bigger picture. I'm doing this for *you*! I'm doing this for *us*! I'm doing this for a better world." He places his hands on my shoulders while standing over me, his wrinkled brow set in determination. He's been like this for as long as I can remember—overly enthusiastic about his next big idea—forever failing to stay on top of his main role as overseer of the realm of souls.

The man is a genius, don't get me wrong. Although, how could he not be, what with all the lives he's lived—all that time to absorb the history, culture, and science the world has had to offer. I understand the need for further exploration and questioning comes with all that knowledge, but for fuck's sake, if I weren't here, all Hel would break loose. Literally.

"In addition to the bigger picture, I believe I have figured out a way to finally stop your endless cycle of reincarnation. I'm close to piecing together how to speed up the process and make you immortal, like me. You won't have to wait any longer to break the cycle! No more lessons to learn, obstacles to face, or having to go through the tedious process of remembering who you truly are with each knew rebirth," he says, his words attempting to form an inspirational speech, but failing to hit their mark or pique my interest.

"Mm-hmm. Yeah. Aren't we not supposed to fuck with the cycle? You know about those silly little things called consequences, right?" I lift a brow and pluck his hands one at a time from my shoulders.

Sensing his irritation, I push my chair back and stand. Walking over to the window, I cross my arms over my chest and stare out into the endless abyss of stars and planets, no horizon in sight. Frustrated, I begin to pace.

"One day, son. One day, you'll look out the window and see what I see. Then you will understand what has been revealed to me as the bigger picture…the great plan," he says triumphantly, as if he has already conquered whatever it is he means to conquer.

I have to give it to the man; he doesn't know when to back down or give up. It's always been something I admire about him, even though it tends to make him appear more like a lunatic than the powerful overseer he truly is. I can't fathom what this bigger picture could possibly be, the one he keeps speaking of. And, quite frankly, in this moment, I couldn't give two shits about it.

"Until then…the souls?" I ask, only to be met with silence and a blank stare. "I need to go check on them, don't I?" I sigh and start to make my way over to the hallway that leads to the viewing station, but I'm cut short by my father's sudden acknowledgment that I most likely visited him for a reason.

"Was there something I could help you with?" he asks with some interest, still clearly distracted by whatever the hell he was working on when I arrived.

"It's nothing. Well, I don't know. I met this woman." I quickly relay to him with one look to keep his mouth shut before cutting me off mid-sentence with twenty questions.

He throws his hands up and gestures for me to continue.

"It's just…there's something about her. Something familiar, maybe? I'm not sure. It's like there's something I know, or am supposed to know, but there's this wall, in my head, keeping me from some memory, either past life or present," I explain, running a hand through my hair in frustration.

When I meet my father's eyes, I swear I see a glimmer of panic. Before I'm able to read further into his reaction, he interjects, "Women will do that to you. They'll make you go crazy in the head."

I stare at him with a blank expression, then shake my head before slapping my hands on the sides of my legs. Brushing off his careless response, I turn on my heels and start making my way over to a hallway different than the one I used to enter the space.

"Don't worry, Aiden; our memory tends to go when we age. I'm sure it's nothing!" he yells after me.

With my back turned, without facing him, I wave him off and head down the second of the three halls that branch off from the central living space. The lights flicker on one by one, leading me down the spiraling hall until I reach the end, where I can oversee the souls who currently reside in Helheim.

"Don't worry, Dad. I'll do your work for you, on top of my own work. It's not like *I'm* the one who juggles life between two places or anything," I mutter under my breath, once again rolling my eyes.

My steps echo and disturb the silence as I make my way down the ancient stone hallway. I swear, each time I come back, this place gets creepier. You would think, after all this time, my father would entertain the idea of hiring an interior designer for down here.

Death doesn't have to be so doom and gloom. In fact, it shouldn't be. There's beauty in death if people could only see it as a part of the soul's journey. People especially have become so attached to the physical world that they've become blind to our purest and truest nature. Death does not mean the end; it is simply a necessary step in moving on to what's next. A soul will come back a thousand times, sometimes more, before figuring this out—and when they do, I promise, any fear of death is vanquished. I'm proof of that. Man, did I fuck around and learn a lot in my past lives before I got to the place I am now. As with piecing memories together after having a regrettable night out with friends, acknowledging past lives can be just as cringeworthy—it's not for the faint of heart.

After my stroll down the winding hall, I finally find the arched entryway and step into the grand room that holds my father's viewing station. The amount of money I could probably get for this house if people only knew its square footage. But it's true what they say about money—you really can't take it with you.

It never fails to take my breath away, this part of my father's hidden realm sequestered beneath my inconspicuous, humble abode. The vaulted ceilings of this cylindrical room are something beyond imagination. Beautifully crafted carvings decorate the supporting stone arches that go from floor to ceiling. Delicate imagery portrays the beauty of what Helheim truly is, not how it has been depicted to the masses throughout history. Man-manipulated history has truly done a number on the truth of existence. After all, throughout history, most influential leaders understood that the easiest way to gain power is through instilling fear and threatening horrific consequences. The truth about death and the afterlife certainly suffered—and still does—the brunt of those consequences.

I step up to the podium situated in the center of the room and place my palm on top of another gold slab, inducing a stream of energy that flows from me to the cold object beneath my hand. Warmth settles in the center of my palm first; then it slowly spreads to my fingertips. A faint light begins to flicker, and soon my hand glows like the warm light of the harvest moon. Images of Helheim grace the smooth sections of wall and ceiling that are not carved. Soon, I'm able to glance into the concealed realm of those who rest in peace while waiting to either return to their original essence or reincarnate to learn—or for some, relearn—the things necessary to transition to a higher plane.

Sweeping my eyes around the protected realm of Helheim—known to some as the underworld, one of its many other names—I take in the souls' temporary home. It is constructed of various wide-open, grassy fields broken up by flowing rivers, babbling brooks, and the occasional mountain range that reaches towards the dusky skies. Bountiful flora as far as the eye can see and Helheim's own species of fauna provide familiar comfort and companionship to all who dwell in this space. It's a place that most might mistake for their concept of heaven to be—if they only knew…if they only understood.

At first glance, everything seems to be at peace; nothing and no one is out of place. Before I'm able to perform an in-depth inspection, the projected image surrounding me begins to flicker out. I snatch my hand back from the warmth of the gold slab to find a small, furry black beast clawing at my jeans.

"Dammit, Void. I wasn't done checking in on things yet," I scold the mass of black fur and scoop him up into my arms. "Did Orthus chase you down here again? Or did you just return from delivering messages?"

The cat vibrates in my arms as he purrs and bats at my face with his paw.

"I love you, but you're annoying sometimes."

With a small, spastic shadow in tow, I lead the way out of the cylindrical room and head back towards where my father most likely still sits, laboring on anything but his actual work. As expected, I find him transfixed, yet again, by his models and his research.

"Everything seem all right?" my father says without even bothering to look up from his work.

Someone needs to work on his priorities, and it isn't me. "From what I could see"—I snap my gaze to my feline companion, who is now concentrating on cleaning his paw—"everything seems normal."

"See! Nothing to worry about. The place pretty much runs itself." He offers me a quick glance and smirks as if to make a point. "Now, if you could take these papers and unfinished maps up to your study to complete them for me." He walks over, arms full, and presses the contents to my chest.

"Remind me again, what exactly are these maps for? Why are they so special to you? Not that I mind creating them, but…" I struggle with the mess that was shoved at me, trying not to drop anything.

"The bigger picture." My father smiles at me, his reading glasses threatening to slide down his long, narrow nose.

"Right." I stare at him with a slightly annoyed expression and continue to juggle all that is in my arms before turning to leave my father to his project. Aware that I did not receive any answers from my old man, I call for Void to follow as I make my way back to my own study…to work on these pointless maps and mull over what I can't seem to remember.

CHAPTER 7
MERCY

"M ERCY! THANK GOD!" A warm body wraps around my own, arms snug tightly around my shoulders. "We were so fucking worried about you!" Tess holds me at arm's length, fingers digging into my shoulders, a mix of concern and relief plastered all over her face. She wraps me in her arms once more, embracing me in a viselike grip. "I thought you were dead," she utters before a dramatic sob.

"Okay, let's not be overly dramatic about this, Tess," Henry says from where he is standing at the island in my kitchen, coffee in hand, trying to play the part of someone who is cool, calm, and collected. The yin to Tess's yang. I know him well enough, though, to pick up on what's left of his nervous energy, which is made apparent by the vein that pops out ever so slightly on his left temple.

At a loss for words, drained of any energy to try and explain what exactly happened, I just shrug, hang my head, and sigh. "It's sort of a long story...but I'm fine! I promise!" Out of habit, I force a smile.

"Fine, my ass!" Tess blurts out. "Henry said you didn't show up for work, weren't answering calls or texts. We drive over here to check on you, thinking you overslept, were sick, or in need of help. I don't know! Assuming it would be something stupid or minor you were dealing with. So can you imagine our horrific surprise, discovering an empty house, a swinging screen door, and your garden ripped to shreds with shattered glass scattered everywhere!" Her voice heightens in pitch, and her eyes become wider, more terrified, as she scolds me, her intentions pure.

What's left of my heart crumbles at seeing the absolute terror I selfishly dragged my friends through. "I'm so sorry, Tess." My brows furrow, and my eyes begin to tear up. I'm shaking, not out of anxiety for once, but instead from immense hatred of myself for the trouble I have caused. "I can explain—" I start to take a breath, a moment to figure out how or what I am going to tell them, but I'm cut off by Henry.

"Mercy, what the actual fuck?" He sweeps his arm around the house to make me really look at what my two friends walked in on.

My house is trashed. Wine bottles litter the counter, the air reeks of stale weed, and the open screen door frames a perfect view of the war zone that is my garden. One look at Henry, and I can tell he is about to explode with a mixture of anger and frustration heavily laced with fear for his friend— for me. *I can't do this anymore.*

Tess snaps her gaze to Henry and curses. "Henry! Back the fuck off! I'm sure she has an explanation for all this!"

Oh, Tess. I do not deserve you.

"She better have an explanation! At this point, we are entitled to one, Tess! We've been absolutely frantic all day!" Henry's voice is almost bellowing, not at Tess, but at the situation. His eyes penetrate mine, and the angles of his face sharpen. Without looking away, he says to Tess, "We didn't hear from her at all last night, and she was a no-show to work this morning. We come looking for her, only to stumble upon this disaster"—his hands furiously motion to our surroundings—"and are finally graced by her wearing… What are you even wearing? Whose clothes are those?"

I'm leaning against the counter now, letting every word sink in.

Burden.

Sensing my discomfort, Tess goes to take my hand, but Henry has had enough.

Of course, he's had enough. I'm too much. Too much of a disaster, not enough of a friend.

"We are leaving; she's fine. Clearly. Just out on a bender with God knows who." Henry is guiding a distraught Tess to my front door.

I don't move. I don't try to stop them. I stand still and drown inwardly from shame, regret, and absolute hatred of myself. Without turning to face them, I whisper under my breath, hoping they won't hear, "I don't want to do this anymore."

"Call me, Mercy," Tess yells as she's ushered through the door by Henry.

The door slams shut behind my friends, and I'm left standing alone in my kitchen. I grab the kitchen towel crumpled up on the counter beside me, ball it up in my fists, and use it to muffle my scream. I feel a combination of nothing and everything, at once, and it's all just too much.

I'm too much. I'm too much and not enough. Never enough. Always a burden. A waste of a life.

I sink to the floor and rock back and forth, hugging my knees tight to my chest. My heart thunders, and the only thoughts I have left are the ones provided by the voice harbored inside my head. I have tried to fight this voice for so long now, and I'm fucking exhausted. The medication I take does little to quiet it, and the recreational substances have become Band-Aids without adhesive. Nothing works anymore, and it's all just too much to handle.

Let go.

Shaky hands help to push me up, off the floor. Once standing, I look for my newest bottle of refilled benzos. With a hand braced on the counter, I eye the pill bottle. Shoulders slumped in defeat, the voice telling me to put an end to all this, I close my eyes and take a deep breath.

Let go.

Eyes set in solemn determination, I go to grab the pill bottle to down all its contents. Just as my fingertips brush the side of the orange bottle, my name so boldly printed on it, I'm startled by the sound of a growl. I whip around, my eyes meeting one eye of gold and the other of silver.

"Orthus?"

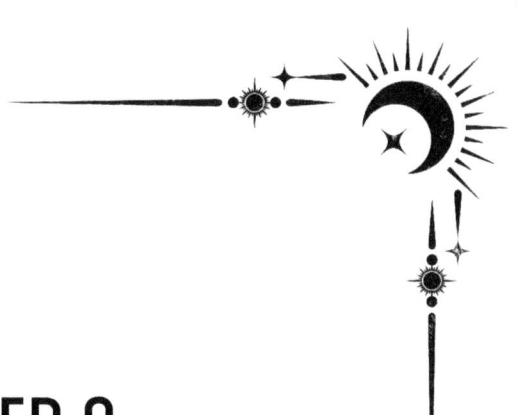

CHAPTER 8
MERCY

My couch now occupied by a dozing and snoring bear of a dog, I busy myself with cleaning up my little house. When I can't clean the mess that is my mind, the next best thing is to clean the mess that surrounds me—in this case, my entire house. Interior today, exterior—mainly the garden—at some point in the future.

I change into my own clothes, tossing what Aiden had given me to wear into the wash with the rest of my dirty laundry. Swapping the oversized shirt and sweatpants for basic attire—black leggings, grey tank, and a knitted blue cardigan. Feeling a little more myself—and snapped out of turmoil by the timely intrusion of Orthus—I pop in earbuds and set my music's volume to blaring to keep the voice at bay.

I start upstairs and work my way down, losing myself in every dust-riddled nook and cranny. What once looked as if it had narrowly escaped its own personal tornado, now, rivals a sanitized surgical suite. Satisfied with the progress and still needing something to occupy my mind, I rummage through my hall closet for fall decorations. For some, it may be a bit early for fall decor, but the leaves are starting to hint at the change in seasons and the start of crisp mornings. While others tend to hold on to every last sun-scorched day, I welcome and eagerly anticipate the transition into the cooler season. Call me a pumpkin-spice basic bitch all you want; I happily embrace this time of year.

Candle in one hand, lighter in the other, I ride the fleeting high I'm on and dance my way to the coffee table. It's only a matter of time before the dopamine fizzles out. AC/DC's "Highway to Hell" plays next in my ears, and I find myself humming along.

After adding the candle to the autumnal centerpiece now adorning my coffee table, I reach over to light the wick. I spin on my heels, eyes closed and smiling, breathing in the scents of apples and cinnamon that take over my household. Losing myself in the energy of the music and the cozy vibes that have settled into my home, I sing out the chorus to what I was expecting to be an empty room…aside from Orthus, who I now realize is awake and alert.

"Awfully cheery rendition you've got there, considering the lyrics." A male figure leans against the framed entry to my living room; he is framed by the warm glow cast by the kitchen lights.

"Hello, Orthus." He raises a single brow at the dog, lips set in a tight line.

Unfazed by the stern look, Orthus greets Aiden with a huff.

This dog really enjoys troubling his owner.

"I knocked," Aiden says as he pushes away from the wall and stands, hands up in placation, no longer casually leaning against the framed entry. "Actually, I knocked a few times and rang the doorbell." He points to his ears and then to me.

"Now I understand the lack of response. In my defense, the door was open."

Frazzled by the second round of unexpected company, I'm about to explain Orthus's presence here, but stop to shake my head and collect my thoughts. "Wait… The door was open? Or the door was unlocked?" I question my intruder.

"Unlocked." As if he owns the place, Aiden saunters over to the couch and plops himself down right beside Orthus. "If you think you aren't in trouble after this latest disappearing act, you are sadly mistaken." He ruffles the fur between the ears of the dog, who knows all too well that he most definitely is getting away with this.

"Unlocked is not the same as open." I'm still standing in the center of my living room, hands on my hips, weight shifted to one side. *The audacity of this man.*

"I suppose you're right. I also suppose that you were eventually going to return my dog?" he asks with a condescending smirk plastered on his face.

Arrogant prick. "Before insinuating that I was intentionally harboring your dog, know that I wanted to reach out to you. However, it's a little hard to do when I don't have your number or any way of contacting you." I stare him down.

From Aiden's features, it appears he is trying not to crack under the pressure; I just know that he's holding back some lighthearted yet snarky response. His emerald eyes dance with mischief and the desire to playfully joke at my expense.

I challenge him with my gaze before ultimately surrendering to the comfort of my chaise lounge, slumping into the soft cushions. Forearm dramatically covering my eyes and nose, I let out a gruff sigh. Moving my arm just enough to see out of one eye, I'm met with a similar scene to the one I awakened to earlier that morning. Formal attire, though, exchanged for something more casual—dark, ink-stained jeans, T-shirt, and brown-leather bomber jacket—Aiden sits at the edge of the couch, forearms resting on his knees.

He tilts his head in a manner that is equal parts curious and wolfish and asks, "Long day?"

"If you only knew." I slide my forearm back over my eyes, entirely blocking my view. I lounge back, completely at odds with how I feel inside, feigning complacency about his company, which is difficult to do, considering he was a stranger just this morning. Honestly, for the little I do know about him, he still is very much a stranger to me.

"Eh, one could argue I might know some of it."

I slap my arm down next to me and side-eye him, clearly irritated by his remark.

"If looks could kill…" He chuckles.

Aiden sits back comfortably in the corner of the sofa, settling in. One arm outstretched along the back of the couch, fingertips pressed to his temple, the other hand supporting his head. Propping one ankle on top the knee of his outstretched leg, he stares at me.

"Can I help you?" I ask.

"Just seems like we are set up perfectly for a therapy session, so let's hear it." He wiggles his fingers at me in such a way that makes it seem as if he really does want to hear what I have to say, but also couldn't care less about my situation.

"You are a complete stranger—" I start, but am interrupted when Aiden corrects me and refers to himself as more of an acquaintance now.

"Yeah, anyway… Stranger, acquaintance—either way— I'm not going to unload my trauma on you." I'm still lounging back in the chaise. Still slightly bothered by my odd sense of comfort between us, but leaning into it for shits and giggles at this point.

Orthus slinks off the couch, abandoning Aiden for a seat beside me. He nestles in tight against my body, somehow managing to find a spot big enough for him to wiggle into. Curled up into a massive ball of black fur, he thumps his head down on my chest and stares at me with endearment. As I gently stroke the soft fur between his ears, he becomes a weighted blanket on my chest and dozes off.

"Who better to vent to than someone who barely knows you and can offer some unbiased opinions?" Aiden prods, encouraging me to open up.

With a heavy sigh, I avert my gaze to the ceiling. "Fine. You asked for it."

He tries his best to mockingly impersonate the posture of a therapist, pushing invisible glasses up the bridge of his nose and giving me a cue to begin with a flick of his wrist in my direction.

"Fucking hell," I mutter, rolling my eyes. I take a deep breath and think about what I am going to say. At this point, I have nothing to lose, so I let loose my words.

"Remember when you were little and you would look at the world through a child's mind's eye? There was never a moment where your dreams were too big. There was never a moment where any obstacle or challenge life had to throw at you could deter you from your ultimate goal. In true ignorant bliss, anything was possible."

I chance a glance in Aiden's direction to see if he's actually listening. Slightly surprised that he is, I return my gaze to the ceiling, unable to look at him when speaking my truth, and continue, "I remember daydreaming about being an artist, or maybe even a vet. I also remember daydreaming about being a rock star, believe it or not." I start to gently laugh at myself. "Artist. Rock star. Vet. It didn't matter what I wanted to be when I grew up. My parents were there to support me in any way they could."

"Sounds like you grew up in a supportive household," he responds.

"Oh, I most definitely did. I grew up with a loving and supportive family, always had—still have—the greatest friends. I could have done anything with my life had I just… This is going to sound cheesy, but…you know…believed in myself." I shrug and cringe at my own words.

"I'm waiting for the moment where this all goes to shit, because as of right now, everything seems fine," he says, lightly judging in a way I think I'm supposed to find funny, charming even.

Clearly not a therapist.

I side-eye him and continue, "The best way I can explain it would be…" I take a moment to think. "Okay, so when I was little, I had this fantasy of becoming a rock star, like I mentioned before. I imagined thousands and thousands of people chanting my name, singing my songs, believing in my art. Believing in me. It was a constant daydream I fell into whenever my mind would wander." I take a moment to let the memories of my past dreams linger, before shoving them down, as I did years ago.

"As I grew older, the stages in my mind grew smaller. The crowds dwindled. The daydream starting to become tainted by reality. Eventually, I stopped seeing myself as a rock star and settled on seeing myself on a stage at a local dive bar on karaoke night."

I look over to see Aiden staring at me as if I had two heads.

"What I'm trying to get at is I realized, as I lost confidence in myself, my dreams became smaller. As a little girl, I was confident I would achieve a rock-star level of greatness. As an adult, I began to lower the bar for myself. I would have to throw back multiple shots before even considering stepping up to the mic for karaoke nowadays."

I sink farther into the cushions, Orthus feeling heavier and heavier on my chest.

"You can sing?" Aiden asks, clearly skirting around the shadow work I'm vulnerably laying out in front of him.

"You suck at this. This isn't about my ability to sing. It's somewhat of a metaphor for my life, okay? Did I imagine myself as a rock star when I was little? Yes. Was that exactly what I wanted to be? No. Did I think of myself as someone who had the potential to become a person of rock-star level in whatever I ended up pursuing? Absolutely. Did I grow up and let the gruesome reality of life ruin my childhood confidence? Yeah. Who doesn't? Did I finally realize that I'm never going to be better than a pathetic woman singing karaoke at her local dive bar, in search of some sort of acknowledgment from hammered drunks, while working a basic job that means nothing to me but pays the bills so I can barely stay afloat?" My rant leaves me breathless.

As I'm catching my breath, Aiden takes the opportunity to interject, "Can I guess the answer?"

Again I give him a look, wishing daggers would shoot from my eyes. Through a tight smile I snap, "I just finally accepted that the voice in my head is right. I'm not whatever version of a rock star I thought I could be. It was never in the cards for me. I'm just…not enough. Not enough for myself… or anyone, for that matter. I'm no one." I would be shaking at this point were it not for the weight of Orthus pinning me down.

There is so much more to it than what I just unleashed on Aiden. My fuckups. My failures. My lack of following things through. The voice that perpetually tears me down, reiterating time and time again that I'm an absolute mess of a human—all by my own hand.

I glare over at the work of art that is Aiden and become even more infuriated. *Why is this man giving me the time of day anyway? Look at me. Look at him. I'm just entertainment for him at this point.* After an awkward moment of silence, I drop my gaze.

Aiden clears his throat and returns to resting his forearms on his knees.

I turn my head to the side, avoiding eye contact and trying to focus mainly on the beast that is now snoring on my chest.

"Have you ever considered the voice you speak of is actually encouraging you, not knocking you down?" Aiden asks, his voice soft.

"Oh, trust me. The voice in my head is not for the faint of heart."

"No. It's not. Because *you* aren't for the faint of heart, Mercy," he says in a tone a bit more assertive now and in a way that indicates he knows me better than I think he does.

"If only you knew what the voice says to me. She's a fucking bitch. Making me well aware of my shortcomings, my flaws, my lack of everything." I'm sitting straight up now, eyes wild, hair disheveled. I can feel the tears start to form.

Orthus leaps off me.

"Ever consider the voice stopped fighting for you when you wouldn't stop fighting it? Denying it? *Maybe* consider the voice was encouraging you to dream bigger, and it gave up when you ran from it. Gave up encouraging you and gave in to what you've been accusing it of."

The intensity in his stare and words pummels me in the chest. I'm left grappling for words that just won't form, mouth open in shock.

When I finally manage to speak, my eyes open wide, and a cold sweat makes my clothes feel too tight and restrictive. He doesn't understand. He's not the type who would ever understand. I stand and point to the front door. "Get out."

"Look, I'm just trying to help." He sits back, looking at me as if I'm the one out of line.

"Help? You ask me to vent to you, and instead of just listening, you basically side with my demons," I say, seething, my voice low and rushed. I've gone into complete defensive mode.

"Side with your demons? That's what we are calling it? No wonder you're in a constant battle with yourself." He laughs.

He fucking laughed! "I don't know why I even opened up to you. I'm such an idiot. Again, I barely know you! Take your dog and get the fuck out." I'm talking through clenched teeth by the end of my outburst.

"Someone gets triggered easily." Aiden sits quietly, unflinching from the tension building in the room. Instead, he calmly waits for my next outburst directed at him. His patience more of a challenge and less for comfort or empathy.

"I don't need someone to baby me and tell me everything will be all right. I *also* don't need someone…let alone a—"

I'm stopped short by Aiden holding up his pointer finger. "AN acquaintance."

My blood boils, and I can feel the heat flush my cheeks. Pure rage over this asshole's inability to read a room overwhelms me.

He's not wrong, though.

I'm about to lay into him, ready to spit out venomous comebacks, when a knock at my door interrupts our fight. A heavy breath forces its way out of me as I redirect my energy to whoever is knocking at my front door. If I were to guess who it could possibly be, my money is on Tess coming to check on me.

A low growl from Orthus catches Aiden's attention, and he immediately gets up to see who might be knocking. Reaching behind himself, he flashes his palm to Orthus, motioning for both the dog and me to stay put.

If Aiden were to turn around, he would be met with my look of disbelief. *How dare he tell me what to do in my own home?*

While Aiden goes to investigate who is at the front door, I get up to grab two wineglasses from the kitchen—one for me and one for Tess…not Aiden. *She's going to be quite surprised when the door opens and it's not me but Aiden standing there.*

Orthus looks at me with worry in his two-toned eyes and lets out a soft whimper.

"You might have to listen to him, but I don't."

From the living room, I begin to walk towards the kitchen. I'm about to reach the cabinet where my glassware is stored when I hear the jiggling of a doorknob. A quick glance to the back door leading out to my garden hints that someone is trying to pick the lock. My breath catches in my throat, and my eyes lock on the doorknob as if my stare could magically help it stay strong enough to hold. I fumble around my kitchen, reaching for something that could be used as a weapon. My hand makes contact with what feels to be the handle of an iron skillet I leave out purely as decoration.

This should do.

Gripping the handle, I ready myself for the intruder to break through and give me a chance to use the skillet for the first time—even if that's not for what it's actually intended. I hear the *click-clack* of nails against the kitchen tile and then feel the warm body of Orthus brush against my leg. His head is lowered, and his teeth are bared.

"Aiden!" I shout-whisper from the corner of my mouth for additional backup.

No response.

"Aiden!" I try once more.

Before I'm able to try again, the doorknob clicks and slowly begins to turn. Adrenaline is pumping through my body at this point, and an overwhelming sense of fight—not flight—takes control. I wind up, the skillet gripped firmly in my hands, ready to strike this fucker down. Preparing myself for battle, I start counting and get to three before the door is smashed open. A man—I swear I recognize him in the brief moment we make eye contact—charges me. Before I know it, I'm being tackled to the floor.

I hit the tile floor hard but manage to keep my head from smacking the ground. I kick out, aiming for anything to debilitate the monster on top of me. I scream in his face like a banshee, swinging the pan at his head with my free hand. I make contact just before Orthus lunges, jaws snapping, and drags the man off me.

The bastard lets out an agonizing cry as teeth pierce skin.

From nowhere, I'm being lifted to my feet. Startled by the contact, I try to scramble and whip my head around to see who has me. Hoping that it's Aiden, I'm crushed when a face I've never seen before comes into view.

A smell as strong as sulfur invades my nose as I'm hauled to my feet. My wrists are bound behind me by one giant, clammy hand, while the other grabs far up my throat. Grime-covered fingers dig into my jawbone, the harsh pressure allowing the intruder to wrench my head into an uncomfortable position. Prickly whiskers of my intruder's beard irritate my skin as he brings his foul mouth to my ear. He jolts my arms and pulls me in tight to his massive body as I, to no avail, try to shake him off. My wrists threaten to snap under his grip.

Again, he brings his lips to my ear. I try to tilt my head as far away as I can from this goblin of a man as he whispers against my skin, "We know who you are. Being here like *this* makes our job *so* much easier. A bit of a disappointment, I won't lie. I was looking forward to a good fight…and maybe a little fun."

My body contorts, and, fighting against the grip this man has on me, I continue to lean my head away from his, my neck straining. From the corners of my eyes, I stare him down and snarl, "There's a special place in hell for people like you."

"HA! Oh man, that's just too good. You're oblivious, aren't you?" His laugh turns into a cackle, and he tightens his grip.

What the hell is he talking about?

His partner starts to push his upper body off the floor. Blood drips from the corner of his lip, and he joins in on the maniacal fit of laughter over whatever sort of inside joke they are sharing.

I can't tell where Orthus has run off to, but all I can do is hope that he's safe and maybe alerting Aiden to what's happening.

"Let's bring her to the woods out back," the goblin man's partner sneers; I'm disgusted as I watch spit spew from his mouth at the end of each word. "We can get things started for the boss. I brought one of the stones with me. The one that should incapacitate her for a bit."

Oh, fuck no.

I attempt to kick out at the man Orthus took a bite out of, but he grabs my ankle. Built like an ogre, there is no way to escape his hold on me. He's quick to bind my ankles and wrists with electrical wire. Then, like a sack of potatoes, I'm tossed over the shoulder of the one who smells like rotten eggs, his hands wandering and grasping at me inappropriately.

I squirm on the shoulder I've been tossed over, while hollering and biting at the hand of the other man who tries to quiet me. I'm slapped across the face before being quickly hurried out the back door. The heat from his touch lingers, turning my stomach.

"LET. ME—"

I'm thrown into a pile of weeds and disturbed soil before I'm able to finish my demand. Due to the momentum, my body involuntarily rolls, and I'm left face-first in the dirt. I wiggle my knees under me and use what little strength I have left to lift my upper body. Ankles and wrists still bound, I want to at least be able to see what on earth is happening. Hunched over in a kneeling position, I take a cursory glance at my surroundings.

Fitting. I would be tossed into my shithole of a garden to die.

Out of breath, my lip split, and body aching, I try to find the cause for my sudden abandonment by my captors. My heart picks up speed when I see a disheveled Aiden bombing around the corner of my house, shovel in hand, lip busted, and cheekbone shining with blood. A car horn sounds off from the street in front of my house, and the ogre- and goblin-like men are seen scrambling to their feet and sprinting off in the direction of the sound.

Realizing he wasn't going to catch up with the two runaways in time to detain them, Aiden diverts his course to me. Tossing the shovel to the side, he's quick to get to work on the wire constricting my limbs. Eyes looking everywhere but at me, he stays on alert and asks if I'm okay. I can barely muster a response before I'm freed from my bindings and being escorted back into my house. Holding on to me with one arm, Aiden uses his free hand to pull his phone from his pocket and dials 9-1-1.

What the actual fuck just happened...

CHAPTER 9
AIDEN

The normal thing to do was exactly what I did—call the police. What I truly wanted to do, however, was chase after the bastards who ambushed Mercy in her home and rip them apart limb from limb. The adrenaline rush eases from my system, but the intrusive thoughts remain. Every worried glance I get from Mercy, as she explains what happened to the police, I meet with a look of support and reassurance. All the while, I fight a surge of overprotection raging inside, tempting me to handle the situation myself.

Orthus lies on the couch next to Mercy, tail gently wagging, eyes softly focused on hers, nose nuzzling into her shaking hands. I stand back, leaning against the entryway and observing him give her the comfort she needs in the moment.

Knowing there isn't much I can do at the time and puzzled by emotions over a woman I just met, I turn to the kitchen for a glass of water. Well, a glass of water for her…and something stronger for me.

Rummaging through the cabinets for glasses, I find myself opening a door to shelves stocked with prescription bottles. Each one labeled something different. Each one marked with her name. Each one looking partially used and then placed back on the shelf for safekeeping. I make a mental note of what I'm looking at before closing the door and finally finding the cabinet filled with glasses.

After finding my way to the liquor cabinet tucked away in the corner of the kitchen, I pour myself a double pour of whiskey. Water in one hand, whiskey in the other, I head back into the living room just as the officer is wrapping up his questioning.

"Do you have everything you need, Officer?" I stand behind him, imposingly but not threateningly. I would very much like the circus of investigators to leave and take their strobing blue lights and intensity with them.

"For the moment, yes. Although, Mercy"—his eyes stay on Mercy, and I take note that they seem familiar to one another and are on a first-name basis—"I would recommend staying with someone for the next few nights. Can Tess take you in?"

Okay, so they definitely are familiar enough with one another for him to also know her friend's name.

"She's going to stay with me." The words are assertive, and they slip out before I'm able to take them back. *What the fuck am I doing?*

The officer stands to face me; he gives me a once-over, before turning back to Mercy. "I can wait here with you while you call Tess. I can even wait until she swings by to pick you up. I'm in no rush." He ends his statement with an accusatory side-eye in my direction.

What a prick.

"John, I promise I'm going to be okay. I'll have something figured out within the hour. I just need to put a bag together, and I'll make my way over to Tess's…if she'll have me," Mercy reassures the officer, who I'm pretty sure is more than willing to throw his offer out for hospitality.

Before he's able to make an offer to host her at his own place, I'm quick to again insert my presence. "I think there's been enough excitement here for the night. We'll be sure to keep you informed if anything comes up. I hope you will do the same." I can't help the smugness that rolls off every word, aware of—and ignoring—the fact that I have no claim on Mercy and have no right to speak on her behalf.

An inquisitive glance is shared amongst the three of us. Refusing to say anything more, I raise an eyebrow at John the Officer. He returns my stare with a defeated huff and places his hand on Mercy's shoulder. His innocent touch makes me heated. He assures her that he and his partners are on the case, and he will get back to her as soon as possible with any updates. A brief hug is shared between the two, and he barks an order for everyone to pack up and leave.

A few minutes later, the house is filled with an eerie silence interrupted only by our breathing and Orthus's snoring. Still standing in the middle of the living room, I face Mercy, both drinks still in hand. She pushes herself up from the couch, takes two steps towards me, and reaches straight for my glass of whiskey.

I can't help my expression as I watch the delicate, little fiend throw back the hard liquor without the slightest hint of distaste. I'm both impressed and slightly alarmed.

"That one was for me," I mutter, pretending to be offended as I offer her the water, which she declines. I follow her to the kitchen, where she refills the emptied glass.

Giving her space, I lean against the counter and watch as she pours herself another generous pour of the amber substance. The only other sound in the room, besides the ticking of the vintage clock, is glass on granite as she slides first a glass and then the bottle to me. I help myself to a healthy pour, take a swig, and break the silence between us. "I was serious about you staying with me, you know. The offer still stands." My voice is low and sincere. I stand, patiently waiting for her response.

Vacant eyes stare back at me, and I notice the little signs of torture I had previously overlooked. The dark, puffy bags that weigh down and overpower the brilliant blue that has lost its desire to shine. The subtle shadows that form from sunken cheeks and unused muscles from forgotten smiles. Had it not been for the dusting of freckles scattered across her face, there would be no hint of color to signify life. She stands there staring at me…and staring at nothing. I can't help but think that I just witnessed a soul forfeit and finally let go of the last bit of will—that last bit of hope.

"Mercy?" I whisper her name as I lower the glass from my lips.

She shimmies her shoulders a bit and shakes away the distress that is plastered across her face. Sorrowful eyes peer up between full lashes as a half-assed, lips-sealed smile attempts to sway me into thinking everything is all right.

"Thank you for the invite, but I'll be more comfortable sleeping in my own bed tonight."

After about an hour of arguing and making sure the locks on every door and every window are secured, I leave Mercy's home around midnight. We are able to agree that Orthus should stay behind with her, much to his delight. Honestly, having him on guard helps Mercy and gives me the peace of mind that she's not alone—not to mention I won't have to wonder where he ran off to in the morning when I wake to find he's missing. As much as I would have preferred Mercy stay the night under my own supervision, I agree to leave and take advantage of her absence to piece together what the hell transpired tonight. After all, I am just her mere acquaintance at this point. I can understand her hesitation or outright refusal to accept my offer.

The night air is brisk, and the occasional streetlight illuminates the cracked and bumpy old roads that lead me home. It's not long before I'm coasting into my driveway with little recollection of the ride, having been lost in my thoughts about all that has happened just within the last couple of hours.

The faces of the men who ambushed Mercy in her home tonight are fuzzy in my mind, which leaves me puzzled and frustrated. I was only able to get a good look at the man who was sent as a distraction to the front door. His face was unrecognizable to me. The others were quick on their feet while fleeing the scene. The sight of me probably spooked them and prevented them from finishing whatever they had planned to do.

My home, cased in darkness, welcomes me as I find my way up the brick walkway leading to the front door. I slip inside, toss my keys on the side table, and head straight to the dry bar in my study. Continuing the night with more whiskey, I fix myself a stiff drink and park my disheveled ass on top of the stool set in front of my workspace. In this first moment of calm, I'm left wishing I had thought to grab ice for my face. I can start to feel my cheekbone swell, courtesy of the prick who managed a swing at me. Extra whiskey will have to do.

As I sip my self-prescribed medicine, I try to wrap my head around what happened tonight. I try hard to piece together a motive behind why a group of men decided to break into Mercy's house, but it doesn't help that I just met her and know little of her background. At a loss, I continue to drink as if it will help me find the missing piece of the puzzle and begin to brainstorm theories.

She lives alone, making her a prime target for a burglary, but they weren't there to take anything. Well, they were in a sense—they were there to take Mercy. But why? Who is she to them? She had no idea who they were. At least, that was what I understood from eavesdropping on her conversation with John.

Ugh, John. I take a bigger sip of whiskey. *Why does he irritate me?*

I stare at the unfinished maps I've been working on for my father; they're scattered across my worktable. Like the start of a Jackson Pollock, drops of spilled ink dot the mahogany table. I push everything aside and grab a pen and paper. Perhaps, I can map out the night in a way that will help it all make sense to me. For what reason, I'm not sure of yet. There's just something nagging at me, making it seem as if there is something I must figure out if this shitty ordeal is to be handled. Maybe it's simply due to my lack of confidence in this small town's police force. *More like my lack of confidence in John.* I roll my eyes. *Well, honestly…maybe more so because of my instantaneous, and perhaps unfair, disdain for the man.*

Pen to paper, I jot down notes of what happened, little details of the night's events, trying to see if anything stands out. Having just met Mercy, there's not much I know about her life, other than what I have seen and what she has told me. From what I have learned, nothing seems out of the ordinary, and from what I know, I don't think she is connected to anyone of importance. We live in a small town in the middle of nowhere, for fuck's sake. I jot down "witness protection" with a question mark, and then proceed to chuckle at the idea. Definitely can't be that, especially with the name Mercy, of all things. That's the last name the government would assign someone. They aren't that creative.

With little coming to mind, I try something I haven't done in quite some time—automatic writing. Thinking that, perhaps, if I just stop thinking altogether and allow my mind to write freely, something might reveal itself from my subconscious. I take another sip of whiskey, almost to the bottom of the glass, quiet my mind, and let my pen flow.

When I finally stop, I can't help but choke on my own breath, stunned at what I've left on the page. Amongst the words and phrases from before is a heavily detailed portrait of Mercy staring straight back at me. I drop my pen and gawk at the accuracy with which I have drawn the face of a woman I barely know. I've managed to articulate every unique detail of her face, down to the light scattering of freckles across her nose and over each cheek.

The accuracy of the portrait has me reaching for the whiskey bottle to pour one more glass. I would be lying if I didn't admit that I creeped myself out a bit. From the drawing, one would assume I know this woman, that she is not someone I just met—not just because of the accuracy, but also due to the emotion that emanates from her eyes on the page. I toss the paper amongst the rejected maps in the trash, worried I might be mistaken for a stalker should anyone happen upon the drawing. Not that I have many people walking in and out of my home to begin with, but better to be safe than sorry.

"I should just go to bed and sleep on it." I blow air out from between my lips and rest my head in my hands. It has been a long day, and my body is begging for rest. I take a final swig of my drink and shove myself back from the table, the stool scraping against the dark hardwood floors. Maybe this is just one of those things I need to sleep on; I'll have a fresh take on it in the morning.

It's a little over three hours past midnight when I wake from a dead sleep and shoot straight up to a seated position in bed. I'm covered in sweat, my heart is racing, and my chest rises and falls at a rapid rate. My jaw hangs open as my eyes scan the room wildly. I try to control my breathing to calm myself and convince my mind of where and when I am.

"I am here," I repeat to myself over and over again. A mantra that has followed me from one life to the next. One of the few things that has attached itself and continues to be carried over with my soul each time I come back. Where it originated from, I've yet to remember.

Tossing the blankets off me, I hastily make my way to the study downstairs. Once there, I'm on my knees by the basket of discarded papers, rummaging through them in search of the portrait I drew hours earlier. I finally find it and fall backward onto my butt. Elbows resting on bent knees, I bring one hand against my temple to support my head as I stare dumbfoundedly at the portrait of Mercy. The realization I came to in my dream now solidifies. I may have just met Mercy in this life...but this isn't our first time around.

CHAPTER 10
MERCY

The early-morning light filtered through the small opening in the drawn curtains, stirring me from a restless night's sleep. An exaggerated groan escapes my lips as I push myself up to a seated position in bed. Knees bent to my chest, I cradle myself, my cheek resting atop my knees.

Eyes closed, I feel the warm breath of Orthus against my skin. "Good morning, friend," I coo, opening my eyes and ruffling the soft fur between his ears. He crawls even closer and wraps his body around mine, nestling his head at my feet. "Thank you for the company and for guarding me all night." He lets out a huff in response, and I take this moment of peace to breathe.

Surrounded by pillows and blankets, I linger in this moment of serenity provided by the comfort of my bedroom, as well as by the company I have. Peeking from the bed, through the gap in the curtains, I catch a glimpse of the rising sun. I watch as the orange glow crests over the hilly tree line in anticipation of the start of a new day. The warmth of its faint glow encourages me to move.

"How about we have an early-morning coffee outside?" I look at Orthus and gesture for him to release my feet from the weight of his snout. I wrap myself in the comfort of my oversized robe and head downstairs to start a fresh pot.

Hair loosely tied in a bun atop my head, I catch a glimpse of myself in the mirror at the end of the stairwell. A ghost drained of any emotion stares back. Brushing off the sight of my reflection, I continue to the kitchen in the back of the house where sunlight had yet to reach. Evidence of last night's fiasco is still scattered throughout the downstairs, most of it in the kitchen. Dirt tracked in by the intruders litters the floor, accompanied by the occasional fallen picture frame and shattered glass. Everything is a reminder of what happened and a nudge for me to clean up and piece back together my life. Focused on my only task in this moment—to brew a pot of coffee—I tiptoe through the debris.

Filling the pot with water from the sink, I lift my gaze to the window overlooking my backyard. Last night's full moon is still visible in the sky, not quite ready to lose itself to the sun's morning light. Transfixed by the sight of time lingering in between night and day, I start the coffee machine and make my way to the barricaded back door. Shoving everything to the side, I leave the comfort of my warm home for the chilled air of the quickly approaching early fall. Each step sends shivers up my spine as bare feet follow the path to my garden. Arms wrapped around myself, I stand with both feet planted in the upturned soil and mangled weeds. Toes digging into the earth below, my chin lifts to the sky. With a soft gaze, I look at the fading full moon.

I admire the beauty of its fullness and let my mind wander in its presence. This moment in time is the perfect balance between night and day, light and dark. The sky fades from warm hues of purple and red in the back of my house, to orange and yellow in the front. A space and time in between. The sheer beauty of this moment is overwhelming, making me want to drop to my knees. Something in me, however, keeps me standing. So instead of kneeling in the dirt, I remain upright, standing tall. Allowing my head to fall back, I close my eyes and breathe.

I am so tired of feeling small.

My arms fall to my side, and my robe softly slides from my frame. I'm left standing in nothing but my silk nightgown, the majority of my skin exposed to the bite of the cold air. Goose bumps cover my body, and I begin to shiver. Feeling exposed, but with no intention to cover up, I embrace the sensations coursing through my body. One breath in and one breath out, I focus on the ground beneath my feet. Another breath in and another breath out, a smile forms on my lips, and the shivering begins to subside. The breath work continues, and I feel my chest lift, my shoulders drop away from my ears, and for once in a long time, I feel sturdiness deep in my bones.

I am so tired of crying. I am exhausted from all the worrying. I am done. Done feeling like nothing at all.

Eyes still closed, face tilted skyward, I feel grounded in this moment. My breathing becomes deeper, my body quiet. Suddenly, my mind snaps, and a sense of clarity takes over. The feeling sends a rush through my body, electricity through my limbs. The images of what happened last night flash through my mind one after the other. Images of me fighting *for* my life, *not* to end it, despite how I've recently felt.

Thinking back to last night and acknowledging the fact I'm standing secure and safe right here, right now, my mind does the unthinkable—it flips the script for the first time that I can recall.

I am not a victim. I never was. I never will be.

I am not this burdensome villain that lies tell me I am. I never was. I never will be.

I simply just am, and I am here. And I finally can start to feel it in my bones.

Last night, I fought. I realize now that I fought because I wasn't done yet with this thing called life, contrary to what I thought the voice had been insinuating this whole time. I fought because the voice truly has been on my side all along, forcing me to become the woman I knew I would be when I was little, just as Aiden had annoyingly stated. Forcing me to face my truths. Forcing me to acknowledge my demons. Forcing me to embrace the darkness so that my light had more reason, more purpose, to shine. I became content with what was comfortable, refusing the challenges that would help me grow. I allowed myself to be seduced by a lack mentality because it was easier than the hard truth. Last night, I could have found the end I had convinced myself I deserved and wanted, but I didn't.

Aiden is right. I know he is. That's why it hurt last night… why it stung.

I needed to break to grow. I needed to fail to succeed. I needed to hurt to heal, to understand. I needed to fall again and again to strengthen myself enough to fly. And now I need to fight for me because I am not done here. I choose not to be done here. Unfortunately, it took my life being threatened for me to realize this.

I. Am. Here.

I allow my eyes to open, and tears stream down my face. The taste of salt dances on my tongue as my lips part, and a laugh frees itself, joining the piercing howl of Orthus paying homage to the now-faded moon. Basking in the warmth of the sun's rays, I stand for a few moments longer in my garden and reflect.

I think back to all that I have accomplished in my life, whether it be something small or significant. I think back to the challenges I have overcome and the fact that I am still here. I realize all that I have accomplished even in my sadness, my frustration, my anger, and my anxiety. And if I was able to get to where I am now, even with all that doubt, all that anger, all that sadness…

Imagine what I can do if I am happy. Imagine what I can do if I accept myself for the woman I am, for the challenges I take on, for the fights I deem worth fighting for. I am worth fighting for.

I inhale a few more deep breaths of the morning air and then turn to head back to the kitchen for a hot mug of coffee, intoxicated by this new outlook on life. One bare foot in front of the other, I know my journey to happiness and acceptance will be full of obstacles and setbacks, highs and lows, moments when I slide back into negativity. But I've made it this far. So today I choose to fight for the life I've always wanted, the one I thought I could never have. I choose to fight for my happiness. I choose to let go of the doubt. I finally choose myself.

I am stronger than I give myself credit for. I will choose to see that now.

Last night was the final straw that tried to break me… and it did. It shattered me into a million pieces amongst the ashes of the life I set on fire. Today, I will take those broken pieces, sweep away the ashes, and start to build myself back up again.

CHAPTER 11
MERCY

Orthus and I hop out of my car and walk down the quiet street. We make our way to the park across from the coffee shop I'm supposed to be meeting Tess at later.

"I think it would be good for both of us to stretch our legs," I say to Orthus, who responds with a playful sneeze and a huff. I dig in my bag and pull out a ball. "I even brought a ball, so we can play fetch." He doesn't miss a beat and side-eyes me at the suggestion, as if I've just insulted his intelligence. "Or not." I toss the ball back into my bag and walk side by side with my new four-legged companion.

Good luck trying to take him back, Aiden.

As if my thought conjured him, I find Aiden opposite us, walking in our direction. I was looking forward to a peaceful stroll through the park, but I guess the universe has other plans for me today. We make eye contact, and my heart skips a beat at the sight of his crooked grin upon seeing me.

Oh, no, no, no. Simmer down, you stupid thing.

I allow the voice to reprimand my involuntary reaction.

Dressed in his usual attire of dark jeans, a relaxed T-shirt, bomber jacket, and combat boots, Aiden swaggers up to Orthus and me. His hands are in his pockets, and he lifts his brows in acknowledgment of us. Eyes shielded behind his aviators, he looks oh so casual. *God, he's so attractive.* I would rate him a ten or above were it not for his arrogant mouth.

There are a lot of men who would be attractive if they just didn't open their mouths.

"Ah! There's the whiskey-drinking fiend who enjoys stealing my dog away from me."

I roll my eyes at his comment. *Here we go.*

"Hmmm. Maybe you should ask yourself *why* your dog prefers my company over yours. I mean, I could make a few guesses," I retort in a snarky yet almost-flirtatious manner. My cheeks flush. *Get your shit together, Mercy.*

"Ouch, no mercy. Your mother must have an ironic sense of humor. Explains the name," he mocks with a smile and a wink.

I squint my eyes and purse my lips at him, unwilling to admit that I enjoy the back-and-forth banter we have. We walk in silence as we cross the street, Orthus slightly in front of us, padding along towards the entrance of the park. People give us plenty of room at the sight of our wolf-like companion.

My body's temperature rises as I become fully aware of our closeness. We continue side by side, following the black mass of fur down the path that twists and turns throughout the little park in the heart of our town. Usually one to break the silence, I find myself self-conscious and instead direct my attention to the view and the occasional pops of autumnal color scattered amongst the trees.

"How are you doing?" Aiden asks, his voice absent its usual smugness and, instead, infused with genuine concern.

I can feel his eyes on me, but I can't bring myself to look at him. "Just brilliant," I retort, forcing a smile and shoving my hands into the pockets of my jean jacket as we continue walking. I sneak a look at Aiden when I'm not met with a witty response. The stubble on his jawline accentuates the tension he's holding in. I can see from this angle that his eyes are closed tight behind his sunglasses. It's a look of apprehension and concern.

We continue our walk, Orthus minding his own business in front of us, until I feel a gentle pull on my arm. Alone on the bridge arching over a stream that runs through the park, I'm brought to a standstill by Aiden's touch. We stand there in the middle of the bridge, no one around except for Orthus, who is more interested in the ducks splashing in the water below. I look at Aiden, and my features soften.

"You don't have to put on a brave face, Mercy. Last night was traumatic, to say the least. I was there. I know. You can talk to me," he says with such sincerity that my rigid posture starts to ease.

Sunglasses now tucked in his shirt, I can see in his eyes the need for me to open up to him or, at the very least, give him a sense that I'm all right. I walk to the side of the bridge and rest my elbows on the railing. I shrug my shoulders up to my ears and stare straight ahead. Aiden turns to join me, and I'm aware of the slight distance he keeps between us.

"You're going to think I'm crazy." I laugh.

"Oh, I already know you're crazy," he jokes.

My eyes narrow and brows lower as I turn my head and glare at him.

"The good kind of crazy, though," he clarifies.

"Ha. Yeah, the good kind." I hold his gaze and can't help but give him a half-hearted smile. "Honestly, though, I think if I tell you how I'm really feeling, you'll think I've lost my mind."

"Try me," he challenges.

"Okay. Well, at the risk of sounding absolutely batshit"—I pause and take into consideration what I'm about to admit—"I'm…happy? No, that's not the word. I'm…appreciative of what happened last night."

I'm met with silence. Aiden now faces me, one arm braced on the railing of the bridge for support. His mouth opens and shuts, like a fish out of water, as he tries to comprehend what I just admitted.

"I'm going to need you to explain, or I might take back what I said about you being the good kind of crazy," he finally manages to say.

I laugh and turn so my back is against the guardrail. Bracing myself with the heels of my hands, I hop up and sit on top of the wide railing, allowing my legs to hang. Hands in my pockets, back to the open air behind me and rocky stream down below, I try to explain myself, "What I'm about to say will probably be difficult to understand. Honestly, it *is* crazy, but…" I take a deep breath.

Aiden steps closer and closes the gap between us, allowing one hand to rest on either side of my hips. "Spit it out, psycho," he gently demands, those green eyes encouraging me to speak my truth.

"Up until last night, my life has been in complete turmoil, to say the least. The past couple of years, I've felt like a complete fraud and failure. My life was falling apart in more ways than one. I became nothing but a complete detriment to myself, both mentally and physically. No matter what I did, I was never enough, and yet somehow too much at the same time. A complete walking paradox. So, naturally, that affected everything in my life. My marriage, my job, my friends..." I take a moment to ground myself, forcing back tears.

"Marriage?" Aiden asks, his posture going a bit rigid.

"Yeah. A failed one," I shamefully admit, my gaze dropping to my feet. "Divorced before thirty! I'm a real winner." I roll my eyes at myself and fight the urge to hide or bury myself in a hole of self-loathing.

No, stay strong.

A hand gently lifts my chin, and I see Aiden has come just a little closer.

"Chin up. Lessons aren't always learned through success. And it sounds like there's more to the story, but we can save that for another day."

A bit of relief settles in, and I find comfort in his lack of good judgment. Encouraged, I continue to explain myself further, "Before last night, I was struggling to bend and not break..." I take a second to collect myself and try to ease the sorrow I've clouded us with. I let out a soft chuckle. "I'm not that flexible, it turns out."

That's met with a light laugh, and I go on when I'm ready to admit why I'm not as traumatized as I should be after last night's upheaval. "Last night I finally reached my breaking point. Hell, I didn't just break; I completely shattered into a million little pieces."

"I'm struggling to see how this is a good thing." Aiden looks at me as if I have officially lost it.

"Because now I get to put myself back together piece by piece. And, this time, I'm building myself back up stronger." A single tear escapes as I hold myself a little taller and smile.

I wait for Aiden to tell me I'm absolutely insane, reckless, or mad. I wait for him to tell me I'm going about this the wrong way or failing to see the event for the horror that it was. I'm ready for him to tell me I *am* crazy, and not in the good way. For him to turn around and walk away. I wait and prepare myself for his judgment and for my feelings to be twisted and worked against me. Bracing myself for the words that I know will sting, I wait for the response I'm sure I'm about to get from him.

But before my chin has a chance to dip back down, he responds. "I told you. You *are* the good kind of crazy," he affirms while wiping away the single tear.

"Yeah, I guess I am."

I settle in at the corner table just outside the coffee shop while Aiden is inside grabbing our coffee order. Orthus is lying behind my chair, soaking in the warmth of the afternoon sun. I perk up when I see a full head of black curls push through the shop's doors and proceed to the outdoor-seating area.

Tess maneuvers her body gracefully around the many chairs and tables between her and me. She is dolled up in a snug-fitting sweater dress that accentuates every curve, and I can't help but smile at my friend who has never been one to miss an opportunity to flaunt her womanly figure. I have always been envious of her body-positive mindset and how comfortable she is in her own skin—both are things I've always lacked. Her confidence at times can be intimidating, but it's her bubbly personality and high-pitched voice that brings balance and warmth to her energy. She has always been my voice of reason, my rock, my best friend, and my sister not by blood, but by choice.

"MERCY! OH. MY. GOD!" Tess's steps quicken as she gets closer. Just as I rise to stand, she throws herself at me. Her arms wrap tightly around my shoulders, pinning my arms to my sides. My breath is squeezed out of me.

"ARE YOU OKAY?" Tess holds me at arm's length, her eyes wide and brows furrowed in distress. Clearly, she has found out about what happened last night.

"I'm okay! I promise!" I reassure her and bring her in for one more hug. "I'm guessing John called you to see if I made it to your house last night?"

"Yes, he did! And, YES, I'm mad at you for not calling me! Of course, you could have…SHOULD have…stayed over at my place last night! I would have made Henry go home!" She gently slaps my shoulder, and we both take a seat at the little table.

"Oh, so Henry is staying over now?" I lean back in my chair and arch a brow at her, trying to bring levity to the conversation.

"Oh no. We'll talk about that later. Right now, I need to know—" Tess stops mid-sentence as Aiden approaches the table with coffees in hand. Closing her mouth after looking stunned by Aiden's appearance, she looks at me, at him, and then back at me. "You must be the guy that John mentioned over the phone."

"And you must be Tess." Aiden smiles warmly at my friend, hands me my coffee, and joins us at the table. "I'm Aiden. It's very nice to meet you, Tess." His voice is low and smooth, and I watch as Tess melts in her seat at the sound of her name on his lips.

Here we go.

Hazel eyes snap in my direction as I lazily sip my coffee… made just the way I like it. "Oh, you have SO much to tell me."

I can't help but shake my head and gently laugh at my friend's reaction. "It's not what you think, Tess."

I smile at her, knowing she's dying to pull any and all information out of me. I can see her mind going back and forth in a great debate of whether to question me first about last night or Aiden. I also see, from the corner of my eye, Aiden as he lounges back in his seat, coffee in hand, and an expression of wicked amusement plastered across his face.

"Mm-hmm. Sure, I'll believe that when pigs fly," Tess says in a sassy tone, causing Aiden to choke on his coffee and then smile wider.

"I like this one." He gestures towards Tess, who is sitting in her chair, arms crossed over her chest. "Tess, what would you like? I'll go grab your order while you two…catch up." He winks after pausing to imply that there is more to catch up on, other than last night's events.

I give him a look insinuating I would love to smack him right now, had I the chance.

Tess gives him her order, and just as he walks out of earshot, she looks at me. I can tell she is torn. "The caring and moral side of me wants to ask you about last night, what happened, and if you're really okay. The other, and much louder, part of me *really* wants to know more about THAT." Her eyes lock on mine as she points her thumb in Aiden's direction.

I sit up in my chair and place my coffee on the table. "Well, THAT…is nothing. Honestly, it's a whole other random-ass story to get into, but not that important." I try to convince her, but clearly fail.

"Bullshit. Also, if that's nothing"—she pauses and takes a breath—"then I'm sincerely, genuinely very disappointed in you."

A look of realization spreads across Tess's face, and I can see her piecing something together. "He's the one who brought you home the other day Henry and I were at your house. Isn't he?" Her doe eyes light up as if she's found an answer that she thinks I'm not willing to give her yet. Smug satisfaction glistens in her eyes. Tess smiles at me and then reaches across the table, her palms facing up.

I place my hands into hers, and she grips them tightly. Her smug expression changes to worry. I can see the tears start to well up in her eyes. Her brows pinch, and she softly whispers, "I'm so glad you're okay, Mercy. When John called to ask if you were with me, and then let me know what happened, my heart dropped. I was so scared."

My heart breaks, knowing the stress I must have unknowingly put Tess through. It wasn't John's place to inform her about what happened. His heart was in the right place, but he should have called to check in with me, not Tess.

"I'm so sorry, Tess. I was going to tell you. I just needed a moment to decompress." I squeeze her hands gently, and my heart swells with compassion and empathy for my friend.

Aiden returns from inside the coffee shop, Tess's drink order in his hand. He joins us back at the table and remains by my side as I divulge all the details of what has taken place over the past couple of days, starting with how Aiden and I crossed paths in the first place. Through it all, Aiden sits quietly, allowing me to tell the story, but he interjects here and there with a few anecdotes of his own. On occasion, I bite back a chuckle as I watch Tess hang on every word that comes out of Aiden's mouth.

"So you have no idea who these people were?" Tess asks, sipping the last drops of her coffee.

"No idea," I confirm, shaking my head. "The whole thing is just...weird." I push my empty mug out in front of me and slouch back in my chair.

Orthus pops up from his sunbathing and places his head on my lap.

"You're the one to thank for this meet-cute?" Tess looks at Orthus and grins.

"Meet-cute is one interesting way of putting it," Aiden comments.

I can't help but roll my eyes. "Tess—" I begin, trying to convince her, yet again, that there is nothing going on between Aiden and me, but am startled when, all of a sudden, Orthus whips his head around and begins to growl. We all look in the direction his nose is pointing and see far off in the distance a glimpse of a cherry-red sports car.

"Hey, that kind of looks like the car you described, the one that almost hit your dog. Can't say I blame him for having a thing against red cars, all things considering," Tess observes, head tilted quizzically to the side.

As if the car in the far-off distance has become aware of our attention, we hear its engine rev as it takes off.

"It sounds like the getaway car from last night, too," Aiden says under his breath. He is on his feet in a millisecond, startling both Tess and me.

"Tess, my dear, would you do me a favor and take Mercy back home with you?" Aiden's tone is eerily calm but demanding.

Tess and I are quick to our feet, frazzled by the sudden change in atmosphere. I look at Aiden, wondering what the hell is going on.

"Do me a favor and take Orthus with you. Lock the doors when you get to Tess's house. Send me her address, and

I'll meet you there later." He starts to list off a series of other demands.

"Aiden"—I try to hide the fear in my voice—"what are you about to do?"

He doesn't answer my question. "If anything, anything at all, seems off once you get to Tess's, call John, and have him come over." His voice is steady, but I see the panic and anger in his eyes.

I grab his arm as he's hopping over the short fence that surrounds the coffee shop's patio. Green eyes meet mine, and I swear I see a cloud of darkness creep over their usual vibrant emerald.

"That's them. Tess's. Now." He turns on his heels and sprints down the street to his bike.

I hear the wheels spin out as he peels out of the parking space and speeds off in the direction of the cherry-red car. Tess is grabbing my hand, pulling me to follow her, and Orthus snaps at me to release me from my daze. My heart pounds in my chest, rattling my rib cage. My body follows Tess, Orthus in tow, but my mind is reeling and stuck in Aiden's direction.

"Hi, Henry. Meet me at my house, will you?" I hear Tess say on the phone.

She opens the back door of her car for Orthus to hop in and gently demands that I get in as well. Within seconds, we are bombing down the quiet streets of our small town, heading to Tess's place.

The entire drive, I'm quiet, my mind trying to comprehend what just occurred at the coffee shop. I knew those assholes were still on the run, but I just ignorantly didn't think that the mayhem of last night would continue to roll over into today. Of course, it would, though. It will continue until they are caught. This is too big for me to ignore and just put behind me or sweep it under the rug.

What the hell does Aiden think he's going to do anyway?

CHAPTER 12
AIDEN

Tears whip across my face as I speed down the road on my bike to catch up with the red car. By the time I reached my bike, hopped on, and raced off, the car was already out of sight. But I must at least try to catch up with the driver and passenger inside. A plan for what I will do if that happens still hasn't sorted itself out yet in my head. At the very least, my hope is to get a good look at the fuckers.

Easing up on the accelerator, I begin to slow my bike to a complete stop and pull over to the side of the road, beyond pissed that the assholes got away from me…again. Cursing, I rip off my helmet and slam it to the ground.

"Fucking hell," I mutter as I drag both hands down my face, at a loss for what to do next. I refuse to admit that John does in fact have his work cut out for him and that I couldn't do a better job at it. I still don't like him.

Knowing Mercy is safe with Tess and Orthus, I reach down to grab my discarded helmet. I turn my bike around and make my way back home. If I can't get my hands on these bastards, I can at least make sure Mercy is protected.

Once home, I head straight to the basement. Storming into my father's realm, I catch him completely off guard.
"Aiden! I wasn't expecting you." He sounds startled as he tries to inconspicuously push whatever he was working on into the top drawer of his desk.

I make a mental note of that before questioning him. "Where's Void?"

The cat circles my feet before my father has a chance to answer my question. I grab Void, lifting him so he dangles in front of me, nose to nose. He releases a sharp cry of annoyance at the sudden movement.

"Sorry, bud, but I have a favor to ask that's important, and I'm on a bit of a time constraint," I explain, trying to justify my abrupt handling of his fluffy body.

His tail swishes and his ears flatten sideways. He's annoyed at me, but not pissed, thankfully.

"I need you to go to the underworld and tell Tari I need her help. I need a protection spell, plant, concoction, talisman…I don't know…something to be used to help protect someone. Can you get her that message for me?" The request rushes from my lips, and it takes everything in me to not shake the little furry creature in my grasp as he blinks at me audaciously. I roll my eyes, take a breath, and through clenched teeth, muster out a forced "Please?"

I lower Void to the ground, and the little guy scampers off down the hall to the little cat door that allows him to come and go from the underworld as he pleases.

Cats. There is a reason why they act all high and mighty, the little assholes. They are one of the few entities able to easily move between realms. When a cat sits in the corner of a room, seemingly staring at nothing, I can promise it's not nothing and most definitely something.

"I don't think those of Helheim's elite messenger service appreciate being manhandled, Aiden. I wouldn't be surprised if he comes back with whatever you asked for…as well as a plague or something to gift you," my father quips, arms crossed, eyes glaring at me over the top of his glasses.

My lip curls at him in annoyance and anger. "My bad," I practically shout at him.

"Asking for Tarini, huh? She's one of Hecate's brightest pupils. What sort of trouble have you found yourself in this time, Aiden?" my father asks, arms still crossed, as he leans against his desk.

I pace, on edge and not in the mood to explain why I need what I need, but I know there's time before Void comes back, and my father isn't one to let things go. I contemplate how much information I want to divulge. Not that it really matters what he knows. If anything, he could be of use and may have a way of helping me figure out the names of the souls who are stalking Mercy.

"It's not for me," I admit, causing my father to lean farther forward as he senses intrigue.

"Who then, might I ask, is this protection spell for? A bit hypocritical of you to step into the Fates' doings after you lectured me the other day about not interfering in your—my very own son's—timeline," he asks, his tone argumentative and to the point.

I come to a halt mid-stride in my pacing; my face, I'm sure, is the picture of vexation. Brows low, lips set in a tight straight line, I close my eyes, take a deep breath in, and then force it out through my nose. My eyes flick open, and I tilt my head to a predatory angle.

"The circumstances here are a bit different. Not as influential as interfering in my own reincarnation cycle," I growl through gritted teeth.

My father's hands shoot up in placation, palms out and open. He dips his chin. "I mean no trouble. I just needed to point out my side of the argument."

I ease my posture, knowing that fighting with him will be of no help to the situation. I run my fingers through my hair anxiously and look back to the hallway Void disappeared down, mentally urging him to hurry the fuck up.

"It's for the woman you met, isn't it?" Not much gets past my father.

I release a heavy sigh, and my gaze meets his. "Yeah, it is."

"She must be someone special to you, then?" he asks as he walks over to me.

"You could say that." I pause, considering whether or not to bring up the portrait I drew of Mercy the other night and the dream that answered a question I hadn't even known to ask.

"What aren't you telling me?" His wispy white brow is arched in curiosity.

My heart pounds in my chest; I'm unsure of what or how much to tell him. After brief contemplation, I don't see any harm in laying it all out there. My hesitation probably stems from the fact that we aren't ones to typically have these sort of conversations. Not to mention I'm a thirty-three-year-old man who has lived many lives. Gossiping about my romantic life, or lack thereof, isn't something I normally do. It isn't something I would ever do.

"I have this pull to her that I can't explain. The other night, I had a dream about her," I begin to explain uncomfortably.

"Son, if you weren't dreaming about women…or men—no judgment from me whichever form you prefer… Everyone knows a soul is a soul; a heart, a heart. It's the soul, anyway, that decides its levels of femininity or masculinity. These meat sacks we're stuck in are just meant for procreation—"

He's about to continue rambling, but I'm quick to cut him off. I throw a hand up to stop him mid-rant, the fingers of my other hand pinching the bridge of my nose in aggravation. I have greater concerns to worry about at the moment.

"First, we discussed this before. The word we both agreed on is 'vessel,' not meat sack." I cringe at his choice of words. "Secondly, clearly you don't leave this place. Otherwise, you would know humanity is a bit more ignorant than you give them credit for."

He shrugs and pushes his glasses back up to the bridge of his nose. "Anyway, needless to say, if you weren't dreaming about someone, I would be a bit concerned. Loneliness is just as much an illness as any disease," he responds with an air of theatrical wisdom.

I squint my eyes at him and let out an exasperated breath. "It wasn't that kind of dream. It was a dream of recognition. A past-life regression, in a sense. She was there. I swear it."

I try to convince him, but his pitying expression shows I have done anything but that.

A second later, Void emerges from the dark hallway, his eyes the first thing to pierce the shadows. A tiny pouch is secured to his back.

I reach down to remove it from the little beast just as my father's hand does the same. "Past lover, or not," he begins to say while walking over to his desk, the pouch now in his possession, "the least I can do for you is add a little extra oomph to Tarini's protection charm."

I watch as he opens the pouch and tosses a stone of some sort into the mix of herbs and spices. He tightly shuts the bag and places it in my hands, holding on a little longer than I feel necessary.

"I can tell you're worried. If there is anything I can do to help, you let me know." He smiles as he releases me.

"Yeah, thanks," I say quickly as I'm turning to leave the study and hurry back to Mercy, Tess, and Orthus.

Quickly, I make my way through the basement door, almost catching Void's tail in the process. He lets out a hiss, annoyed that I didn't sense him behind me. He's really going to have my number after today.

By the time I make it up the stairs, Void has scurried to the front door and hopped up on the side table. As I reach for the keys I tossed there, he swats at my hand and growls.

"You're not coming with me," I argue with him.

He sits on the table, swishing his tail over my keys, and puffs out his chest.

Craftily hidden in his long fur, I see a piece of paper rolled tightly and woven into black tufts. Gently, I remove the paper.

Void, now finished with his mission, leaps off the table and hurries off to my study, most likely with the goal of ruining some of my works in progress as payback for the way I handled him earlier. Well deserved, I suppose.

Eager to get back to Mercy, I unravel the rolled-up paper and furrow my brow at the words written elegantly by Tarini's hand.

Things are not as they appear, Tari.

"Well, that's fucking cryptic, Tari."

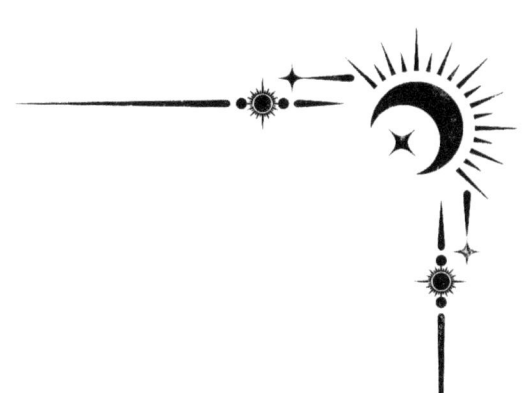

CHAPTER 13
MERCY

Tess and I sit around her kitchen table, both worried and unsure of what to do next. Orthus lies by the front door on high alert, nose facing towards any unsuspecting visitors. Silence fills Tess's home, tension and fear palpable in the surrounding atmosphere—so different than the usual coziness of the home Tess and her sister inherited from their mother.

I have fond memories of Tess, her little sister, and me gathered around this same table, decorating cookies for their family's annual Christmas party. One of the many family events I was always wholeheartedly welcomed to and made a part of. Christmas music played in the background as Eleanor—or as I called her, Momma Nell—danced around the table, sprinkling flour over our heads when the song "Let it Snow" played on the kitchen radio. And then Lily, Tess's sister, always joined her mother and took the mess a little too far.

Momma Nell made every holiday special for her daughters, even more so after their father passed away from a freak accident that occurred while he was using large machinery at work. Momma Nell made sure to make every day of life after her husband's death a day worth honoring because "life is a gift worth celebrating every second of every minute, of every hour, of every day."

Those same words are etched into the headstone that sits right next to her beloved husband's—a heart attack took her away right around Tess's twenty-first birthday. We celebrated Tess's birthday that year with Momma Nell's favorite bottle of wine and her husband's expensive bottle of whiskey at their gravesides. We made sure to bring extra glasses to leave at their graves, filled to the brim, in hopes that a heavenly wind would come to topple the glasses and pour out their contents, serving the bodies below.

Before that tragedy, Tess and I were inseparable. After that tragedy, we made a pact to never leave the other's side—a 'til death-do-us-part sort of thing.

Those memories are now distant as the two of us share an occasional look at one another, unsure of what to do in this situation in which we find ourselves—well, in which I find myself. Thankfully, Tess is far removed from the chaos that is happening in my life right now…or at least she has been.

"Maybe we should call John?" Tess asks, worry in her eyes.

Before I can answer her, Orthus starts to growl and explodes upward onto all fours.

Our heads snap in his direction, both rattled by the disrupted quiet that had settled throughout the house. Orthus is about to pounce when we both see Henry's head pop through the doorway. I'm quick to call Orthus off, just before he charges a very confused Henry.

"Whoa! Is that a fucking wolf?" Henry's eyes bulge out of his head in terror as he presses his body firmly against the front door.

Considering we both worked—well, he still works there—at the veterinary clinic, I want to laugh at the horrified look on Henry's face. After taking a look at Orthus, though, swear he has doubled in size. With his fur standing on end, teeth bared, ears pinned, and tail out taut, he looks like a hellhound straight out of myths and legends.

"He's not a wolf, I swear. He's actually a big sweetheart, I promise. Just maybe a tad overprotective," I say while walking over to Orthus to calm him down.

"When did you get a dog?" Henry asks as he seems to be trying to regain his composure and bring his heart rate down.

Tess rushes to his side, reaches up to wrap her hands around his neck, and pecks his cheek.

"Aw, how cute." I lovingly mock them, hoping to bring the energy of the room back to normal—or at the very least, make it less chaotic.

Tess guides Henry over to the couch in the living room. I make myself comfortable on Tess's father's old La-Z-Boy. Orthus sits proudly, still on guard, at my feet.

"Who is going to tell me what is going on?" Henry looks to both Tess and me, demanding answers.

"Where do I even begin?" I glance at Tess, in need of help to reiterate the story as to why we are where we are in this very moment. Before I manage to get one word out of my mouth, Aiden comes bursting through the front door, startling us all.

"And who the hell are you?" Henry shoots a hand out in Aiden's direction, clearly still unnerved by his own unwelcomed entrance.

"*That's* Mercy's new boy toy." Tess maniacally giggles, temporarily forgetting the disturbing reason we are all gathered in her living room.

"Tess!" I start to reprimand her but am stopped by Aiden shoving something into my hands.

"Keep this on you at all times," he tells me with no explanation.

I hold the strange but lovely-smelling pouch in front of me. "This is…?" I look at him in utter confusion.

"I'll explain later. Just shove it in your pocket for now, all right?" His voice is demanding yet concerned, so I do as he tells me.

Aiden stalks to the kitchen to grab a chair and then joins us in the living room. He looks slightly disheveled. I've never seen him like that; he's usually bursting with an air of smug confidence mixed with complete indifference.

"I know I'm starting to sound like a broken record, but what the hell happened earlier? Were those the men who attacked me? Did you catch up to them? Are we safe? Did you do something it would be best for me to not know about?" The questions keep coming, one after the other. My rambling, frazzled state clearly becomes amusing to Aiden, who hasn't even tried to fit a word in, instead choosing to sit and watch me spiral.

Oh, look—there goes the recently found confidence I felt earlier.

Words stop tumbling from my mouth. I see Tess clutching Henry's hand and arm, her eyes wide with concern and fear. Henry looks as shocked and confused as ever, while Aiden now wears his usual smirk and cocked eyebrow, waiting patiently for me to give him a chance to speak.

"Run out of oxygen yet?" he asks me playfully.

I squint my eyes at him, my mouth open in frustration. Taking a second to collect myself, I finally droop, hunch my shoulders, and rest my elbows atop my knees. I force my shallow breathing to become deep again as I try to focus my mind on one concern at a time.

Before I'm able to say anything, Henry pipes in, reminding Aiden and me that we aren't the only two in the room. "I don't care which one of you it is, but someone has to explain to me what is happening." Henry makes eye contact with Aiden and then me. His stare insinuates he'd prefer to hear my version of events first.

"I'll tell you everything, Henry, I promise. First, however"—I snap my attention to Aiden—"tell me what just happened with you."

Aiden leans back in his chair, one ankle resting on the knee of his other leg, hands shoved into his pockets. "I tried to chase after the car we saw at the coffee shop but couldn't catch up."

I nod my head, reach into my pocket, and pull out the little pouch he handed me after bursting through Tess's front door. "Okay, and when you couldn't catch up to the people who tried to abduct me the other night—"

I'm about to ask what Aiden did next, but Henry cuts me off mid-sentence. "WAIT… WHAT?"

I throw a finger up, signaling that I will get back to that in a moment and explain, my eyes still locked on Aiden's.

"I went home quick to charge my phone so I could let John know that we had seen the car that was at your house the other night," he tells me matter-of-factly.

"And in the meantime you decided to put a little trinket together for me before reaching out to Tess and me to let us know you were okay, or ask if we were okay?" I dangle the scented pouch between us.

"There's lavender in it. That's supposed to help calm you down," he responds as if that's a perfectly acceptable response.

"PRIORITIES, AIDEN!" My expression is one of incredulity, I am sure, amidst my outburst.

"Seems like you need to take a good whiff of that right now," he says, pointing to the pouch pinched between my fingertips.

Before I explode, Henry clears his throat to grab our attention. "I want to hear every detail. *Now*," he demands. He is always the person willing to step in and assist when shit hits the fan, no matter the circumstances.

Together, Aiden, Tess, and I retell the story of what happened at my house the night before. Henry interrupts every so often, trying to both understand and bring a new perspective to our own investigation. Tess speaks as if she were there, too.

Despite the topic of conversation, I can't help but smile at the flow and ease of everyone's interaction. I feel comfort in their support and at ease in their natural connection—it's as if they've known each other all along.

A moment of silence descends once everything has been thoroughly divulged to Henry, who is settled across the room. The quiet is soon disturbed by Tess clapping her hands. "Now, let me tell you how they met!" she exclaims giddily.

"Tess—" I start, only to be quieted by Tess pouting her lips at me.

"Come on, Mercy. Everything has been so serious and nerve-racking. Let me have this," she pleads, hands pressed together in a praying position at her chin.

"Fine, but I'm going to the kitchen to make coffee." I stand in defeat and watch as a bright-eyed, smiling Tess twists around in her seat to face Henry. "Just know that she's been jumping to conclusions and making assumptions," I say over my shoulder to Henry while making my way to the kitchen, knowing that he is well aware of Tess's tendency to romanticize things. It's one of the qualities we both love about her, and only occasionally find annoying.

While I hear Tess enthusiastically tell the tale of how Aiden and I met, adding her own romantic embellishments to the story, I rummage through her cabinets for coffee supplies. Caffeine is probably the last thing my adrenaline-shocked body needs right now, but the activity helps me escape Tess's dramatization of my past couple of days.

"How are you holding up?"

I jump at Aiden's voice, unaware he followed me. "Better than one might expect." I smile at him while pulling four coffee mugs from the open shelves.

"We are going to figure this out," he tells me, pushing himself up to sit on the counter.

"Isn't that what the police are for?" I ask as the coffee machine gurgles to life and the aroma of ground coffee sweeps through the house.

"Yes, but it doesn't hurt to do a little digging ourselves. It will keep you from letting your guard down," he suggests as if I'm not well aware of the potential danger I'm still in.

"I appreciate the concern, but I promise I'm okay." My words, I know, do little to convince him.

"Just do me a favor. Please keep that pouch on you at all times. Sleep with it. Bathe with it. Take it everywhere with you. Just don't let it out of your sight," he says, his eyes pleading for me to listen and obey.

"What is so special about this thing?" I toss it into the air.

He grabs it before I have a chance to and shoves it back into my jacket's pocket. "Don't mock me." For the first time ever, I sense a bit of modesty in his voice. "It's a…talisman… a protection spell…wrapped up nicely in a convenient little pouch for you."

I gawk at him.

"I said not to mock me," he growls, irritated embarrassment darkening his eyes.

"I swear I'm not." I chuckle softly. "I just would have never guessed you to be one who believes in this stuff. If anything, I would take you for one of those assholes who makes fun of others for believing in woo-woo shit," I explain.

"And do you?" he asks, head tilting to the side ever so slightly.

"Do I what?" I take a sip of coffee, eyes flirting with him from behind lowered lashes.

"Believe in this 'woo-woo shit,' as you called it?"

"For one, I didn't call it 'woo-woo shit.' I was referring to what I thought *you* would call it," I correct him while placing my mug down on the counter.

Reaching into my pocket, I retrieve the pouch and turn it in my hand, examining it. I wonder what else is in it, besides herbs and spices, since it feels so heavy.

Aiden reaches out and cups his hands around mine, as if making sure I don't let go of this precious pouch he's gifted me.

My eyes lock on his, willing him to see my honesty when I tell him that I do somewhat believe in what others call nonsense. I've always had an open mind and been curiously drawn towards things some might call witchcraft or dabbling in the occult. The farther down the rabbit hole my curiosity took me, the more I saw such things as misunderstood and unimaginably intriguing. It's amazing how even just a little bit of research can start to change your perspective.

"Told you," Tess says, nudging Henry in the side with her elbow. I wasn't aware that the two of them had joined us in the kitchen.

"For fuck's sake." I pocket the pouch and sigh in Tess's direction, not missing Aiden's amused smile.

"I think you should stay a few nights here with Tess. I don't think it's safe to go back to your house just yet,"

Henry says before I have a chance to deny any relationship Tess is convinced Aiden and I have.

As much as I would love to sleep in my own bed, I understand his concern, and appreciate the subject change.

"I would feel better if you just accepted my invitation to come stay with me," Aiden grumbles before sipping the coffee I just handed him. He stares me down, clearly annoyed by my continued rejection. I catch a slight glimmer of pleading in his green eyes, though, which makes me think twice about his offer. That little glimpse of concern also causes my stomach to flip slightly and my cheeks to flush.

"Mercy, you know you're more than welcome to stay with me. It would be fun! We can have a sleepover like when we were younger," Tess says, and I can see all the ideas of what an adult slumber party might look like running through her head. There will be plenty of drinking, talking, entire-series TV binges, and at-home spa treatments. She's bristling with anticipation at this point, and I would be a horrible friend to turn her offer down. Plus, it would be nice for us to reconnect...to laugh together.

"Help me pack a bag?"

Tess throws her arms around me in excitement. Over her shoulder, I catch Henry's look as he mouths the word "sorry," knowing that I'm in for a few nights of endless activities and very little of the alone time that my introverted self craves.

Aiden's shoulders and eyes drop slightly in... Defeat? Disappointment? I'm not sure which one, as he's quick to mask his emotions. "Tess, would you mind if Orthus stayed with you ladies? I would feel a bit better having him here on guard," he finally says.

"Oh, of course! Orthus, you can even join us when we do our spa day. I'm sure I can get my hands on some brushes for that thick coat of yours. And I'm sure I have some oils that are animal friendly and will help to bring out that shine in your black fur!" Tess claps her hands together while looking straight into Orthus's eyes.

I hold in a laugh as his ears go flat, out to the sides, and he gives Aiden a look as if to say, *You fucking owe me.*

CHAPTER 14
MERCY

"Do you mind if I just borrow your shampoo and conditioner?" I shout to Tess while putting together an overnight bag in my bathroom.

"Of course not, what's mine is yours!" I can hear her rummaging through my closet and drawers. "Oh, how many pairs of underwear do you want me to pack? I'll make sure to pack some of your *sexier* options in case you spend the night elsewhere at some point." Tess snickers.

I've decided that ignoring her at this point might get her to ease off her matchmaking tirade. Clearly denying anything between Aiden and me is going in one ear and out the other with her.

"When was the last time you wore *these*?" I turn in time to have two pairs of silky-lace thongs thrown at my face as Tess pops her head into the bathroom, wiggling her eyebrows wickedly.

"Honestly, anytime I wear yoga pants and don't want any panty lines to be seen."

Tess scoffs at my reply as she stomps back to my closet. "You're no fun."

I've heard that before.

Nope. We aren't doing this.

Silence fills the hall between us for a few minutes as I battle with the voice in my head. Finishing up in the bathroom, I join Tess in my bedroom. Seeing that she has stuffed my duffle bag with what looks like more than the essentials for a few overnights at her place, I take a moment to flop down on my bed.

It's not long before I feel the bed shift as Tess takes her place next to me. Her black curls spill across the bedspread and mix with my disheveled blonde waves. We lie there for a moment, staring at the ceiling. The silence is loud between us while I wait for her to release something I can sense has been weighing on her.

"Mercy? Can I ask you something?" Tess turns her head to face me.

I meet her hazel eyes, aware of the concern they reveal. "Anything." I grab her hand, and we lie there side by side.

Her eyes scan my face. Behind them, I can tell her mind is busy calculating how to broach whatever is troubling her. "Are you okay?" she asks with a furrowed brow as she squeezes my hand.

The honest question is simple to ask, but complicated to answer. The short answer is yes; I *am* okay. We both know though that it's more complicated than that. Each day brings its own challenges and obstacles to face. Challenges and obstacles that at times give me the almost-impossible task of forcing me to convince my own mind that it's all going to be okay. That I am going to be okay.

Just because I recently started to befriend that voice I had fought with for so long, it doesn't mean that I'm not tempted each day to be consumed by the negative, as I have always been before. This whole relationship with myself is new, and I'm still trying to figure it out. No other person abused me; I abused myself—and that's going to take time to heal and change on the deepest levels. And I've only just broken through the surface.

"I am, Tess. I promise. I know things are a bit...chaotic right now," I say, failing to find the proper word to describe the current uncomfortably horrific situation I find myself in.

"Ha! Not the word I would use to describe recent events, but go on." Tess's eyes drift back to the ceiling as her head, framed by a crown of curls, gently rolls back to its centerline.

I stare for a moment and then smile at my friend; love for her bursts from my chest. All that she has been through, and still she remains the warmest, most caring soul anyone would be lucky to simply just meet.

"I mean it." Turning my head back to its center position, I close my eyes instead of zoning out while staring at the ceiling. "Last year was miserable after the divorce was officially finalized, even though we had been separated already for a year. I thought I had lost everything. Thought I had thrown my whole life away and was doomed to live out the rest of my days alone with many stray cats." I sigh, and we both chuckle. "But, instead, I've come to realize it was all just one big lesson I needed to learn. A fucking shitty way to learn a lesson, but necessary nonetheless."

"And what exactly was this lesson you so wisely speak of?" She turns her head once more to look at me. Her eyes welcome me to explain so she can try to understand.

"That somewhere, at some point…I forgot who I was. Who I *am*. And, unfortunately for me, I needed to remember and get back to that person…" I pause, stretching out my free hand and reaching under my pillow. I feel the edges of the card I had glimpsed poking out from under my bed the night I found—what I would consider to be—my personal deepest pit of rock bottom. The night I finally broke, crumbling into a million shattered pieces amongst the weeds and decay I call my garden.

I feel the tarot card beneath my palm and, without even looking, know exactly which card it is. Know that drawn in gold-colored ink is a tower struck by lightning and set ablaze by merciless flames. People are depicted falling from the highest windows of their once-imposing structure. It's a card symbolizing radical destruction of everything once felt or possessed—but it also foretells ultimate liberation and change for the better.

Card in hand, I refocus my thoughts and try to explain myself further to Tess. "Medication and therapy can only do so much. In the end, it's always been me that has to save myself." I pause for a moment of relief from this heavy conversation. "I had to burn it all down and pick myself back up from the ashes. I had to destroy what I created because somewhere along the line, I lost myself in the process of my own creation."

A single tear falls down Tess's cheek, but her lips form a soft smile. "I'm just happy to finally have you back. Broken pieces, ashes, and all."

We begin to chuckle, and the sound is music to my ears. Overwhelmed by a lightness I haven't felt in so long, I'm possessed by unstoppable laughter. Tess joins the insanity. First, she's laughing at my loss of sanity, but then she's laughing with me. Soon, tears of happiness stream down our faces, and despite everything that has happened, we can't stop smiling.

Each day will be different, but in this moment, I know who I am. I know I am here. I know I am happy.

"Fuck, I love you," Tess says while wiping tears from her eyes. A toothy grin proudly spreads across her face.

"'Til death," I choke out through laughter and the last of my own tears.

We arrive back at Tess's; the home has been brought to life by the crackling fire, stoked by Henry, that is bringing warmth to the house's old bones in this late-September evening. The snaps of splintered logs and pops of sparks dancing from their flames are soothing to the senses.

"I'm getting marshmallows to roast over the open flame! Mercy, you make the hot chocolate. And don't forget to add the peanut-butter bourbon."

I raise both thumbs high above my head dutifully as I eagerly follow Tess's commands.

"Henry, we need pillows, blankets, and anything that looks comfy."

Henry is off with a salute to our self-appointed, fearless leader.

"Orthus"—he lifts his head from his curled-up position on the couch—"you just keep being cute," Tess coos.

He responds with a groan and settles back into position.

The three of us convene around the fire's hearth, popping toasted marshmallows in our mouths or adding them to our hot-chocolate, peanut-butter-bourbon concoction. Any worries and concerns are left behind the locked front door. In this moment, it's as if we have traveled back in time to when the only responsibilities we had involved schoolwork and household chores.

As we share stories, reminiscing about our past shenanigans and teenage debaucheries, I swear I can hear the faint tinkering of Momma Nell in the kitchen. It feels as if the three of us were patiently waiting for Tess's father to walk through the door and wrap his daughters in a warm embrace. That was always the unspoken signal for Henry and me to rush and set the table for dinner before we enjoyed a home-cooked meal while discussing our plans for after high school. Tess and Lily's parents beamed with pride for their daughters, and even shared that pride with Henry and me. Sitting in the warmth of this memory, I wonder if Tess and Henry feel it, too.

Sitting shoulder to shoulder, knees touching, I watch Tess lean into Henry's side, his body adjusting to form around hers. I sip my hot drink, my eyes softening as I take in the scene. *That. That right there is love.*

Before I'm able to open my mouth to tell my friends how sickeningly perfect they are together, we are jolted from our moment of peace by Orthus. His hackles are raised, and once again he appears doubled in size. A low growl vibrates through him as his lips scrunch upward exposing sharp canines. The three of us collectively stop breathing.

My heart pounds violently in my chests. I can feel my rib cage rattle as fear settles over my body. "Orthus? Bud, what's wrong?" I utter in barely a whisper.

His response of leaping off the couch and positioning himself at the front door, crouched low and ready to pounce, unnerves us even more.

"Mercy! Mercy, call Aiden." Tess's eyes are wide and focused solely on her front door.

"Aiden? What is he going to do? I'm calling the police." Henry leans back to have better access to the phone in his pocket.

"Wait. Tess is right. I'm going to call Aiden." I'm quick to retrieve my phone from the chair behind me.

"Mercy—" Henry begins to argue, but I shut him up with one look.

"I don't know why, but my gut is telling me to call Aiden. So, please, can you just fucking trust me."

Before I'm able to find Aiden's number on my phone, silently thanking him for adding it into my contacts list without my asking, the front door swings open. The three of us are on our feet faster than a cat spooked by a loud noise.

"Grab a bag. Quick. Get in your car and follow me to my place. Now. Orthus, you go with Henry and Tess. Mercy, you're riding with me."

A wave of relief washes over all of us at the sight of Aiden and not some stranger.

"My door was locked," Tess says looking puzzled.

"Apparently not. Let's go."

We get the not-so-subtle hint of urgency from Aiden, and the three of us are quick to collect our things and follow him out the front door. I'm thankful for Tess's and Henry's willingness to just follow Aiden's instructions and not question him. Questions can be answered later.

As I sling my duffle across my body, adjusting it on my back, I catch Aiden's attention. Fear is not etched across his face; only determination and calculated planning are there. "What is it?" I can't help but ask. I need an explanation for the urgency.

"I was on my way over to check in with you all. I know; I know; I'm a nice guy," he quips with a cheeky grin. His tone switches back to nothing but serious when he explains how, on his way over, he caught sight of the red car once again, this time cruising Tess's neighborhood.

The four of us, Orthus in tow, are out the door within minutes, having taken no time at all to collect our things. I watch Tess open the back door of Henry's sedan for Orthus to squeeze into it. Satisfied that everyone is ready to go, I swing my leg over the pillion seat of Aiden's bike and wrap my arms tightly around his waist. For a moment, I'm unsettled by the familiarity and comfort I find in our closeness; then I try to shake it off.

"Looks like this little pouch you gave me is a dud," I joke, trying to ease the tension that has made itself at home in my bones.

He brings the bike to life with a twist of the throttle. At the end of Tess's driveway, he stops to look for traffic. Before we take off down the main road, I can feel his body shudder against my own. "That's the problem. There's no way that that talisman wouldn't work."

Before I'm able to make any remark or tease him for his absolute faith in this little pouch of protection I've been given, we peel out of the driveway. At high speed, we whip through the twists and turns, eventually pulling off the main road and onto unlit back roads. All I can do is pray that Henry and Tess are able to keep up.

We sit together in Aiden's grand living room, which boasts high ceilings with exposed beams that draw the eye up. Oversized tanned-leather furniture crowds around a massive fireplace framed by floor-to-ceiling windows overlooking the secluded property. Light-colored faux-fur blankets are draped across the furniture, and gold accent pieces break up the warm but dark color scheme that runs throughout the house. In all honesty, throughout, his home is beautifully decorated with sophisticated art and furniture of masculine and luxurious taste—all words I would use to describe Aiden.

Except for sophisticated, only because I need to keep him humble, and I refuse to inflate his already-enlarged ego. I smirk to myself at the innocent yet teasing thought.

Aiden joins us with a bottle of whiskey tucked under one arm and four crystal glasses clutched between fingertips, offering one to each of us. As he serves each of us a generous pour, I tuck myself into the corner of the recliner, which is large enough to swallow me whole. I pull one of the blankets over my knees and cover my toes, getting settled and comfy with my now-full glass of whiskey in hand.

"Scoot over." Aiden stands in front of me, back to the fire framing him in a soft glow.

"I was here first, thank you very much. And I'm quite comfortable," I say just before I sip my drink and peer at him over the rim of my glass.

"I can see that. And because you look so comfortable, I'm being nice about sharing *my* seat with you." Without permission, he fits his body around mine while I glare at him and hold my glass out in front of me to avoid any spillage.

The recliner proves to be big enough to fit two comfortably if one slightly rests atop the other. After a few adjustments, Aiden has himself positioned comfortably beneath me, my ass wedged into the corner of the chair and my legs draped over his lap. He props one leg up on the ottoman in front of him and rests one arm across my lap.

"Now, aren't we cozy?" He tilts his head and smirks, pleased with himself; then he takes a sip of his drink, his eyes shimmering deviously.

I meet his stare and roll my eyes, shaking my head incredulously. *The audacity of this man.*

Tess's lack of response to the scene we just acted out, one I know she would have considered flirtatious, causes me to refocus my attention on her. Something I do gratefully, considering I was involuntarily starting to enjoy our little back-and-forth moment as my blood began to heat—and not because of the heat from the gas fireplace.

I can't allow myself to be distracted or bothered by any emotions and feelings other than my own right now.

"Tess, you good?"

Henry sits close to her, his hand rubbing soothing circles on her back. Her breathing isn't short or labored, but her stooped shoulders and fidgeting fingers wrapped around her glass display signs of her distress.

"Mercy, what have you gotten yourself into?" Concern flashes in her hazel eyes as worry knits her brow, her eyes pleading for answers I don't have.

"Tess—" I begin but am interrupted by Aiden.

"I promise you *are* safe here. It's hard to explain, but think of us as…off the grid, so to speak, when we are here."

His words only raise more questions and feelings of uncertainty for Tess. I can see it in the way she looks at me and then Henry, unsure of what to trust.

"Trust me, Tess. I have no clue why these lunatics are after me. I mean, you know me! Can you think of any reason at all why they want me? My only thought is that I'm being mistaken for someone else."

I watch as she churns thoughts in her head and mulls over any explanation she can think of...and comes up with nothing.

"I would never do anything that would put me or any of my family and friends in danger. Can you trust me on that, at least?"

Her eyes meet mine, and I can tell her busy mind has settled a bit. She softens her gaze but gives me a tight-lipped smile.

Yep. I have, of course, managed to make my best friend lose all trust in me. And here I go, leaping to the worst-case scenario, as usual. I know it's not that she doesn't trust me. She is just worried about me.

I let go of a breath I've been holding, afraid of Tess's reaction, when I see her face brighten up a bit and a mischievous smile form on her lips in an attempt to mask the worry I know is still weighing on her.

"On that—of course, I trust you." She then points between Aiden and me. "On *that*—let's just say I remain skeptical of your denial."

I don't argue or disagree with her. I'm just happy to see her relax a little, but I can't stop my heart from clenching when I think of the unease she and Henry feel because of me.

As if sensing my moment of heartache, Aiden gently squeezes my leg in a show of support. The subtle gesture causes my body to react and relax against him. *Fuck.*

"Ummm...is that an inlay of a Ouija board on your coffee table?" Henry leans back as if the board can somehow reach for him; his eyebrows rise to his hairline.

"Let me guess. And the planchette is what you normally use as your coaster?" I joke, which elicits a low chuckle from Aiden.

"Ever used one?" The question is thrown out to all of us, but green eyes focus mainly on me, as if my answer is the only one that matters to Aiden.

"Mercy and I tried once."

Henry looks to Tess in shocked surprise.

"I definitely moved the planchette to scare Lily," I admit, snickering at the memory.

"Maybe that's why she moved to the other side of the country as soon as she could," Tess responds, lightheartedly laughing.

"What do you think? Want to give it a real try this time?"

My dare evokes an array of reactions. Henry balks and responds with a "fuck no."

In need of something to distract me from the abductors still on the loose and the guilt I feel over dragging my friends into whatever this is, I click my tongue, wiggle off Aiden's lap, and set myself up at the table. "Tess?"

Tess stares down at the display of letters and numbers, the Hello and Goodbye, the Yes and No, with what looks to be sadness mixed with a hint of hope. Her expression stirs feelings of unease in the pit of my stomach as I realize whom she might be hoping to talk to if this actually works.

"Let's do it," she finally responds, which forces an agitated groan out of Henry.

CHAPTER 15
MERCY

The room is dark, lit only by the warm glow of the fire and candles I've placed around the space. *If we are doing this, we are doing it right.*

The four of us sit around the rectangular coffee table—Aiden across from me and Henry across from Tess. Mixed emotions about what we are about to do bring a certain kind of energy to the room that's a mixture of excitement and apprehension. Apprehension mainly from Henry.

"All right. So…are we reaching out to just anyone or someone in particular?" Aiden's question rattles us a bit as we take in what we are about to do. There's a moment of silence as each one of us meets the eyes of everyone else around the table, looking for a spark of interest in anyone's expression.

"Let's just get this over with. It's not like they really work anyway," Henry says, rolling his eyes in irritation. The tension in his shoulders fails to convey his forced skepticism; instead, it reveals his nerves.

"I-I," Tess stutters, "h-have s-someone in mind."

We all turn and look at her. Aiden, not knowing much about Tess's life, is unable to grasp the weight of her words. I feel my chest tighten and know Henry is feeling the same as I watch his chin dip and his eyes softly close.

I reach across the table to squeeze Tess's hand in a show of support and understanding. "Okay, Tess. Let's do this."

Acknowledging the heaviness that has fallen upon the room, Aiden clears his throat. "Two fingers on the planchette, please," he instructs us, shaking us from our moment of sorrow.

Once we've taken our positions, he casually announces to the room that we are here to chat with the deceased, as if what we are doing is as normal as meeting up at a bar to catch up with friends. The way he goes about doing this is so nonchalant that I hope, if this is works, no spirit is offended by his lack of enthusiasm. The last thing we need right now is trouble on another plane of existence, especially when there's so much going on already on this one.

We sit there patiently, our fingers resting atop the planchette. A collective breath is held by all of us, and then it is released when the planchette refuses to budge and not a single chill runs up our spines. I, for one, am left a bit disappointed.

"Maybe we are doing this wrong?" Tess's face scrunches up; she looks puzzled.

"I told you these never work."

"Shut up, Henry," I scoff, frustrated by his continued cynicism and now determined to prove him wrong. No one lifts their fingers from the planchette, and before anyone has the chance to back out, I pipe up, "Let me try."

"Think you have a better way with words?" Aiden asks.

"*Maybe* the spirits would be more willing to talk if they were welcomed with more respect and eagerness...like we care." The last bit I say while shooting a deadpan look towards Aiden.

"The floor is yours, my dear." A mischievous grin lights Aiden's face.

A challenge. Always a challenge.

Centering myself in whatever way I think might work—and failing at it because I truly have no clue what I'm doing—I jumble phrases and words together in a way that, to me, sounds spiritual.

"Namaste," Aiden interjects.

"Aiden! Come on!" I snap at him as he fights back laughter, poking fun at my obviously failed attempt to come up with some profound greeting.

Henry and Tess laugh a bit, and I shoot each of them a look as my cheeks flush. Soon, I too can't help but laugh.

"Okay, fine! Let me give it a go." Tess rolls her shoulders, stiffens her spine, and places her two fingers back on the planchette, lifting an eyebrow at us to join her.

After a quick sip of our drinks, the three of us join Tess and attempt round three.

"We gather here to call upon the spirit world in hopes of communicating with loved ones who have left this world… left our side." Tess's voice falters towards the end and becomes barely a whisper. And then she asks the question I knew she would; it still causes my heart to beat solemnly in grief for my friend. "Mom? Dad? Are you there?"

For a long, drawn-out minute, there is nothing. No flickering of the candles' flames. No drop in temperature, as described in all the paranormal shows and movies I've seen. I look up to see Aiden watching Tess. Her focus is dialed in on the planchette, willing it to move.

He looks at me, and I can see the regret in his eyes, as if he, not I, were the one to suggest we fuck around with the board in the first place. The look of regret quickly flashes to wide-eyed surprise a moment before the planchette moves.

He's looking at me as if I suddenly grew an extra eye or something.

Our eyes release each other's gaze, and we divert our attention to the planchette. My breathing quickens, and I feel a chill begin to creep up my spine. I look over at Tess, whose jaw hangs open in delight. Then I look at Henry, who is definitely shitting himself right now.

"Who's pushing it?" Henry demands, horrified.

The planchette lands on Yes.

"My mom," Tess chokes out in answer. Tears begin to well up in her eyes, which makes the golden browns of their hazel glow.

I feel the weight of Aiden's gaze on me as the chill in my bones settles deeper. My core twists; I chance a look down and see a foggy black figure hovering over my midsection, looking as if it's trying to find a way inside me. Frightened, I snap my gaze to Aiden's, wondering if he's seeing the same thing I am. His blatant stare focused on my face tells me I'm the only one who can see it. I start to feel another sense of terror as I begin wondering what *he* is seeing that is causing him to stare with such a look of rattled awe, as if he's been struck by the revelation of a once-hidden secret.

One second I'm sitting around the table with my friends. The next...

CHAPTER 16
AIDEN

Tess's call to the spirit world was a plea for comfort and an attempt to perhaps one more time feel her mother's presence. When nothing happened at first, I immediately started hating myself for not simply brushing off Henry's question about my table. Its purpose is to do more than just be a placeholder for things—sometimes, it's just easier to communicate directly with those in Helheim I need to talk to, instead of relying on Void all the time. It's basically texting.

Had I known about Tess's parents, I probably would have suggested something else to entertain us and to distract Mercy from her troubles. Anything else. Honestly, I'm wondering now why I didn't just suggest strip poker. Not that I want to see Henry strip, but Mercy and Tess, on the other hand… Now *that* would have been a fun distraction. But no. I had to go along with talking to the fucking dead.

There's a torturous pause of nothing, as if no one actually feels like talking. Go figure, the one time I actually offer up conversation, the chatty bastards don't want to talk. But then, as I apologetically look at Mercy for traumatizing her best friend, I see the blue of her left eye flash silver and her pupil become cloudy. It's for just a few seconds, though long enough that I know I'm not just imagining things, and the sight unearths a vision buried deep in my subconscious mind. Right after the flash, the planchette slowly slides to Yes.

Overwhelmed by the movement of the planchette, Tess and Henry fail to notice Mercy's brief transformation. Before the color returns to her eye, her eyelids shut tightly. I watch as her eyes move rapidly from side to side beneath their lids. My fingers, which are next to hers, feel her skin turn cold. All I can do is sit and observe. This vision is something I will definitely have to revisit at a later time.

"Tess?"

We all look at Mercy as a voice not her own calls out for Tess. For her daughter.

"Mom?" The heartfelt sob that comes with Tess's question is from the depths of her soul.

Mercy's hand lunges for Tess's wrist and latches on tightly. The impulsive movement is a bit too violent to be a mother's warm embrace. Her head swivels to face Tess even though her eyes are still closed and moving rapidly within their sockets.

Any bit of happiness leaches from Tess's face. Any bit of hope or positivity is replaced by shock that quickly progresses to absolute terror as Mercy tilts her head to the side in a predatory manner.

"Mom?" This time Tess's voice lacks the joyous love it carried just seconds ago. Her simple question is now laced with fear.

Mercy's body convulses slightly, and she looks to be fighting off something that we cannot see. Grip firm around

Tess's wrist with one hand, the fingers on the planchette turning white on the other, her arms cross over her body and leave her in what must be an uncomfortably twisted position. I watch as her shoulders hunch forward and her stomach beneath the tightly fitted shirt flexes and constricts in what appears to be a painful way. The internal struggle suddenly stops, and I watch her body soften.

"Tess!"

Mercy's grip eases around Tess's wrist, but temporary red marks remain. Mercy's head twitches, and her features release any tension they held. It's as if two entities were fighting for the use of her voice, her vessel; Tess's mother—I'm cautiously hoping—is really the one who won the fight in the end.

"My beautiful girl. Your father and I miss you so much," the voice speaks through Mercy, any trace of hostility gone. "We both love you more than you could ever know. Please tell Lily we love and miss her, too."

I watch as a glimmer of hope peeks through a longing daughter's watery eyes. And I silently swear to any gods, to whoever is listening, that if the spirit contacting us through Mercy is not Tess's mother, I will be making a quick trip to my so-called basement when this is wrapped up. Void will have a very unpleasant message from yours truly to deliver to the fool who is deciding to fuck around. After all, there *is* punishment in Hel for those who deserve it.

"Mom? Is this…is this really—"

"Don't remove your fingers from the planchette," I warn her. "We don't know for sure if this is your mother."

Regret is not a strong enough word to describe how I feel about my damn decision in agreeing to this group-bonding activity. The number of things that could go wrong… I use my free hand to take a much-need gulp of liquor.

Each flame of the surrounding candles begins to flicker, evidence that the connection between worlds is becoming weak. The dancing shadows they cast push Henry closer to the edge of losing his shit. I'm pretty sure one of us will have to perform CPR on him in a second if his heart doesn't stop beating like a frightened rabbit's. And I'll definitely be writing a check to the best therapist in town for Tess after this. Clearly, it's been a while since I've dabbled in the how-to-host-newly-made-friends department.

My eyes scan the room, and the flickering flames come to a standstill in eerie unison, their flames reaching higher in one last-ditch attempt to connect the dead and the living.

Two worry lines from hurt form between Mercy's brows, her eyes still closed, the corners of her mouth tilting down in sorrow. She sighs before speaking, displeased by the doubt I shared with Tess.

"Take a look at you now." Mercy's brows remain fixed in a state of worry, but her lips form a smile meant only for Tess. A simple phrase shared, intended to convey a more significant meaning.

A breathy laugh whispers out from Tess's lips, and her smile meets her eyes, tears now sliding down her heart-shaped face. "Take a look at me now."

"I love you, Tess."

"I love you, too, Mom." Tess's voice cracks and is barely above a whisper.

Mercy's head twitches once again, and her loosened grip around Tess's wrist becomes a vise grip once more. Her head cocks to the side, and her features sharpen in demanding urgency. Through closed eyelids, a distant soul's stare bores straight into Tess's wide-eyed gaze.

"We are all dust with no way of going home or coming back. The wheel is broken." The voice coming from Mercy is dry and pained, as if it is coming from a prisoner whose water has been withheld.

Tess's face pinches into a look of confusion; she tries, to no avail, to shake Mercy's constricting grip from her wrist. "I don't understand!" Her voice rises in bewildered fear.

"The wheel. Is. BROKEN!" An audible gasp rushes out of Mercy. Her eyes slam open, and her body jerks as if she's been punched in the gut.

My attention snaps to Tess. "Goodbye. Say it. SAY IT NOW, TESS!"

"Goodbye!"

On my instruction, I guide everyone to push the planchette over to Goodbye and fall back, bracing myself on my hands. I reach for my glass and down the last few sips of whiskey it held. That was more intense than I had anticipated. I've only ever seen the Ouija board work by spelling out words and short phrases. Never have I witnessed a possession in which the possessed person's voice is not their own and two spirits battle each other to come through. I've also never seen someone's body react as Mercy's did; it looked as if she was battling more than just the two spirits on the other side. There was something else *here*. Something I'm not sure any of us but Mercy could see and feel.

"What the actual fuck just happened?" Mercy's voice is finally her own.

Henry, Tess, and I all stare at Mercy. Henry is wide-eyed, staring at her as if he were a deer and she the headlights. Tess is crying. I think they are a mix between happy tears and frightened tears, but that is yet to be determined. And I...I'm intrigued. Not only by what just happened, but the effect it had on a mental block I can now confirm is there after having felt it slip at the sight of Mercy's silver eye.

I know more than I think I do. There's an understanding of something more, something bigger. Though blurry, something revealed itself to me; it needed me to acknowledge it. I just can't seem to completely access that information in my brain. And I need to know what and why.

CHAPTER 17
MERCY

As I'm being dramatically told what the fuck just happened to me and to everyone else, I don't feel the least bit shameful about the third glass of whiskey I'm currently pouring down my throat. Between the *thing* I saw swarming around my core and the place my mind took me, I'll need more than just three glasses to take the edge off.

After feeling ill at the sight of the black cloud pulsating at my stomach, and while everyone was speaking to Momma Nell and some random unhinged spirit, I was…not there. Physically my body was, but mentally I was in a place I had never been before. A place of permanent twilight and endless horizons where the sun and moon linger together in time and space. I was both something and nothing at the same time; I had a body that I could not quite feel and a mind that was fully aware.

I force myself to look focused and interested in everything Tess is telling me. Henry occasionally jumps in to provide logical and rational reasoning for it all in an effort to calm himself. In reality, I am lost in my racing thoughts, trying to cling to any memory that tries to slip away like sand in an hourglass. Once the last granule falls through to the other side, I know most of what I just experienced will become a fuzzy memory lost amongst many others in my subconscious.

Aiden has remained quiet, only interrupting on occasion to help Tess's and Henry's retelling of the events. Deeply concentrating, the muscles of his square jaw twitch as he scratches at the stubble that frames his face. His green eyes lack their usual vibrancy and have become a darker hue, which I've come to realize as a sign of mental gymnastics or conflict he's internalizing.

It's as if I've known this man for a lot longer than just this week.

"And no one thought to have their phone recording this whole time?" I sarcastically lament, shaking my head and trying to hide my discomfort.

I'm met with nervous laughter and looks of uncertainty from Tess and Henry.

"Well, between dodging the fuckers that are out to get Mercy—"

I interject, mumbling under my breath, "Ugh, thanks for the reminder."

He side-eyes me and continues, "...and speaking to the spirit world." Aiden pauses before slapping both palms on the floor beside him and launching himself to his feet. "I think it's time we go to bed."

Oh, sure. I'll have no fucking problem sleeping after all that.

"Tess. Henry. I'll show you to the guest room. Mercy"— envious of the way Aiden is able to easily lift just one brow, I lift both of mine at him and wait to hear his suggestion as to where I will sleep—"you can have my room. I'll sleep on the couch down here. I'm sure Orthus would love to share the bed with you again," he says with a grin that pulls to one side.

It's Tess's turn to side-eye me before following Aiden down the hall to the spare room, Henry in tow. I know she's thinking that Aiden's offer to sleep on the couch is just for show. I imagine she suspects he will be joining me in his bed once she and Henry are behind the closed doors of the guest room.

I answer her with a shake of my head in denial.

As if he understood everything that was just discussed, Orthus stands, stretches in front of the fireplace, and then plods over to me. He lets loose a gentle sneeze and nuzzles the hand at my side.

"Lead the way, bud." I take a second to scratch behind his furry, pointed ear before he guides me to Aiden's room.

I turn over in the bed that's not mine, unable to get comfortable. Not because the bed itself isn't something worthy of the royal family, but because my fucking mind won't stop overthinking every little thing that has happened today, yesterday, the day before, and so on.

I thought I was past this. And of course I forgot my meds at home.

A faint ticking sound from the grandfather clock down the hall echoes into the bedroom. Its low metronome—*ticktock, ticktock, ticktock*—is anything but soothing; instead, it makes my skin crawl. Orthus kicks my lower spine with his back paws as he sleeps soundly, off in dreamland; that's the last straw, and I accept that sleep isn't going to happen anytime soon.

My bare feet hit the cold floor, and I groan as I leave the warm bed. The longer I lie there, though, the more my mind is just going to abuse me with worries and thoughts I have no control over at the moment. So I've decided to distract myself by poking around the kitchen and helping myself to a midnight snack.

Knowing that Aiden is asleep on the couch, I do my best to stay quiet and tiptoe through the living room without waking him. Once in the kitchen, I open cabinets at random in search of anything that might satisfy my hunger, which stems simply from restlessness. Aside from salted peanuts, artisanal crackers, and some stale biscuit-type cookies, there's not much to eat that could be considered a snack. And I'm not about to make myself a full meal.

A simple glass of water it is, then.

Curiosity gets the best of me as I start to make my way back to the bedroom, so I make a detour to the study. A desk lamp has been left on, and I'm drawn to it like a moth to a flame.

French doors painted black open to a room of walnut shelving that lines the side and back walls from floor to ceiling. I walk the perimeter, eyes browsing the titles of books that fill the shelves and are piled on the floor in every corner. The first unit of shelving is filled with books on astrology, spirituality, and religion. As I move to the next unit, the categories change to more science-based literature of astronomy, physics, and mathematics. *Boring.* Continuing on my cursory exploration, I find books on history, psychology, and art. The man sure does like to read—assuming these aren't all for decoration—but it doesn't seem for enjoyment, considering the lack of fiction housed here.

My fingers lazily brush along the tomes as I browse, stopping on no title in particular. As I reach the end of the book-filled shelves, I find myself staring at a wall covered in an array of beautifully inked celestial maps. The ones that appear to have been pinned first are orderly and positioned with care, but are now covered by what look to be more recently created renderings that overlap and hang askew. The visuals are absolutely stunning and created in such fine detail.

"See anything you like?"

Startled, I whip around to find Aiden leaning against the door frame. My cheeks heat from a combination of being caught snooping and the sight of him shirtless. Not only does he have bone structure worthy of sculpting, but the rest of him just adds to his unnatural beauty. His muscles are taut and lean, as if he's been training for a battle that certainly will never happen in this town, or even era. And those piercing green eyes of his continue to have me questioning if it's desire I'm feeling or a warning to be heedful of trouble.

Either way, I'm fucked. Curiosity killed the cat. And I'm that stupid cat.

"Ah, maybe *now* you see something you like." He winks and strolls over to the wall I am standing in front of, but not before calling me out on my traitorous roaming eyes.

I clear my throat and blink a few times, returning my focus to the inked maps. "Don't flatter yourself. It's just been a while since I've seen a guy shirtless, all right?" I try to sound nonchalant, yet can't manage to hide a tone of embarrassment.

Pathetic.

"Whatever you say." The corner of his lip turns up, which causes my pulse to quicken, thanks to both the undeniable attraction I've been fighting and the mortification over my blatant eye fucking.

That's the only type of fucking I will be able to manage when he looks like that and I look like...well, me. I can't even fake the confidence I would need to be with someone like him. But fuck it. A girl can dream.

I change the subject, bringing the focus back to the maps pinned to the wall. "These are all...actually impressive pieces of work. You drew them yourself?"

"Yeah. Everything here is mine. This is...I guess what you can say I do for work. And it's not just pretty; it's also accurate." He brings his hand to the back of his neck.

I use every bit of control I have to keep my eyes zeroed in on the maps, not him. "You mean to tell me you pay for *this* house by selling artistically illustrated maps...of space?" I tease him with a glance over my shoulder, attempting to arch one brow skeptically. "Because there are so many people going on vacation in the solar system these days."

"I guess you can say that I found that one unicorn of a client who appreciates my work. Any other buyers are just a bonus."

His response is suspicious, but nothing I haven't heard of happening before. People who have stupid amounts of money tend to obsess and collect strange things.

"And these are only a few examples. The bigger, more creative pieces are actually being prepped for an art exhibit later this month."

I'm officially impressed and annoyed that this new knowledge about him makes him that much more attractive—and unattainable for someone like me.

"Oh, trust me. What I've seen so far… Well, I'm more than impressed. I'm not taking away from your talent, but… damn…a unicorn client is—"

"I know I lucked out," he says with a smile and sits at the oversized walnut drafting table in the center of the room.

I can't help but shuffle over to him, the blanket still tightly wrapped around me, and peer over his shoulder. Curious eyes now fixed on the work in progress in front of him, I lean in and examine it from over his shoulder, the occasional tendril of short, tousled wave brushing my cheek. The smell of cinnamon and pine hit my senses the closer I get to him.

What the fuck is wrong with me?

I jump slightly as Aiden swivels in his seat so that he faces me, positioning his knees on either side of my thighs.

"Cold?" He pulls at the blanket I now have wrapped so tightly around me that I'm willing it to make me disappear. The gentle tug shifts me off-balance, causing me to lean more into his hold and quickening my breathing. His hands, now on my hips, anchor me to the spot; I couldn't flee if I wanted to.

Aiden tilts his head to the side inquisitively. "I'm curious."

"About?" I have no clue what that mind of his wants to know.

"You."

Well, that catches me off guard. Now, *I'm* curious. "Why?" My eyes narrow.

"Maybe so I can understand better why those men are after you." He hits me with his own narrow-eyed gaze. "And you don't seem like someone who has any shady business dealings you're keeping secret. So...tell me, Mercy, what is it about you that has someone out to get you? What makes you so appealing to them?" He lifts his chin, and though he's sitting and I am standing, we are just about at eye level with each other.

I shrug my shoulders and grimace at thoughts of my life up to this point. "No shady business here. I live a pretty average, slightly depressing life. To tell you the truth, I think those assholes think I'm someone else. Someone definitely a bit more important than I am."

"You're important," he counters with a look that tells me there is no room for argument on the matter.

But, naturally, I do because I'm new in this battle to better myself. *I want to get better.* "Ha. Yeah, pretty sure if I disappeared, no one would notice. And even if they did, after a short amount of time, they would realize, whether I'm in their life or not, it makes no difference to them."

Yup, there's that negative self-actualization coming out strong. So much for kicking that habit to the curb.

Baby steps, Mercy. Baby steps.

The color of his eyes dims, and his brows pinch together in a show of concern, of all things. Everything I've been working on over these past couple of days is starting to feel like a facade I've created in order to believe the lie that I can do better. That I *am* better.

It's not a facade, is it?

No, it's not. I am working on this. It's not fake.

Shit, maybe it is.

"Tess would notice," he counters, breaking my train of thought. My lips part, about to argue that over time, she would find life no different with me than without, but he shushes me as he holds up his index finger in the little space between us.

"Henry would notice."

My chin drops and eyes become heavy as he continues his list of people who I know love me but would be no worse without me. *He doesn't understand.*

"Your family? I don't know them, but I bet they would notice. And to that point, if each one of these people notices… doesn't that mean you're important to them? That you hold significance in their lives?" he questions.

I know he's asking rhetorically. I fight the urge to deny his argument as the depression-induced pressure building in my skull starts to thrum.

"It doesn't matter how big or small a role you play; we all have a purpose that helps each other along this unpredictable *thing* we call life. It just matters that you are playing your role. So, yeah, in laymen's terms, you're important." He finishes his speech and refuses to look away as I fight back the tears that threaten to fall.

"That's a lovely way to look at it, and I'm sure that it's true for most. But I've proved through experience that someone can walk away from me and be all the better for it. I've lived through…am living through…proof of my lack of importance. I am no one. And I just have to be okay with that. And I am." I continue to fight back the tears as I try to convince him of my truth.

Silence fills the little space between us, and I watch his eyes flick back and forth as he takes in the hurt I can't hide on my face. A hurt that isn't the result of anything he said, just a pain that I've let fester and dwell inside for so long that trying to rid myself of it feels as hard as cutting off a limb. I've became so comfortable in my pain that my recent attempts to break free from it have proven to be more difficult than I expected.

"If you think you are of no significance, of *no* importance, to someone who walked away, you are looking at it all wrong." There is no trace of his usual tough exterior; instead, I catch a glimpse of the Aiden with whom he surprised me the other day on the bridge. He offers me a side of him I doubt he lets many others even know about. And I'm not quite sure he even realizes he's doing it.

"Because you *were* important for that person. Still are. You were a lesson they needed to learn, and that person wouldn't be where they're at today had you now been part of it. It's up to them to see it as an experience to grow from, just as it is for you." His grip tightens around the blanket, pulling me in just a bit closer.

I'm fighting with all my strength to internally hold myself together. "Okay, so *that* person grows…but what if *I* break? Because I did. More than I had ever broken before." I pause, remembering the conversation I had with Tess not too long ago, telling her that I was going to be okay. I laugh at the confidence and certainty I had convinced myself would be mine again.

"I told myself that I burned it all down for the better. That I will build myself back up from the ashes that are left, the broken pieces that are scattered. That I will find the self I lost along the way of living amongst the ashes and pieces of me. But what if all that's left are ashes and broken things that can't be put back together as I have hoped?" My heart hammers in my chest as the confessions about my fears tumble out, and I am unable to take them back.

"There's a freedom in recreating something from nothing. A freedom in picking up those broken pieces and placing them back together in a way that leaves cracks to allow light to shine through." He brushes loose strands of hair away from my eyes, which burn from grief and restored hope. "Those ashes are meant to be scattered in remembrance of who you were before…and appreciation for what it took to get to where you are now."

I'm quiet as I take in everything he's just said to me. I begin to feel the sensation of self-worth and self-preservation trickle their way back into my mind. I think back to the tarot card and the conversation with Tess. I force myself to see it as truth and not the facade I fear it to be. I remind myself that I am enough and make a mental promise to keep telling myself that until I finally believe it.

I am here. I am enough.

"I promise there is freedom in breaking."

I tilt my head back, forcing the tears to slide back into my tear ducts. When I believe I have my emotions somewhat under control, I meet Aiden's gaze again. "Here I was, thinking that all these books were for decoration. Come to find out, you've been hitting them hard. Especially those psychology books."

He shoots me a look of unabashed reverence for himself. "You think I'm only beauty and no brains?"

I can't help but laugh, thankful the weight of all that we just spoke about is lifting.

"I still would like to know more about you. There has to be some explanation as to why Frick and Frack are so obsessed with you." He stands from the stool and walks over to the French doors to leave the study.

"Why does there have to be some *obvious* reason for them to be obsessed with me? Other than my weird-girl charm and alluringly feral appearance?" The confident tease is a bit forced, but still progress.

Aiden stops in the doorway to face me while holding his arm out towards the living room. "Care to join me by the fire for a drink?" He brings the hand of his outstretched arm to the top of his head, shoves his fingers into his hair, and gives me a wry grin. "I don't think either of us is going to find sleep anytime soon. And you can humor me with your tales of rising, falling, breaking"—I drop my eyes and scoff at the latter part of his suggestion, having little interest in revisiting any part of my life up until this point; when I look back up, I'm caught off guard by the hand he is now reaching out to me—"and finding your freedom."

I release a sharp exhale and take his hand.

An orange glow paints the living room and announces the start of another day. The room is toasty from the fire that continues to burn. Basking in the warmth of another body, I stretch my limbs and am the very portrait of a cat waking from a long nap. Not ready to open my eyes, I roll over to find another position of blissful comfort and am lulled back to sleep by the steady rise and fall of Aiden's chest.

Realization strikes, and I snap awake, planting my palms firmly against the bare chest of the man I mistakenly used as a pillow after drifting off to sleep late last night…or maybe it was early this morning. Launching myself to a sitting position, I force air from Aiden's lungs when I push against his chest, rattled and not thinking about waking him.

His eyes fly open for a mere second before he squints to block the morning sun. "Fuck. Good morning to you, too."

He covers his eyes with one hand, avoiding the now-glaring sunlight.

The blanket is still wrapped around me, just not as tightly as it had been when we originally sat down to talk. I'm suddenly feeling very self-conscious about my morning appearance.

"I'm sorry! I didn't realize we had fallen asleep." I groan as I pull the blanket snug around me once again.

"What time is it?"

He's clearly unbothered by the whole ordeal, as he's barely moved a muscle to get up and seems quite comfortable with me still between his outstretched legs.

When the hell did we get into this position? I can't trust myself even in sleep, apparently.

"Umm"—flustered, I look around for a clock and find a phone that was left on the Ouija-board table—"it's quarter to seven."

Nervous energy continues to build, and I'm unsure of what to do with myself. After little sleep, I'm still tired, and the thought of going back to the bed currently occupied by Orthus crosses my mind. I shift my weight to leave the couch—and the limbs of a man I woke up tangled in—but I'm stopped as fingers wrap around my wrist.

"I was comfortable and warm…and then you moved." The complaint, a low grumble, is directed at me and meant to elicit some sort of sympathy. Aiden stares at me through one open eye; the other is covered by the bicep of the arm he drapes across his face to avoid the light pouring through the windows. He pulls my arm to force me back down into a comfortable position, my head once again using his chest as a—rather hard—pillow.

"Relax, would you?"

My body is rigid against his, and I am far from the tired, liquor-induced relaxed person who would have snuggled into this position last night. Strands of my hair gently snag on the stubble of Aiden's jaw, and he brushes them away, but then he leaves his fingers in my hair and threads them through the long, loose waves. The touch is intimate, and I melt into the light pressure as he massages my temple. The small, slow circles he makes cause my mind to be at war with itself over whether or not to give in and just enjoy the moment.

"I can stop." His fingers pause for all of two seconds before I reply with a quiet and quick "No!" My head right under his chin, I can feel the knowing smirk forming on his lips.

In five minutes, my racing heart has slowed. In another two minutes, my body is heavy and fitted perfectly against his. In another five minutes, despite the morning sun beaming down on us through the large windows, I'm sound asleep.

CHAPTER 18
MERCY

I awake to the flash of someone's phone camera and scowl at the sight of Tess sitting on the couch across from where I am lying on top of Aiden.

"For the next time you deny that there's...ya know...*nothing* going on here"—she flicks her finger between Aiden and me—"I can just shove this in your face." The smug pride in her smile has me sticking my middle finger up at her, while I bury my head under my arm and—due to my position—against Aiden's chest.

The flash goes off one more time.

"We made coffee. Hope you don't mind." Tess snuggles into Henry, making herself right at home with a hot mug of coffee between her hands and Orthus curled up at her feet.

"I don't mind at all. I'm going to grab a cup myself," Aiden says while sitting up, lifting me in the process. "Were you two comfortable last night?" he asks over his shoulder as he walks to the kitchen.

Bringing the coffee mug up to her lips, Tess stares at me, her eyes twinkling. "Oh, very much so." Refusing to lose eye contact, she continues, "Although...I might argue not as comfortable as Mercy." She does the thing where she wiggles her eyebrows at me, and I glare back.

As Aiden approaches with a coffee mug in each hand and still shirtless, Tess gives me a nod of approval and then gestures for me to fix my hair.

I can't believe her right now. I mean, I can. It's Tess. But still.

"Tess and I were actually talking this morning and think that it would be safe if we were to go back to my place," Henry says, joining the conversation, thankfully, with a topic that doesn't revolve around where and with whom I just woke up. "We figured my house is an unknown location. And it's not like they're after us." He winces as the words come out of his mouth, unable to take them back.

"Relax, Henry. I agree with you. There's no need for you two to be any more involved in this than you already are." I sit cross-legged on the couch, coffee in hand, content with the idea of my friends being as far removed as possible from my current troubling situation.

"We *do*, however, think it would be a good idea"—Tess starts giving me a look that tells me she's anticipating a strong response from me—"for *you* to stay here. With Aiden. In this house. Under supervision. Where you're safe. Not that we think you can't handle being alone. We just worry about you, and we need to get back to our jobs before they start wondering where we are. Not that we've been gone long at all, but how could we leave your side knowing what we know now! And with everything we talked about yesterday at your place, I think being alone really isn't a good idea for you anyway. Again, not that I think—"

I throw a hand up to stop Tess's rambling and, honestly, to simply force her to take a breath before she passes out. "Tess, you and Henry need to get back to your lives. I agree. And I love you both so much for being by my side throughout this whole…escapade," I say while tossing my hand in the air. "You don't need to worry about me, though. The police are investigating things still, so it's not like I'm completely vulnerable. And I—"

"Will be staying with me until everything is settled." The very casual assumption is made before I can even finish my sentence.

I snap my attention to Aiden—whose go-to facial expression, I've decided, is a permanent smirk—and then I get whiplash when I jerk my head back to Tess, who has put her coffee mug down and is clapping her hands in agreement as if everything has been settled.

"Perfect!" Tess chimes, her hands clasped together in satisfied delight.

"Excuse me! Do I not have a say?" I give each person a well-earned look of disbelief.

"The jury has spoken," Henry states matter-of-factly, and my jaw drops slightly in frustration as I was relying on him to have my back.

Overwhelmed by the need for control over my own situation—control that clearly I'm still struggling to gain—and by the incessant guilt of becoming someone else's burden, I rack my brain for any excuse that will convince everyone that I am perfectly fine taking care of myself.

Henry and Tess watch as I struggle to come up with an ironclad excuse, while Aiden lounges in the corner of the couch, relaxed and patiently awaiting my response he, without a doubt, already has a rebuttal for. He barely tries to hide the wicked grin behind the coffee mug at his lips, assuming, I am sure, that I have no leg to stand on in this fight.

But I refuse to be holed up in someone else's home like a damsel in distress in need of protection. Fuck that. Everyone here is more than welcome to call and drop by my home to make sure I'm still alive, still here. Other than that, I'm not going to let the unfortunate inconvenience of being someone's mistaken target, or whatever they were planning on doing with me, to interrupt a much-needed period of personal growth that I need to do *on my own*. Not to mention I need to start looking for another job so I can pay my bills. My savings is only going to last me so long.

I narrow my eyes at Henry, knowing my excuse won't be enough to win Tess over, but perhaps it will be rational enough to get Henry on my side. "You both just met Aiden. How do you know I'm any safer here with him than I am in my own home?" I hold Henry's attention, my eyes brimming with stubborn defiance. A part of me hopes Aiden doesn't take offense to my selfish argument—after all, I can't deny everything he has done for me even though we know very little about each other.

"I think we can all argue, here, that he made a pretty damn good first impression. *And* we both have known you long enough to know this is the least questionable decision you've ever made," Tess begins before Henry even has a chance to speak.

I catch Aiden's nod of appreciation towards Tess, and I slightly choke at her dig. I know I'm fighting a losing battle. "Well, it's not like I'm exactly making any decision—"

I'm not even allowed to defend myself before Tess cuts me off. "And be honest with yourself, Mercy. Do you really think going home is safe for you? What's the other option? Your parents? You're telling me you are going to pack up and leave to go stay with them down South until this all blows over? You hate the heat. And who's to say the fuckers don't follow you down there!" Tess's nostrils flare, and the look in her eyes leaves no room for argument.

"First, if anyone informs my parents about what is going on here…" I suck in a breath to steady myself, refusing to think of the relentless surveillance and overprotectiveness that would come from the parents of an only child—even if that child is now a grown-ass adult. "Just don't. There is no reason for them to be involved right now. I'm still here, safe, and perfectly healthy. Second…" I can't form a thought, and words escape me as my mouth opens and closes like a fish on dry land.

"Second?" Aiden's tone is teasing, knowing I have nothing to argue.

"It's settled, then. Aiden, good luck." Tess salutes Aiden with her mug of what, by now, must be cold coffee.

Henry chances a look of empathy, but I know, given the chance to say anything, he would agree with Tess, just a little less harshly. Awkward silence fills the room, but it is disrupted by the clicking of Orthus's nails on the hardwood floor, followed by a soft thud as he takes his spot in front of the fireplace.

"It's only temporary, roomie," Aiden says, breaking the silence and reaching an arm along the back of the couch to playfully tug on the braid I had busied myself with during the uncomfortable break in discussion. "Let *Officer John* do his investigating and crime solving, and let me provide you with a safe house. It will be fun."

"Good. She could use some *fun*," Tess snipes as she pops to her feet and storms off to collect their belongings.

"She says it with love, Mercy. She's just worried for you and knows there's nothing she can do, and that bothers her,"

Henry, the peacekeeper, says, trying to explain Tess's outburst, even though I know deep down that Tess only means the best. Always has, always will.

I hug goodbye a worried Tess, reassuring her for the hundredth time that I'm not upset with her, just the situation. Not that staying in an extravagant home and knowing I'm safe with a man whom I could happily stare at all day is anything to complain about—so long as he keeps his haughty attitude in check. It's just the amount of unknowns and lack of familiarity that has me battling to keep another breakdown at bay. I'm not mentally equipped to handle this sort of thing on a good day, never mind during such a tumultuous time the universe gifted me as if to say, "What doesn't kill you makes you stronger!" I understand the whole tough-love ideology, but now just is not the time for it. I'm hard enough on myself already.

"I hope you know I plan on visiting. Just because we are forcing you to hide away for the foreseeable future, doesn't mean Henry and I can't come hang out with *Aiden*, the only person we would be visiting here." Tess nudges me with her elbow as I walk her to the front door.

"You don't need to speak in code, or whatever it is you're trying to do." I laugh at her. "It's not like we are being watched or overheard here."

She follows my line of sight to the endless tree line that surrounds the property and the long driveway that can only be found if one knows where to look when driving down the twists and turns that make up the labyrinth of roads throughout this part of town. I would be lying to myself if I didn't admit that a small part of me is looking forward to the solitude that this house provides. The fact that I can't do much of anything at the moment—having a bounty on my head for some reason I can't even fathom—even plays to the needs of the introverted hermit that I am.

I just need to look at this as a mini vacation from life in general.

"Not only are we actually in the middle of the woods… but I'm pretty sure, from the speed we were going last night and the number of random back roads we took to get here… Honestly, do me a favor and text me when you guys find yourselves at Henry's."

An impatient honk is heard from Henry's running car, eliciting an eye roll from both Tess and me. We embrace each other one more time before Tess hurries to the passenger door. As she opens it and glances over at me, her eyes light up and a smile spreads across her face, rosy cheeks pink from the chilly autumn air. It takes me a second to realize I'm not the one she's looking at, but then I feel the presence of a warm body mere inches behind me.

"We'll be back at some point soon!" Tess waves a hand, her black curls bouncing as if energized by optimistic enthusiasm about something she's sure will happen.

"Planning on it." The sound of the voice behind me is deep, but I can hear the smile in it. "I really like that one."

We watch the car until it's out of sight, which only takes a few seconds before the density of the surrounding trees obstructs our view. I inhale a sharp breath before turning to face my new normal, for the time being, and am forced to tilt my head back so as not to be staring directly at the hollow of Aiden's throat.

"Of course you do. The two of you have been on the same page this entire time, making my life that much harder."

I stand with my arms crossed, weight shifted to one leg, doing my best to look frustrated, yet still determined to regain control. "I *am* fully capable of making decisions concerning my own life."

He closes the little space between us even more, forcing me to lift my chin higher in defiance. Now towering over me, he cocks a brow, his mouth close enough that if I were to lift my heels, I could add to the list of my many poor decisions Tess has already so mercilessly brought up.

"According to your friends, I would argue otherwise," he counters while extending an arm out and ushering me back into his house.

Begrudgingly, I brush past Aiden and enter the place I'll be calling home until John can find the culprits and take them in for questioning. He needs to hurry and wrap up this investigation before he has to add a homicide to the mix, and I'm forced to go on the run. I'm not sure how long Aiden's and my combative personalities can coexist. There are many ways that this can play out.

CHAPTER 19
AIDEN

The first few days together are awkward—for Mercy. For me, it is pure entertainment I haven't had under my roof, or in my life, for a long time. I know eventually we will fall into a pattern—as everything in life always does—but until that pattern is comfortably established, it is as if I were watching a feral cat try to settle into a new home and adjust to new surroundings. So I happily sit back and watch as my newly acquired feral cat grows comfortable and accepts her current situation. Each day, her guard comes down more, allowing us to know each other better and her to not be so defensive or on edge.

There is an unspoken understanding that we already have a certain level of trust between us, a level only slightly higher than what is found in people who have just met. Our undeniable pull towards each other is most likely the main reason that extra layer of trust even exists. Whether Mercy is aware of this, too, I'm not entirely sure. The moments when her defenses are down and she allows herself to simply just be,

I notice a hint of awareness in her eyes and in her energy, further supporting my suspicion that she feels the same pull I do.

With what I know so far from the visions I've had, the gut instinct I can't deny, and the experience with the Ouija board, I know there is something more to understand between the two of us. Unfortunately, I'm at the mercy of...well, Mercy... waiting for her instincts to kick in and entice her to stop denying whatever it is between us and start asking the questions I need her to ask. Whenever that time comes, I...*we*... will better understand why the fuck I suddenly realized I had a mental block...and why she seems to be part of it.

I wish I could sit her down and tell her everything, but she would think me a crazed lunatic, and that would endanger any chance of her mind being truly open, which is necessary for her to realize her true essence. I can tell that there's a crack in the door of her mind already, one caused by a lifetime of questioning herself and the world around her. Curiosity mixed with personal trauma have shaken her enough to make her question what she's been taught to believe and trust. With that door slightly ajar, the need for understanding builds, and that's when the questioning begins. Were I to disrupt this fragile path to discovery, I would risk her mind being scared shut, plummeting her back to the comfort of limited belief, limited understanding.

It takes a certain kind of strength and vulnerability to face and accept the truth of our existence, the way the world works...the way the universe works. These past couple of days have enlightened me a bit about her readiness to step into the path of awakening, enlightening, understanding, or whatever you want to call it. But I can't expedite the process...her process. It's all on her. So I will wait.

It's late morning when I walk from the kitchen to my study—third coffee of the day in hand—and catch a glimpse of a moment that has become part of my new normal. Sprawled out and taking up a majority of space on the couch is Orthus, and huddled beneath blankets in the far corner with a book in hand is Mercy. The lit fireplace and the view of the fall landscape through the expansive windows create the perfect background to the cozy tableau. I sip my coffee and smile at the sight. Sensing my presence, Mercy turns the page and forces herself to lift her gaze to me.

"I didn't mean to disrupt your reading."

"No worries. I was actually thinking about lying down for a bit, anyway," she says.

I realize her face is a bit pale. "Everything all right?"

"Yeah, don't worry about me. I'm all good. This happens… a lot. Especially if I don't have my meds, which I somehow forgot to grab when Tess and I were packing." She balls her hand into a fist and begins knocking gently on her chest, the fingers of the other hand gently tapping the book on her lap.

"You don't look…good," I observe from the opening to the kitchen and make a show of scrunching my nose in doubt.

"Thanks. That's what every girl wants to hear." Her eyes narrow at me, and her fingers stop tapping, but her knuckles keep knocking.

"I don't mean to offend. Is there anything I can do?"

It has been a few days since I've felt that dark cloud that seems to linger around her. Moments in which her spirits are high—when she assists me in the study with my art, when she's busy walking with Orthus, exploring the yard, or when we find ourselves engaged and lost in conversation—I can feel that cloud on the periphery, attempting to get close, but with little success. I know it waits patiently, however, for her spirits to drop, as if in eager anticipation of coming home to her.

"I know you don't. I'm finally getting used to your way with words. I'm just"—she forces herself to inhale heavily mid-sentence. I watch her whole body still as she holds her breath and closes her eyes. After a few seconds, she exhales through her nose, and I catch the slightest shake in her small frame as she opens her eyes and softly smiles—"teasing."

"Honestly, though...*are* you all right?" I question her, unable to hide the concern in my voice. Unaware of walking, I draw near to where she sits on the couch. I watch her place both feet on the floor and lean forward, hands braced on her thighs, her shoulders hunched over.

"I'm fine. I just need to lie down and let it pass," she tries to convince me while attempting to stand. She sways on her feet, and whatever color is left leaches from her skin. One hand presses to her chest, one arm wraps around her waist, and her core sinks in towards the back of her spine, making her hunch over.

Void appears from nowhere and is instantly circling Mercy's feet, rubbing his body against her bare legs. I shove him aside, which elicits an angry hiss, but I don't think twice before I lift Mercy into my arms.

"Let's get you back to bed," I whisper into her hair.

She shakes in my arms and tries to focus simply on breathing. She herself is light in my arms, but there is a heaviness to the air around her. The skin left exposed by the knit slip she has yet to change out of since waking is cool to the touch, yet sweat beads around her hairline.

"I think it's just your run-of-the-mill panic attack made more aggressive by withdrawal from my medications," she tries to explain through quickening inhales and an unconvincing chuckle meant to brush off what's happening. "I swear this happens, and it's no big deal. Like I said, I just need to let it pass."

"I'll text Tess to have her drop by later with your medications. She will know which ones to grab, right?"

I lower her onto my bed, and before I'm able to drape a blanket over her, Void hops up and makes himself comfortable, his body taking up most of Mercy's torso and his head resting on the center of her chest.

"I can kick him out." I reach down to grab the furry beast, the movement causing him to switch from purring to growling the moment my hands are on either side of him.

"Leave him. He's helping."

Her eyes close, and I notice she has finally stopped shaking. I turn to leave and give her the privacy she needs, but I stop when I feel her fingers try to wrap around my wrist. I look down; her eyes are open, and they convey embarrassment.

Her lips part, and the voice that comes out is pained when she says, "You saw the cabinet of pill bottles." It's not a question, just an acknowledgment of something she picked up on when I asked about Tess and her medications.

"No judgment, I promise. I know it takes a while to find something that works." I keep my voice low and soothing—something I wasn't aware I was able to do. "Can I ask… why you keep them all? Why not just toss them if they don't help?"

I feel the skin on her fingertips warming as they linger on my wrist, and I notice a bit of color returning to her features. Whatever Void is doing seems to be helping because not only has she stopped shaking, but her breath is no longer so labored. Fucking cat. If this doesn't go straight to his head, I will be more than surprised. He'll probably only respond to being called Dr. Void after this.

"I don't know why I keep them. I've tried to toss them, flush them…even considered emptying them down the garbage disposal. But the second I pull a bottle from the shelf, I get a sudden need to hoard them… I guess just in case?" She avoids looking at me, choosing instead to stare at the newly self-certified "doctor" in the house. Then she says in barely a whisper, "Maybe I do know why."

My chest clenches at her admission of the grim thoughts that have plagued her mind. I don't know what to say, so I choose to release my wrist from her fingers, take her hand in mine, and squeeze. "Rest. Come back out when you're ready, and we can"—I run my fingers through my hair, trying to think of something we can do to distract her—"do something. I'll figure it out."

It's hard, but I let go of her hand and leave her to rest in the company of Void. The second I leave the room, I instantly feel lighter. A weight I wasn't aware of is lifted off my chest, which leaves me confused and bothered.

In need of visiting my father to see if he's even checked on Helheim, I take advantage of Mercy being tucked away in my room and make my way to the stairs leading down to the nuummite door. While I'm down there, I'll see what herbs and incense I can steal from him to cleanse this space. Something is off, and it's better to cleanse than not to cleanse.

CHAPTER 20
MERCY

Aiden shuts the door behind him when he leaves the room, and I roll onto my side when the sound of his footfalls disappear. Void crawls out from my hold and chooses to position himself like a crown atop my head on the pillow. His little body vibrates with a hearty purr that echoes in my ears, which makes him a living white-noise machine.

Knees tucked towards my chest, I loosen the tight ball I curled myself into and look down at my stomach. The black cloud I briefly saw forming around my midsection is finally gone, but I run my hand over my stomach just to be sure.

This is not the first time I have seen this thing, and I have a feeling it will not be the last. When we were gathered around the Ouija board two weeks ago—actually, maybe three weeks at this point; damn, I've been here for a while—I saw it circling around my core right before I lost consciousness. Overwhelmed by everything else that happened, I didn't think again about the black cloud until a week later when I was sitting on the window seat, worrying about what my life had become and what the hell I was going to do about it. I felt myself slipping back into my old habit of fueling the voice in my head that spews negative thoughts of self-doubt, despair, and loss of control over my life. It was then that my chest started to get tight and my stomach began cramping, warning me of the oncoming panic attack settling into my body.

Remembering I hadn't brought any medication with me, I felt the panic start to consume my mind and body, but knew there was nothing I could do but ride it out. It was then, when I stood to pace away my worries, that I looked down at my waistline and watched as the dark cloud pulsed around me, wispy tendrils reaching out like fingers invading my space and touching my body. The sight forced me to sit back down helplessly; I did not know what to do as the dark cloud and its wispy tendrils sought ways to embed themselves in me.

Just before I yelled to Aiden for help, Void appeared out of nowhere, hissing, growling, and batting away the cloud until it became mist disappearing into the air. He then crawled into my lap, and I cradled him to my chest, my heart rate decreasing as my breathing eased.

This is now the third time I have seen this thing—this entity. The first time was when I was much younger, in kindergarten, and when I described it to my mom through tears, she simply chalked it up as nothing more than my overactive imagination. Now an adult, I know that is not true.

Lying in bed in the present moment, I wonder why all of a sudden I'm seeing this thing again and so often. I also wonder what the actual fuck this thing even is and why it seems that only Void and I can see it. It's not lost on me that it's only around when I'm feeling low. Why can I see it now, though, as opposed to before? It's not as if the years between childhood and now haven't been a miserable roller-coaster ride of climbs made solely for the purpose of gaining momentum for the slamming, soul-damaging falls, twists, and turns. Something happened the night of the Ouija-board experience. I just don't know what.

Made restless by my own thoughts, I sit up in bed and thank Void for the assist by scratching him under the chin and leaving him to his nap. I rummage through my duffle bag and pull out an outfit to wear that's more appropriate than my night slip. Once my clothes are on, I stand in front of the full-length mirror and fashion my hair into a high ponytail, allowing the flyaways to frame my face.

Ugh, I look like death itself.

Grabbing my bag of toiletries, I make my way to the bathroom, hoping to freshen up and look a little less like the living-dead girl I feel I am. I take all of five minutes before giving up and accepting that at least my breath is fresh, and I look clean.

Staring at myself in the mirror, I look into my own eyes and see nothing inside. *Where did I go? I'm working on this… but clearly not hard enough.*

With a heavy sigh, I grab my wand of mascara and apply it to my lashes in hopes of bringing at least a glimmer of life back to my eyes. I twist the wand back into the tube of black cream, toss it back into my bag, grip the edges of the sink with my hands, and stare down my own reflection.

"I am here." The words are said out loud and in defiance of everything I've been feeling. With that, I leave the mirror image of myself to deal with my problems, as if I could hand them off or rid myself of them that easily. I smile to myself, grateful of being able to shake off whatever had come over me earlier, and go to see what Aiden is up to.

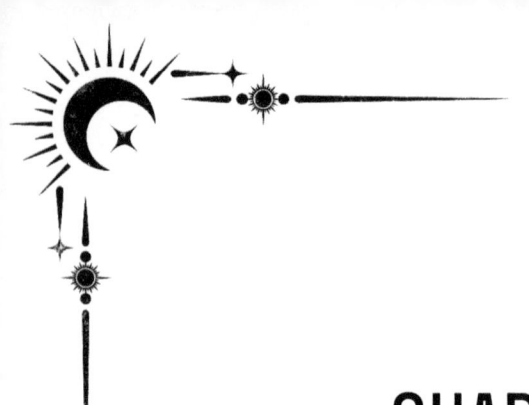

CHAPTER 21
AIDEN

I slide my phone back into my pocket after receiving a text back from Tess saying that she and Henry will stop by for dinner later, Mercy's medications in hand. Look at me, making friends and inviting them over for more than just an errand run.

Struggling with the many rolled-up maps I want to take to my father, I drop them to the floor so I can draw blood from my finger to draw the runes on the gold plate sealing the door to his lair.

"Fuck," I mumble under my breath, having cut myself deeper than I intended. I place my hand on the gold plate and quickly draw the three symbolic runes with a very bloody finger. The blood drips and smears when I flatten my hand against the cold metal. The door slowly creaks open, and I think once again, *One day I'll stop forgetting to oil these damn hinges.*

Just as the door opens completely, and I'm about to bend down to gather my things, I hear Mercy's voice behind me.

"Where in some secret, hidden tunnel does that fucking lead?"

I whip around and find Mercy with her jaw slack and eyes bulging, taking in the view of the rune-covered tunnel that leads to my father's realm. Having been caught in this compromising position and fearing the foundation of our trust will be broken, I guess that this must be the time to come clean and risk that cracked door in Mercy's mind closing. It's time to sit down and try to pull the questions out of her that I need to answer in order to help her better understand. In order for *me* to better understand.

"I think we need to talk," I say, letting the door slide shut behind me.

The souls of Helheim and my father will have to wait.

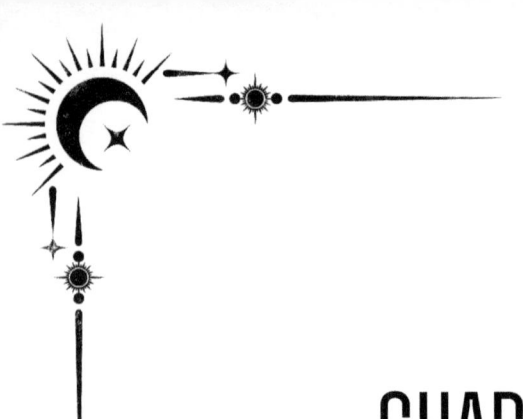

CHAPTER 22
MERCY

"Where should I begin?" Aiden asks, sitting at the drafting table in the center of his study while I pace along the wall showcasing his work. He's unknowingly positioned himself to look like a disheveled version of Rodin's *The Thinker*. However, instead of his hand being tucked contemplatively under his chin, as Rodin sculpted his masterpiece, Aiden's fingers pinch the bridge of his nose in frustrated concern.

"How about you tell me what the fuck you're keeping down there in your creepy dungeon space, Aiden?" I'm almost yelling the question when I halt mid-pace and throw my arms out to the side, my eyes wide and demanding answers.

"I'm not *keeping* anything down there," he says, and before I'm able to form the words, he adds, "or any*one*, Mercy." He drops his hand away from his face, and his brows lower as he glares at me, offended by the need to explain this.

"Okay, so then…what *is* down there? Why did it look like you got caught when you spun and saw me? And *why* were you finger painting on the door with your *blood*?" I point to the hand he has wrapped in an ink-covered handkerchief.

There's a long, drawn-out moment of silence while I watch Aiden sit and stew over what he wants to tell me. He sits perched on the stool at his drafting table, swiveled to the side to face me, the balls of his feet balancing on the bottom rung, and his forearms bracing his upper body as he leans forward. He locks eyes with mine and answers my questions with his own, "Do you practice any sort of religion? Have any sort of particular belief system? Faith?"

Caught off guard, as that was not what I was waiting to hear, I stumble over my words and give him an answer, "I was…I was raised Catholic." I look at him and wonder where this is going.

"Okay, so you—"

I cut him off before he can continue. "I was raised Catholic. That does not mean I consider myself to *be* Catholic. I've…um…let's just say that religion has always intrigued me. Fascinated me, actually. To the point where I've found myself lost in my own research, obsessing over the many different types of faiths and belief systems in the world. Over the years, it's led me to question everything I've ever been taught to believe while growing up. It's led me…" My voice trails off, and I stop before I go any further, embarrassed by my rambling and self-conscious about sharing my beliefs. Internally, I reprimand myself for feeling the need to try and explain my theological ideologies in such an unhinged way.

How the fuck did we even get on this topic?

"Please. Keep going," Aiden encourages me.

The way he says this makes me certain of his lack of judgment. If anything, Aiden seems relieved that we jumped right into the topic without the need to beat around the bush. The tension that had been evident throughout his body earlier now softens. I can feel my guard start to come down a little more because of the sincerity in his voice and the look in his eyes that tells me he needs me to explain further.

I slide down the wall behind me, careful not to ruin any of his art, and plop down on my butt with my back against the wall, knees pulled up to my chest. With a heavy sigh, I close my eyes and try to figure out where to even begin with what I have to say. I have rarely ever discussed this with anyone... except myself, silently in my head.

"There was a time in my early twenties when I was trying to figure out how to settle my anxious mind and find some sort of relief from the depression that latched on to me like flies to shit." Staring at the ceiling, I take a second to mentally scan the long list of ways I tried to cope over the years. "I sought help and relief through doctors, therapists, various hobbies, self-help books, excessive exercise, talking to friends and family... I tried everything."

I fall silent for a bit, thinking back to my early twenties and seeing it as the time when all the mental chaos within me really started ramping up. A time when everything seemed to be at my fingertips, but I allowed it all to slip away simply by getting in my own way.

"I, of course, even tried the toxic route of numbing my mind with alcohol and chasing highs that I knew were only temporary." My eyes fall to my feet as the sharing starts haunting me with old and recent memories. The weight of the discussion begins to overwhelm me.

"*Tried* the toxic route? Or are *still* trying the toxic route?" Aiden teases with a wink, trying to lighten the heavy weight that tries to settle on my chest.

"So I've clung to a few vices. At least, I'm aware that I use them as a crutch and a temporary Band-Aid. And I have them under control now, as opposed to before."

"Let me guess what happened next. All out of ideas, you finally decided to lean into faith and turned to God for some sort of comfort and help?" He lifts a brow and smirks as if he knows where this is all heading.

"I did." I laugh at myself. "I tried to find God."

"And did you?"

"Well…I found myself reading passages in the Bible first and becoming angered by descriptions of the females being lesser than the *superior* males." I clear my throat and wince as the remnants of any Catholic guilt left in my bones stirs at my criticism of what is believed to be sacred Scripture by many.

"The scare tactics used for manipulation. The freedoms denied. The contingencies that accompany this system of belief… I could go on, but I think you get the point. All this is to say I did not find God. I found anger. I found distrust. I found a need to dig deeper, to learn more. There had to be more. So I started doing the one thing you're not *really* supposed to do as a Christian or a person of faith." I hold Aiden's gaze with my own, my heart rate quickening at the light I can see dancing in his eyes, which encourages me to continue.

"I questioned everything. First, I questioned God. Then, I narrowed my train of thought, questioning how people put all their faith and trust in stories written by men *ages* after the events took place. Stories written by men who, we choose to naively assume, have no other intention than relaying to the world the supposed word of God. I questioned if anything we've ever been told to believe throughout the history of us…the history of religion…has truth to it, or if it has all been corrupted by people's conscious, or unconscious, desire for advantageous answers, for power, or to evolve."

Met with respectful silence after confessing my sin of questioning, I pause to read the room and find that I haven't ruffled any feathers yet, so I feel it's safe to continue. "I questioned the translations, the different adaptions rewritten to suit those who rose to power over the centuries. I wondered what stories were redacted over time to manipulate our way of thinking…of believing. *Who* was redacted from the stories and why?" The many thoughts and questions rush out of my mouth in an explosion of relief over finally sharing and being heard.

"And I know this can be found in other religions, too. Religions that pigeonhole people into one way of living, what is truly right, and what is truly wrong—forcing people to believe their way is the only way. The imbalances disguised as rules to abide by…" I pause to make sure Aiden is following, and then I proceed with my explanation.

"Raised Catholic, I couldn't help but start to look into the Christian faith first, but soon I found myself looking into others for more answers. Instead of answers, I only gained more questions and a deeper demand for understanding." I furrow my brow and look at Aiden, who is sitting there and hanging on to every word that leaves my lips, almost as if he is anticipating and waiting for me to bring this around to a specific conclusion he's hoping for.

"So in your search for guidance and support…unlike many people…you didn't find God. You found questions," he says matter-of-factly. Then he continues with, "What else did you find?"

"First"—I feel my face heat, unsure of how to further explain myself—"I asked myself who I thought was right and why it could only be one belief system that has the answers to existence, to our purpose, to…I don't know… *everything*." Shaking my head, I try to organize my thoughts into one easy-to-explain, linear progression of how I came to the conclusion that no matter what teaching, what religion, what belief people held, I could constantly find parallels and connections between them.

If he doesn't think I've lost it by now...

"I found myself randomly researching and studying a variety of theistic and nontheistic religions in search for answers I came to realize I hadn't even known I was looking for. I remember studying Eastern literature and being fascinated and connecting to the concept of rebirth and liberation represented in the Wheel of Life. I then dove into religious beliefs, like that of the Vikings, Egyptians, and tribal cultures who believed in the existence of multiple gods who have specific roles in governing the universe and their people's way of life. I even thought to look somewhere that had always piqued my interest, somewhere society has been taught to fear. I looked..." I pause and hold my breath, realizing I'm about to be ridiculed. I feel an overwhelming sense of paranoia and regret for allowing myself to open up this can of worms I've carried for so long.

"I promise I won't laugh." Aiden smiles, clearly having read my thoughts, and nods for me to spit out what is now caught in my throat.

"I looked into witchcraft. I looked into the occult. I looked into spiritualism and astrology. I looked into everything that people might call woo-woo or demonic." Afraid to look him in the eyes and be tormented by laughter or cynicism, I keep my chin tilted down and my gaze downcast.

I hear Aiden get up from the stool, and my pulse races with each footstep I hear come closer to where I sit on the floor. I feel his body heat as he lowers himself to sit in front of me, positioning himself so that the ball I've tucked myself into is cradled between his bent legs. Waiting for him to cautiously ask me if I've ever been committed to a psych ward or something of that nature, I refuse to meet his stare.

Instead, he surprises me by taking my chin between his fingers and forcing me to look him in the eyes. Without an ounce of judgment or trepidation, he simply asks me again, "And what did you find?"

I take a steadying breath. Then, without fear of his reaction, I tell him, "I didn't find the one and *only* God." I shift my eyes away from his before ultimately looking back to the emerald green I've become unnervingly attached to. "I found *many*. And I found nature. I found balance. I found patterns, parallels, and connections. I found freedom and strength. I found frequencies and energies…" I smile as a tingling sensation runs up my spine with every proclamation I make. "And for me? With this broadened outlook on faith that I allowed myself to see, to feel, to embrace…I found what, or *who*, spoke to me most—the Morrigan. From her, I found the guidance and support I had been looking for. I found the warrior I needed to help guide me through the war I had within myself. I found the uncomfortable truth, the need to face my shadows"—I cringe—"something I admit to obviously still struggle with today."

"You found answers," Aiden says, our eyes locked on each other as we sit close enough to share a breath. The electricity between us is chaotic, intoxicating, and fueled by the shared unhinged delirium brought on by the depth of the conversation we've spiraled into.

"I grew up with an understanding that I should embrace and search for answers from the Father, the Son, and the Holy Ghost when facing trying times, or just throughout life in general. I instead found the guidance and support needed in the Mother, the Maiden, and the Crone. So, yeah, I found the answers that spoke to me…or at the very least, a path to follow. In the end, isn't that the one piece of truth I could at least take away from all this?" A small smile eases itself across my face.

"And what is that? What is this truth you believe you have found while you were searching for your answers and finding your path?" Aiden urges me to continue unraveling the web of theories, epiphanies, connections, and questions that have crowded my mind for so long. His hands find mine and grip me with excitement and a hint of what I can only describe as relief.

"What connects everyone is a shared underlying kernel of truth that can be found amongst everyone's belief system; it exists and is untainted and pure, but it has been lost amongst our misinterpretations and misguided intentions simply because we are…human." I shrug my shoulders and tug one corner of my lips towards my ear.

For a moment, we sit there in each other's silence. Aiden's eyes dance around my face; I can see he is contemplating what to ask or say next.

"I can confirm one thing that you found." The twinkle in his eye prepares me for a witty response that is sure to ruin the oddly intimate mood that has settled around us.

"And that would be…?" I ask, tilting my head slightly to the side and raising my eyebrows at him.

"The paradox that is religion." He grabs my hands and hauls me to my feet in one swift movement.

"Wait… What?" I'm suddenly confused and flustered by his remark.

"That everyone is right, *and* everyone is wrong," he says simply, as if that is a reasonable answer that is easy to digest and understand. "People limit themselves, their knowledge, without even knowing it's what they're doing. This causes the creation of this paradox that even though people's beliefs can contradict one another…they still can hold a shared truth. So everyone is right, and at the same time, everyone is wrong. Everything people believe, in a sense, does exist, but it doesn't the way they think it does."

"I-I'm l-lost," I stutter and spin around in place as I watch Aiden whir around me, gathering in his arms what he previously held and then dropped when I unexpectedly appeared—rolled-up maps depicting constellations and anything beyond Earth's atmosphere.

"No, actually. You're not. Religion has become a paradox because of the involvement of people. When, in reality, in its purest form, religion—faith, belief…what have you—is actually something of a greater whole in which differences don't exist separately, but instead bleed into one another. You've just been unable to see beyond religion; it's kept you from seeing the bigger picture, kept you from the answers you seek."

Aiden's words flood my head, and I try to make sense of it all. For a second, I think I understand, and then I lose that understanding just as quickly as I grasped it, which only makes me feel more ignorant by the second.

Why does he suddenly sound wiser and older than he is? Why is he even bothering with me and my surface level of understanding about whatever the fuck this all boils down to?

"Fuck, I sound like my father." He rolls his eyes at himself and then looks to me, maps under one arm, his other hand stretched out and reaching for mine. "Let's go."

With nothing to lose, I place my hand in his and give him a quizzical look, not of distrust but of curiosity. "Where are you taking me?"

"To my creepy tunnel that leads to my even creepier dungeon space."

I chuckle at his response and then find myself quickly schooling my features into a look of apprehension at the dubious grin he gives me. I had completely forgotten how this conversation started in the first place. I asked questions I'm realizing now I don't think I want the answers to. Questions revolving around what's behind that mysterious fucking door.

PART II
AWAKENING THE GODDESS

CHAPTER 23
AIDEN

Just outside the solid black door I take the armful of rolled maps intended for my father and dump them haphazardly into Mercy's arms. I watch her gently handle them, cradling them close to her chest, careful not to damage the delicate paper covered in intricately inked star maps. The gesture so thoughtful that I can't help but crack a smile at her care for something I created. Something she deems worthy to be handled with respect and gentle mindfulness. My chest tightens, and instead of fighting it, I give in, slightly intrigued by the feeling.

"Are you squeamish when it comes to blood?" I ask her once she has herself situated.

I'm met with eyes the color of the bluest skies and taken back by their vibrancy. It wasn't that I had never noticed their varying beautiful hues of blue before—it was the fact that at this very moment, they are the clearest I've ever seen them, almost as if a light has finally flickered on within her.

"Aiden?" she says, snapping me out of the dream state I'm apparently lost in because of her bright-eyed gaze.

I close my mouth—finally aware my jaw had become slack—and shake my head to regain a sense of focus. "Sorry, what did you say? Was that a no to being squeamish?" I ask, but do not give Mercy time to answer before I flick my wrist and free the sharp blade of my pocketknife.

Mercy's eyes widen at the sight of the knife in my hand. "Squeamish of blood? No. Squeamish around sharp objects… in your hands?" A hissing sound escapes from between her teeth as she looks down to the sudden slashing movement of the knife across my palm.

"Reopening fresh wounds is never fun," I mutter under my breath, refraining from reacting to the hot, searing pain now pulsing in my palm.

"So that's why your hands are so scarred and rough."

"Sexy, I know." I wink and turn towards the door as a well of blood pools in the palm of my hand. One after the other, I paint the stacked runes in blood on the gold plate and finish by pressing my hand flat against the precious metal.

"Sexy? Sure…had they been scarred and calloused by hard work or some secret fight club you're part of," she teases nonchalantly, and I think, if I were to look back, I'd see her standing there absentmindedly picking at her nails. "Not by some weird unlocking device." I hear the playfulness and smirk in her voice.

"Who's to say I'm not part of a fight club? I mean, don't you know the first rule of fight club?" I joke, but she quiets behind me, I assume wondering if I'm pulling her leg.

There's a brief moment of familiar heat under my palm, and then the door creaks open. Turning towards Mercy, I reach my hands out to collect the maps she still holds.

She takes one look at my bloodied hand and fingertips and then holds the maps a little closer to her chest. "How about *I* hold on to your artwork so that you don't ruin any of it with bloodstains."

I nod in agreement, step to the side, and stretch out my arm in welcome. "Shall we?"

"If you think I'm going in first..." She snorts as if I'm ridiculous to believe she would walk right through the door without hesitation. Though I know she trusts me, she's not an idiot who throws caution to the wind, and I can tell she is still skeptical about the "secret dungeon" I'm revealing to her.

"Follow me."

Just before the door closes behind us, Void scurries through. He winds himself around Mercy's legs, purring and rubbing his face against her shins. Clearly still upset with me, he brushes by without so much as a glance at me, puffing his chest out and twitching his tail straight into the air as if to say, "Fuck you."

Point taken. I'll have to figure out a way to get back into his good graces if I want his help in reaching out to Tarini anytime in the future.

Mercy, too, then steps around me and falls in step behind Void.

"I thought you weren't going first," I remind her.

"I'm not. I'm following my fearless leader, Void."

With that, I see Void attempt the closest thing to what I would consider a gleeful skip down the hall with an unnecessarily boosted ego, thanks to Mercy's comment. I'm going to be kicked out of my own house by the animals who have clearly decided that, no matter how many lifetimes they've lived with me, they will choose Mercy's company over my own any day. I can't be mad, though, because I can't blame them. So, unable to release the upward-turned corners of my lips, I shove my hands into my pockets and follow the pull that grows stronger every day.

"Throw those maps right on top of that large desk. Don't touch anything, but feel free to look around. I'll be right back."

I begin to turn and leave, wiping my bloodied hand on my pant leg, when Mercy pipes up.

"You're telling me not to touch anything when you're the one with blood on your hand?" She hesitates for a second—clearly something has come to mind—and then asks, "Is that how you got into Tess's house the other day even though it was locked? By using some weird, dark blood-magic spell that unlocks doors?"

The quiet laugh I can't hold back warrants the narrow-eyed glare she gives me. With hands raised in placation and a twisted grin on my face, I explain to her that it doesn't quite work like that. "I guess you could call it magic, for lack of a better word, and as an explanation that wouldn't involve a lengthy lesson about the science behind it all. But to answer your question about Tess's front door…yes. It only worked, though, because of the sheer luck that her home has apparently been warded before. She must have a witch in the family she's not telling you about…or one maybe she isn't aware of. Hell, maybe she's a witch."

Mercy scoffs, throws her weight onto one leg, and starts listing off reasons why that couldn't be true. She points one finger in the air, waving it at me, and says, "For one, if

Tess were a witch"—making air quotes with her animated fingers—"she would probably never shut up about it and would turn crafting love spells into a full-time job. And two"—she shrugs as if to emphasize how absurd my thoughts are—"she would have told me. Simple as that."

I look at her, my mouth opening and shutting, caught in a state between not knowing what to say and needing to catch my father and explain to him what's going on before he walks in on a surprise guest and me in his secret abode. Running a hand through my hair, I remember something and ask, "She has a sister, doesn't she?"

"*Lily?*" Tess's sister's name comes out of Mercy's mouth in comical disbelief.

"You never know. Now, look at this"—I grab Mercy by the shoulders and spin her around to face the window—"while you wait here for me to return. I'll be right back. Stay here."

Before she can protest being alone, I leave Mercy staring awestruck at the window and hurry down the hall, at the end of which I'm both surprised and relieved to find my father. Surprised to see he's returning from actually doing his job of checking on the souls of Helheim, and relieved to get to him before he becomes aware I allowed someone other than the two of us to be down here. Something he's always warned me not to do.

"Aiden! I was beginning to get worried about you. I haven't seen you for some time now. Is everything all right? You look…anxious. Why do you, of all people, look anxious?" My father's brows knit together in worry as he questions me, resting his hands on my shoulders—his signature move when expressing any sort of concern or sympathy.

"I-I…" I stutter and inhale a deep breath, knowing there's no turning back now. On the exhale, I let out an exasperated sigh, slap an open hand to my forehead, step out from my father's hold on my shoulders while sliding my palm down my face, and lift my hand and point in the direction of the living space at the center of his realm, where each spiraled hall meets. "I'd like you to meet someone."

When I finally look at my father, I can see his face fluctuate between paling and reddening. I might tower over him, but that doesn't mean I don't fear the repercussions of breaking a rule made by the overseer.

He forces himself past me and walks down the spiraled hall at a brisk pace. I easily keep up with him and try to find some way to douse the fire I wanted to prevent by speaking to him before he actually saw Mercy. Had he been in the center space, at his desk, when we arrived—as I hoped—my thought was that he would be so caught off guard that he would have had no choice other than to be pleasant in the presence of an unexpected guest…and he would have had no time to think about what I had just done. Instead, I was granted the opportunity to give him a heads-up and explain the situation, but failed.

"We have *one* rule, Aiden. ONE!" he yells, reprimanding me, as he hurries to the main space.

I wince and hope that Mercy can't hear his booming voice filled with anger as it echoes down the hall. "Here me out, though—"

We reach the end of the hall, and I catch myself before slamming into my father's rigid back. I look past him and watch Mercy turn on her heels to face us; our commotion appears to have disrupted a trance into which she has fallen. Her long hair whips around her shoulders, and her figure is framed by an aura of stars that seem to have come alive, shimmering and dancing in her presence, as she stands with the window as her backdrop. The sight causes yet another memory of mine to stir, as if it had been deliberately buried alive in my head, begging to be uncovered.

"Ummm. So, Dad, I'd like you to meet—" He cuts me off before I'm able to finish the introduction.

"Fucking Hel."

CHAPTER 24
MERCY

"Dad, I'd like to introduce you to Mercy," Aiden says, stepping from behind his father's smaller frame to stand next to me. "Mercy, this is my father, Leo."

The man standing in front of me looks nothing like Aiden. He's not short, but compared to his son, Leo is a good six inches shorter than Aiden, his skin tone more caramel. Aiden, on the other hand, were it not for his dark hair, looks to have come from a family line descending from Scandinavia or Ireland, and certainly not from wherever Leo's ancestors may have originated. Aiden's mother must have had some seriously dominant genes, assuming he takes after her.

"It's very nice to meet you, Leo." I walk the short distance between us and extend my hand out of common courtesy. I smile pleasantly in hopes of breaking the sudden tension that billowed in with Aiden and his father upon their arrival from the hall Aiden had disappeared down earlier.

"It has been quite some time since I've met any of Aiden's...acquaintances," Leo says while taking my hand in his, not to shake but to place a gentle kiss atop it.

The gesture causes an uncomfortable knot in my stomach to form, both from being surprised by the move and from feeling the iciness of his thin, withered lips against my heated skin. He drops my hand suddenly. The second my hand is released, the knot in my stomach starts to disappear, and I try my best to hide the faint feeling that washed over me when I touched Leo.

Void sits between us, his tail swishing over my feet, ears back flat against his head, hissing at Leo.

"Oh, Void, don't direct your temper at me when I know it's most likely Aiden who's the cause for your unpleasant mood."

Void narrows his eyes at Leo's comment and proceeds to serpentine his body between my ankles almost territorially. I bend down and scoop him up, cradling the massive cat in my arms, grateful for the emotional support his presence provides.

"Ah, I see how it is. Looks like you have some competition, Aiden," Leo says with a wink before walking towards the kitchen area. "You two sit and make yourselves comfortable. I'll put a kettle on for tea, and you can tell me all about yourself, Mercy."

With Leo's back turned and distance between us, I jab Aiden in the ribs with my bony elbow and glare up at him. He returns my glare with a look of innocent confusion that I am sure he is faking. I know all too well he is amused by my discomfort with the surprise introduction to his father.

"Why couldn't you just tell me your father lives down here?" I whisper angrily under my breath.

"Would that have explained the reason for the blood, the mysterious-looking door, th—"

I wave him off before he can finish. "It still doesn't. If anything, it just adds to my growing list of questions, but *fine*. You could have at the very least warned me, though. I wasn't anticipating meeting anyone. Let alone your *father*, of all people," I snappishly whisper through a tight jaw. I cross my arms over my chest, narrow my eyes, and lift my chin.

His only response is his usual devious smirk—fully aware he pulled one over on me—accompanied by a look in his eyes of pure entertainment over my frazzled state. The surprises continue when he reaches out, untangles my crossed arms to take my hand in his, and leads me over to the leather furniture staged in front of the gigantic fireplace.

My heart skips a beat, and I silently curse myself for the heat that I feel flushing my cheeks. *Ugh, I'm an idiot.*

"Joke's on you. Parents have always *loved* me," I quip, following Aiden as he directs us to the couch and pulls me to sit beside him.

"I wouldn't have introduced you had I thought otherwise," he tells me, causing my heart to skip yet another beat as I wonder exactly what he meant by that—what his intentions are behind this surprise introduction.

I might be completely overthinking this... I definitely am... My heart can't handle any more surprises, never mind the headache that comes with trying to understand whatever the fuck is going on between us. I'm not ready for whatever this *is...if there is a* this.

Aiden gracefully falls back into the corner of the couch, positioning himself so that he lounges with one leg stretched out, propping on it the ankle of the other. One arm draped over the couch's back and the fist of the other under his chin, supporting his head, he lazily observes me as I stand and explore the objects and maps on display in the space. He straightens upon the sound of footsteps and clanging of porcelain against silver that rattles on the serving tray his father carries over from the kitchen.

I stop my perusal and walk over to one of the two empty leather accent chairs that bookend the matching couch, ignoring Aiden's silent invitation to sit with him. As I take my seat, Leo serves us tea with a smile and a softness in his eyes I had not witnessed until now; they ease the wariness that I've felt since our introduction. I accept the hot cup of tea, returning the smile in hopes of some sort of acceptance from him, and watch as Aiden does the same, just to place it on the side table and ignore it.

"Mercy—what a beautiful name," Leo says, breaking the ice, and follows it up with a sip of tea, careful not to let the steam fog up the glasses that balance just above the tip of his nose.

"Thank you" is the only reply I can conjure, unsure of what to follow up with to start a conversation. It's not as if I can ask what I truly want to know—*So, care to tell me about this space we are currently in? And why does it feel weird down here, like I'm in some sort of other realm, like I traveled through some portal? Oh! And why does your locking mechanism require blood?*

"I'm happy to see Aiden has found someone to put up with him," Leo says, turning his gaze to Aiden. "Looks like you've found the angel of mercy you needed."

"Oh! We…we aren't…we aren't together…like that." I trip over the words that fumble from my lips. The need to clarify this for Aiden's father is secondary to my own rejection of the idea that *Aiden* would want to be with *me*. Not that I want to be with him, anyway. He's nice to look at and all—okay, he's *really* nice to look at—but it's only been a year since my divorce; the wound is still fresh. And, again, I still have to work on myself before adding another person into the mix, considering how well that turned out the first time. I roll my eyes at myself, not caring if anyone notices.

"Ah, I see," Leo responds. A smile that's neither happy nor sad spreads across his face. If anything, it appears contemplative.

Saving us all from the awkwardness created by Leo's assumption and my rejection, Aiden clears his throat to get our attention. "Actually, I've brought Mercy to meet you because she has some interesting thoughts about faith and religion. I thought you could maybe help clarify or even answer some of her questions on the subject."

Wait… What? I lower the cup of tea at my lips and give Aiden a look that says, *What the fuck?* He knows from our earlier conversation how vulnerable this type of discussion makes me feel. Not only am I meeting his father for the first time without warning, but I'm also about to be mocked and made fun of by him. *Angel of mercy? He's going to rethink that and see me more as a spirit of the unhinged.*

"Aiden—" Leo begins in a tone that could be considered reprimanding, but he is cut off by his son before he can finish.

"Before you say anything, considering what you do for work"—Aiden leans forward in his seat and raises a single finger to his father, whose mouth has gone slack and eyebrows have shot up in disbelieving shock—"considering the *research* you do for work, I thought maybe it would be informative for Mercy to bounce a few of her ideas off of you. Help her feel a little less of that Catholic guilt and give her reassurance that questioning everything is far from a mortal sin. Also, I just wanted you to meet her…and for her to know that I'm not keeping dead bodies in my basement." Aiden finishes with a grin and a dip of his chin in his father's direction.

Eyes still fixed on Aiden, as if a secret conversation is taking place mind to mind, Leo noticeably forces a smile and asks,

"What are some of these ideas and questions Aiden speaks of, my dear?" He turns his head as he addresses me as "dear" and focuses his attention solely on me.

I fight the urge to cringe at both Leo's cryptic behavior and his use of "dear" in lieu of my name. *He's just an old man bothered by his son's arrival with a surprise visitor who he's never met before. I can't blame him for the twinge of annoyance in his tone. I would feel the same way. Actually, I do. Fucking Aiden.* I blink a few times, frozen by being put on the spot.

I must look like a deer in headlights because Leo's demeanor softens towards me, as if he realizes my unpreparedness is due to our mutual friend here. He softly exhales through his lips and tries to thaw me from my frozen mental state by saying, "I promise there are no questions or ideas that might offend me or lead me to believe you to be insane."

My lack of response and obvious hesitation lead him to try one more tactic to convince me to share my thoughts. "I mean, you've met my son. Trust me when I say I've heard it all…and then some. There will be absolutely no judgment on my end."

Oh, fuck it. You want me to share my unhinged concept of existence to your father, Aiden? You asked for it.

"So…I had this thought a while back, and since then, I've come to my own conclusion that…" I speak my version of the truth for the second time in my life and reiterate everything I previously said to Aiden.

Every so often, Leo politely apologizes as he interrupts my flow of thought with his own theories, which are supported by his own extensive and impressive research. His interruptions and interjections intrigue me and increase my confidence in the theories and ideas I have kept to myself for so long in fear of embarrassment and criticism. A spark within me comes alive the farther we venture down the rabbit hole that is science, history, religion, mythology, and lore. Aiden occasionally jumps into the conversation but leaves his father and me to do most of the talking.

Eyes—framed by lines of wisdom gained throughout his many years of dedication to research—gleam as our conversation starts to come to an end. And I can only hope this man understands how much I appreciate his willingness to listen without judgment and to contribute without patronizing. During these moments, I forget everything that is happening in my life. The greater mess that it has become. I hold on to this moment and stash it into the chaos that is my mind, in case I ever need to come back to it for a sense of feeling heard and understood.

"The Bible, the Dead Sea Scrolls, the Torah, the Quran, the Vedas"—Leo rambles off the list of sacred and religious texts that come to mind, and I hang on to every word he says, anticipating the point he's about to make—"they all hold pieces of truth. Honestly, I've always said, perhaps, if we just burned them all together, the details that hold no weight will turn to ash, leaving within the rubble the purest, most indestructible pieces of untainted knowledge that have always been meant to be understood as a whole. Were people not so incessant in striving to be right or in feeding their hunger for power, perhaps we wouldn't have so many questions. So many wars. So much corruption, suffering, and pain."

Silence fills the space between us after Leo's somber outlook on humanity's inability to put ego aside and find common ground reminds us that this search for enlightenment, understanding, awakening—whatever the term for it is—is a mere fantasy.

"Well, what can I say? People are going to be people," Aiden chimes in, breaking the silence with a frank and pessimistic—albeit accurate—point. The words, a bucket of ice water poured over me, pull me out of my own head.

"Not all people, Aiden." Leo gives Aiden a look that any father might give to his son when he knows something is not worth getting into or debating any further.

I take this as my signal to interject and thank him for his time and willingness to not only listen, but also share his own findings and theories with me.

"Before you leave, if you have just a few more minutes to spare, I'd love to leave you with one more thing to think about."

Leo stands and invites us to follow him to the large screen I was entranced by earlier. The crystal-clear quality of its imagery could easily convince someone they are simply looking through glass and out a window…were it not for the view it reveals. The cosmic imagery obviously must be transmissions from satellites floating in the atmosphere.

Eager for this last bit of information Leo is willing to share, I hop out of my seat and follow him as if I were a puppy who has just been asked if I want to go for a walk. Aiden takes his time getting up, but when I turn to see if he is joining us, I see him watching me with a knowing smile on his face, as if this moment is the whole point, the reason he brought me down here.

Definitely no dead bodies. Still wary about the blood thing, though.

Leo gently places his hands on my shoulders and steers me so that I am standing front and center of the massive display. Once again, I'm sucked back into a trance, overwhelmed by the beauty before me. The stars shimmer and dance amidst their dark, endless surroundings, creating the view we have before us of the Milky Way. A view that leaves me speechless, not just because of its beauty, but due to the spiraling mystery it holds, the black hole at its center.

"What if I told you"—Leo's voice cuts into my trance—"that everything we just spoke of goes far past sacred texts, history, and tradition? What if I told you that not only would we have to merge everyone's truths together, but also the truths that are found in science and in space, to find the answers to the questions we ask?"

My heart races in the cage of my chest. Excitement pulses through my veins, and I swear the stars shine brighter in response to my reaction. I walk closer to the display and reach a curious hand to the glass, as if I could touch the gas and dust that shimmers behind it. My face illuminated by the light, I stand awestruck once more, lost to the marvel in front of me.

"There is a reason we all find ourselves looking to the stars to make wishes, to dream, to wonder, to feel *something*." Aiden stands with his body mere inches from my back, causing me to startle at the sound of his voice and the feel of his warm breath at my ear, unaware that he had snuck up on me. "Because, deep down, we know amongst them is where we will find our truest selves, our purest forms, the start and end to our infinite cycle. Deep down, we know we look up because it's a moment our soul, our essence, remembers and recognizes home."

I turn to look at Aiden, the angles of his face made more prominent and beautiful—godlike even—in the light cast from the stars shining brightly in space. I gawk at the sight in front of me.

I am quickly snapped from my daze when his father says, "The stars hold the truths, Mercy. Maybe not all of them…but a lot—of that, I am certain. We ourselves, in fact, are made up of stardust, in a sense, as scientists have discovered. Every atom that is the reason for our existence—whether it be the atoms of oxygen in our lungs, carbon in our muscles, calcium in our bones, or iron in our blood—came to creation inside a star before our Earth was born. They are indeed where we all came from and will go back to. And understanding *that*, my dear, is how we can start to find our answers, come to know the truth, and become enlightened."

The door closes behind us—Void included—as we leave what felt like a whole other world. The weight of panic I felt earlier is completely forgotten, as is the sight of the dark, shadowy cloud trying to enter my body. A wave of gratitude—for spontaneously meeting Aiden's father and discovering what's behind the mysterious door—washes over me. Usually, spontaneity is not my cup of tea, neither are last-minute introductions. I'm a creature of plans, routine, and knowing what to expect in advance. However, this time, being blindsided helped to snap me out of the rut I was slipping back into. The rut I have been constantly fighting. Now, I will accept it—not as my home, but as something to climb out of. How I was able to handle this experience is a win in my book.

"Tess just texted back saying that she and Henry will stop by later tonight with takeout and your meds," Aiden tells me.

I nod in silent acknowledgment and continue to follow behind him as we make our way back to his study. I sit behind the drafting table quietly observing Aiden pull a few books off the many shelves and stack them on an end table by the accent chair in the corner of the room. Other than Aiden informing me of Tess and Henry joining us later in the day, neither of us has said much since the black door sealed behind us.

What is he avoiding? I think what just happened went better than I would have anticipated, considering my earlier outburst when I discovered him with a bloody hand at the door he previously told me was nothing to be concerned about.

"So…what did you think of my dear ol' dad?" Aiden asks without turning to face me, still focused on whatever task at hand he's given himself. "Relieved you didn't stumble upon any bodies? Dead"—he finally turns to look over his shoulder; eyebrows lift and fall in a wicked tease, accompanied by a sly smile—"or alive and being held captive?"

"I still want to know more about the blood—"

"Again, as I mentioned before, it would take too long to explain how that all works. Just think of what most call magic as a form of science that hasn't been explained or understood yet by most of humanity." Aiden waves a hand in the air with a flick of the wrist, suggesting an end to that topic of conversation.

"I guess I'll accept your explanation…for now." I store that bit of information in the recesses of my brain, to mull it over at another time. Then, I clear my throat before continuing my interrogation. "On another note, thanks for the heads-up that I would be meeting your father! You never said *anything* about him before, especially the fact that he lives in your…" I pause, tilting my head to the side in contemplation, trying to think of how I want to broach the subject without sounding insane. "I want to say basement, but I can't. Why does it feel as if we entered a whole different world when we passed through that door?"

Aiden's back goes rigid, shoulders tensing, the thin fabric of his shirt teasing the hint of muscles that constricted and tightened when I voiced my curiosity and—probably delusional—observation. His reaction catches me off guard.

When he turns, he makes the excuse, "I guess that's what happens to someone who is sensitive to going belowground."

I snort at this poor excuse, completely not buying it. "Let me guess. Getting the real answer from you as to why I felt that way would involve you having to explain yet another topic of discussion that's too much to get into right now?" I cross my arms over my chest and try to master the look I've seen my mother give my father a thousand times before when trying to pull the *whole* story out of him—the time he returned to the family farm with not one, but *two*, horses for me in the trailer comes to mind.

"Fine. I'll explain liminal spaces to you…just not at this very moment. We will both want a drink for that one," Aiden says in compromise.

Mom would be proud. I give Aiden a nod in agreement.

"How was I supposed to say no to taking them both? They're a bonded pair," my father explains to my mother, who has enough on her plate already with all the other animals he has accumulated throughout the years.

"Oh, I don't know, Lou. Maybe just a simple *no* could have done the trick? Even *'no, thank you'* would have worked. We could have looked around for another horse who doesn't come with a friend. Mercy is only six! I was okay with the idea of a pony, not two rescue horses! We aren't made of money!"

I bound to the front door, hand on the doorknob, impatiently waiting for the nod of approval so I can introduce myself to the newest additions to the family.

"One pony would keep her busy from being interested in boys for only a little while. Don't give me that look!" My father chuckles at my mother.

She can't help but roll her eyes at the reasoning behind my father's decision, his preemptive attempt to keep me, their only daughter, from the dreaded boy-crazy phase that will eventually come—signaling my transition into a young adult. She knows he sees each birthday celebration, each milestone, and each time I insist I don't need their help as another step towards their little girl growing up. She accepts the inevitable and knows they still have plenty of time before I reach that difficult age when I am no longer their little girl, but an independent woman they can be proud of. But she also knows my father will do anything he can to delay the inevitable at all costs—which apparently includes purchasing two middle-aged horses in desperate need of my care and his assistance. I am their only child, after all.

"I know you are doing this so you two have something to bond over. Why not a beat-up truck that you two can rebuild together?" My mother questions Dad, arms crossed and one eyebrow lifted in challenge.

I watch them calmly argue as if I weren't right there, listening to every word they say. Bouncing on the balls of my feet, flicking my eyes between them, desperately willing my mother to agree to my father's surprise purchase and not make him take them back to wherever they came from.

"Rebuild a truck that she would eventually use to drive away in? No, thank you. Plus, she's been begging us for riding lessons, and I do miss having the stalls filled in the old barn out back. I'm sure my parents would love to see the old horse stalls put to some use again."

My parents were so young when they had me that they jumped at the offer to move into the guest house near the old barn on my father's family's property, in exchange for helping to run the cow farm and keeping up the property.

"*Two* horses gives us that much longer before we have to worry about that next phase in life, and it will teach her responsibility. She'll even understand the value of hard work at such a young age! Distraction from trouble. Responsibility. An introduction to the benefits of being a hard worker...*and* she's happy." This final explanation is given with a kiss on the forehead and a warm embrace.

At the sight of my mother's nod over my father's shoulder, I run barefoot out the front door to the trailer. Swinging open the side door, I see the two emaciated horses staring back at me, scared and shaking, their fates unknown.

I envision what my life is to become with them in it. "It's okay. I've got you," I promise them, my small hands reaching for the nose of the one closest to me, offering him the chance to investigate my scent and eliminate me as a threat.

My father is right. Those two horses teach me everything. Give me everything. Give me a purpose, life skills, and an understanding of responsibility in the disguise of gentle nuzzles, big brown eyes, and four legs that carry me through the highs and lows of growing up.

They are with me for twenty years before succumbing to old age. Growing up, I pour everything I have to give into them and ask nothing in return, but I receive more from them than I could have ever asked for. They are my therapists, my shoulders to cry on, and my beacons of light when my mind drags me into darkness. They are the ropes I cling to and my reasons for not letting go when the voice tells me otherwise.

They are the medicine that brings me balance before I have to rely on prescription medications to help adjust my serotonin and dopamine levels when my brain can't accomplish that on its own.

The day they leave for greener pastures shatters me; they take with them a piece of me I refuse to ever replace. It is then that I decide I need to walk away from the family farm, from the life I know and love, the passion that holds me together when the voice tries to tear me apart. I allow the pain of their absence to consume me, choosing avoidance instead of acceptance.

I shut out that part of my life. The decline in my mental health accelerates and tightens into an unavoidable spiral as I desperately search for purpose in my life. Their deaths mark the death of my childhood, the death of something I gave myself completely to, and the birth of daunting realities about life itself. It becomes the start of losing myself in the trap of living up to impossible standards of perfection I have built up in my mind, based on societal pressures, and the start of my inability to dull the self-critic within. The start of not becoming too attached to anything, so as to protect myself from any feelings of loss, rejection, or failure. The start of trying to reinvent myself in all the wrong ways—such as following a man to a city and getting trapped in a big corporate job at a marketing firm that bleeds me of any passion I have left, effectively destroying the last few things that make me who I am.

A few years go by as I try to convince myself that this is the new me. The improved me. The me society said I needed to be in order to have the sort of value that equates to a respectable life. It is the start of numbing the pain of a broken heart and lost soul who was fooled into believing that the little things and a simple life lack value, lack purpose. In this attempt to become someone I never was meant to be, forcing on myself a lifestyle I know will never make me happy—but *will* please other people—I eventually realize I have done exactly what I set out to do when I decided to run away from, rather than face, myself—I lost myself in a job that means nothing to me, lost myself in a marriage I rushed into for fear of otherwise being alone, lost myself in a value system that measures worth by only money, and lost myself by desperately building a life not meant for me at all.

I lost myself all right. So much so that the only way to find myself again is to set my life on fire and then send out a distress signal.

Everything must burn, and if it destroys me in the process... so be it.

Aiden walks over to me with a leather-bound book. He pauses, standing a couple of feet in front of where I sit, and stares at the cover of the book he is holding, clearly contemplating whether or not to hand it to me, as if it holds secrets he's unsure of sharing. As he continues to hold the book in the space between us, I reach out to take it from him…only to have him tighten his grip. My eyes meet his, and the intensity of his stare sends shivers down my spine.

"Let's have dinner with Tess and Henry first. Tonight, when they leave, do me a favor and read this. I'll explain what I can to you after…and hopefully answer any questions you might have had as you read it."

He releases his grip on the book, and the implications about its importance create a heaviness in my hand that is beyond physical weight. No title graces the cover, which increases my curiosity and ignites a spark of fear of whatever knowledge it may hold.

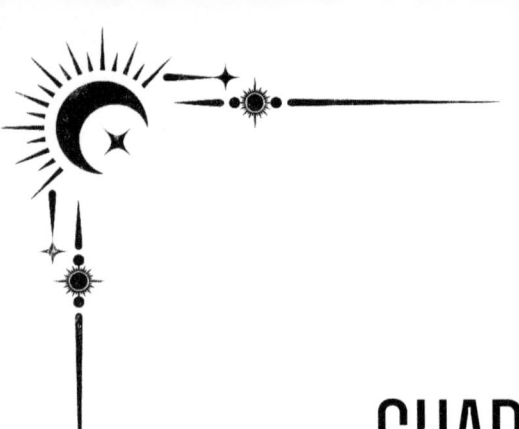

CHAPTER 25
MERCY

Tess enters Aiden's home by throwing herself through the front door, wrapping her arms around my neck, colliding into me, and forcing me to stumble back into the foyer. A smile spreads across my face at her way of greeting me, and I laugh at Henry, who stands in the open doorway, takeout in one hand and wine in the other.

"Missed you, too, Tess," I say when she finally releases her grip and pecks me on the cheek. Since I moved back to town, this is the longest we've gone without seeing each other.

"Can we not go that long without seeing each other again? I had flashbacks from when you left us to move to the city, and we lost you to the bastard who kept you from us." Her singsong voice loses its softness when she speaks about my ex and the life I lived with him. Her pout forces me to chuckle instead of sigh and roll my eyes at the lighthearted— yet intentional—jab.

Tess hugs me one more time before making herself at home and walking farther into the home as if it were her own.

"I've brought the goods," Henry says while using his foot to nudge the front door shut behind him. I take the items from his hands, thank him, and gesture for him to follow me to the kitchen.

"How are you doing?" His voice low and quiet beside me causes the question to sound genuine and sincere; he doesn't pressure me for a response. The question comes from the pure heart of a friend.

"Despite everything, I'm actually doing okay," I say, turning to look at him when we stop and stands in the open entryway of the kitchen.

He scans my face, looking for any sign that I might be lying to him, and then softly sighs as he exhales through his nose and smiles down at me. "I believe you," he says, acknowledging that I know he was scrutinizing me to make sure I wasn't lying.

"Quit holding the wine captive and bring it over!" Tess yells from her seat at the large island in the center of the industrial-style kitchen.

Henry makes a joke about her needing to learn patience and walks over to join her and Aiden, placing the food on the counter. I stay back for a second to take it all in. The golden light from the hanging fixtures paints the faces of my friends in a warm glow. Their voices become nothing but muffled chatter and gentle laughter as they pass the bottle of red wine between them, loading up their plates with food from the takeout containers scattered across the counter. The beauty in the simple and wholesome moment brings a smile to my face and forces me to prevent a building tear from escaping.

And in this very moment, despite how and why we all got here, my chest expands with overwhelming emotions of happiness. I catch myself gripping the fabric of my shirt, my hand pressing firmly into my chest, as if trying to hold on to the feeling, afraid to lose it. For the first time in a long time, I feel a sense of home within me.

"Are you going to join us? Or just stare at us like a creep?" Aiden asks before shoveling food into his mouth; he's standing bent over a plate of food, elbows on the counter that supports his upper body. Both his tone of voice and the look in his eyes are playful. Any notion of seriousness from our earlier conversation has been replaced by the satirical charm that, against my better judgment, I'm finding obnoxiously attractive.

I'm fucked, aren't I? the voice in my head says matter-of-factly instead of questioningly. *It's okay to be happy,* the voice adds more quietly.

An electric shock runs down my spine; I'm surprised by the voice's atypical…support? *Was that support I just heard from within?* I ask myself. But then I mentally shake myself. *Stop fucking questioning it, and just go with it.*

I pull out the stool next to Tess and gently nudge her with my shoulder, meeting her laughing eyes with a smile of my own as I take a seat.

She tilts her head and rests it on my shoulder for a brief moment before lifting her glass of red wine in the air and saying, "Well. Isn't this nice?"

Properly stuffed from the burgers and fries we paired with the bottle of merlot Henry and Tess brought, the four of us reconvene in the living room. My two friends lounge in the cushions of the same couch, as they did weeks earlier, snuggled in each other's embrace. Both perfectly comfortable, as if hanging out like this, with Aiden in his home, were something they've done countless times before. Aiden sits sprawled out on the oversized recliner nearest the fireplace—the spot he claims as his—swirling the remaining red wine in his glass. And I walk around the room with a newly opened bottle of red I found in the wine racks and offer everyone a refill.

"Expensive choice," Aiden drawls from his seat behind me. The remark forces me to glance over my shoulder mid-pour, to find Aiden with his usual smirk and raised eyebrow.

"Oops." I shrug, topping off my glass with the dregs of the bottle.

Since Henry is the designated driver, and I do not have to leave the house, both Tess and I enjoy the buzz we feel after finishing our second glass of wine and starting on our third. I place the bottle on the coffee table and stand with my back to the fireplace, warming myself in front of the roaring fire that is fighting the late-October chill outside. Surprisingly, the massive windows overlooking the dark forest outside do a good job at containing the heat within. My shoulders lift to my ears, and I sip my wine, backing closer to the fire to warm a chill that has settled into my bones.

Aiden clears his throat to garner my attention. "Sit," he demands, motioning to the little bit of space left in the corner of the recliner he's sprawled out on; he has no intention of moving to make more room.

I glare at him and scoff at the command. *I'm not a dog.*

As if he read my mind, he sighs and gives me the look a puppy would make when begging for scraps. "Would you *please* do me the honor of cozying up with me on this recliner so that we can share body heat and both be comfortable?" he asks, instead of demands, this time with forced sincerity, batting thick eyelashes at me and mock pouting.

"Only because I'm cold, and you said please," I tell him, the growing buzz from the wine giving me unnecessary encouragement to give in and oblige. I plop down on the corner of the recliner, glass raised high above my head so as not to spill, and drape my legs across Aiden's lap.

"Comfy?" Aiden asks, arching a brow.

I stare at him over the rim of my glass and sip more wine for the confidence I suddenly feel lacking. I will the corner of the recliner to swallow me whole. *What am I doing?*

Aiden adjusts himself around me, lifting me slightly so that my legs now drape across the arm of the recliner and my butt rests right on his lap. I feel my face flush and take a bigger swig of wine before accepting my fate and leaning back into his chest and the crook of his arm.

"Looking awfully cozy over there," Henry says, breaking the silence that has fallen over the room.

I shoot him a look and ask, "Want to play with the Ouija board again, Henry?"

Henry quickly loses the sly smile on his face, replacing it with a straight, tight-lipped expression and horrified eyes.

I feel Aiden buck a bit beneath me, clearly holding back laughter and choking on a sip of wine.

"Only *I'm* allowed to make unwelcome comments about those two in front of Mercy, Henry." Tess looks over at Henry, lightly smacks him on the shoulder, and scrunches her nose at him.

God, they're disgustingly adorable.

"Excuse me! She's my friend, too! I think that entitles me—" Henry is cut off by the ring of Tess's phone.

She lifts her hips, giving herself access to her back pocket, takes the phone out and answers, "John? Hi! I didn't know you had my number. What's up?"

A few quiet seconds go by, and Tess nods while making eye contact with me. "Yeah, she's right here. Would you like to talk to her?" Tess gets to her feet and walks over to hand her phone to me.

I take it and turn it on Speaker so that everyone can hear John. Everyone is invested, in one way or another, in what happened to me earlier, so it only makes sense that everyone hear what John has to say.

"Hi, Mercy?" John's voice comes through the speaker.

My heart beats a little faster in anticipation of what information he has to tell me. My anxious mind is distracted only for a moment as I feel Aiden's body tense beneath me at the sound of John's voice.

"Hi, John. What's up?" I ask as casually as possible, trying my best to hide any nervous energy in my voice.

"We found traces of blood and fingerprints, at Tess's house, that we are having analyzed and compared to what we found at your house."

The room goes silent, and the four of us exchange blank stares, unsure of how to react to this new information.

John continues, "I just wanted to inform you of where we stand in the investigation so far, in hopes of offering you some sort of relief and hope that we *will* find the people who are harassing you. When the results come back, we are hoping they will point us in the direction of someone to question. We won't stop our search until they are found and detained. I promise you that, Mercy."

My breath catches in my throat as a flood of emotions washes over me at being reminded of what led to the four of us sitting together in this room in the first place. Why I have found myself living in the home of someone I met not very long ago, instead of in the comfort of my own. How I came to know the owner of this house. The abnormality of the whole situation. It isn't that I had forgotten the whats, whys, and hows. I simply set the facts aside in an attempt to prevent the fear, which threatens to consume me, from taking control of my already-spiraling life.

"Thank you for the update, John. I appreciate all that you and your team are doing."

"Stay safe and—"

Aiden cuts John off, his words clipped and agitated. "She's perfectly safe with me. No need to worry about her. Just worry about the task at hand."

There's a pause before John speaks again, his tone doing little to hide the edge in his voice. "Mercy, is that Aiden? You aren't staying with Tess?"

"He offered me a room to stay in until this all gets sorted out and it's safe for me to go back to my own home. Between him and visits from Henry and Tess, I'm doing just fine," I tell him, internally questioning, *Why do I feel the need to explain this?*

Irritation begins to prickle through me at feeling the need to explain the choices that I've made. One look at the taut expression on Aiden's face lets me know he's feeling the same way, if not more so; he seems to be verging on anger.

Another pause occurs, this one long enough to make us wonder if the call was dropped, until we hear John let out a breath. "I'll call back when the results are in and let you know of any new leads. Keep your phone on you so I can get in touch."

"You can always call my number as well," Aiden speaks into the phone, doing little to mask the haughtiness behind what should have been a simple suggested alternative. "She might not always have her phone on her, but she's always near *me*." His words sound as if he's staking his claim, just as a dog pisses on a tree to mark his territory.

John and I say our goodbyes before ending the call. The second the screen of Tess's phone goes black, I whip my head around to stare Aiden in the eyes. "What the fuck was that about?"

"I don't trust him" is the only answer I get from Aiden.

"He's a *cop*."

"And?" He tilts his head at a predatory angle, looking at me as if no additional explanation were needed.

Tess's light chuckle catches both Aiden's and my attention. The two of us turn to see what she finds so funny.

"Jealous much?" Her question is directed at Aiden with a wink and another sip from her wineglass.

All of a sudden, that brief bout of happiness and peace I felt earlier is doused by the cold chill of reality and a discomfort I can't seem to shake, which is brought on by Tess's observation. The cold I had denied, now, slides into place with ease and claims residency in my bones. I don't have to look down at my stomach to know the black cloud only I can see is back, also in search of a place to call home within me.

Sensing the tension taking over my body, Aiden circles his thumb against my thigh. But what was meant to be a comforting touch is, instead, too much to handle. Catching everyone off guard, I attempt to pop to my feet with as much grace as I can muster, untangling myself from the limbs

I hadn't realized I had become entangled in. The heat of Aiden's body is replaced by a preternatural chill, even before I manage to clamber out of his lap and stand.

My buzz now gone, I stand uncomfortably in front of everyone and inhale a deep breath before announcing to the room, "On that note, I think it's time for me to go to bed."

"Mercy, are you all right?" Tess questions quietly, but I know it is what everyone is thinking after my sudden mood change; all three stare at me with looks of concern.

"I'm fine. I promise. It's all just…" I rake my fingers through my hair. When they get stuck in the loose knots, I take a second to finger brush my hair, which creates a distraction and gives me time to come up with some sort of explanation for my sudden shift in energy. "It's all just a lot to take in at the moment—what John said. It's just been a crazy few weeks, and I was just reminded of the reason behind the craziness. Not that I had forgotten. I just…"

Tess is on her feet as I struggle with words; she wraps her arms around me in a comforting embrace. She squeezes me gently, and my face is buried in her mass of curls, the scent of lavender wafting into my nose.

My vision blurs, and I fight back the tears. My mind is on the verge of spinning out of control, readying itself to obsess over everything all at once—the investigation, what the hell I'm going to do about my life once it's over, what to do about my life while everything is still happening, and…Aiden. Just Aiden in general.

What am I doing?

Heat from the fire caresses my back as Tess grips my shoulders and pushes me back so that I'm at arm's length. Flames from the fire dance and reflect in her eyes, emphasizing her look of determination. Her brows furrow and eyes slightly narrow as she tells me, "Mercy, you are not alone. You do not have to handle this on your own. We are here to help carry the weight of what life has thrown at you, just as you do for us when we need it. Every day, we *choose* to be in each other's lives. We *choose* to be here *with* you. We *choose* to be here *for* you. We *choose* you, for better or for worse, just like you do with us. We are here, Mercy. Let us be here for you. You are not our burden. You are our friend. We. Love. You."

I stare up to the ceiling, struggling to hold back the tears that want to stream down my face. Whether or not Tess knows the entirety of what is causing the chaos to take over my brain, I know she speaks the truth. I know that, no matter the obstacles or challenges I face, she will choose to face them with me, just as I would for her. Right now, she might think that it's only this investigation that's causing my anxiety to spike, and I'm more than fine with her thinking just that.

"'Til death." The words a quiet whisper on my lips to the friend whom I will forever hold in my heart and consider to be blood, even if biology says she's not.

With my hand in hers, Tess turns her gaze to Henry, who looks at both of us with just as much love in his eyes as I have for both Tess and him. I offer him a knowing smile, understanding the look in his eyes to be the same as the heartfelt words spoken by Tess. The three of us linger in the moment for only a few more seconds before Henry rises to his feet, wraps his arms around both Tess and me, and plants a kiss on Tess's forehead.

"We love you, Mercy," Henry says while taking a step back. The corners of his eyes crinkle slightly as his lips pull upward in a soothing smile. "We also know how cranky you can get if you don't get any sleep, so we will be heading out." Laughing, Henry nudges my shoulder. He then gently tugs

Tess away from my side, leading her to collect their jackets before saying their final goodbyes for the night.

I will be forever grateful for Henry's ability to read the room without judgment and fully understand whatever the situation may be.

An unusually quiet Aiden stands with me in the doorway while I wave to Henry and Tess. When their car is no longer visible, I close the door and triple-check that the lock is secure. A twinge of surprise hits me when I turn to see Aiden is no longer near, but instead he has situated himself at the drafting table in his study. Orthus lies at his feet, softly snoring, exhausted from being chased around the house all day by Void, who decided to take out his ongoing frustration with Aiden on someone who doesn't have thumbs and the ability to lock him down below with Leo.

Standing in the middle of the open double doors, I instinctively find myself crossing my arms over my chest to make myself feel small, burying myself inside my oversized sweater. Wanting to say something, but not knowing what it is I want—or need—to say, I cautiously enter Aiden's space. My mouth shut. My mind overthinking to the point that every thought has become a whirring blur. Heart pounding for a reason I can't understand. I quietly sit on the chair in the corner so that I'm facing Aiden, but close enough to the doorway that I can easily escape if needed.

The silence is broken by the soft tap of Aiden's pen being placed on to the table. Our eyes finally meet, and I open my mouth to fill the space between us, but he beats me to it.

"I'm sorry if I overstepped earlier. With John. With you."

Not knowing how I want to respond, I close my eyes and pick at the skin around my thumbnail. When my eyes open, I see Aiden looking at me, willing me to say something. Anything.

"It's okay." My gaze is soft, and I lift one corner of my mouth in a half-assed attempt at a smile.

"No. It's not. I'm sorry." He offers me his own unconvincing smile, as if to say we can put whatever this is behind us, and then he goes back to distracting himself with adding unnecessary finishing touches to the work of art he's recently finished.

With a soft exhale, I rise and walk to the wall of book-filled shelves, absentmindedly running my fingers across each spine and stopping with splayed fingers on two books. The spine of each book is aged and worn, their titles barely legible. The first is titled *Cosmos*, and the second starts with *Pale Blue Dot*, the rest of its title lost to wear and tear throughout the years.

"You didn't overstep," I say, breaking the awkward silence.

His pen once again makes a soft tap as it's dropped from the hold he has on it. When I turn away from the wall of books to look at Aiden, I find him glued to his seat, eyes now on me instead of his art, and I swear I can see the gears turning in his head as he decides how to respond next.

"I did. Tess called me out on it in the way that she does." A spark of humor briefly lights up his face—his self-awareness dulling the smugness that would typically reside there.

"Maybe you overstepped a little," I admit with a lilt in my voice as I walk slowly over to where he sits. My eyes soften, and I smile. "But I won't lie to you and tell you there wasn't a part of me that *wasn't* upset about it."

A breathy laugh escapes him, and he responds with a questioning look that's brightened by a mix of curiosity and playfulness.

I step closer to him and settle right behind where he sits, leaning over his shoulder to admire his latest creation. "This is beautiful."

We stay like this for a minute or so. I take in every little detail of each star cluster he's artistically depicted and worked into a composition that would take any viewer's breath away. Part of the piece grabs my attention, and I find myself leaning closer, farther over his shoulder, to observe.

Lost in the art, I'm startled when his voice, low and soft, pulls me from the trance I've lost myself to. My heartbeat intensifies with the faint touch of his lips against my ear when he asks what caught my attention, causing a rush of heat that flushes my cheeks. I jump back, fully aware of the personal space I invaded without invitation.

"Sorry, I just got lost in the art." My words fumble from my lips, rushed and clearly trying to cover any embarrassment I feel for being the one to overstep this time. As casual as I can make myself appear, I make my way back to the wall of books, creating distance between us.

"Never be sorry for getting lost in the art." His emerald eyes shine as bright as the stars that inspire each piece he creates, and they hold me, a willing captive; I'm unable to look away, unable to move. Frozen to the spot, I rack my brain for something to say. Something to disrupt the tension that has started to build between us and around us.

I fall back slightly, my upper back resting nonchalantly against the hard edge of one of the many shelves. One leg crosses over the other. My arms wrap around myself. My body language is just as confusing as the emotions and thoughts rampaging in my head.

"Is that one of the pieces that will be going to the gallery to be included in your exhibit?"

He nods and stands to walk over to where I awkwardly lean, not standing to my full height—not that I'm anything above average. When he finally stands before me, I'm forced to lift my chin and look up.

"I actually wanted to ask if you would be willing to be my plus one for the opening-night event." His eyes scan my face, trying to read my thoughts on the matter. And for the first time, I see a subtle splash of redness appear on his cheeks, softening the hard angles of his features into something that gives me a glimpse of the boy he might have been in his past.

"Will there be free drinks?"

"Of course. Even a few charcuterie boards to be picked through," he says, that single corner of his mouth curling upward.

"It's a date." My stomach churns the second the words are said. *Date? I had to say date?*

"It's a date." Both corners of his mouth lift, and his lips partially expose a bright-white smile that causes my heart to beat faster and the acid in my stomach to transform into a kaleidoscope of butterflies. Dimples I had barely noticed before are made prominent by the genuine smile that graces his face. The sight of his happiness caused by my slip of words and agreement to join him brings a smile to my face as well, and I sink into that feeling, unwilling to let it go.

Hold on to this feeling. Let it wash away the panic from earlier. Let that go, but hold on to this.

Not knowing what to say next, I simply just look at Aiden, the corners of my lips lifting slightly, my eyes tracing every detail of the face in front of me. Comfortable, we linger in the silent moment we share. His smile falters for a brief second, though, and I'm unable to hide the worry in my eyes, wondering what could have happened within these past few seconds to cause his smile to fall.

Before I'm able to ask what's wrong, both of his hands find their way around my neck, and his thumbs dig softly into my chin, angling my face up and towards his. Inhaling sharply, my eyes stare at him and watch as his dart around my face in a manner that is both frantic and longing. I realize he is searching for signs of any hesitation or dissent from me, especially after having just apologized for overstepping earlier.

What he might have seen was surprise. I can't believe he sees me this way, no matter how many times Tess and Henry have told me otherwise. Perhaps he saw confusion, because why me when he could have anyone else. Anyone far better than I could ever be. Assuming he is not blind—which I know he is not, although now I do question that, especially after the way he's taking in the sight of me—he definitely must see disbelief. Again, because…why me? Why me, when I am nothing compared to anyone else he could have.

All of these things he must see plastered on my face, and as if in answer to my silent questions, he draws me closer in one swift motion until our lips collide. The taste of him is unlike anything I've ever experienced. I can taste the wine we had drunk earlier that night, but it's dulled by a sweet tang of what I can only describe to be—

A jolt of electricity strikes between my eyebrows, and a vision first clouded by mist is all that I'm able to see. Feel. Smell. Even the whirring sound of silence hums its way into my ears. The mist parts, rolling away lazily, tendrils of it lingering a little longer over certain areas, forcing attention to the tiniest of details as the view is revealed. For a split second, my vision goes black, back to the view of what can only be seen behind closed eyes.

Then Aiden, still holding my face with one hand, takes the other behind my head, driving his fingers into the mass of unruly waves. He pulls me closer, kisses me deeper, and steals my breath. Another jolt of electricity strikes.

It's as if my mind has become an old favorite toy of mine—the viewfinder—only this one is a bit more high tech; instead of snapping through stills, I'm seeing snippets of scenes from what feels like old memories. Open fields of tall grass sway in the breeze as if they were rolling waves in a deep sea not completely calm, yet not raging. Just after allowing me to take in the beauty of the open space where the dancing blades of grass reach as far as the eye can see, the scent of lavender overwhelms me in the most soothing way possible, easing my mind's eye as it moves on to another scenic vision.

For a few more seconds, I'm gifted one last look of the open land I now notice is surrounded by trees with sinewy trunks and branches that twist and stretch in whimsical ways, reaching outward and upward to a sky worthy of worship. Warm golds, oranges, and pinks start at the horizon and transition into the richest turquoises, teals, violets, and deep blues generously dusted by shimmering stars high above. The vision soon fades to black as I experience another deep kiss and an exhilarating loss of breath.

The jolt of electricity this time is welcomed and hungered for, as it opens new scenes in the forefront of my mind. My very essence wills grappling hands and prying fingers into existence to reach for more visuals, to reach for more insight. My heart thrums with an energy I've never felt before as I'm gifted with what my newly freed essence cries out for—more visions and scenes of a place so beautiful, so ethereal, so otherworldly, yet welcoming, like home.

Grand visions consisting of various breathtaking landscapes ranging from snowcapped mountain ranges to the bluest oceans, tides ebbing and flowing on shorelines made of sand the colors of moonstone, citrine, and rose quartz flood my mind, which beckons for more. Within these scenes, I catch glimpses of clusters of dwellings and cities crafted from the natural sources of the environment, proclaiming the existence of civilizations blessed to call such places home. All existing beneath a never-ending astronomical twilight sky.

More refined imagery then takes over, closer, replacing broader views with those more intimate and personal. The welcomed flood continues in my mind, vision after vision, such as winding paths dappled by light from the moon and stars that filter through the crowns of every kind of tree imaginable. Etchings depicting stories glisten in granite that has been carved into steps leading up to the mouth of a cave set behind a waterfall. Silhouettes of figures dancing around a roaring fire, their limbs a blur of meaningful movements. Every step, every twirl, every whirl of the wrist, every fluttering of fingers holds divine purpose and energy. Vision after vision overwhelms my mind as I willingly become intoxicated by them and am unwilling to let it all come to an end. But then it goes black once more.

My heart stops beating in my chest, and I feel myself flatline for a beat or two. One last jolt of electricity settles in the center of my brow, and I'm left with a final vision that's startling. As if I'm standing nose to nose with someone who stands before me, my view is only that of a pair of eyes. One with an iris a shade of blue I know looks all too familiar, the other with an iris translucent and white, it's pupil opalescent and slightly milky. Had I the chance to step back, there would be only the slightest indication that the eyeball even consisted of any iris or pupil at all. The eyes that stare back send a shudder up my spine, but the longer I stare, the more familiar they feel.

Suddenly, my curious essence feels chaotic and twisted, as if it's being pulled in two different directions. One second, I'm looking into the eyes of someone I do not know; the next, I'm looking into my own. This back-and-forth continues until it finally hits me. The visions are not imaginings; they are memories. The eyes that stare back at me aren't those of a stranger; they are those of someone I know personally. Intimately. Wholly.

As if in answer to my sudden realization, I feel a chaotic energy vibrating within me, coaxing me to accept this insane conclusion. It does not allow me to second-guess or deny the revelations unfolding before me and within me. Whoever she is and whoever I am, I am she, and she is me. And it's only when we are together that we are whole. That we...I... am free.

What the actual fuck.

My eyes slam open, and I find myself abruptly shoving Aiden away, suddenly feeling trapped between him and the wall of books behind me. My hand clutches the fabric of the sweater above my heart as it races and rages in my chest, contradicting the flatlining experience of mere moments before. I hyperventilate with an open mouth as if I've just ascended from the deepest depths of a body of water in which I had been forcefully submerged. Shock pales my face and rattles my bones, leaving me lightheaded and reaching a hand out for stability.

After having been aggressively pushed away, Aiden looks at me warily, seeming unsure of how to help or offer a hand for support.

"Did you see that?" The words rush out of me in between gulps for air; no doubt the look on my face is wild and feral. "Tell me you saw that, too." The tips of my fingers turn white as my grip on the shelf tightens. In desperation and fear that

I have finally lost it, through clenched teeth and with manic eyes, I yell, "TELL ME," at Aiden, who stands in front of me with his hands up in a defensive posture and ready to catch me should I fall. The words come out as a frantic demand through labored breaths.

Only when my breathing ceases to be so labored does he finally speak. His eyes soften, and he drops his hands, reaching to grab the untitled book he had handed me earlier. Cautiously, as if I were a predator he's trying to survive, he approaches with the leather-bound book. He towers over me, only inches away, but I find myself feeling larger than he. My body is small, but the essence of my true nature looms large—a feeling that is unnatural and strange to me.

Aiden places the soft-leather book in my nearest hand, and I release my grip on the shelf to place the other on top of his, both our hands securing the book in my possession. I blink, trying to force a sense of calm over me; I relax my gaze, which is held captive by eyes of emerald green that rival the beauty of the forests from my visions…my memories.

"I'll answer any question I can. Any question you have to throw at me," Aiden says and then pauses on an inhale. On the exhale, he pushes the book closer to me, his eyes still locked on mine. "First, I just need you to read."

CHAPTER 26
AIDEN

Surprise struck the day I found her. Slight suspicion settled in my mind when little things, such as knowing how she takes her coffee, were second nature, even though I had just learned her name. Curiosity was piqued when I couldn't quite ignore the energetic pull that continued to lead me to her. Then a need for answers consumed me when I finally witnessed that first flash of something different, but somehow familiar, transform her face in the blink of a second. Intrigue and a need to understand finally claimed ownership of me once unknown repressed memories were brought to light through dreams and little moments spent with her.

What I thought to be true after piecing together the fragments that had revealed themselves—intentionally by Spirit or fate—has just been confirmed in this moment, in this kiss. It is not just Mercy whom I taste on my tongue. It is Hel.

CHAPTER 27
MERCY

Speechless, I make my way to what once was Aiden's room, now temporarily mine, with Orthus at my heels. The leather-bound book is clasped tightly to my chest. Everything that just happened overstimulates and confuses my system; the heat that flushes my cheeks from Aiden's advances is in direct opposition to the icy shock and wash of paleness caused by the LSD-like hallucination I just experienced.

There is no way that was real. It was just the wine talking…or making me see things.

I toss the book on the bed and make my way over to the corner of the room where my duffle bag of clothes is stashed. Emptying what's left of its contents on the chair next to it, in search of clean sleepwear, I can't help the annoyed sigh that escapes as I pull the only option that I have left—a lacy piece that still has the tags on it.

"Why did I leave Tess in charge of packing?" I hold the sheer-lace baby-doll garment—that's meant for anything but sleeping—at eye level before crumpling it into a ball and shoving it back into a deep recess of my bag. "I should have known better," I grumble.

I look over my shoulder and zero in on Aiden's dresser across the room, where I know he keeps his T-shirts.

"Don't mind if I do."

Without even having to rummage through his drawers, I find exactly what I'm looking for and help myself to one of his many T-shirts to wear to bed. I strip out of my day clothes and pull his shirt over my head, the hemline falling mid-thigh.

The sight of my reflection in the mirror above the dresser catches me off guard. I lean in for a closer look at the bags under my eyes and subtle worry lines etched in my skin between my brows. I can't help but focus on the emptiness that has crept its way back into the sea of blue reflecting back at me. The years of depression and anxiety forever linger there; no matter how hard I fight it, no matter how good life is at any moment, they linger. Even in times when all seems well and happiness sparks its light, their darkening presence patiently waits in the shadows, only to be brought forth for no other reason than they are simply parts of who I am.

A flash of silver amongst the blue in my left eye causes me to jerk back from the mirror, and my hand flies up to touch my face. I step forward, lean closer to the mirror, and gently brush my fingertips over the delicate skin around my eyes. Silver flashes again, this time fading to a milk white that slowly leaches any blue left around my pupil. I watch closely as the blackness of my pupil transforms into a misty, opalescent color—or lack thereof. What surprises me most, however, isn't the sight of my eye, but the steadiness of my heartbeat and the absence of panic.

Stepping back enough to see more of myself in the mirror, I search for any other changes and transformations, but

I quickly come to realize there are none. Captivated by the sight of my left eye, I can't help but stare at the strange woman in the mirror—at *my* reflection looking back at me. An energy reminiscent of a muffled adrenaline rush eases its way into my body, almost as if does not wish to startle me, but it demands attention.

Just read the damn book.

And there it is again—the voice within my head that is my own yet not my own, all at the same time. The voice I have come to know, the one that has chastised and critiqued me for so long. The voice of the mental illness that has been, and always will be, the reason I'm never alone, even when I technically am. The voice that is the reason for the shadows that hide or reveal themselves in my eyes every day. It is that voice again…but at the same time, it isn't. This time, it feels different, just as it did earlier when it surprised me with a tone of unlikely support.

The reflection in the mirror shows me eyes that have turned back to blue, and the steadiness of my heartbeat leaves. In place of the calm, my heart rages inside my chest as if it were hammering fists on a locked door, begging for release, unsure of what the hell is happening. I clutch my chest, my hand balling the soft fabric of Aiden's T-shirt in a tight fist, and stumble backward until the backs of my thighs make contact with the edge of the bed.

After sitting down, my one hand still gripping the shirt above my chest, the other hand falls to the side and lands on the worn leather of the untitled book. My wild-eyed gaze drifts to the volume just as Orthus nudges me with his nose while placing his large head on my lap. Releasing my grip on the shirt, I reach for the top of Orthus's head, and an ease washes over me with each stroke of his soft fur. Finally feeling somewhat grounded—as much as I can be at the moment—I turn my attention back to the book. Curiosity taking control of my emotions, I flip the cover open and find a handwritten note tucked inside.

> *Think of this as a brief summary of everything. An intro of sorts. A foundation for all that there is to know...for now. Potentially a way for you to understand things that you're having trouble accepting or understanding.*
>
> *I really hope you aren't a slow reader. There are things I would like to tell you, but can't until you've at least read this. So hurry up. I'm impatient.*
>
> *—Aiden*

"Be happy I'm curious and desperate for answers, asshole," I mumble under my breath to the currently absent author of the note while scooting my butt back and slumping into the mass of pillows behind me. "Otherwise, I'd be reading this one page per day."

I pat the open space next to me, and Orthus leaps onto the bed and curls his massive body by my side.

"I hope you're up for a bedtime story," I tell him, tucking Aiden's note back into the book and flipping to the first page—hoping that, if anything, reading will at least help me fall asleep.

> *A lethal predator about to catch her prey, I sprint through the woods on nimble bare feet, aware of every root, rock, or ditch that might cause any other to stumble and fall. This forest, however, is as familiar*

to me as my own reflection. The vast expanse of this entire place—from the dense forest, through the open fields, to the crystal shores—is a part of my very essence, created by the same stardust responsible for my own existence. This place is more than just my home; it is also home to some others like me who share the responsibility of guarding those who reside here temporarily, resting and reflecting for as long as they need before transitioning or ascending.

Rage sets fire to my very soul and fuels me, allowing each of my strides to be faster and to cover more distance. I know it's not his time yet to join me, even though I can't help but count down the seconds until we can be reunited again. Even we are not allowed to tip the scales in our favor or toy with the balance of the universe, as tempting as it may be at times. The consequences of cosmic destruction aren't worth the risk. No one and nothing is above the need for balance.

If anything that threatens the balance is set in motion, existence will slowly collapse. It won't be noticeable at first, but as time progresses, so too will the speed at which we will be crushed into nothingness and implode into nonexistence.

Our destruction will begin slowly, unnoticeably even. Conscious life on places like Earth will notice a subtle shift in temperature that will be confused with what most will argue to be a natural phase in Earth's infinite cycles, which are still trying to be understood by many. The subtlety will fade, though, as the rate of destruction speeds up exponentially. What once was thought to be something that could be ignored will send tremors throughout the planet, dismantling all that makes up her foundation. The waters will rise, mountains will crumble, and vegetation will wilt and die. Violence and terror will consume the masses to the point that the divine chaos responsible for creation will become corrupted and unravel beyond its own power, obliterating everything and leaving only the essence of something that once was. And this will happen like a domino effect throughout the expansive universe.

It is true that light cannot exist without darkness. Warmth cannot be fully understood without knowing what it means to be cold. Happiness cannot be felt without knowing what it means to feel anger. Success means nothing without failure. These opposites must coexist for energies in the universe to continue to vibrate and perpetuate itself. But when the balance is disrupted and ignored, the motion of the spiral that progresses outward weakens. The rhythmic, humming vibrations propelling the universe forward become unhinged, and the outward spiral shifts to inward, pulling us faster and faster into nothingness.

There is the belief—and hope—that chaos will survive and come out the other side, that everything will begin again, as we believe has happened before. But I'm not ready to let that happen. I like these lives of mine. I love these lives of mine. I'll do what I must to preserve them—for me and for all. If only others would think and act the same, would respect the need for balance.

Finally, I reach the end of the path, and the thundering sound of water cascading over the cliff's edge into the lake below reverberates in my ears. I fight the urge to weep in relief. With no time to lose, I bound to the cliff's edge without slowing my pace and leap up the masterpiece of granite stairs carved from the surrounding natural elements. Once behind the waterfall and in the mouth of the hidden cave, my feet slide from under me on the wet, slippery surface. Delicate hands catch me before I fall, hauling me upright and keeping me from bashing my skull on the hard surface.

Almond-shaped eyes look at me in panic, their amber glow lack the usual calming effect. The small, shimmering bindi squeezed between the wearer's furrowed brows catches my eyes and reminds me to control my frenzied energy and return to rational thinking—the only way I can possibly restore the balance that's about to be thrown off-kilter by an idiot who's overcome by relentless jealousy and the delusional need for undeserved power.

"Tarini, I need to get a message to the mortal realm… now!" My plea comes out as a mixture of uncharacteristic sobs and short breaths.

Without hesitation or questions, the tiny female grabs my wrist and hurries me into the depths of the cave, beyond its library, and into her hidden sanctum. But just as we enter her sacred space, my breath catches in my throat, and my stomach drops. Frozen in place, my eyes open wide in terror at the vision depicted in the scrying pool a short distance from the sanctum's entrance. I feel a pull of my arm as I force Tarini to a standstill beside me, stopping her from reaching her ink and paper.

"I'm too late." The horrid realization is uttered as a mere whisper from my lips, causing Tarini to whip her head from me to where I stare ahead of us.

Unable to watch, I turn my gaze to Tarini and see the dark-caramel color of her complexion drain in understanding horror. Her hand around my wrist tightens, fingernails digging into my skin and drawing blood. Her other hand clutches her chest above her heart, exactly where I know the sharpened twig has been aimed and embedded in the chest of the one whose soul is not destined to join me so soon.

"She forgot about the mistletoe." Tarini's words hang between us in the heavy silence, paralyzing us where we stand.

The ground beneath us trembles from the shift of the universe sliding off-balance as a result of a single soul's choice. A single soul who, like others before him and after him, thrives on the mayhem it creates, who shakes the universe at its core without a care as to the severity of the infinite number of consequences. That is one of the unfortunate things about balance — wherever there is a positive, there must be a negative. With the negatives come those who just enjoy seeing how far they can tip the scales.

Such cataclysmic events have happened before, and balance has been restored—albeit to a drastic extent—before an ultimate end was reached. But this time something is different. Something is off.

Sharing the same suspicion, my frantic eyes catch sight of Tarini's. I watch as her face goes blank, and then I feel myself falling back into an inescapable darkness.

I snap upright in bed, drenched in sweat. Heart pounding. Breath labored. Rattled by a dream that felt more like a memory—one I can't place…but know I have to. The leather-bound book lies open on my lap, having been flung from my chest during my panicked awakening. I look down and read:

> As above, so below. As within, so without.
> So long as balance remains, the universe shall maintain.
> When ignored, disrespected, shaken, or tempted,
> Should it not be righted, destruction will be incited.

A soft meow grabs my attention when Void enters the room, hops onto the bed, and lands in front of me. Still in shock from the fever dream I just woke up from, I watch him position himself at the foot of the bed and puff his chest out. Something nestled in his fur pokes out just enough for me to see it. He notices the object has caught my eye and puffs out his chest farther, as if in encouragement for me to pluck the object from him.

I hold in my fingers the small piece of paper that has been rolled tightly and craftily nestled into Void's fur, gently pull the string loose, and open the tiny scroll.

I saw it, too. I'm beginning to remember now. Are you?
—Tarini

"What. The actual. Fuck."

CHAPTER 28
AIDEN

She's sitting with her knees tucked to her chest, on a chair facing the window; I make sure to cautiously approach Mercy so as not to startle her. Her hair, still mussed from what appears to have been a fitful night's sleep, overwhelms her delicate features, which are pinched into an expression of distant thought. Her delicate chin is resting on her knees, eyes trained on the view ahead.

I sink down in front of her, balancing on the balls of my feet. I wrap my fingers around her ankles. The touch is meant to be a gentle reminder that I'm here—physically and emotionally—just as much as it is to help steady myself.

Impatience taking over, I break the silence. "My guess is that you did indeed read the book I gave you and that you must have some questions."

Another moment of silence lingers between us, and I watch as she collects herself and her thoughts. When she finally releases her distant gaze from the window, I'm met with the brightest blue eyes to which I realize I've become hopelessly attached. Eyes—I'm realizing more accurately now—I've been subconsciously searching for as more memories emerge from a fog that has been trying to clear itself from my brain since our first encounter.

The sunlight filtering in through the window accentuates every vibrant shade of blue in her eyes. The life that had slowly started to brighten them over the last couple of weeks is now in full effect, holding me captive and at full attention. I see her soul in them. Her essence. Her true self.

"I read the book."

My eyes widen. "The whole fucking book?"

Her bright eyes narrow at the surprise in my question as she says, "I read long into the night." Clearly feeling insulted by what was meant by me to be impressed disbelief, not skepticism, I watch as she rolls her eyes before returning her gaze to the window.

"So I'm going to guess the distant, lost-in-thought look is the result of you having consumed the overwhelming amount of information I condensed into that one book," I say, pausing when she whips her head back to me and widens *her* eyes this time in disbelief. I do little to help hide the smug smile that has my mouth quirking to the side at her shocked reaction to my claim. "And of course the crankiness is the result of little sleep," I add. The corners of my lips pull ear to ear in a shit-eating-grin as I brace myself to be slapped or shoved after the playful jab.

I snicker, watching her mouth open and close. Her mind clearly is searching for a comeback, but she's too exhausted to find one. The tight ball in which I found her eases, and she looks at me. I lift my chin to her, encouraging her to speak her mind.

"I have even more questions now."

"Can we go somewhere more comfortable for me to answer them? My knees are starting to hurt, and I know this won't be a quick conversation." I groan, pushing myself up to stand, knees cracking. The sensation in my body reminds me I'm not a spry teenager or young twenty-something any longer. Not that I'm old. It's just that my body reminds me of the stupid shit I put it through during the time when bouncing back as if nothing happened was the norm. I don't care whom you talk to, or what they're selling, there will always be a difference between a twenty-year-old's body and that of someone who has finally reached their thirties. Recovery time is just never the same after a certain point, and the ground suddenly becomes harder. I swear, that must be why many gods and goddesses only stay so long in their vessels on Earth before they discard them. Kill them, to put it bluntly.

I hold out my hand in invitation; Mercy grabs it, and I pull her from her seat and guide her to the kitchen. She makes herself comfortable on the barstool, while I walk around the island to start brewing a fresh pot of coffee. It gurgles to life, interrupting the contemplative silence Mercy sits in, no doubt wondering where to start with her questions.

"You. *You* wrote that?" The disbelief on her face might have been insulting had it been a book about anything other than the attempt at a brief summary of the universe, its creation, and how it works. I get it. Sacred texts like the Bible of Christianity, the Tripitaka of Buddhism, or the Vedas of Hinduism—to name only a few—weren't created and written by one person during a single lifetime. Then again, neither was this book.

I place two coffee mugs on the counter and pull up a stool so that I'm sitting in front of Mercy. This is the type of conversation that needs to be face-to-face. The gurgling of the coffee maker continues, and I take my seat, schooling my face into something that comes across as both serious, so that she is prepared for the impact of what I'm about to say, and calm, in hopes she won't run out the front door thinking she's been staying in the company of the world's next up-and-coming cult leader.

"As much as I would love to impress you and tell you that I wrote that within a single lifetime...I'd be lying. It's taken many. A few gap lives, if I'm being completely honest, may have delayed its completion. Even now, I'm still learning things that I know need to be amended or added." I angle my head and smile while watching her face, waiting for the words I just said to sink in.

A drawn-out beep signals the coffee is ready, but I wait for Mercy to say something.

"Yeah, about that. I guess I'll start there with my questions. When I talked to you before about my belief that there must be some sort of truth in regards to past lives and reincarnation..." Her voice trails off almost in a question, as if she in fact can't quite believe in the very truth she had embraced in the first place.

I smile at her, satisfied that my words have indeed hit home. "Want me to grab something stronger to mix with your coffee before we start?"

"I feel like I should be clearheaded for this."

"Suit yourself," I mumble, shrugging my shoulders and standing up to retrieve the coffee pot and creamer, pouring us each our first of many cups.

Elbows propped on the counter, steaming mug between my hands, I wait for her to take her first sip before asking, "So where would you like me to begin? Would you like to hear about the past life when I finally first earned the ability to figure it all out? Or would you like me to just jump right into how the reincarnation part of this all works? I could definitely share a few stories about crazy shit that has happened to me in other lifetimes."

Mercy chokes on the coffee, and I know it's not just because it's hot, but because of my nonchalance on the subject matter at hand and the simple fact that this is indeed what we are discussing. As if it's real. As if it's fact. Because it is.

"How about I surprise you and wait to talk about myself until after going over everything else?" An anxious smile spreads across my face. "I know. I know. Look what you've done to me. My arrogance is fading." That earned me another eye roll.

"I was right, though? This whole time. My suspicions about past lives and reincarnation are true?" A mix of awe, excitement, and a healthy dose of terrified wonder awakens the life in her eyes. Caffeine apparently was not needed to pull Mercy from her earlier sleep-deprived state.

"Look who's the one all high-and-mighty about themselves now? Are you sure you don't want anything stronger to go with that coffee?" I lift my brow and sip from the mug.

"Aiden. Please, would you just get on with it, already? I'm sure I can handle whatever it is that you have to tell me."

Placing my coffee mug down, I lean forward, brace myself on the counter, and ask her, "Remember when I told you religion is a paradox? That everyone is right, but also wrong at the same time?"

Bright eyes stare at me, locked in and ready to listen to—and I'm sure question—every word that is about to come from my mouth. She gives me a subtle nod as my cue to begin.

"I think it would help if we started with talking about structure first." I press the heels of my palms to my eyes and slide my hands down my face. *Fuck, this is going to be...challenging.*

"Structure?" Her eyes narrow and head tilts in a manner of curiosity and confusion. The mug of coffee in her hands is now simply a solid object for her to hold on to. An object that's subconsciously giving her a way to keep her grip on reality—even though everything I'm about to tell her, crazy as it sounds, is indeed just that, real.

"Think of the universe as infinite, in a way; it was never created because it was always here to begin with. It just started off smaller than it is now. Since its debut performance, it's been expanding, creating more space. So…there is no true beginning and no true end because that would insinuate that there was a time before the universe. It's just simply always existed." I try to read her expression, wondering if she follows so far, and I'm met with a dip of her chin to continue.

"All right, now let's take the universe as a whole and look at the pieces it's constructed of."

"Like our galaxy?" she says through sips of coffee.

It's no surprise to me that she has knowledge of the universe at a basic level; that's not what causes my eyebrows to lift or my hesitation. It's the fact that I know where this conversation will eventually lead, the seriousness of it all, and the consequences of attaining this knowledge. I take a moment to think twice before continuing, considering things she's meant to learn, not from me, but on her own time.

Realization hits me. I may be doing exactly what I tell my father not to do—manipulating someone's cycle of awakening and enlightenment. I'm doing just that by revealing all that I've learned over my many lifetimes. Maybe, though, this is part of her process. Maybe I'm meant to be a part of it, and this is my role. Either way, I decide there is no going back now.

After a steadying breath, I continue, "In the early stages of the universe, there were no galaxies. The universe was comprised of every speck of energy jammed into an infinitesimal point, otherwise known as a singularity. Due to the extremely high density of this point and its high temperature, an explosion occurred. The force behind this explosion drove the condensed energy outward from its original primordial point, and gravity continued to do its thing, drawing the once insanely condensed matter into newly scattered formations. Once shit started to cool down and stopped being so soupy, these new formations took the shape of the first stars that, in turn, created the first galaxies. It was creative chaos."

I'm about to continue when I'm interrupted by the sight of Mercy dramatically smacking her forehead onto her arms that are crossed on the counter. I stop and stare as I barely make out her muffled voice as she says, "I hated science class."

"Bear with me, will you?" It comes out a bit more sharp than I intended it to. "I promise, in order to answer the questions I know you must have, it requires you to have as much understanding of how it all started first." My voice is a bit more empathetic by the end of this statement.

"Sorry. Continue with your lecture on the Big Bang." She sighs, peeking out through hair that has fallen in front of her face, and cracks an apologetic smile.

Flipping over a discarded piece of art I had lying on the counter, I grab a pen and begin to sketch a visual of what I'm trying to explain. Unable to keep myself from poking fun at her claim of an irreverence for science, I clear my throat and do my best impersonation of a past high school science teacher, diagrams and all. "As the first stars clustered by way of gravity, forming individual galaxies, they would continue to branch out farther away from their original location in the primordial singularity."

Lines of black ink reach out in multiple directions like spokes of a wheel as I try to convey the movement of the scattered clusters of dots I've added around the center point. Mercy leans closer to watch as I then begin drawing a spiral over each extended line, beginning at the center point and uncoiling tightly at first, then more loosely as it expands outward.

"I probably would have paid more attention in science class if my teacher had taught more like this. The monotone drawl of his voice as he read from the textbook, word for word, just put me to sleep."

I crack a smile at her words and take what she said as a compliment. Looking up from my drawing, with the point of my pen positioned over the center dot—my representation of the primordial singularity—I gesture for her to keep looking at the drawing as I speak.

"With the force of the explosion, the energy dispersed was intense and strong enough to allow the stars that eventually were formed to move away from their point of origin. Despite the immense power of gravity that was still within and surrounding the primordial singularity, there came a point where the direction of stuff was allowed to change." I start to explain, hovering the tip of my pen over the tighter areas of the spiral, "Anything that had been blasted past a specific boundary, where this expanding spiral of energy starts to become looser, can be looked at as out of range from the force that pulls stuff back in towards its point of origin." The ink of my pen leaves spastic dashes expressing a back-and-forth motion. "It's not that the energy is any less as the spiral expands—remember, energy cannot be created or destroyed, just transferred—it's just that at this boundary, after the explosion occurred, anything that was not forced beyond it is unable to reach the velocity needed to escape the gravitational pull of that exploded primordial singularity."

Her eyes start to glaze over, so I try to simplify what I'm trying to explain. "At this boundary line, we find an ebb and flow of things; everything is still in motion, just delicately balanced. Go too far over the line one way, you get drawn in towards the singularity. Find yourself on the other side of that boundary line, you enjoy a cosmic lazy-river ride spiraling away in orbit."

Mercy lifts her head finally and leans back in her chair.

Eyes focused on me once again. Good.

I smirk as I tell her, "Was it a big bang? Yes. However, with everything I just explained to you, what other type of event fits this same description?"

Her eyes light up, and I can tell that she's made the connection I wanted her to make before I expected her to. "So... you're saying that the Big Bang was also in a way the formation of the first black hole?" she asks me.

Her question gives me hope that I truly am meant to reveal this all to her and not totally fucking over her karmic timeline.

"The Primordial Black Hole of the Big Bang." I shrug at hearing it said out loud. "I know it doesn't roll off the tongue as nicely as just the Big Bang, but...I deem it a more informative title."

Mercy hops off the stool she's seated on and grabs the pot of coffee, leaving me to question my title choice.

"I have a feeling we are both going to need more caffeine for the remainder of this discussion," she says while refilling each of our mugs.

I take one sip, clear my throat, and once again continue with my lecture. "Now, fast-forward to the universe continuing to expand and being compromised of more than just the initial clusters of stars that formed the first galaxies. At this point, we need to think about how the universe is expanding and the structure it's becoming."

Another sip of coffee by each of us, and once again I continue. "Consider that every galaxy has a supermassive black hole within it. Envision from the singularity of this black hole to its event horizon—that encompassing boundary line—the top of a cone. The stars that have been forced past the event horizon, escaping that pull of gravity inward, spiral farther out and away as they age. The width of the structure enlarges as they continue to expand outward, forming the rest of that particular galaxy and giving it its conelike structure."

I'm stopped mid-explanation by the sight of Mercy's raised hand, and I can't help the side-eye I give her. "Yes, class?"

"Before we continue, I think I need to take preventive measures and pop something to help the inevitable migraine all this information is going to cause," she mumbles.

"I offered you whiskey to mix in with that coffee, might I remind you. Anyway"—I wave my hand at her and attempt to get back to the topic of discussion, but am derailed once more by a raised hand catching my eye—"let's leave the questions to the—"

"So that would mean, at some point, at the edge of each individual galaxy—"

"The halo."

"Sure, the halo. There would be black holes from older stars that have spiraled farther away from that particular galaxy's event horizon as they age."

I nod again. "There would."

"Then a galaxy, massive or small, would form out of that black hole's transfer of that star's energy? The energy of that star never truly dies, just…rearranges itself amongst the star's discarded debris?" She says this in the form of a question she knows she has already answered. "And this pattern would then continue…infinitely."

"Infinitely," I confirm, smiling. "And the farther out in space that galaxies form from that primordial singularity point, the more 'stuff,' for lack of a better term, gets diluted. This means, after the universe expands to a point that a massive star explodes and a black hole is formed, the new galaxy could be made up of more than just star clusters and gases. It could also be made up of planets with rocky terrain…and eventually life as we know it."

If there were crickets in this room, they would be the only things you hear. At this point, Void has decided to join the conversation, and he leaps into Mercy's lap. I watch as she mindlessly strokes the fur on his head and under his chin. She is clearly lost in deep thought as her brain works overtime to piece all this information together.

"When you say everything is created from a star's explosion…" Her words begin to drift off, leaving me to pick up and confirm where her thoughts were taking her.

"We are connected to the stars because we are the results of their explosion and transfer of energy, just as they were the result of the first explosion of the primordial singularity that caused the Big Bang. The energy that once held them together never disappeared, just as the energy that once held the primordial singularity together never disappeared. It simply dispersed and transferred to whatever that star was made into. Our energy and essence are those of that star. And that star's energy and essence are the same as that of the primordial universe."

The only sound that can be heard is Void's purring from Mercy's lap. Her gaze leaves mine, chin dipping down, and her focus shifts to staring at the patterns left in Void's fur by her fingers that trail from between his ears to the base of his tail. I recognize this version of her silence as—not panic, sadness, or fear—deep contemplation and mental gymnastics in order to try and connect the dots.

"When I was reading the book...*your* book...there were moments that I couldn't quite tell if what I read was meant to be taken literally or metaphorically."

Silence returns to the room, settling around us in a welcoming embrace, offering space to allow the mind to wander and question, observe and answer. When I see that Mercy has quieted her inner thoughts and is taking a second to mentally rest, I meet her meditative stare. Speaking out loud the written words I know she is referring to, my voice just above a whisper, I recite, "The universe isn't just a thing out there. It's also a thing in here," and I press my hand flat against my chest.

"Everything your father said about being made up of stardust..." she begins to say, her words trailing off as she connects one thought to the next. "The words you wrote, the ones you just spoke, they weren't a metaphor at all. Just a poetic way of explaining what your father said is true. We *are* made up of 'star stuff,' just as the stars were made from everything that the universe ever was, ever will be. We are just as much a part of *it* as *it* is a part of *us*."

I nod and brace myself, knowing where the end of this part of the conversation leads next.

"But where does religion tie into this? How can *every* religion tie into this? Especially considering that this denies the varying religious beliefs that we are creations of whatever divine being each claims to be its sole creator?" Mercy asks, bringing us back to her original question, perhaps because she thinks I'm just talking around the subject and using this astronomy and cosmology lesson to avoid it.

Just as I'm about to try to reignite the discussion about the science behind black holes, in order to get to the religion part, Mercy unknowingly asks one final question that to her might not seem connected. But I know that it will later indeed link everything together. My mouth opens, and before I'm able to get a word out, she adds, "Wait. What about the energy and information that isn't able to escape the draw of the black hole's gravity? If it's all infinite, unable to be destroyed, then the black hole must lead to somewhere if those things continue to exist."

I hold Mercy's gaze for a few moments. The puzzled look on her face begs for answers I'm about to give her. I can only hope she's ready. "It does continue to exist. Mercy… why most haven't been able to figure out what lies beyond the event-horizon point of a black hole is because they aren't meant to know yet. They haven't reached the point in their cycle at which they are meant to finally understand. To know the truth."

"Understand what? The truth about what?" she fires her questions at me, one after the other.

"Understand that black holes simply just lead to the other side of the infinite structure that is the ever-growing universe. Simply put…well…they lead to the…*other side*." The last two words I draw out a bit in an attempt to emphasize exactly what I'm referring to as the other side.

As I expected, silence fills the room. To say the concept of conformation of life beyond the one we are in now, beyond what people call death, can be—is—overwhelming, no matter how relieving and beautiful the conformation may be. It's a shock to the system, to say the least.

"You mean to tell me that the pearly gates of heaven, paradise, whatever you want to call it, are actually just the event horizons of black holes?" The disbelief and shock in her voice is almost comical.

Void chirps in her lap, stretching upward from the ball he had made himself. His chirp rolls into an abrupt *meow* as if to say, "Duh."

So I back up his sentiments with a simple "Um, yup."

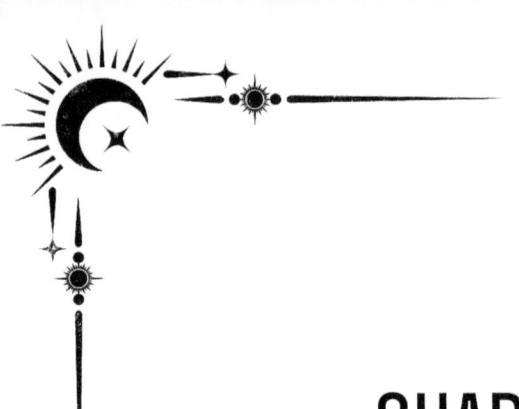

CHAPTER 29
MERCY

I'm about to pace a trench in the kitchen floor after asking Aiden for any sort of visual proof to back up his conformation theory of the other side. I'll admit that the pacing didn't start when he began to explain to me in further detail, "The reason for the bloody passcode to enter into my father's space isn't because of some fancy DNA apparatus he's obsessed with." No, no. The pacing started when he followed that up with, "It's actually part of the process—quick opening ritual, I suppose—that allows someone to enter a liminal space of a higher kind. Think of it as magic backed by science."

What the actual—

Oh, but wait... There's more! He then includes this little extra bit—the hall he disappeared down and returned from with his father leads to an observatory. Not just any observatory, but the Observatory of Souls, he calls it. Just a casual place where one can get a peek at the other side—heaven, the underworld, Helheim, whatever the fuck you want to call it.

No matter what it's called, he describes it to me as a place of many names that serves only one purpose—to allow those whose energy has moved on from their earthly vessels an opportunity to rest and a place for the chance to reflect. Yeah, that part did have me finally stopping dead in my tracks.

"Show me." The demand a challenge meant to call his bluff—his claim—that under us at this very moment is a way to basically confirm life beyond our time on Earth. I cross my arms over my chest and throw my weight onto one leg. I'm not about to let him pull one over on me and make me look like a gullible fool. I'm not some idiot.

He truly had me there for a while—the Big Bang, black holes, elements in common with the stars and this very universe. I believed him. Hell, I *still* want to believe—at the very least, *that* part of the story he wove. That beautiful thought that we are all connected makes even the simplest of things still hold great significance. I will happily accept that. Believe that.

It was this last bit, however, about what lies beneath our feet that made me double back and rethink everything I've been told. Everything he mentioned before was easier to accept and believe when there was still room for questions. Still room for that blissful ignorance we all take advantage of to avoid a worried mind. But when he told me that *visual proof* of the *other fucking side* is right beneath our feet, that's when things became unsettling. That's when the blissful ignorance that had once unknowingly provided comfort was ripped from under me.

I'm convinced the only plausible explanation is that Aiden is indeed mocking me somehow. Mocking the theories I vulnerably shared with him—the ones he even persuaded me to share with his father.

Is his father in on this, too? He played along with it all in a way that set me up for what Aiden just told me. And if so, for what reason other than simply wanting to humiliate me?

"I can't show you—"

I point a finger at him with a wicked grin and think I caught him red-handed playing some sort of fucked-up mind game on me. "Ha! You thought—"

"*Now.* I can't show you *now*. Perhaps tonight, though."

My arm slowly lowers as I watch the corner of his mouth pull up into a smug smirk of righteousness. Smug enough that it forces one of his subtle dimples to make an appearance.

"I promise you, Mercy, everything I'm telling you is true. Everything you've read in that untitled book and everything I've told you so far is only a fraction of all there is to know." Those emerald eyes of his hold a new glow I hadn't seen within them until now, as he promises me his honesty, any pridefulness gone from his expression.

And, dammit, I fucking believe him. *What the fuck is wrong with me? I am either gullible as fuck, or…I don't even know anymore.*

"Okay, fine." I return to my pacing while Aiden continues to sit on the stool at the counter. With a glance up as I pivot to continue making my laps around the kitchen, I catch the sight of two pairs of eyes following me with amusement. One pair belongs to Aiden and the other to Void, who sits on the counter right at Aiden's shoulder.

"I suppose you're also going to tell me that Void has some sort of special abilities?" I ask with a sarcastic chuckle, stopping mid-pace with a hand on my hip, unsure of whether to laugh at myself, at Aiden, at this whole situation, or just at everything that my life has become at this point.

The two turn to look at each other then back at me. Aiden tilts his head to one side, and Void lets out a dramatic sigh in a huff.

"Right, silly question. Of course, he doesn't. He's a cat." I throw my hands in the air to emphasize my joke and the absurdity of it all, only to be answered by a low growl.

"Not that I'm ever one to boost Void's already-inflated ego, but—" Aiden begins, but I can't take it.

"Stop." I pinch the bridge of my nose with one hand, the other raised, begging for a moment to pause and think. "Let's tackle whatever *that* means after I've wrapped my head around this," I say, twirling my hand around over my head and reaching towards the sky.

I pace back and forth a few more times before returning to my seat. Elbows on the counter and fingers tented at my temples, I look at Aiden through my lashes and scrunch my brows. "So how do we come to the conclusion, then, that all religions, belief systems, and so forth are *both* right *and* wrong? If there is proof of an afterlife, one of them had to be right. So…which one is it? Who is right?"

Aiden watches me thoughtfully, emerald eyes scanning my face with a slightly devious smile, as if he knows what he is about to tell me will change my life forever. He locks his eyes on mine, and in a voice deep yet quiet, he answers, "No one."

In a moment that I believe was meant to blow my mind—leaving me awestruck and speechless—I suck in a breath, confused, and release the captured air through my nose. "If no one is right"—my eyes narrow, and I can see slight disappointment at my uneventful reaction—"then how is it that everyone is right and wrong at the same time, as you've repeatedly told me?"

"Fair. Let me elaborate," he tells me, standing up from the stool and reaching out a hand to guide me. The gesture is a bit intimate, which creates yet another thing for me to overthink and worry about.

Don't be stupid. This means nothing. Stop overthinking. There are bigger things to wrap my head around at the moment. Much *bigger things.*

Nevertheless, I take his hand and allow him to guide me into the living room and over to the window seat that has become one of my favorite spots in this house. The blanket I left tossed in the corner the day before is still there when I wedge myself into the one corner that gives me the best view of the expansive backyard and tree line for critter watching.

Aiden takes a seat in the corner opposite me. After a few unsuccessful seconds of trying to get comfortable, he finally settles on pulling the knee of his leg closest to the window towards him and letting the other stretch out and cradle me.

If anyone were viewing this scene from the outside looking in, they might believe they have caught a glimpse of a private moment between a cozy couple huddled up together, still dressed for sleeping or lounging the day away in each other's company. Enjoying each other and the view of the last of the vibrant fall foliage from the comfort of their home, which boasts character and warmth. That may be what a stranger would think, but they would be incredibly wrong.

If the observer only knew…that the couple who sits behind the massive windowpanes is not a couple at all…that in all actuality, they truly are only a step beyond being strangers… that within the mind of the woman huddled in the corner, an oversized blanket pulled tightly around her body, is pure chaos made up of unsettled emotions, newly acquired truths that are hard to believe, and an ongoing war between a voice and her that started decades ago…that the words being spoken by the man with emerald eyes, who has seen more than can ever be imagined, are hard to believe. More than *I* could ever believe…but somehow I do.

If the viewer had been a fly on the wall, instead of some lost hiker or passerby on the outside, they would have heard Aiden's explanation start in the realm of science and, by the end, be tied into the realm of faith and the divine. Would have heard how, after the earliest stages of the Big Bang—or whatever the long-ass fucking title was that he wants to call it—as the stars continued to form and planets were made, cosmic energy and particles transformed into something more. A conscious soul.

The more Aiden speaks, the more I find I'm losing myself in all that he confesses to me. With unblinking eyes, I stare at Aiden as he tells me how those first conscious souls that formed from the earliest and brightest stars were basically thrown into the deep end of the pool. Their sink-or-swim scenario unfolded with their becoming something tangible made of flesh and bone, tasked with the responsibility of figuring out what it is to think, to live…to exist. Forced to figure out what to make of the chaos they were born from and into, they had no other choice than to gain knowledge through endless failures and successes, trials and errors.

After springing to life closest to the origin point of the cosmos—in terms of both time and space—and going through countless trials and tribulations, these primordial souls eventually became the ones who future souls would look to for guidance and answers. Eventually, they were the ones deemed to be our goddesses, gods—the divine.

My lips remain sealed tight, and all I can do is continue to listen, taking in each word he speaks out loud. Things begin to make sense in my mind as he describes how more souls formed as time continued, the universe ever expanding. Explaining in more detail how the primordial souls who came first were relied on by others to share their wisdom, their truth, and their understanding of how—and what it means—to exist. Theirs became the answers to questions asked. Examples for what can't be seen but must be understood. Guides to those in need. And as the universe expanded, so too did the divine, as needed, increasing to assist in the ebb and flow of life as it became grander in nature and size.

"That would explain and give some sort of proof as to how there can be so many different gods, goddesses, deities..." My voice drifts off, the thoughts in my head still churning. I finally blink as if to lock all the information in my head.

"Exactly. At the start of it all, there was never *one* almighty being who was meant for us to worship and follow. There was the primordial singularity. And that singularity has always been the source for *everything*. We are a part of that *everything*, as large a part as the divine and all that creates the cosmos. We are all just part of the scattered pieces and information that was the universe in its most basic moment. Strip away all the misinformation from people's beliefs, and even then, you're only a little closer to what's actually true. Everyone's story has to start somewhere. It's just unfortunate that each story has been influenced by opinions and assumptions that, throughout time, have manipulated the truth beyond recognition."

"So that's what you mean when you say that everyone is wrong, and at the same time everyone is kind of right. There is truth in everyone's belief. It's just hidden behind a misguided and distorted understanding of what they were told to be true." My heart races and a soft throbbing starts behind my eyes. I'm unsure if it's in response to all this information, the dangerous amount of caffeine sloshing around in my empty gut, or a combination of both.

Aiden nods and explains that, if anything, it is the collective belief and acceptance of untainted knowledge, unbiased understanding, and wisdom that has always been meant to serve as something for *all* to believe in and to follow—an idea more than an individual or group of individuals. The divine were always meant to be our teachers, our guides, and our compasses in this eternal cycle of existence. Always meant to be respected—just as one respects their elders and the people who raised them.

"Those who were placed in the role of the divine never intended for their existence to be used for control, power, or manipulation, and yet..." Aiden takes a deep breath, and I watch that glow in his eyes disappear for a moment. He lets the words he didn't speak hang in the air between us.

I unravel myself from the blanket that's starting to feel constricting instead of comforting, as it was before these revelations. Knowing there is so much more to hear, I reposition myself on the window seat and crumple the blanket into a ball that I hold tightly in my arms, pulling it into my torso. Leaning forward with the balled-up blanket for support, I look for that light that I know can still be found in those green eyes that have suddenly gone dark.

"Tell me more. Before it all went to shit," I say with a smile. "Tell me more about the beginning," I quietly request, and the light that had faded begins to flicker again.

A smile tinged with sadness makes me think the conversation may be over for now, to be resumed at another time. Much to my relief, however, I watch that sad smile transform ever so slightly into one hinting at hope, thanks to memories of a once-promising past.

So I remain quiet and still, eyes trained on Aiden's, encouraging him to continue enlightening me, as those primordial souls once had done for others eons ago.

Aiden drags fingers through his mussed-up hair, taming the occasional rogue curl as if that alone will bring order to the whirlwind of thoughts I can sense him trying to organize in his brain. Giving up on the stray tendrils, which I personally think help soften the sharp angles of his face, he refocuses himself and continues in a voice that is both quiet and profound. "Hierarchies were established, not for the purpose of power, but for the purpose of maintaining progress, finding balance, and existing in an ordered fashion for all to thrive. Everyone shared the same belief, not necessarily with regard to a single higher power or idea, but about the preservation of the world, the universe, and everything as a whole. Living in constant harmony, in balance, and advancing knowledge for the better of all were the ultimate truths and the purpose for existing.

"In the beginning, all was well. But just as there was continuous striving for balance and harmony, there was, by nature, the chaos that threatened to disrupt the harmony. After all, you cannot know what balance and harmony are without knowing imbalance and chaos. As it is with everything in existence, one cannot exist without the other. That's the hard part about obtaining knowledge—you must learn both the pros and the cons, and then decide how best to apply that knowledge.

"Unfortunately, while some kept an open mind and acknowledged the concept of yin and yang, using it as a way to better understand how to be and do better, others found themselves conflicted. They were either unable to accept that one cannot be without the other, or they were seduced by advantages they believed only one side could promise. Those individuals found themselves drifting, their minds closing, their energies dimming, and their souls trapped in an endless cycle of eventually trying to return to what they had once been.

"Some were able to escape this cycle by learning from their mistakes, their failures. Others, however, were not so lucky. Power, greed, doubt, and envy kept them from escaping their karmic cycles, corrupting the truth of what once brought everyone and everything together. The knowledge of what once brought the conscious soul into existence was forgotten by many, and there was a threat that soon it would be forgotten by all and replaced by intentional and unintentional distorted truths created by man.

"The history of the divine eventually became twisted by the tongues of those who spoke their own versions of a truth influenced by ego. What once established understanding and balance was forced to be considered myth, and the hunger for power over others grew insatiable. Then, during the times of early civilizations, organized religions arose, and the stories of divine figures were reinvented even more elaborately—a far cry from the truth in the beginning—so that they could serve the purposes of those in power and authority.

"The truth of the universe became lost and was replaced by rhetoric shoved down the throats of those who became conditioned by the corrupted, and in turn the history of the divine was rewritten. Fearing the consequences of noncompliance demanded that the people accept the lies as fact, only furthering the distance between humanity and nature's divine truth.

"The further society strayed from the balance of nature, in favor of power, the further they strayed from the divine and the truths of the universe. Religion is not a creation of the divine, of nature, of the cosmos. Religion is nothing but a societal creation that has been developed and warped over time to manipulate and control others through the misrepresentation of divine figures. It is the closed-minded, trapped, and corrupted souls that created division in the name of religion. Those who fought to prove themselves right, to damn those who disagreed, to redefine the reason a hierarchy had been established in the first place...*they* are the ones who turned the divine into categories that could be falsified or validated, denied or accepted."

Silence hangs between us as Aiden gives me time to process everything he just unloaded on me.

"So...the gods and figures of all the belief systems exist or once existed? Even those of the Greek, Norse, and Egyptian pantheons..." Even though my words trail into silence, I know Aiden can tell that the list continues to prattle on in my head.

"Precisely. They all exist or existed at one time, as we do now." That smile returns, as does the full light in his eyes with this revelation; it drops only for a moment as he adds in a single breath, "Except for some that I won't name, that were definitely made up by psychotic individuals who wanted a creative way to exploit people for money and grant themselves immunity from taxes. You know who they are."

We both laugh at this, and I roll my eyes as I think back to all the documentaries I used to binge-watch on the exact groups I know he is referring to. I was always shocked that people actually believed in such things. It took time for me to understand it's a slippery slope you can suddenly find yourself accidentally careening down; the mind is so fragile and easily manipulated. Aiden's explanations make me better understand how time can alter what our minds decide is true and how just the slightest misunderstanding or change of phrases can lead everyone further away from the actual truth.

"What people need to understand is that *we* wrote the stories that we are told to believe. *We* decided on the facts based on discovered ancient artifacts, manuscripts, artwork, and more. Those stories once held some, but probably never all, of the truth, but the combination of time and human interpretation and translation gradually altered and even obliterated the initial facts—just as easily as a phrase can be altered in a game of telephone."

Aiden's comparison of the history of all things divine and sacred to a game of telephone strikes something in me that sparks a bit of rage. Not because of how ridiculous it sounds, but because of how simple and blatantly true it is. Of course, what we've come to know throughout time has been altered. How could it not be when you look at it through a lens as simple as that of a child's game? A game that has proven time and again just how easy it is for words to be misheard and retold differently. There's always that one kid who changes the phrase on purpose, just because they can. In a game, that behavior is funny or entertaining. In life, it causes problems, creates belief in false claims, results in the loss of information, and can even result in war or civil discord.

"Our mind, body, and soul—three separate things—create what we are as a whole. The body eventually dies, as it's only meant to be a temporary vessel for our soul, which is made of energy, to call home. The mind, however, is just as important as the soul. It is what gives us consciousness. And as you know…the mind is both powerful and fragile. It doesn't take much for it to be swayed one way or another, which leaves the soul at its mercy."

Aiden's words cause the little hairs on my body to stand on end. "All it takes to get to someone's very soul is to break their mind," I say, sharing the thought that sends a freezing shiver up and down my spine.

CHAPTER 30
AIDEN

I'm seconds away from standing up from my uncomfortable position; my body is cramping from sitting in too small a space for such a long conversation. Leaning forward to help reposition my limbs so that I can slide off the window seat to stand, I'm stopped first by Mercy's voice and then by the sight of her beautiful eyes shining brighter than I have ever seen them before, transformed by curiosity. I notice the tip of her nose is pink from the chill that has settled over the house, now that the once-steady sunlight filtering through the window has been blocked by clouds. I then feast my eyes on the dusting of freckles across her face; they remind me of the same stars we are talking about, the ones that light the night sky. Her full lips, just inches from mine, now parting to ask a question, elicit a flood of memories. This very face has haunted my dreams since I scooped her up, bloodied and bruised, weeks ago.

Frozen, I look at the woman in front of me. The sun's light filtering through the window once more creates a halo effect, bathing her in a heavenly glow. I'm overwhelmed by a need to worship her, offer her my praises and devotion, and beg her to be with me. My heart pounds in my chest as if it's calling—screaming—for her heart to hear my own's song. A song that has only ever been meant to be sung to her. A song made of lyrics, somehow forgotten for so long, now creeping back to the forefront of my memories and reminding me of who this woman has always been to me, lifetime after lifetime. My heartbeat thunders, and I can hear it ringing in my ears, begging to be heard by Mercy. Begging to be remembered, even though it's all still foggy in my mind—nevertheless, the images of our past lives together get clearer each day I spend with her.

"Where are they now? The divine? Where have they gone?"

Her questions snap me out of my trance. I release my gaze, which has been trained on her lips, and meet her eyes. I sit back in the same cramped position I had been trying to escape before becoming paralyzed by the sight of Mercy glowing in the sun's light and the memories that image unveils.

"They are still here. They are still with us when they need to be, or feel they need to be," I start to explain, and then it hits me—we are close to the point that I have to tell her what all this time I've wanted to share, but have not for lacking of knowing how.

"How so?" she asks, tilting her head to the side and narrowing her eyes. I know she's readying herself to call me on any bullshit, as if she knows I'm about to tell her that they can, and will, walk amongst us.

On an exhale, I offer Mercy a soft smile in hopes that it will comfort her as she hears what I'm about to say. "Just like when our souls have tired of their earthly forms, they leave this realm of existence that you and I are in currently. Most souls will return to the other side and continue their cycle of reincarnation until enlightenment is reached. On the rare occasion when a soul has reached the ultimate state of heightened awareness to the truths of the universe, they are then faced with a choice to make. One choice is to remain in their karmic cycle, choosing the path of reincarnation throughout eternity—many prophetic souls choose this route. The other choice is a bit more sacrificial; that's why it is only chosen by a select few."

Orthus startles both of us as he places his large head in Mercy's lap, having crept on silent paws to the window seat.

Good. She's going to need some sort of emotional support after I finish explaining this.

Orthus flicks one of his pointed ears in my direction, and in that moment, I realize how important it is that Mercy know this truth, not just for her, but for him as well. Orthus was instrumental in revealing who Mercy truly is. It was made abundantly clear—and I overlooked it—the day she saved his life and unknowingly rediscovered an eternal bond he's since been keenly aware of. The hound of Helheim knew he had finally been reunited with his forgotten queen.

"Sacrificial?" The disturbed look on Mercy's face as she questions my remark makes me all the more relieved to have Orthus here by her side.

With a dip of my chin, I continue and try to explain, in the best way possible, how this other choice is as much a gift as it is a sacrifice. "To end your cycle as a physical form by returning to a state of pure energy, as a star, is a sacrificial choice. With this option, there are two ways for the soul's freed energy to continue to exist. Once the energy is transformed from flesh and bone to star form, it continues to exist until the balance of the inward pressure against its own dense gravity is threatened and inevitably collapses. The collapse of the star will result in an explosion. The explosion can be significant enough to form a black hole—as we discussed earlier this morning—that, in turn, will create more galaxies, continuing cosmic expansion.

"The other possibility, however, is a supernova explosion in which the star's particles are blown away and only the core of that star remains. Remember, the core of the star is the energy of the soul. This new state of existence after the supernova explosion is scientifically known as a pulsar. No new galaxy is formed; the universe does not expand. Instead, the energy remains within its current galaxy as a timekeeper."

The fact that Mercy hasn't had a mental breakdown yet, even with all this information being thrown at her, gives me hope that the ultimate revelation I'm about to hit her with won't totally dismantle her. I'm not sure there is a pill to help with that.

"A *timekeeper*?"

I pause after her question, anticipating what her reaction will be when I tell her what a timekeeper is *and* how it relates to her. *Fuck. Well, here goes nothing…*

"Pulsars act as cosmic lighthouses. Each beam of light pointed towards the Earth gives us a way to keep track of the universe's history by keeping track of its time. These timekeepers…*they* are the gods, goddesses…the divine you asked about. We look up to the sky, unaware that deep down it's simply our soul in search of guidance from those who came before. I mean, who better to seek help from than those who bear the infinite weight of the knowledge that is the universe's truth?"

I watch Orthus, with his nose, nudge Mercy's hand, which she lifts to scratch behind his ear. The action seems disconnected from her mind, which I can tell is spiraling in an attempt to organize and understand all that she's been told.

Before her mind has a chance to disassociate, I decide to fuck with it all; there is no better time than now to let the cat out of the bag. When I see her fingers slow in the rhythm of stroking her hound's black fur, I blurt out, "There's one other thing that I should mention."

"Oh?" she asks timidly.

I close my eyes for one final moment before ripping away the blissful ignorance that Mercy has lived in her entire life, knowing I'm about to turn her whole world upside down. As my eyes flicker open, I don't think as I prepare to shove her into the deep end in hopes that all I've told her so far is enough to keep her from drowning.

"As timekeepers, part of their responsibility in ensuring the continuation of time is to assist in maintaining balance and cosmic expansion. Timekeepers need a way to observe and continue sharing their knowledge and wisdom, with those who work their way through their karmic cycles, in hopes of keeping the universe on the right track. They need a way to stay connected to everything; that involves doing more than just pulsing light at those who look up. A more hands-on approach, so to speak."

Mercy remains silent, but appears calmer and more with it than she was seconds ago. She returns her fingers to Orthus's fur and twirls black tufts around them.

And with that slight observation—that I have her attention and she hasn't gone catatonic—I shove her into the deep end and pray that she swims. "*So*," I start, clapping my hands together and putting a bit more oomph behind the word than necessary, "the vessels—the minds and bodies—of some chosen individuals who appear sporadically throughout civilization serve as home to not just one soul… but two. By sharing a single vessel, the divine has the ability to take over, so to speak, during times when their intervention is needed."

She cocks her head to the side before asking, "Why must they share a vessel with another soul on Earth? They are timekeepers. They are *the* actual *divine*, for fuck's sake. They don't have the ability to manifest their own earthly form, or whatever?"

"Remember? The sacrifice of choosing to break free from the karmic cycle of reincarnation upon enlightenment is giving up a planetary vessel for all of eternity. Being constrained to a vessel limits the ability of what energy in its purest form can accomplish and threatens the balance of nature. When the choice to stop reincarnating is made, the soul is choosing to uphold the balance of the universe over living amongst humanity. Even for the divine, there is a give-and-take," I remind her.

"So… I'm going to use Jesus as an example, to try and wrap my head around what you're telling me. He's the first one to pop to mind, having been raised Catholic. He is divine, but walked the earth in actual form. That form held both Jesus, the divine, and…some poor bastard who had no choice in the matter?"

"Mm-hmm." *Oh boy, this is going to be fun when she figures it all out.*

She snorts and laughs, trying to mask the weight and discomfort of this newly discovered information. "So there really are people out there who speak the word of the divine…and most of us are reporting them to the loony bin?"

"To be fair, it only happens on rare occasions, this sharing of vessels. Most people that believe themselves to be speaking the word of whatever god they believe themselves to be communicating with do actually need, at the very least, a good therapist…an intervention…rehab—" Before I can continue, my rambling is brought to a halt by Mercy asking the question that, when answered, will determine if she sinks or swims.

"How would we even know? How would a person know they share a body with another a soul? A divine soul?"

Please. Please. Swim.

"Mercy?"

"Aiden...?"

Swim, Mercy. Flail, kick, do whatever you need to do to keep your head above water. I beg of you.

"Have you felt anything different lately? Seen anything different? About yourself...within yourself? Maybe think about that other voice inside your head..."

She's quiet for a long minute before breaking into laughter. "Okay, okay. I see where you are going with this. You're funny. I have anxiety and depression and a whole bunch of other shit going on in here...not some divine entity."

My lips pull into a tight line. As my head subtly nods up and down, I mumble, "I would argue otherwise."

There's a bit of back-and-forth that proceeds between us. She is in complete denial, and I am trying to convince her that what I've told her is true. It's not until we revisit the memory of the Ouija-board fiasco, the visions that flooded her memory during our kiss, and her revelation to me of what she saw while looking at herself in the mirror that she finally allows things to add up and considers the possibility that what I've been telling her is true—she is one with a goddess of the underworld.

"It's true. You are both Mercy and Hel."

CHAPTER 31
MERCY

Ever since our conversation, I've been keeping myself busy by making sure Aiden is ready for his exhibit tomorrow. No matter how many checklists I go over and rewrite, it's still not enough to completely distract my mind from spiraling down the newest rabbit hole that Aiden dug for me. At this point, I have so many things going on in my life that if I don't distract myself, I'm going to go numb—which might sound lovely for a person who feels everything all at once, every day, but trust me when I say…it's not.

"We don't need another checklist, Mercy. The museum already has my pieces that will be on display, and I've already rechecked that the room in which they'll be installed is assembled correctly. Just relax. Take Orthus for a walk or something," Aiden tells me in passing while I sit at his drafting table surrounded by discarded, balled-up pieces of paper I've written and scribbled all over.

He walks over to where I sit and squats down to reach into a drawer where he has stashed the rolled-up star map that he's been meaning to take down to his father. What his father then does with all those maps is still a mystery to me—even with everything that I know now.

Sitting on the stool with him below me, I look down at the crown of loose curls level with my knee, and all I can think about doing is reaching down and running my fingers through them. Before my intrusive thoughts take over and my fingers bury themselves in the rich dark-brown tendrils of his hair, I'm struck with a twisting sensation in my gut as he places his hand on top of my thigh and squeezes gently.

He turns his head to look at me, green eyes shining. "And don't worry about the alcohol. That's already taken care of. Open bar for the night." He winks, his hand still on my thigh as he gently presses down to assist his standing back up.

Between the chaos running rampant in my brain and the lingering sensation of his hand's weight on my thigh, I can't stop myself from fidgeting with a piece of crumpled-up paper that litters the top of the drafting table. "There must be something left I can do to help."

"I promise you, there isn't anything left for you to fixate on or micromanage." He shrugs. "Why don't you take Orthus for a walk or something? I have to take this down to dear ol' dad, anyway."

"Don't you remember? I'm living with you because there are two men still not accounted for that want to kidnap me for some stupid reason," I remind him while resting my chin in my hand and blowing out air to scatter the loose strands of hair that have fallen in front of my eyes.

"Right. To think, I started to forget all about that and had begun thinking how incredibly relentless squatters are nowadays." He shoots me a look and then cracks a sly smile at my expense.

"Dick," I mutter at him, lifting the only finger I'll ever lift for another man again.

He chuckles at the flip-off. "What if you and Tess take Orthus and go into town to pick out something to wear for tomorrow's event? I'm sure you will be safe in a public space, especially with Orthus and Tess right by your side," he suggests, leaning back against the drafting table so that I'm no longer looking down at him. "Well...mainly Orthus for safety. Tess will be there for the much-needed socializing you've been lacking and needing."

It's actually not a bad idea, especially considering that I don't have anything to wear for the opening of his solo art exhibit. I'm pretty sure it's an event that requires attire a step or two above my nicest jeans paired with a flattering blouse. Considering the tux I saw hanging in the studio earlier, I think a shopping trip is necessary.

"I could do that. I probably *should* do that," I admit sheepishly. "While I wait to hear back from Tess, though, I could just go with you and finally see this observatory you promised to show me last night, but conveniently weren't able to." I flutter my lashes and throw him a mocking grin.

"I told you, something came up that made it impossible to go down below last night. Hopefully tonight, though, we will be able to."

"Fine. I'll hold you to it, then." I slide off the stool and call out to Orthus, "Be ready in twenty minutes, Orthus! You, Tess, and I have some shopping to do." I have no clue where in the house he is, but I'm clued in slightly when I hear him respond with a dramatic huff.

CHAPTER 32
MERCY

"There is no way in hell they are letting that beast into the boutique, Mercy."

Tess and I sit in her car, which is parked in front of one of the handful of boutiques in town. Normally, we would have gone into the city or the nearest mall to shop, but we figured it would be smart to stay closer to home, with all that is happening and still unknown.

"I said the same thing to Aiden once I realized any high-end shop owner would probably faint at the sight of their expensive dresses being in the same room as an extremely large, furry dog whose black fur spreads like glitter."

"And what did he say to that?"

We simultaneously open our doors and climb out of Tess's small car. When I go to open his door, I can't help but chuckle at the sight of Orthus crammed into the back seat.

"He handed me his credit card. Told me to buy myself and you"—I point to Tess and close the car door, making sure it's locked—"whatever expensive dresses our hearts desire. His

299

argument being that they won't turn down customers who show up with a black card and no spending limit."

Tess's face is just visible over the roof of the car. Her eyes pop out of her head, and her jaw hangs slack when I flash her the credit card Aiden shoved into my pocket before we left. A smile slowly spreads across her face in shocked delight, and I know we won't be leaving the boutique until she has had both of us try on every single dress they have to offer. The shopkeepers will be worried about Orthus causing chaos in the store, but in reality, Tess is the one they should really be worried about. If only they had seen what my bedroom looked like after she went through my closet to help pack a bag for my stay at Aiden's.

"How on earth does he have a black card?" she asks, linking arms with me as we make our way down the street to the boutique's entrance. "He's an artist. A very alive one, at that. I thought art wasn't worth much unless you were already famous…or dead."

I ignore the very true—yet still hard to swallow—joke, thinking back to my time in marketing, creating designs for advertisements instead of for pleasure and meaning. Bills had to be paid, and being a starving artist until the day I died wasn't something I was interested in doing—still isn't. Inevitably, reality set in; my childhood dream of creating meaningful and inspiring art for a living died, and I sold my soul to capitalism and aided in the manipulation of consumers, convincing them they needed to buy whatever bullshit product was new on the market. So, yeah, I get where she is coming from with her remark. Doesn't make it sting any less, though.

"Apparently, he's just one of the lucky ones to have gotten noticed early in his career." I shrug. My gaze remains fixed forward to give no hint that I know it's not just his art that's responsible for his wealth. It's also the many lifetimes he's had to fine-tune his financial-planning skills from past experiences. Perhaps, he even has some secret bank account he's been adding his money to throughout each lifetime. Maybe he sells collectible tchotchkes he's tucked away to sell once enough time has gone by and they're considered ancient artifacts that have skyrocketed in value over time. Hell, the reasoning behind his wealth could be a combination of all of the above.

All I know is that it will be easier for Tess to accept he earned his money as a hit man, rather than by using the knowledge he gained during multiple reincarnations. So I avoid explaining any further.

"However it is that he makes his money, who am I to question it when he's being so generous." Tess looks at me with a devious grin that I return with a playful nudge of my shoulder and a laugh.

The bells dangling above the door jingle when we step into the immaculately clean, blindingly white boutique. Two employees distracted by their phones extend their welcome in our direction, but are immediately brought to attention by the *click-clack* of Orthus's nails against the tiled floor, which is clean enough that it could be used as a mirror.

Before they are able to tell us to fuck off, I whip out Aiden's credit card and wave it at them. "We are here to do a bit of damage to"—I inwardly cringe—"my boyfriend's credit card."

The two employees glance at each other, clearly having a silent debate on whether to allow us in any farther or to tell us to shove the credit card up our asses and leave with our beast of a dog in tow.

"He forgot their anniversary and is making up for it by giving Mercy his card with no spending limit!" Tess abruptly shouts into the silence, adding to my lie.

As soon as the two employees hear the words "no spending limit" blurted from Tess's mouth, their demeanors change, and they wave for us to join them at the back of the store, where the most expensive dresses are kept.

Tess practically drags me along, as I'm apparently not moving quick enough for her. She buzzes with impatient excitement, itching to try on dresses and spend Aiden's money.

Risking tripping over my feet, I glance back at Orthus, who is very carefully following us to the back of the store, fully aware of his size and the simple fact that he doesn't belong in such a place. I offer him a smile, hoping he reads it to be one of appreciation, not pity—even though I do pity him for being forced to be my guardian.

When we find ourselves surrounded by beautiful dresses, Orthus finds himself the only empty space available and curls up into the tiniest ball he can manage. I wish I could tell him we won't be long, but Tess hands me one of the two glasses of champagne we were offered, so all I can offer him is an apologetic pat on the head.

CHAPTER 33
MERCY

By the end of our visit to the boutique, even Orthus has won the employees over with his polite behavior, which earns him a light-blue ribbon they tie in a perfect bow around his neck. They even gush over how handsome he looks with it on and how it brings out the "exquisite uniqueness" of his two-toned eyes. I have to bite back laughter, knowing he is doing all he can to refrain from snapping at the hands responsible for adorning the hound of Hel with a whimsical bow.

Later, after spending some ungodly amount of money, Tess and I walk the path to Aiden's front door. Tess still has a bounce in her step, elated by the dresses she picked out for both of us. My dress is gold to bring warmth to my pale complexion; it is complete with an open back that exposes the lunar-cycle tattoo that is intricately inked down my spine. Tess's is a pale-green tint of silver that makes her hazel eyes pop and hugs every curve of her hourglass figure.

I open the door to allow the three of us to enter and am not surprised to catch Aiden walking out of his study. Orthus shoves past Tess and me, head low in embarrassment, his paws stomping across the symbol of the ornate witch's knot inlaid on the floor.

"Nice bow," Aiden tells him, eliciting a soft growl and side-eye in return.

Once Orthus has disappeared into the other room, Aiden snaps his eyes in my direction and proceeds to scan me up and down. He crosses his arms over his chest, and there's a sense of relief and lingering tension in the stance that makes me wonder if he's pissed that Tess and I—mainly Tess—took his offer of having no spending limit too literally.

"That was…not quick at all, actually."

Taken aback by the edge in his voice, I retort, "I didn't think I needed to rush back anytime soon. You told me there was nothing left for me to help with."

Tess stands by my side, not awkwardly like a normal person, but instead invested in the drama unfolding in front of her. All she is missing is a bowl of buttery popcorn.

"As you mentioned before you left, there are still two idiots out there—no thanks to *Officer Johnny Boy*"—he says the name with intended annoyance—"who want to get their grimy hands on you for some reason we still don't know."

Was he worried about…me?

"Which is why we took poor Orthus along with us, remember? To be our guard dog on the slight chance we ran into said idiots." I would be crossing my arms were it not for the dress carefully draped over them. So, instead, I'm confined to expressing any sort of irritation by narrowing my eyes and angling my head.

"All I'm saying is you could have sent a simple text telling me you'd be home late."

My chest tightens at his choice—or, most likely, it was a slip of the tongue—of the word "home," as this is *not* my home. I know the word didn't slip past Tess, either, as I hear her softly choke on the invisible popcorn I imagine her to be eating. My shoulders and chin drop slightly as I realize we were out for a few hours, and I hadn't once sent Aiden a message to let him know we were fine.

I can't be upset. If our roles had been reversed, I would have wanted to hear from him. No, not him. Tess or Henry, sure. How can I be worried about someone I wouldn't have met had it not been for those stupid idiots chasing me in the first place?

"I'm sorry."

Before Tess is able to unleash her inner feminist to tell me I don't owe anyone an apology, Aiden beats her to the punch. "Don't be sorry. There is nothing for you to be sorry for. I didn't ask you to check in with me. I'm not your keeper. I just…started to get worried." His arms fall from their crossed position, and he drags one hand through his hair before shoving both hands into his pockets. "I'm sorry for overreacting."

Tess's mouth shuts into a tight line as she shifts her eyes between Aiden and me.

"Don't be sorry." I offer him an empathetic smile, understanding more than some how it feels to worry.

"Well, on that note," Tess pipes up, clapping her hands together and startling us from the silent, shared moment of understanding, "I just wanted to stop in to thank you for the generous donation to my ever-growing closet before heading back to give Henry a private showing of how sexy I look in my dress." She winks at me.

Aiden's facial features soften, and he walks over to take the dress and hang it alongside his tux in the study. With careful hands, he plucks the golden silk from my arms while offering Tess a smile. "My pleasure, Tess. I'm happy you were able to accompany Mercy and get her to leave home for a bit. And I appreciate that you and Henry are coming tomorrow."

There it is again. Home.

When he turns to leave us to our goodbyes, after offering Tess one final smile, I follow her the couple of steps to the front door. We hug and go over our plans for the next day, deciding on the time she and Henry will be picking me up to carpool to the event. I have no plans of hopping on Aiden's crotch rocket in a dress or shoving a helmet over whatever I manage to do with my hair. He needs to be at the museum an hour before the exhibit starts, anyway.

"Henry and I will pick you up tomorrow around six thirtyish."

"Thanks, Tess. I'll see you guys then. Love you."

She squeezes my hand before walking to her car. "Love you, too."

I watch until she's halfway in her car, at which point she pauses to whip her head around and give me a shit-eating grin. "If you need a ride *home* tomorrow, we can give you a ride back here afterwards."

With a roll of my eyes, I gently bang my head against the door, and she laughs while climbing the rest of the way into her car.

CHAPTER 34
AIDEN

I need to make up for overstepping earlier. Just because I offered Mercy my house and protection, doesn't mean I'm allowed to keep tabs on her and be upset when she doesn't update me on her every move. As I told her, I am not her keeper. I am not her master. I am... Well, I am *someone* to her, but even this, she hasn't realized yet. Even *I* have holes in my memory as to how we knew each other in our past lives. The only thing I do know for certain is that, throughout each lifetime, Mercy has always been there; she's always meant something to me. I recognize now the sad song my soul has sung for so long, from one life to the next. Begging to be understood. Begging to be heard. It's finally found the audience for whom it had been longing, only to be gut-punched when the pleading lyrics fall on deaf ears.

I find Mercy where I knew I would, nose buried in a book, tucked into the corner of the window seat in the living room. Blankets form a cocoon around her petite body, making her look like some fragile porcelain doll wrapped in bubble wrap. Looks are deceiving, though. I'm aware of the soul within. Aware of the fire itching to be ignited in her bones. Aware of the strength she denies she has, the power she wields—and I'm not talking about the portion shared by Hel.

A tail pokes out from under the blanket, swishing violently the closer I come. *Sorry, Void, but I'm absolutely going to interrupt your snuggle time with Mercy.*

Alerted by the growling monster wrapped around her feet, Mercy lifts her eyes from the pages and meets mine. "What's up?" she asks, her voice quiet and sleepy from a long day out with Tess.

"Dad's locked himself in his study, working on whatever the fuck he's working on that doesn't have anything to do with what he's supposed to be doing."

My words cause Mercy to close the book and set it down beside her. Her eyes flicker to hopeful-anticipation of the intrigue hinted at by my words. "Oh?"

"I figured there isn't a better time than now to sneak you back down into my creepy dungeon to show you the observatory."

She eyes me, clearly still unable to believe that portion of what I revealed. "Have you ever been to Plymouth Rock in Massachusetts?" she asks, completely throwing me off.

"Huh?"

"There's this rock in Plymouth that people will go to visit because it supposedly marks where the Pilgrims got off the Mayflower and symbolizes the founding of a new nation."

I stare at her blankly. "What the fuck does that have to do with the observatory?"

"I remember the first time I visited it on a school trip. The entire class and I were expecting this larger-than-life monument or some sort of incredible sight. The second we were allowed off the bus, we ran over to where this momentous rock was said to be. To say we were greatly disappointed in what we finally saw would be an understatement."

Again, I stare at Mercy blankly, waiting for her to get to the point.

"What we were expecting to see turned out to be nothing more than a rock barely big enough to sit two or three of us kids. Extremely underwhelming and not nearly as interesting as we had all imagined it to be."

I'm about to ask her why she brings this up when she asks, "I feel like this observatory is going to be the equivalent of Plymouth Rock—overrated or simply just not what I'm imagining it to be. So…are you taking me to your version of Plymouth Rock, Aiden?"

Arms crossed over my chest, I smirk down at her. "How about I show you, and then you can tell me if it is or not?"

"All right, then. Back down to the creepy dungeon, it is."

The blankets that had been wrapped around her are now being tossed into the opposite corner of the window seat. Still warm from her body, Void pounces on the pile of fabric and circles until he plops himself down and curls into a ball of fur, whiskers, and claws.

"Follow me," I say, grabbing Mercy's hand without thinking and flashing her a knowing smile. I'm about to show her something that will indeed live up to the hype.

Despite everything I have told her, I can still see the skepticism in her eyes. Even after watching me unlock the nuummite door with blood-inked runes…after feeling the difference in atmosphere when stepping into the liminal space...and after seeing the carvings along the spiraling hallway's walls...the skepticism is still there. For the time being.

A soft gasp has me looking over my shoulder and questioning the cause for her reaction. The reflection of twinkling stars in her eyes gives me an answer before I even have to ask; I know the visual impact of the window's celestial beauty. No matter how many lives I have lived, even I can admit that the view never gets old; it always steals the breath from anyone lucky enough to stand before it.

"I could sit in front of this screen for hours every day and just stare." Mercy's voice is quiet and awestruck. She walks closer to the window so that she stands perfectly in the center of it. The stars react to the sight of her; just as they did the last time she was down here, they shine brighter and create an aura of starlight around her silhouette. I stay back for a few minutes to give her time to bask in the glory of the universe's light show. The growing brightness of the stars that dance around her, their flickers outlining her figure, cast her in a dark shadow edged with bursting starlight. The vision is emblazoned in my mind for the next time I pick up my pen to ink something worthy of creating.

After a minute or so has ticked by, I stroll up to stand next to her. I'm quiet for a few breaths, enjoying the quiet moment and the view. Eventually, I redirect my gaze to look at Mercy, and I smile as her eyes meet mine. I allow myself a moment to gaze at the constellation of freckles scattered across her face.

"Would you believe me if I told you that this isn't a monitor hooked up to a computer and satellites somewhere?"

"Are you about to tell me that this is some sort of magical window that allows its viewers a glimpse into the cosmos?" She snorts and turns back to continue taking in the view.

"Magical window. Portal. Whatever you might want to call it. What it's *not*, though, is some sort of monitor connected to a satellite far off in space that is sending back images."

Mercy crosses her arms over her chest, and I'm ready for her retort, denial, or accusation about thinking she's gullible. Instead, I'm met with silence as she thinks about whatever it is she is about to ask or tell me.

"Is it always the same view?"

That was not the question I had been anticipating. I can't tell whether or not she believes me, but I answer anyway. "No, it changes depending on who is standing in front of it. I've come to learn that it shows the observer their soul's location, their home within the universe. That's why the stars that surround you shine a little brighter when you are near the window—like a beacon of light showing you where your soul's home is amongst the other stars."

There is a steadiness in her breathing as her gaze returns to the window, her chest rising and falling in a way that shows she is at peace in this moment. We continue to stare at the stars and the dark abyss they float through, enjoying the quiet view together. I'm at ease until she quirks her head in my direction and hits me with a question I'm unsure how to answer at this time.

"When you walked up beside me…why didn't the view change for you?"

Always so observant. My mind scrambles for a response that isn't "because your home and my home are one and the same." She has to figure that part out on her own. I'm still figuring it out, too, albeit just a bit quicker than she is. It helps that I already know much that she does not.

There's a clattering of instruments against tiled floor that echoes down one of the three spiraling hallways, and I'm grateful for the distraction. "Sounds like Leo is still tinkering with whatever the fuck it is he's piecing together. As much as I would love to stand here all day and just stare, I think we should hurry along so I can actually show you what we came down here to see."

"Leo?" She arches her brow at me.

"I call him by his first name, instead of Dad, when he annoys me. Let's go." I grab her hand and pull her along at a brisk walk, leading her to the Observatory of Souls.

CHAPTER 35
MERCY

The hallway I'm led down is darker than the one we entered through. A subtle chill winds its way through my body the farther along we travel, and I start to regret my incessant pushing to see this hidden space I still can't believe is real. That doubt, however, starts to vanish when I stop in my tracks after catching sight of a grand arched opening that marks the end of the spiraling hallway.

My gaze is drawn up to the keystone, which is a stone carving of a genderless face that seems both alive and dead at the same time. The eye on one side is sculpted like that of a bust from Ancient Greece; the other, hollowed out like a skull. One side depicts a facial structure of plump flesh and youth; the other has chiseled-out areas, with hints of exposed mandible and cheekbone, to show decay. As horrifying as the image is, I'd be lying if I said it wasn't hauntingly beautiful.

I'm not sure how long I stand still, my eyes transfixed by the keystone, but it is apparently long enough that I do not realize Aiden has left my side. Standing the twenty or so feet in front of me, beneath the stone archway, I hear him clear his throat to grab my attention. Behind him shines a subtle glow of light that's not warm and bright enough to be from the sun, but also not the cold of a full moon's soft-white light. It's the light of a time that's perfectly balanced. A time of somewhere in between.

"Coming?" He reaches out his hand.

I fill my lungs with the cool air that flows through the halls, and before I'm able to second-guess my decision and turn to flee back to the safety of the known world up top, my feet move of their own accord, closing the distance between us. My hand slides into Aiden's as if it were something that happens routinely and with the same amount of thought that's needed for breathing. The little hairs on my arms stand on end, not from the feeling of his skin against mine, but from the sudden wave of anticipation that washes over me. But then I remember that the world up top is not safe for me, anyway. So I let Aiden lead me the rest of the way and leave all worry behind.

Once through the archway, we find ourselves in a ginormous cylindrical room, empty except for the limestone podium that stands at its center. One look around the expansive space and I'm overwhelmed by the detail in the intricate carvings that cover the stone pillars that create a rib cage of sorts to support the domed space. In between the pillars are calcite walls, smooth and blank, so white that they brighten the space enough to make me forget for a moment that we are underground, deep beneath Aiden's house.

I'm given time to walk around the space and take in my surroundings. My mind tries to comprehend the imagery carved into the stone pillars and arches that reach from the floor, made of a black marble scattered with veins of gold and blue, to the breathtaking gold-plated ceiling high above.

After a few laps around the room, I believe I have figured out the meaning behind the carvings and the story they intend to tell.

"Definitely not like Plymouth Rock, I'll give you that." My voice echoes throughout the domed space. I'm not yet ready to take my eyes off the imagery carved into stone before me, but I ask Aiden, "This is the proof, though, right? The description of what the other side looks like?" I turn to look over my shoulder at Aiden, who is standing with his hand hovering over a gold slab that sits atop the limestone podium that's anchored in the center of the cavernous space.

"You really thought I dragged you down here to show you my version of Plymouth Rock, didn't you?" His eyes light up, and he smirks at me as he slams the palm of his hand on top of the gold slab.

The room around us comes to life as visual images bloom and are projected onto the calcite walls. I stumble back a few steps, and my jaw goes slack as I take in the same scenery I have seen only two times before—the first time when Aiden kissed me and the second time that same night in a dream.

"This…is my proof," he croons in a voice that drips of milk and honey.

As if I'm peering through the eyes of a bird flying high in the sky, the visuals before me swoop through a land that should not seem familiar to me at all, but it does. Tears begin to well up, and I fight to blink them back, unsure of why they started in the first place. I see the green hills, open fields, crystal shorelines, and snowcapped mountain ranges. I see the forests I ran through in my dreams and the outlines of figures dancing in the softness of the never-ending twilight's light. I see the rushing waters of the waterfall that veils a set of nature-made stairs I know lead to the entrance of a cave.

And then I see her. I see the ochre eyes of the woman I remember from my dream. The woman whose note found its way to me by way of a messenger cat. Those eyes stare back at me in shock and awe, as if she, too, can see me.

"Hel?" Her voice echoes throughout the open room and is like velvet when it penetrates my ears. Her eyes are wide in shock and lit with a sudden sense of relief and hope.

I'm shaking, but I reach out with my hand to touch her. To feel on my fingers the warmth of her soft caramel skin. To run through the strands of black, silky hair they know they have felt before when braiding those tresses. But instead of a living being, all I feel is the cold, smooth surface of the white-calcite wall. The image flickers the second my fingers lift from it, and there's a stirring behind me.

"Void!" Aiden yells, swiping at the mass of black fur that springs out of nowhere, knocking his hand off the gold slab.

Void responds with a growl and hiss, his ears lying flat against his head while he stares at Aiden. Void becomes a blur as he skitters across the slick marble floor, slipping occasionally, his paw pads not providing enough friction. When he reaches me, he twirls his body around my ankles as if insisting I move. Aiden and I watch him bound towards the open archway; he pauses only for a brief moment to turn and see if we are following.

"I think we might need to go now."

I don't hesitate to grab Aiden's hand and allow him to lead me back through the archway and down the hallway from where we came. When we find our way back to the general living area, Aiden tells me to take Void and wait for him in his study above.

Without asking any questions, I do as I'm told, scooping Void into my arms and hurrying down the spiraling hallway that leads back to the nuummite door.

CHAPTER 36
AIDEN

My pulse has finally evened itself out after closing the heavy door behind me. I'm not sure what induced the spike in my heart rate more, seeing Tarini call out to Mercy—well, Hel—or narrowly avoiding what would have been an unpleasant run-in with my father.

Don't get me wrong; I understand the need for secrecy about his whole domain below my house, but I think a damn-good argument could be made that Mercy, of all people, should be welcomed down there—especially now that I know for certain who she truly is. Had there been any doubt at all before, the last two days and Tarini's recognizing her were more than enough confirmation for me. Still, following their first introduction, I could tell there is something about Mercy that makes my father uncomfortable. Luckily, Mercy did not pick up on it, but I've known my father long enough to read his tells. And there is definitely something that he is not telling me.

When I make it to the open doors of my study, where I told Mercy to wait for me, I find her pacing the length of the room. I know she's had a lot thrown at her, and what just happened in the observatory has clearly done little to calm her nerves.

Keep treading water, Mercy. You haven't gone under yet.

"Everything all right?"

She halts abruptly, head snapping in my direction. The move causes her hair to whip around her shoulders, the pieces that land across her chest accentuating the rise and fall of her distressed breathing. An icy fire erupts in her eyes, and I wince at the glare she gives me.

Right. I suppose, had I been in her position, that would have been an annoying question to have been asked.

"Am I…am I…all right?"

Here we go.

"Oh, Aiden, I don't know…" She laughs a bit maniacally.

Here comes the sarcasm.

"Would you believe me if I told you?"

Oh, she's fired up. Hearing her use my own words to drive the point home, I can't stop the playful smirk that pulls the corner of my mouth to one side, fully aware that it is only going to provoke her more. My chin lifts, as do my eyebrows, and I cross my arms over my chest as I stand in the middle of the doorway.

Let it out, Mercy. Let me have it.

"Ahhh!" Her hands fly up to cover her face and dampen the sound of the yell she can't help but let out. "Would you believe me if I told you that what you just showed me I've seen before?" She's back to pacing again, her words coming out almost in a shout. "Would you believe me if I told you I've met that woman before? That I couldn't help the tears in my eyes from welling up at the sight of a place I swear I have *never* been before, but it calls to me as if it wants me to come home? Would you believe me—"

"Yes." I don't move from where I stand in the doorway, and I don't take my eyes off her.

"Would you believe me," she continues this time in a voice of broken whispers, "if I told you I believe it all?"

This is the toughest part about waking up to a truth that's been buried and hidden for so long. The truth that's always been deep inside our minds, just waiting to be discovered, acknowledged, and understood. It is the part when the soul finally breaks through the mind's barrier, shattering the very walls it had always felt safe behind. It's the moment when the floodgates open, and we have to make a choice to either let the waters drown us or find a way to float.

Mercy's eyes turn glossy, and I'm under her before she collapses to the floor. I scoop her into my arms. There is no choice for her, I've decided. She's going to fucking float.

The fireplace roars in front of us as we sink deeper into the corner of the oversized leather couch. I have her positioned between my legs, my knees bent on either side of her, like a barrier of protection. The back of her head rests between my collarbone and jaw, leaving me to fight the urge to brush away her long blonde hair that continues to get caught in the stubble of my unshaven face. Her body presses against my own, tight enough that I'm aware that her breathing has calmed; she's finally backed her toes away from the tempting edge of the precipice she was inching toward.

"I ask this fully aware that you are positioned in such a manner that could be a detriment to my balls, but"—I brace myself and then gently whisper into her ear—"are you all right?"

I'm met with silence. Not even a twitch of her muscles.

"Mercy?"

"Why me? I am no one...nothing special. Why choose me?" Each word she speaks slowly and quietly. Each word is spoken in a tone of confusion mixed with lack of self-worth.

I take a deep breath before answering, "Believe it or not, there are some things I don't have an answer for." I crack a smile, my cheek resting on the side of her head, hoping some light humor will shake her from falling into a catatonic state.

She pushes air out through her nose in a silent, subtle laugh.

Good. It worked.

"Honestly, though. I'm an absolute train wreck of a mess. I am..."

She inhales heavily.

"I am..."

Another inhale.

"I am broken. Broken in so many ways. Why on earth would a goddess want to share a vessel, a mind...with *me*?"

I don't answer her question directly. Instead, I ask her another. "Have you ever heard of dark matter and dark energy?"

Her head turns to the side, and I can feel her brows furrow against my cheek, clearly wondering where I'm going with this.

"Dark matter is said to make up over eighty percent of all matter in the universe, even though scientists have never been able to actually see it to prove this. They assume it exists to explain the behaviors of stars, planets, and galaxies. They believe it was created from black holes. The Big Bang—the Primordial Black Hole—is thought to be the initial source of all dark matter and all other constituting elements of the universe as we know it today."

She's quiet, and her breathing is even, my brief science lecture clearly taking her mind off the weight that the universe so clearly keeps piling onto her shoulders.

"What's your point?"

"Before I get to my point, let me also tell you about dark energy."

Her body vibrates in a joyless laughter as she tells me, "Oh, trust me, I know all about dark energy."

"So…you know then that it's necessary for the continuing expansion of the universe because it is strong enough to fight the pull of gravity?"

She becomes heavy against me, as if defeated by the information that keeps coming, prompting more questions than supplying answers. I'd be lying, however, if I said I wasn't enjoying the closeness of her body pressed up against mine as a result of her being so overwhelmed.

"I still don't see where you are going with this," she murmurs as she adjusts herself, having just become aware of how much her body has started to melt into mine.

"Unlike the scientists out there, I believe *you* see more than you think you do. See, dark matter and dark energy aren't just out there in space," I begin to explain, "but they are also here with us. With you."

Tentatively, I take her hands in my own and place them over her racing heart and clenched stomach. I refuse to lift my hands off hers as I fight the urge to pull her as close to me as she was a moment ago.

As things seem to connect in her mind, she does her best to twirl her body around between my legs so that she can look me in the eyes as she asks, "You see it, too? The dark cloud?" Her eyes are shining bright and hopeful. Hopeful that she's not alone. Hopeful that she can stop calling herself crazy.

"No, I cannot," I tell her and watch that brightness vanish. "*You* can, though. I know you can. I've seen the look on your face when it makes itself apparent to you, even if it's surrounding others. That's part of Hel's gift. To see things others can't."

"How do I get rid of it?" she asks me.

Her question rips at my heart. As do her eyes as they plead for me to have an answer that will offer her relief from the pain and exhaustion this gift forces her to endure. She is seeking an answer I wish I could give, but I do not have a solution to offer.

"You can't. That dark matter, the dark energy, they are responsible for your emotions, your frustrations, depressions, and anxieties. Everyone has a cloud of dark matter surrounding them. Some just have a bit—or a lot—more than others."

"Fantastic." She frowns.

I laugh gently. "It is, though. It is fantastic because it's what causes us to break. It's what causes us to be vulnerable. To grow. Without it, there is no expansion of us. No expansion of the universe." I don't think as my fingers grab her chin so that she has no choice but to look at me as I tell her, "The perk of being broken, of being vulnerable, of feeling and becoming self-aware is that it only makes you stronger, not weaker like you may think. The only time you are weaker is when you deny yourself these things."

"I don't feel strong, though."

Her whispering voice does something to me; it invokes a raging fire and a need to destroy whatever or whoever is the cause of her self-doubt.

"Hel would argue otherwise." Again, I crack a soft smile, but this time I do so in a show of support. "I think that's why she picked you. I think that's why she has always picked you. I think the more you learn to accept yourself, the wider you allow the door to open for her to come through. The less you fight yourself, the less rigid you become, and the more willing you are to embrace the balance of everything that makes you, *you*, then the more supportive that voice in your head becomes. The stronger you become."

I say, tapping my finger to her temple softly, "Don't underestimate yourself, Mercy. Never underestimate broken things. Everyone is broken in one way or another. It's all about what we do with the shattered pieces of ourselves that matters. Embrace everything; each piece stands for something."

CHAPTER 37
MERCY

We haven't moved from our spot on the couch, and it's getting late. I want to ask what he meant when he told me that she always picks me, but I'm exhausted and not sure I'm ready to dive into that. Not entirely sure what *that* might even entail and how deep it goes. What it might mean about his past lives and my own being somehow connected. Otherwise, how would he know she picks me every time? How does he know *I* am the one every time? It's too much to get into right now, and my body, just as much as my mind, is begging for rest.

"What if I don't want the responsibility that comes with sharing myself with Hel? Can she choose someone else?" I ask him in hopes there is a way out of this mess; I need a simple yes and a promise that we will talk about that later.

I want to lift my head to read his expression when he tells me his answer, but exhaustion weighs heavily on me. Instead, I find myself sandwiched between Aiden and the back of the couch, too tired to reposition myself so that I'm not using him as my personal body pillow.

There is no one else to choose when I am just as much you as you are me.

I jolt at the voice in my head. At Hel in my head. *Our* head.

"Based on that sudden reaction to seemingly nothing, I think she answered that question for you already," Aiden says. He's clearly known all along that the voice I often criticized is more than just the internal demon I've thought it was for so long.

The voice was always a part of me. The voice has always been mine. The voice has always been Hel's. I am Mercy, but I am also Hel.

Aiden's voice is low and quiet as he begins to paint a picture of the other side to try and ease my troubled mind. His words create a montage of beautiful scenery that flashes before my closed eyes, and I find myself drifting off to the lull of his voice. I wonder for a time, before exhaustion finally consumes me, if it's his description that paints such detailed imagery in my mind's eye or if it's my buried and forgotten memories that are now being resurrected from their graves. Those memories now freed, gasping for air, rushing to the surface and vowing to never be buried alive or forgotten again.

In his arms, my body goes limp. My head rests heavily in the crook where his shoulder meets his chest. My breathing steadies. My heart matches the easy rhythm of his, and I allow sleep to take me with the hope for peaceful dreams.

Behind the curtains of the willow tree's branches, I sit and wait, knowing he should be arriving anytime now. It's a bittersweet moment, knowing that his return to me means the end of another life lived. All I can hope for each time is that his end is peaceful and without pain, just as I know he hopes the same for me when my time comes.

My chest tightens, and there's a sudden sharp pain that takes hold of my heart as if it's fighting to beat while strung up by a noose made of barbed wire that tightens with each pulse. The pain increases, taking my breath with it. My eyes roll backward, leaving only the whites to be seen. A death rattle releases from my lungs, and then I feel myself flatline.

One second goes by.

Two seconds.

Three.

"Hello, my sweet shadow."

My eyes don't have a chance to open, and the smile spreading across my face is stopped by the collision of lips I have spent a few too many years longing for. With his forehead pressed to mine, I breathe in his familiar scent, and my eyes flutter open. I allow myself a quiet moment to hold his comforting gaze, reminding myself I will have plenty of time later to get lost and explore in the forest of greenery that are his eyes.

"I've been waiting for you."

"Patiently?" The corner of his mouth quirks upward, revealing his subtle dimple.

"Depends on who you ask." I smile, thinking of Tarini and how she still can't decide if being our third wheel is any better than dealing with my lonely impatience.

One moment, it's my back against the tree; the next, it's his. His hands wrap around my waist and don't let go, positioning me so that I straddle his lap. I reach out and let my fingers dive into his crown of loose curls; I run them rhythmically and repetitively through the soft tendrils. His head arches back in pure enjoyment, eyes closed, and I watch the strong column of his neck bob as he swallows a satisfied moan. I don't stop. I just sit there in his lap, his knees tented behind me for support and to keep me close.

"At least it seemed quick this time. Painful. But quick."

At the sound of my voice, he lifts his head to look in my eyes.

"Heart attack?" I ask, wincing.

He sighs. "I wish you didn't have to feel it, too." He furrows his brow and frowns.

"I welcome the feeling when I am here. Whatever it may be, I know the pain is temporary, and it means we will be reunited soon."

I place a kiss between his brows and turn so that my back presses against him, leaning my head back to rest against his chest. He leans his cheek against the crown of my head, and I can feel my hair get caught in the stubble that contours the strong, angular features of his face. We sit like that for a long time, melting into each other's body. Two lonely pieces finally placed back together again.

"I'm not sure how we can tempt fate to do so, but it would certainly be more convenient for us if we could simply pass on together, at the same time each go-around." He groans, which breaks the comfortable silence we have settled into.

"I know. I find comfort in telling myself that time apart helps to make the love grow stronger." I chuckle. "At least, this time around it was only three years we had to be apart, not a whole decade like last time."

He presses his lips to the top of my head, and I feel them part as he mumbles, "Always putting the positive spin on things."

"Someone has to," I say, smiling up at him.

"Oh, my darling Hel. How I missed you." He pulls me in tighter, and I let him, encourage him. "Perhaps, we'll stay here a little longer this time around—not that it's entirely up to us. I think we've earned it, though."

"Whether it's here or there, so long as we are together, I won't complain," I say, adding to his sentiment, as if putting the thought out into the atmosphere could alter our fates.

"Who is going to listen even if you do complain?" he jokes, his body vibrating with gentle laughter.

I teasingly jab him in the stomach with my elbow. "Good thing you're here, then."

"Oh, I see. So that's all I'm good for? To listen to your complaints?"

"Of course not! You're good for other things, too." With a wink, I pop to my feet, grab his hand, and pull him through the cascade of flowing branches of the willow tree.

CHAPTER 38
MERCY

Early-morning sunlight eases me awake, and I find myself comfortably wedged between Aiden and the back of the couch. My head and hand rest on his chest. One leg is draped across his midsection, held there by his hand gripping my thigh. The steady rise and fall of his chest beneath my hand and cheek let me know he's still sleeping. If I move, I will wake him.

Were this the first time I woke up with my face pressed against his chest—back when he was still somewhat of a stranger to me—I most certainly would have moved. Would have wiggled my way out of his grip. But then I remember that, even that first time it happened, I did not extricate myself from the situation I found myself in. So I check to make sure I hadn't drooled on Aiden while I slept, and then I remain exactly as I am. Comfortable. Safe. Peaceful.

I'm not surprised that I have awakened where I am, or that we never woke in the middle of the night to move to separate beds. After everything that happened yesterday, my mind wasn't going to let me simply go to bed and sleep or be at ease if left alone all night.

Alone?

I jerk at the voice in my head. *Right. Not actually alone.*

I don't hear but feel the voice smile in appreciation of my acknowledgment.

I'm insane. Aren't I?

If you are, then so am I.

This makes no sense.

Oh, but it does.

Care to explain?

Think of the trinity.

What? Like the Father, Son, and Holy Ghost?

I'm thinking more along the lines of a triple goddess—the Mother, Maiden, and Crone. But yes, that trinity works, too. One goddess or god. Three aspects or faces that together represent the one as a whole. You, Mercy, being the Maiden. I, Hel, being the Mother. The universe being the Crone. Those three aspects together make us whole. Make it impossible to be one without the other.

So…I haven't been talking and fighting with myself this whole time? You're the one I've been arguing with?

Oh no, you have. I am you, and you are me. So in a sense, you have battling yourself this entire time. It's truly exhausting, if I'm being honest. But you know that already. One day, hopefully, you'll stop seeing me as separate from you and instead as part of you. Part of us. Part of me.

I understand…and I don't.

Some things are just better left embraced instead of understood. Just embrace it. Embrace us. Realize you've always been whole, even when you felt you were not. Know that you have always been enough. Release yourself from this war you've created against an enemy that exists only because you let it. Stop being your own worst enemy.

A low-grade migraine starts to work its way behind one eye, causing me to lift my hand from Aiden's chest and press it to my temple. The movement stirs him, and I feel his breath rush against my skin. His body tenses under mine as he stretches his limbs to shake out whatever stiffness has settled into his joints and muscles from sleeping on a couch that, though comfy, is not meant for a full night's sleep. I'm sure having me crammed against him all night didn't help, either.

"Has this become our new thing?" He yawns as his morning greeting.

"A *new* thing?" I ask, my hand still pressed against my temple. "You ask this as if we had an *old* thing."

He ignores my question. "How long have you been awake?" His voice is gravelly from just waking. "Judging by the little bit of sun poking through the window, it's too early for you to sound so alert." He brings one arm behind his head for support but keeps the hand he has on my thigh exactly where he's had it all night. His fingers gently dig into my skin as he subtly squeezes me three times.

"Not long. I've just been…talking to myself." I adjust myself so that I can look at him.

He tucks his chin down to look at me, one eye still closed, the other open, staring in my direction, and crowned with an arched brow. "Ah, I see," he says.

It hits me then that my eye must be that odd translucent color that I've come to recognize as Hel's.

Confirming my suspicion, Aiden grins and addresses that other part of me. "Good morning, Hel."

My mouth involuntarily curves into a seductive smile, and the words that come out next are more Hel's than they are Mercy's. "Good morning, handsome." My tone is uncharacteristically sultry and confident.

I can't help the mortified gasp that whooshes out of my mouth. "That was Hel. That wasn't me."

"You are Hel," he points out in a voice that's low and teasing, clearly enjoying my obvious bout of embarrassment.

"I am Mercy" is all I can think to say.

"Mm-hmm" is his only response. His eyes remain closed, and his usual smirk makes its first appearance of the day. His grip tightens around my thigh and then loosens, but he still keeps his hand exactly where it is.

I am your confidence, girl. Embrace it. Embrace me. Embrace us.

Not long after waking up on the couch, we find ourselves quietly sitting at the island in the kitchen. Had Orthus and Void not nudged and pawed us to finally get up and feed them, we might still be in the same positions in which we woke earlier. Admittedly tangled and comfortable.

At this moment, Void lies sprawled out on the counter, belly full, letting me twirl his tail around my fingers while waiting for the coffee to finish brewing. At the sound of the last few gurgles of the coffee maker, Aiden gets up and proceeds to fix each of us a cup. As he does this, I turn my gaze to look out the window above the kitchen sink and watch as Orthus finishes his morning routine, which consists of making one final round of his three-lap perimeter check. A responsibility he seems to have taken upon himself recently.

A steaming-hot mug of coffee made just as I like slides in front of me, and I offer a sleepy smile in exchange. Aiden takes his seat across from me, coffee mug in his hands, joining in on the activity of watching Orthus plod around the property. He chuckles when one of the three crows who seem to call this place home swoops down from a tree, trying to spook the large hound. A chorus of cackling caws erupts from the trees when Orthus jumps, startled by the black-feathered bird.

I snort, bring the coffee mug up to my lips, and watch as Orthus pins his ears back and snaps in the crow's general direction, not quite able to figure out that the bird tricks him by hovering and hiding in his blind spots. It's comical until I start to wonder if it's innocent play I'm watching or the perfect example of toxic gaslighting in nature.

"Sleep all right?"

I shift my gaze away from the window and back to Aiden. "Not bad, actually. You?" I take a sip of my coffee.

"Only woke up a few times due to you twitching in your sleep." His eyes take on a brightness I now know to mean he's in a playful mood—meaning I'm about to be teased and poked fun at. "Must have been some dream you were having."

My face flushes, heat warming my cheeks. I try to brush it off and sip my coffee.

"You were dreaming about me, weren't you?" he says matter-of-factly, as if he were in my head last night, seeing everything my mind dreamed up. It catches me off guard to the point that I go eerily silent, hold my breath, and try to figure out as quickly as possible if he's trying to get a rise out of me and teasing, or if he has some higher-level mystical-Illuminati, star-power, or alien kind of bullshit ability where he can read my fucking mind—at this point, nothing is starting to surprise me. So why the hell not? Paranoia seeps into my bones.

This minuscule moment of pause, this little glitch in my own matrix, adds fuel to a fire I would prefer to have prevented by *not* throwing the first match. But just that stupid little moment of hesitation is the match that lights the fire.

To my horror, I watch Aiden's playful demeanor take on an edge of deviousness. A tight-lipped, cocky, and satisfied grin grows wider across his face until white teeth are revealed, and he's smiling ear to ear. That little blip of mine was just enough time, somehow, for him to see the glitch for what it was, and for me to realize too late that he was indeed just teasing.

What the sci-fly fuckery, made-for-TV drama do I really think I'm in? Dumbass. Of course, he was teasing.

Let the existential spiral begin. I swear I feel Hel's eye roll while she's muttering this thought in my head.

I choke on my coffee. It's too late to redirect the conversation.

Aiden's eyes widen in curious delight. "You *were*!"

There's a fluttering sensation in my stomach that's a mixture between embarrassment and involuntary arousal—the latter I blame Hel for.

Blame me all you want, but, remember, the feelings are just as much yours as they are mine.

"Don't flatter yourself." The redness I feel lighting up my cheeks isn't helping my attempt at denying his claim. I wash down my embarrassment with another swig of coffee and change the subject by asking, "Don't you have last-minute things you need to do before your exhibit tonight?"

"No." His voice is smug; the glimmer in his eyes leaves me wishing at the moment that one of Hel's gifts was invisibility. After an uncomfortable—for me, delightful for him—pause, he gets up, coffee in hand, and admits, "Actually, I do, now that you mention it."

I stay seated on the stool, too mortified to move. Clutching the almost-empty coffee mug in both hands, I hold it up to my face in some feeble-minded attempt to hide behind it.

Aiden walks around the corner of the kitchen island, and when he reaches me, he stops, leans down, and whispers in my ear, "I can't wait to hear all about this dream…later tonight…when we have a moment to ourselves in the gallery."

With that, he and his inflated ego saunter out of the kitchen, leaving me to sit and stew in my own self-conscious discomfort.

Shaking my head in an attempt to clear my mind of everything, I throw back the last of what's left in my mug—as if it were a shot of something stronger—get up, and make my way to the bathroom to freshen up and start my day of doing…well…nothing at this point, until Tess and Henry come to pick me up later this evening.

I need to get my life together.

I am.

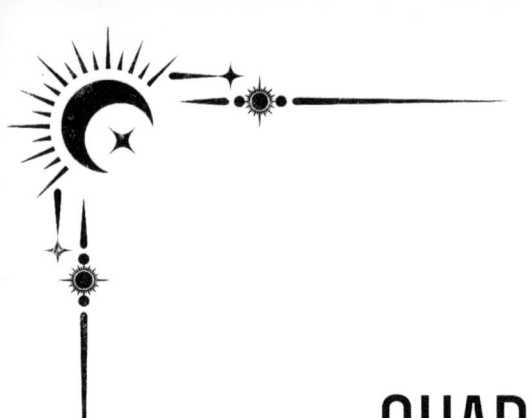

CHAPTER 39
MERCY

"I want *all* the details," Tess demands after I regretfully mention my dream from last night. We sit side by side at the counter in her bathroom, applying makeup and fussing with our hair, just as we used to do when we were younger.

When lunch rolled around earlier, I decided I needed to get out of Aiden's house to keep from spiraling down a rabbit hole of my own making. So I called Tess and asked if she was up for company while getting ready for tonight's event. She, of course, gleefully agreed without hesitation and had her car keys in hand before hanging up the phone, eager to, as she put it, "prep and pregame" as we had done so often in the past. I can always count on Tess.

I can always count on Tarini.

"Honestly, I've already forgotten the details," I lie. "All there is to tell is that I had a dream, and Aiden was in it." I tick the two facts off on upheld fingers.

Tess leans in closer to the mirror, applying another layer of mascara to her already-thick lashes and eyes my reflection.

"I'll ask again later, after you've gotten a few more drinks in you." She winks. "If *I'm* being honest, I'm surprised you haven't jumped his bones yet. Tell me you have at least kissed, for fuck's sake. Don't disappointment me, Mercy. Tell me you've at the very least swapped spit."

Lovely way of putting it there, Tess.

I pause my hand's back-and-forth motion while applying the dark-maroon lipstick I picked out earlier; it hovers over my darkened lips. I part my lips to speak, but nothing comes out. I stare at the now-prominent points of the Cupid's bow on my upper lip, then quickly glance at Tess in the mirror, but hope she doesn't notice—or if she does, she takes it as all the confirmation she needs and drops the subject. I return to my own reflection and touch up the edges of my lower lip.

In a silent way of insisting on a different topic, I focus on the makeup I've truthfully outdone myself with, emphasizing my two favorite parts of my face. For all the things I never liked about myself or never thought beautiful, I have always, at the very least, been able to appreciate the fullness of my lips and the color of my eyes.

It's time to start appreciating more.

"Oh no, you don't. Details. Now! Who kissed who first? How many times did you kiss? Did it just end there? Wait… *Have* you had sex and haven't told me?"

I'm unable to look Tess in the eyes, for fear of her uncanny ability to always pull every last detail out of me, no matter the topic of conversation. I swear, there have been times in which she has gotten me to admit to things I hadn't even realized about myself.

Instead of replying, I take the safe route and look at my eyes in the mirror, acting as if I'm inspecting the accuracy of the winged black eyeliner that frames my top lid and the dusting of golden-brown eye shadow that brings out every hue of blue in my eyes. I lift my hand to apply mascara and focus on the task at hand while admitting to Tess that Aiden and I have indeed "swapped spit."

Tess squeals like a schoolgirl who has just heard the latest gossip spreading around the class. "It's about time!" She throws her hands into the air, her voluminous black curls bouncing in her excitement and dramatic show of relief. "I need to know everything."

"I-I don't know what to tell you." I shrug and offer her a half-ass smile.

I could tell her how it made my stomach drop when he grabbed me and crashed his lips into mine. How when our lips parted and I took his tongue into my mouth, I tasted the alcohol we had both been drinking, mixed with something sweet and familiar that made my heart thrum. How the sensation of his skin against mine sent electricity throughout my body, teasing and caressing every part of me. Or how it quite literally transported me to a whole other world. A whole other life.

I could tell her how, for the first time in what seems like forever, I feel wanted, needed, and—

"Nope, you've gotta give me something, Mercy." Arms crossed and curvaceous hip jutting out to the side, Tess stares at my reflection in the mirror and refuses to release my gaze until I give her something to satisfy her need for juicy details.

"It was"—I pause, thinking of what to say—"everything you would expect it to be, but better." I stand and turn to look at her face-to-face, hoping my eyes and the suggestive upturn to the corner of my mouth relays enough information to quench her thirst for now.

She eyes me for a second, but then gives me a devious grin; there's an amused gleam in her eyes. "That's my girl. It's about time you get back in the game. Granted, I still expect more details later, but don't worry. I'll be patient and wait for the liquor to do the talking."

"Tess—" I begin, but she holds up a hand to stop me.

"Look, before you start making up excuses and lose something incredible just to avoid being hurt again or trying to talk yourself out of it because you don't think you're *whatever* enough for Aiden—or anyone else, for that matter—I need you to know…I know." Her gaze softens. "I know it's scary. I can't even imagine how scary it might be for you. The last time you let someone in and felt safe, that same someone then went and pulled the rug out from under you so many years later and let you fall."

There's a rustling of fabric as we both slip into our dresses. "And you know what, Mercy? You fell. You were bruised and scraped up. You were terrified and self-destructive. You were hurt, betrayed, and broken into—"

Stopping her in the middle of her rant about my past trauma, I signal for Tess to turn so I can zip the back of her dress. "I get it, Tess. I lived it. Still do. What's your point? If there even is one."

She pulls her hair to the side, so it doesn't get caught in the zipper. "That's it. Stop living it, Mercy. It's time to accept you've stopped falling. Remember the tarot card you spoke to me about weeks ago? The Tower card? You fell from the tower that was set on fire, and I've watched you slowly start to pick yourself up from the ashes these past few weeks. Why stop there? Why not rebuild?"

She returns the favor by signaling for me to turn so that she can adjust the loose fabric that falls just above my lower back. A chill runs up my naked spine from the graze of her fingertips against the exposed skin. "All I'm trying to say is, everything you've been through has been scary, but you're still here. You've made it this far, even through the trials and tribulations *we* all know you didn't deserve, but for some reason, you always believed you did...and still do."

Tess turns me, satisfied with whatever she felt she had to do with the fabric at my back, and faces me towards the full-length mirror. My hair is left in long, loose glamour curls that are pulled to one side, cascading onto my chest from over one shoulder. Tess strategically takes the mass of golden lengths and places them just so.

From behind me, she grips my shoulders in her hands, rests her chin in the crook of my neck on the opposite side from where my hair has been pulled, and sighs thoughtfully at our reflections. "It's time, Mercy. It's time for you to allow yourself to be happy, to shake off this dark cloud that you welcomed to swallow you whole. You deserve to be happy, whatever that happiness might entail. And if you don't trust yourself to think that way, then at the very least, trust me."

I don't know if it's Tess's words or our reflections, but for the first time in a very long time, I see a glimpse of the woman my younger self envisioned I would one day become.

I am the woman who has always been here, waiting to be seen, acknowledged, believed in, and trusted. I. Am. Here. *Embrace it.*

"Holy fuck. You two clean up nice," Henry says in greeting as he lets himself into the room, Orthus in tow, and I welcome the levity he brings.

Tess twirls us around, her smile reaching from ear to ear. She takes in the sight of Henry, who is fussing with the lapels of an emerald-green tux that only he could pull off. The rich color of the fabric draws out the warm, deep, rich color of his skin. Tailored perfectly to hug and compliment every lean muscle of his body, the tux emphasizes his natural beauty and athletic build.

"I think we can say the same about you, Henry." My lips part in a bright smile. I'm impressed again by the beauty of both my friends. A beauty that can both be seen and felt.

Tess gracefully leaps over to Henry and throws her arms around him, tilting her head back so that she can look up at his smiling face. "I would kiss you right now if it weren't for the lipstick I just applied."

After a second of thought, Tess lifts onto her tippy-toes and plants a kiss just above Henry's clean-shaven jaw. She giggles at Henry's reaction to the lipstick stain he can't see but knows is there. Quickly, she licks the pad of her thumb and aggressively tries to wipe her mark from his face.

"Tess! Really?" He fights against her grip and scrunches his nose at the feel of her wet thumb trying to wipe off what's left of the lipstick still on his cheek. "Ow! Okay, easy. Let me go clean this off myself, and I'll meet you two"—he looks at Orthus—"sorry, you *three*, at the car. By the time you fit Orthus into the back seat and make enough room for one of you, I'll be at the car, ready to go."

Tess grabs the keys from his hand. "Ha! Look at us!" She waves her hands up and down in a dramatic show of our dresses. "We aren't sitting in the back with the dog. You are."

Orthus huffs as if offended by what Tess just said. I squat down as low as my dress allows, bend from the waist, take his gigantic head into my hands, and look into those two-toned eyes. "I, for one, am honored to have such a handsome man escorting me to such an event." With that, his ears perk up, and I ruffle the fur between them. "Let's head out."

CHAPTER 40
MERCY

It's only a twenty-minute drive from Tess's side of town to the small neighboring city that's known for its music and art scene, just as much as it's known for its progressive history, culture, and charm. It's a far cry from the soul-sucking city I fled from after the divorce from an equally soul-sucking excuse of a man.

We pull up to the front entrance of the museum, the three of us stepping out of the car unnoticed until Orthus leaps from the back seat and shakes, fluffing his long black fur after being cramped in the back seat with Henry. The wolf-like hound's appearance garners surprised looks from the other gallery attendees and drains any color from the valet attendant's face as Tess tries to hand him the keys to her car.

"He doesn't bite. Promise," she says while placing the keys into the scared man's outstretched and shaking hand. Her smile does little to ease the man's obvious fear of dogs. "Unless you give him a reason to," she adds.

The valet attendant's reaction to Orthus has me rolling my eyes for a second, until I see Orthus standing on the walkway near the man, waiting for me to join him. His massive size is something I easily overlooked, having grown up on a farm and being used to the company of large animals. But seeing him in a city atmosphere, as opposed to the woods at Aiden's, I now realize just how intimidating he might look to any other person. I suppose the stares and pale faces that quickly walk by us, whether from fear or fascination, are understandable. I can't imagine the conversation Aiden must have had with the museum's manager to allow Orthus to come.

"Come on, Orthus," I call to him, stepping up to his side. "Let's get inside before we scare away Aiden's audience and potential buyers. I'm sure the two of us can hide in a corner once we've done our rounds."

"You talk to that dog like he understands you," Henry teases while attempting to fasten a loose cuff link.

Orthus throws Henry a side-eye, and Tess laughs. Grinning, she walks up to Henry and swats at his hand to take over fastening the cuff link his fingers keep fumbling with. "I'd be careful, Henry. I think he just might."

I'm about to say something when I hear my name being called from just outside the grand entry doors. I snap my head in the direction of the voice and find that it's coming from John. "What is John doing here?"

"Maybe he's a lover of art," Tess suggests, linking her arm through Henry's as we all four walk up the ornate stairs leading up to the entrance.

I snort and mumble under my breath for only Tess and Henry to hear, "Maybe. However, I would argue that since it's Aiden's art and they obviously don't like each other—"

"Mercy!" John yells my name one last time, even though there are just a few more steps before I reach him.

"Hi, John." I force a smile, truly not feeling any desire to hear what he might have to say about the ongoing case.

"May I borrow a moment of your time?"

Tess glances at me in a silent way of asking if she and Henry should stay or wait for me inside.

Considering the two of us chose to forgo our jackets to avoid coat check, I give her a subtle nod that she takes as her cue to wait inside with Henry, away from the late-October chilly air.

"I can spare a few seconds, John, but keep in mind the dress I'm wearing and the temperature outside." I try to keep frustration out of my tone, but fail. I understand he's only doing his job by keeping me up-to-date on any findings, but I'd rather hear about whatever it is he has to say another time. Not now. It's the first time I've felt somewhat excited to be out and about like a normal person.

"I'm sorry to do this here, but the results came back from the blood test only a half hour ago, and you weren't picking up your phone. I realized today was Aiden's art exhibit and hopped in the cruiser, hoping to catch you before you entered the museum. The timing isn't ideal, but..."

I sigh and pinch the bridge of my nose. "It's all right, John. You don't have to be sorry. I appreciate all the hard work you've been doing to find the guys that are after me for whatever stupid reason. It couldn't wait until tomorrow, though? I'm not here alone. I am safe in the company I keep."

"That's the thing. It couldn't wait until tomorrow because I don't think you are."

At John's comment, Orthus steps closer to my side, his head coming to the height of my lower ribs. I rest my hand just behind his triangular ears, which are pointing skyward on alert.

"What do you mean?" I ask, angling my head to the side and narrowing my eyes. I have an uncomfortable feeling that I'm not going to like what I'm about to hear from John.

"The blood. We found a perfect match. It's Aiden's blood, Mercy. He has something to do with whatever it is that's going on. I'm afraid I'm going to have to bring him in for questioning, and you will need to stay away from him."

I know there must be a perfectly reasonable explanation, but the shock tightens my chest. My fingers, which were just gently resting on Orthus's head, now clench in his fur. My mind begins to spiral, and I feel the panic attack coming on.

There is no way that he is in on it. Whatever "it" is.

Of course, he's not. It feels as if that other part of me, the one in my head, is rolling her eyes at the present physical part of me.

"John, I'm sorry, but there has to be some reasonable explanation behind why the blood matches Aiden's. He had nothing to do with that night I was attacked. He was there that night *helping* me. He's *been* helping me ever since. Hell, I can't go anywhere without him, or at the very least without Orthus at my side for protection. He's just as eager to catch those two assholes as we are." My body begins to shake, and I'm not sure if it's because of the cold or due to the information that has just been dumped on me.

"Some criminals enjoy hiding in plain sight, Mercy. It's part of the thrill. This could all be a sadistic game to him. The second you let your guard completely down will be when he strikes. And we don't want to find out what happens when he does."

I shake my head. "No, that's not possible."

"Mercy—"

"John, I'm telling you. It's not possible. I"—I close my eyes and catch my breath before it gets away from me and the panic wins—"I know that's not true because I—"

"You what, Mercy?" John does what he can to mask his clear frustration with me, but I know him all too well from years of growing up with him in the same town.

"Because, John. Because I've already let my guard down with him, and look." I throw my arms out to the side, heat beginning to flow through my veins. "I'm still here. In one piece. Quite frankly, doing better than I have in a long time. It's not Aiden, John. You're wrong."

"The results, Mercy—"

"*Fuck* the results, John!" Frustration and anger flood through me. I direct the energy at John, who is probably thinking I've been brainwashed into trusting my alleged captor. My outburst causes a few nosy people to stare in our direction.

Tense silence fills the air between us as I stare John down. My mind runs a million miles per hour, trying to make sense of it all as I scramble for some sort of explanation to settle my nerves and convince John he's wrong.

Stop spiraling for two seconds and think. I know why his blood could have been found at Tess's house. I just need a second to figure out—

"Wait." I shake my head and breathe a sigh of relief as the realization hits. "There's an explanation for it."

John crosses his arms over his chest, his brows lowering into a pensive look as he clearly wonders how he is going to convince the person who he believes is a brainwashed victim that she's wrong.

My tongue is tied, though, because how am I to explain that Aiden's blood was on Tess's door because he used some sort of blood magic to unlock it. How that magic worked because, apparently, someone in Tess's family has knowledge of witchcraft or is in fact a witch. Oh, and yes…magic *is* real, and it's just a form of science that hasn't been discovered by most of humankind…yet.

"I can't explain it to you without you thinking I'm batshit crazy, but I need you to trust me when I say Aiden has *nothing* to do with this. You can't arrest him."

"Mercy—"

"John, please. I beg of you… Don't." I can't keep my voice from cracking. "He's not your guy. Give me a chance, a couple of days to prove you wrong. I don't know how I'm going to, but I'll figure something out that shows without a doubt Aiden is innocent. You need to keep looking. Just because his blood showed up at Tess's, that doesn't pin him to my attack. He could have cut his hand on something, and it was fresh enough to bleed when he gripped the doorknob to enter. I would think you need more evidence than that, anyways, to tie him to the crime."

John's face softens as if my attempt to clear Aiden's name on faith alone makes him feel sympathy for me. His gaze never leaves mine, as if he's trying to imply he has more evidence than he's allowed to divulge just yet. Even if he does, I still know he's wrong. So I continue to stare back and plead with my eyes.

"Well, I can't arrest him here because we are out of my jurisdiction. But I *did* plan on meeting him at his house after the event tonight. If you can think of something between now and then to convince me otherwise, you have my number."

That's not enough time.

"Two days. Give me two days to bring you solid evidence that Aiden had nothing to do with my attack and has no ulterior motives other than offering me a safe place to stay while the investigation continues." I allow my emotions to take over and feel the tears begin to build.

Convince him. I need to convince him. Make him feel sorry and obligated to trust me.

John brings his hand to the back of his neck and appears to be rubbing a tension knot, clearly unsure of how to handle the situation. I know, had I been anyone else, he would have ignored me and followed Aiden home tonight to arrest him.

But it's me he's talking to—his former high school crush whom I know he would still do anything for. Ugh, I'm being manipulative.

No, you are making use of the advantages you have in a time you need them. You're being strategic.

Right. I'm being strategic.

See! Now we are thinking as one!

"John, please—" I'm cut off from my pleading when he groans in contempt. Contempt I know isn't directed at me, but at the current situation and Aiden in general.

"Fine. I'll give you until Monday, early morning. That leaves you tonight and all of tomorrow to bring me something that takes Aiden out of the equation."

A wave of relief washes over me. I thank him and seal the deal with a peck on his cheek. His face looks flushed when I pull back to thank him one more time.

Okay, that was a little manipulative, but I had to really solidify his offer.

You did good. We did good.

"Be safe, Mercy."

I nod and smile at him before turning to escape the conversation and the cold. "Let's go, Orthus."

With Orthus at my heel, I shake off the uneasy feeling brought on by John's conversation, and I remind myself of the woman whose reflection I saw earlier in the mirror.

Be strong.

I roll my shoulders back, take a deep breath, and stride through the museum doors with my chin held high.

I am here.

CHAPTER 41
AIDEN

I'm catching up with Henry and Tess—they're telling me John pulled Mercy aside just before entering—when the sound of the gathered crowd quiets. From my angle, as I stand with my back towards the staircase, I watch as, simultaneously, everyone's champagne glass seems to halt mid-flight, before reaching pursed lips. The chattering in the large open-gallery space quiets and is almost silenced altogether. All eyes stare at whatever is happening behind me.

Henry and Tess fall silent, as well. Their focus shifts from me and our conversation, to staring along with the captivated crowd.

That's when I turn.

At the top of the stairs, framed by a soft glow that floods through the open doors, stands the silhouette of a woman and her four-legged protector. The darkened silhouette holds her chin high and shoulders back, scanning the crowd for her company. It's only when the doors softly close behind her that the silhouetted pair becomes completely visible.

I swallow the sharp inhale I pull through my nose as the silhouette is replaced by a woman whose eyes shift from an icy hue of blue to one kissed by the light of a warm summer sun when they finally find whom they are looking for. I watch her walk down the stairs as graceful as a sure-footed deer, but with the unmistakable confidence of a lioness walking back to her pride, emblazoned with purpose—to protect.

A goddess in the flesh.

The golden color of her hair is lighter than I've seen it before; that and the dark makeup—which I know she applied as armor to mask any weakness she might feel—brings a sharpness to her features that would warrant any person to think twice before underestimating her. Even if a fool were tempted to take a chance, the gentle giant who never strays farther than an inch from her side would demonstrate how fatal his bite can be. Confirming, to those who think it, that he is indeed as dangerous as they believe him to be.

I reach the bottom of the stairs just as Mercy takes her final step. I offer my arm, and she takes it, her eyes meeting mine—a self-conscious smile the only chink in her armor. I lean down, bring my lips close to her ear, and whisper Shakespearean words I hope will mend that armor. "Though she be but little, she is fierce."

When I pull away to take all of her in once more, I'm pleased to see a smile both daring and reserved on her face. A smile filled with pride that's more discreet than it is boastful. The perfect balance of everything that makes this woman whole.

Pleased with what I see, I lead her to the center of the gallery space. Orthus follows just a few strides behind us, choosing to fall back now that I stand at her side. I bring us to a halt, clear my throat, and raise my glass to garner everyone's attention.

Not that it isn't on us already.

"I just wanted to thank everyone for coming out tonight in support of my work."

Everyone in the room quietly claps their hands, as they would at a golf tournament, then join in raising their glasses as I had done with mine.

"All pieces, except for the installation in the other room, are available for purchase. Know that all proceeds will be divided equally amongst the charities of Mercy's choice" —I tug the corner of my mouth upward as I feel Mercy tense on my arm at the surprise mention of her name—"and a sponsorship for a deserving young artist's residency of choice."

More applause follow this announcement.

"So mingle. Enjoy. Drink...*and* spend money if you're able to, knowing it's going towards a good cause. Cheers."

Sipping from my glass, I watch as the crowd does the same, eventually parting to grab another glass of the complimentary champagne and to peruse the artwork that hangs on stark-white walls. As the focus of attention disperses, I guide Mercy over to rejoin Tess and Henry.

"Well, that was quite the entrance," Tess says in way of greeting Mercy.

"Completely unintentional and embarrassing," Mercy responds.

Her obvious discomfort with the attention, which is clearly evident in her tone of voice, stirs my jester side and tempts me to lightly poke fun and disrupt her bout of unnecessary tension. "People will always stop and stare at shiny things. Especially when that shiny thing looks like you tonight. So I, for one, couldn't imagine a better way to get the crowd's attention." I focus on Mercy, my lips pulling into a mischievous grin, and watch her squirm from the faintest of compliments.

Tess doesn't hide her smile as she watches me toy with Mercy. Henry, next to her, squeezes Tess's waist, failing to contain her obvious enjoyment of Mercy's and my interaction.

A subtle buzz of chatter fills the room as guests flit around the gallery and take in all the artwork. The four of us stand together—refilled champagne glasses in hand—and people-watch for a couple of minutes.

Henry takes a sip from his glass, clears his throat, and asks, "So what did John have to say, anyway? Seeing as he didn't come in right after you, I'm sure it's safe to assume he wasn't here for the art."

Mercy's entrance into the gallery was so dramatic I didn't even think to ask about John. *Thanks for asking, Henry.*

"Apparently he found a match to the blood sample that was found at your house." Mercy nods her head at Tess just before taking a deep swig of champagne.

That wasn't a pleasant, relaxed sip.

"That's...great! Right? We are even closer now to this being all over!"

Tess's excitement is something I expect to also be emanating from Mercy. Instead, I catch her gulping down another mouthful of the bubbly liquid.

By the look on her face, she wishes that were something stronger.

"Considering his main suspect right now is, Aiden—"

I widen my eyes in disbelief and snap my head around to look at Mercy. "Wait... What?" My voice comes out choked from the champagne that catches in my throat during her pronouncement.

That is not what I was expecting her to say.

"Don't get me started. That's what took me so long. I was outside pleading with John to not arrest you tonight when we get home."

I know it should not be her last words—"when we get home"—that catch my attention. It was most likely a slip of the tongue. But I can't help myself; that little slipup of hers distracts me from what I should be more concerned about—the whole "arrest you tonight" thing.

"Okay, but even if the results are a match"—Tess's eyes dart from side to side as she tries to piece together whatever she can to clear my name—"they need more evidence than just that. Don't they? How does he know the blood isn't from defensive wounds or something completely random?"

Tess's lack of hesitation in rejecting the idea that I am behind the attacks causes me to blink a few times in surprised relief. It hits me that the relationship I've formed with these three is new yet somehow already way beyond superficial—especially considering the short amount of time we've known one another. This is all completely unexpected.

The fact that Tess, Henry, and Mercy aren't even questioning my innocence has me at a loss for words, if I'm being completely honest. For all they know, I could be the culprit. Truly, they've just met me, and I them. For all they know, I could have been scheming and conning them this whole time. For all they know, I could be taking advantage of a woman—their closest friend—who has been broken by her very own negative thoughts throughout most of her life, only to eventually be discarded by someone who offered her the false promise of a lifetime together and support. For all that they know, John—a man the three of them have known since childhood, far longer than they have known me—could be right.

He's not. I know that, and—thankfully—they know that, too.

As we stand here questioning what to do next, I realize that in the grand scheme of things, proving my innocence is not what terrifies me. Neither do John's suspicions about me and what he believes to be my true nature.

When have I ever cared what others think of me? I know who I am.

What does unsettle me, though?

This. Mercy.

Truthfully, in the short amount of time we've spent together these past weeks, the relationship between Mercy and me has evolved into something neither of us was expecting. Something we both assumed at first was unknown and new has turned out to be something we simply forgot, something that has been patiently waiting to be rediscovered…something that has been multiple lifetimes in the making.

I've been standing by Mercy's side, watching her break down her walls, brick by brick, and encouraging her every step of the way, whether through obvious support or by challenging her. I've completely exposed myself to her without hesitation or fear, the repercussions of our relationship either unknown or blatantly ignored by me.

Vulnerable. I've become vulnerable to her…because of her. I will not deny that vulnerability. Neither will I deny the fact that it terrifies me. Vulnerability means weakness, just as it also means strength. Mercy makes me aware of the weakness I have worked so long to guard. To protect. To bury.

So, no, it's not the trouble that life is throwing at me that is causing this adrenaline rush I'm just becoming aware of. It's not John coming to arrest me or the idea of having to prove my innocence. What scares me is the trouble that threatens to keep me from the missing piece of my soul…whom, until recently, I had no idea I was missing.

"Tess is right. He needs more than just my blood being at the scene to pin this all on me."

I take a swig from my almost-empty glass and start to keep an eye out for someone to replace all of our glasses. I have a feeling we all need more champagne.

"That's what *I* said, but *apparently* he has more proof that he isn't willing to divulge just yet," Mercy says, cocking an eyebrow at me.

For the first time in a very long time, I feel my heart skip a beat out of fear of shattering. That rush of adrenaline now bubbles with fear, instead of the restless excitement it started with. "You don't actually think—"

"Really?" she questions me, a bit of hurt in her voice. Her eyes soften, and I can feel them tracing every angle, every curve, every line of my expression. Her brows pinch together in a show of warmth and sincerity. "Of course, I don't. I know you had nothing to do with this, just as much as Tess and Henry know that."

I can't help but look at Tess and Henry, trying to read them, hoping to find their earlier take on the matter unchanged. Hoping for the reassurance that they do stand with Mercy on this, that they believe her over John. Believe me.

And I see it. I see the unwavering trust they have in Mercy's belief in me. Deep down, I know this has little to do with me and everything to do with the change they have seen in Mercy since that day our paths inevitably collided.

A change we can all agree is for the better. A change brought on by simply encouraging her to accept herself as she was and as she is. A change brought on as each brick of that wall she's built is torn down, piece by piece, revealing a sense of happiness within that I knew was there all along. That happiness was just waiting for the chance to breathe and the space to come alive on its own terms.

They know, as do I, that I am not responsible for providing Mercy with this newfound happiness that grows brighter every day. All I've done is simply offer her the space to find it on her own, along with any encouragement she has needed along the way. I know this is why they trust me.

"So what's the plan, then?" Henry asks, shaking me from my own thoughts.

"I have— *We* have until Monday to figure out how to redirect John's focus or convince him that Aiden has nothing to do with those two assholes that caused this mess." Mercy's chest rises and falls with a deep breath. "For now, I suggest we enjoy our evening. There's nothing we can do at this very moment. We can think of something later. We will. We have to."

Everyone nods.

"Well, man of the hour," Mercy begins, eyes staring up at me, newfound energy of unshakable confidence and unflappable determination settling over her features, "care to show me around?"

I offer her my arm. She instead grabs my hand, intertwining her fingers with mine. It's intimate. It's everything. So I embrace the adrenaline and all that comes with it.

With that, Tess and Henry part ways to walk the gallery perimeter on their own, leaving us in each other's company. The giddy smile on Tess's face at the sight of Mercy's hand tangled in mine is anything but subtle.

Mercy takes a step ahead of me before looking over her shoulder, our fingers still laced together. "Come with me?"

"Always." I fall into step beside her.

We walk hand in hand around the gallery, and I think to myself that Mercy has for so long walked through darkness alone. Her friends and family hoped that she would find that light of happiness and peace within herself, but they did not understand that what she truly needed—wanted—was company. Not answers. Not solutions. Just company and a hand to hold while she found her own answers while toiling in her darkness and experimenting with the light that's just finally broken through.

I am that company. I will always be that company. My hand is the hand she will always hold. And even if she drops it, I won't stop reaching for her. Making sure she knows I'm always there when she needs something or someone to hold on to.

I will be the one who walks alongside her, content in that darkness for as long she chooses to linger there. Reveling in the shadows just as much as the light whenever she decides to let it in. Embracing whatever answers she finds and enjoying whatever path we journey to find them.

Whether it be in light or darkness, wherever she leads, I know I will follow. That decision and choice—I now know—was made by me long, long ago.

CHAPTER 42
MERCY

"I would be lying if I said I wasn't slightly unsettled about your lack of worry about only having until Monday to figure out a way to clear my name." Aiden shoots me a quick glance, keen eyes angling down at me. The sudden movement jars a rogue curl free, the tendril falling from a swept-back hairstyle, and it hangs just above the apex of the sharp brow he has raised at me.

"I know. *Normally*, I would be worried," I counter, fluttering my lashes towards him at the expense of mocking myself. Going even further to emphasize my self-awareness, I flash a playfully psychotic smile, attempting to be lightheartedly snarky, and for once not caring how much of a fool I am making of myself.

Is this me flirting? For fuck's sake, I need help.

I earn an eye roll and throaty chuckle as Aiden's response.

"I suppose my unusual demeanor tonight, the newly discovered optimism, might come across as unsettling to you." A dark and humorous laugh slips free for one breath, but then I continue and ask Aiden what I can only imagine he's already thinking—knowingly baiting him with an opportunity to give me some satirical response. "Probably anticipating I'll have a public mental breakdown any second now, aren't you?"

We stand side by side in the extra room that holds his installation piece. With no one having reached this end of the exhibit yet, I take advantage of the still-private moment and keep speaking. "Normally, I would be worried. Very worried. Sickeningly so..." I acknowledge out loud, my voice trailing off as I turn my head to face him. "I know it doesn't make sense, but I just—" I shake my head, my tongue suddenly caught in my mouth.

At the center of the dark room, we stand. The only light comes from the projector, which casts a steady stream of flickering soft-white dots on shadowy walls—an artist's own rendition of a celestial planetarium.

"You just what?" Aiden's eyes dance around my face, looking for the answer before I give it. His lips twist into a smile. "Know exactly what to say to John to stop him from closing the case simply because—let's be honest here—I make a convenient and easy suspect?" His question is voiced as he intends it to be heard—more like a scoffing statement. His tone, deep and hushed, is at odds with the obvious and out-of-place playful energy he chooses not to hide.

With my hand still in his, he spins me around, pulling me in close so that my back is pressed tightly against his body. His arms tuck under mine in an embrace around my waist, and we continue to stand there. The only ones in the room for the time being.

My head falls back to rest against his chest. Any remaining caution about my feelings is decidedly thrown to the wind.

His chin moves from the top of my head to nestle against my ear so he may speak quietly for no one but me to hear. "Tell me, Mercy. What is it that's on your mind that has magically given you the ability to relax and feel sure of yourself for even just a quarter amount of this time?" I'm not looking at him, but I can picture the playful look he has on his face right now. I can especially picture it when he readily adds, "New record, I bet."

Still held tightly in his arms, I turn and lift my chin, eyes closing briefly at the touch of his lips grazing my temple, then my forehead after a subtle change of position. My breath does not hitch; instead, it remains steady. The rhythm of my heart is bold, sure, and unwavering.

I blink a few times and pull back just enough to look Aiden in the eye as I tell him with every ounce of conviction I have, "I guess it's this gut feeling that I somehow know this isn't something we need to worry about. I just know that things are going to be okay for you. For us."

"I was hoping for a bit more factual validation than that, but…" He chuckles, not finishing the thought.

I let out a breathy laugh. "I know. I know. Not exactly the answer you were hoping to hear from me, but I'm telling you that things *are* going to be okay because…well…I just know that they will be. For once, my mind isn't trying to convince me otherwise." I hit him with my most convincing smile.

"It's a good thing you aren't a lawyer. If you were…and I end up needing one…I hope you would understand my choice to seek help elsewhere."

I pout, acting insulted, before joining him in quiet laughter. The moment of amusement is brief before I extricate myself from his tight hold so that I can turn to face him completely. "It *will* be okay." My words become just as much a mantra as they were meant to be factual—they are what

I currently choose to believe. "We will figure this out. There is no other option. I won't allow there to be." I fix a look of determination on my face to emphasize my sentiments.

That determined look, however, falters as people start to filter into the room, and I feel this moment of confidence, of happiness, of optimism start to shrink back into the recesses of my brain. Fleeting moments, just as I expected them to be. But at least, for once, I enjoyed those moments while they lasted.

"Where are you going?" Aiden asks, his eyes drilling into mine.

"I'm right here." I look at him, confusion warping my face.

"That's not what I'm talking about." He taps my temple with his finger. "Here. Where are you going here?"

"What do you mean?"

A shadow of that dark cloud begins to make an appearance around my stomach—an invisible wall only I can see—trying its hardest to force space between Aiden and me. It becomes more opaque as the familiar feelings of doubt and negativity slink back into my mind, reclaiming what has always been its place—its home. My only comfort is that these negative emotions are as familiar to me as is the mindless act of breathing.

"You were just living in the present for the longest time since I've met you"—he smiles—"and it was beautiful."

Well, fuck me. Let's hope this freshly mended heart can handle another mistake. There's no choice at this point is there?

Nope.

A tear threatens to escape, and though I try my best to keep it from rolling down my cheek, I fail. But before it can slide down my face and onto the ground, as so many tears have done before, it is instead wiped away by the thumb of the hand I suddenly realize is caressing my cheek.

"No more tears. Come back to the present, with me." A simple request.

In the room that's starting to get crowded, we remain as we are—at its center, ignoring the commotion of the world around us, and trapped in a spell of our own making. The spell breaks only for a moment when Aiden catches sight of something behind me. The smile that appears on his face, crinkling the corners of his eyes and exposing his dimples, has me tilting my head in admiration and need—no—desire for the vision before me.

As I'm drinking in the sight of him, Aiden interrupts my exploration of his features and spins me around more eagerly this time. When I see the cause for that breathtaking expression of his, my chest tightens in a way it never has before.

The projection of stars throughout the room has been slowly transforming, throughout the night, into different patterns in this man-made night sky. Constellations and star clusters rearranging themselves into striking arrangements that represent varying forms of life. The message being driven home is that we are all connected. All made up of the same stuff—star stuff.

"In every lifetime I remember, I have been an artist," Aiden starts, freeing me from my transfixion by the star art. "Some lifetimes, I have been a struggling artist; others, more starving. More recently, I've thankfully fallen into the realm of thriving artist—much to do with the fact that my art has been able to mature over time, thanks to knowing and understanding the things that I do in such a way." He says this offhandedly, as if to brush aside the importance and priceless value of the knowledge and experiences he has had.

We both know he isn't wrong. One look around the gallery space, and it is hard to imagine that someone of his age could create those pieces. Not that either of us, in our early thirties, would be considered young—especially in the art world, I might argue—but there is an essence in his work that goes way beyond his current thirty-plus years. His work emotes passion and a sense of understanding life in a way only someone who has lived many lifetimes would know and could convey. "A new artist with an old soul," critics call him.

If they only knew.

His voice is just a whisper in my ear as we both stand still. "Every lifetime, I have always been an artist. Every lifetime, no matter the medium, I find myself creating one particular portrait over and over again. Almost as if, subconsciously, my mind has always fought to never let it go, refused to let it become a memory that fades with each lifetime."

The tears I didn't realize were building start streaming down the sides of my face, leaving trails of salt in their wake. I break away from Aiden's hold on me and step closer to the pointillistic portrait of me projected overhead. My head falls back slightly to take in the full sight. The crowd around me murmur words of genuine awe.

I feel the presence of someone behind me, but I do not turn to see who I already know it is. My hands cover my mouth, jaw hanging slack in shocked reverence.

Aiden's hands are in his pockets, but he stands so close behind me that I feel as though he is embracing me, as he did before the room started to get crowded.

"I don't know why it's taken until now to remember this, or what time has passed since the last time I knew this to be true, but for many lifetimes this vision of you has haunted me. I catch myself creating it even when I don't mean to; it has caused me frustration and at times bouts of insanity, wondering whose face this is that stays with me. Why it is that I can't stop seeing it and creating it, using whatever tool I find at my fingertips."

I'm silent. My body involuntarily leans into his for support, for comfort.

"It eventually hit me, as if a locked safe of memories, one I was unaware of, had finally burst open." He curls his shoulders, dropping his head so that his words can't be heard by anyone but me. "You've always been my timekeeper, Mercy. You've always been my muse, no matter the relationship we had. I'm not sure what happened to make me forget that…to make *you* forget that…but I'll be damned if it happens again."

Like a cat basking in sunlight, completely at peace with the world, there's a purr that vibrates within my soul, and I can feel warmth from a light seeping through the many cracks that resulted from years of breaking. That light shines brighter than it has ever been able to before, thanks to the shadows that I've allowed to remain.

Light cannot be seen without the dark. And light cannot stream through solid walls. The only way the light can reach the dark is through the cracks in the walls that we build and through the holes that we willingly punch in them.

As if just noticing my tears, Aiden angles his head and narrows his stare. "I thought we agreed no more tears?"

"What if they are happy tears?"

He removes his hands from his pockets, steps up to my side, and places one hand on the small of my back. The gesture is intimate. His skin is warm against my own, yet chills still run along my spine.

"I suppose I'll allow it, then."

With the tears now dry on my face, I look up at him and smile.

"I think the museum can take care of whatever needs to be taken care of for the rest of the night." There's a shine in his eyes that sends my heart into a chaotic frenzy of overwhelming anticipation, and I choose to dive headfirst into that energy without worrying about drowning.

Maybe it's Hel. Maybe it's Aiden. Maybe it's me. Perhaps a combination of all three. Whoever or whatever is responsible for this moment, I am forever grateful. If this moment is the only one in which I feel this way, I will take it. I will embrace it. I decide to allow myself to overindulge in it to a point that far surpasses gluttony. Because, deep down, I know it will be fleeting.

So I will hold on to it far past the point of white knuckles, broken nails, and bloodied palms. This brief glimmer in time. This hint of happiness. This unusual—for me—moment in time in which, despite everything, I remain fully present. I do not wallow in the past or worry about what is to come, neither of which I can change.

I am here.

"Home then?" I ask.

The heat that just flared in Aiden's eyes softens as he responds with a smile that reaches from ear to ear, "Home."

CHAPTER 43
MERCY

Between the sheets and under the covers of Aiden's bed, my bare skin presses against his, our body heat counteracting the early-morning chill of fall that has settled throughout his home. His arm drapes over me, holding the warmth beneath the comforter. Warmth—as my teeth begin to chatter—I need more of.

I start to shimmy closer to his body, wanting to absorb more of his heat. He subconsciously reacts to this, pulling me in even tighter in such a way that's both possessive and protective. Long limbs intertwining with mine, he wraps around me as close as possible. I feel each of his muscles start to tighten and flex, slowly squeezing my tinier frame.

Honestly, if this is how I go—being lovingly squeezed to death by a very attractive man—I won't complain.

Caught between the slight terror at being suffocated by Aiden and the genuine bliss over the same thing, I accept my fate, focus on the rhythm of our breathing, and relax. Well, relax in a way that also includes trying to convince myself to keep up that optimism and confidence from last night. Old habits die hard—I should know.

With all the current chaos and mayhem that has been adding fuel to the unpredictable fire that is my life, I can't help but be greedy and pray for this moment to last as long as possible.

This isn't greed. This simply is. Accept it.

Aiden begins to stir, and I find myself wiggling in closer to his body—not for warmth this time, but to satisfy my unapologetic need for this limited time of comfort and peace.

Just before that last spark of calm and positive energy flickers out and leaves my body in the blinding darkness of unsettling emotions, surprise reignites that flame. My breath is squeezed out of my lungs as Aiden's hold tightens into a warm embrace. I feel his lips against the skin of my neck, causing tiny hairs to stand on end and electricity to buzz through me. When he loosens his hold, my body remembers how Aiden's hands and body felt as he roamed and explored my entirety last night in a welcomingly forceful and needy way. Rough and calloused hands alternated between possessively hungry grabs and worshipingly tender caresses—an intoxicatingly perfect balance of love and lust. For once, I felt desired for everything I am, demons and all.

"I'm not sure about you, but last night has left me parched," Aiden drowsily whispers into my ear as his way of saying good morning.

"Good morning to you, too, and yes"—I laugh, turning over to face him, his arm a heavy weight that resists letting go, and then tightens as I curl in closer, tucking my head under his chin—"me, too."

Neither of us moves.

I release a teasingly huffy sigh, warm air rushing out through my nose. "Is this your way of asking me to leave the comfort of this nice warm bed to run to the kitchen to fetch us water?"

An insulted scoff rattles Aiden's chest, which makes my lips tug into a subtle smile. "Excuse me! Do you think I'm not a gentleman? I would never ask that of you," he teases, and I can't help but giggle like some sort of lovestruck teenager.

It's a little pathetic. It's slightly disgusting. But I'm not denying myself this moment.

A chill replaces the warmth of Aiden's spot next to me as he makes his way to the edge of the bed. I pull in close the mass of blankets—nothing but the top of my head and eyes are visible.

"I would never ask that of you…at least during the first couple of dates." He winks before pulling a sweatshirt over a head of rich-brown, unruly waves. Last night's newly discovered and explored skin of permanently inked symbols is hidden once again beneath clothing.

As jaw-dropping as he looked last night, this current version of him is what makes my blood pump most. For many reasons—some clearly obvious just by looking at him. But to be honest, the most genuine reason is simply because, in this moment, he is completely himself—vulnerable and raw—a truly beautiful balance between the best and worst versions of himself.

"You've got maybe two more before my chivalry is dead. And then these free courtesies come with a price." He shoots me a look and gestures to what his idea of currency is.

I squint my eyes and briefly pull the comforter down just enough to stick my tongue out at him while flipping him the middle finger. He laughs, and I watch him leave the room, staring at what just shared a bed with me…smirking and feeling shamelessly proud of myself.

I am here. I am happy. I am at peace.

My heart surges, and my eyes close softly.
Everything is going to be okay.

A few minutes slip by before I feel a presence in the room. I'm about to make a witty remark and tease Aiden about being quick, but then instinct forces my eyes to fly open in terror. Immediate recognition hits me—the dark figure is one of the two men who attacked me what feels like forever ago. He stands, looming over the foot of the bed.

At first, I am paralyzed by fear. But then adrenaline kicks in not a moment too soon, and I regain a bit of sensation throughout my body. Lurching up, determined to fight, my lips begin to part in an attempt to scream Aiden's name. Instead, panic overrides my system as I'm silenced by a hand that smothers me by covering my nose and mouth from behind.

The dynamic gremlin-and-ogre duo have finally found me. The gravity of my situation sinks in when my vision blurs, and darkness creeps in around its edges. Head woozy, my body becomes deadweight in my captor's arms. I feel myself being lifted and awkwardly cradled by the one I deemed ogre-like. The smell of rotten eggs and cigarettes lingers on his breath and skin.

Incapable of fighting back this time—thanks to what I assume to be chloroform on the rag with which they covered my face—I helplessly accept my fate. The voice is the only thing that remains as I try to hold on to my rapidly dwindling consciousness.

At least I was able to rediscover happiness.
Come on. Fight this.
At least I finally found myself again.
I've been here all along.
At least I was able to shake hands with my demons and see them for what they truly are.

They were never demons.

At least I finally accepted my shadows and understand they're needed for there to be light.

Those shadows can be wielded. Use them now.

At least I was given that chance.

Don't give in.

At least I allowed myself that chance.

I'm so tired.

At least there's a next…

That voice. Hel's voice. My voice. The voice I finally learned to accept.

Silenced.

CHAPTER 44
AIDEN

The glass in my hand shatters on the floor in the kitchen when I'm whacked over the head by something heavy and blunt. Dropped to my knees by the pain pulsing in the back of my head, temporary blackness leaves me unstable and disoriented. I swear I hear my father's voice tell my assailant to take it easy, and then something about needing me alive. Confusion floods my thoughts as I try to understand the lack of terrified distress in my father's orders. Unease and distrust hit me in the gut harder than the object that cracked my skull. My father should be begging for my safety, not ordering the asshole to take it easy on me as if he's under my father's command.

Black dots distort my vision, and I'm having trouble trying to focus. I wince as I examine the back of my head with my hand, only to pull it away and find it covered in blood. To say I'm not looking forward to that inevitable headache would be an understatement. The world stops spinning enough for me to try and ease myself up from the floor. I brace a hand on a bent knee for leverage to rise. It takes everything in me to stand, but once I'm upright, what feels to be the barrel of a gun is jabbed into my lower back, not aimed to kill, but certainly to paralyze.

The hood of my sweatshirt is balled into the fist of the gunman. He twists and pulls it tight enough to restrict my airway. "Hands up, you pretentious fuck."

I do as I'm told. My eyes find my father's, and I see nothing of the man I thought I knew. Now, there's nothing but maniacal calculation in his eyes. The whimsical mask of a loving father who encouraged curiosity and creativity has fallen, revealing the look of a man with a deranged soul. His frail shoulders are suddenly rigid, commanding authority as he walks up to me, hands clasped behind him. He holds his chin arrogantly high, devious eyes staring down at me through corrective lenses that up until now made him appear kind. Misplaced hatred radiating from that stare penetrates deep into my soul.

"I've been patient with you, boy, letting you live life after life while I researched and experimented with ways to accomplish the impossible. It's time for you to accept the fate I've finally been able to create for you." He begins to pace in front of me, his hands striking the air, accentuating the impatient rage in his false claims of care and generosity. "You should be on your knees, thanking me right now for being given the amount of time you've had." His voice shakes with bitter anger, each word spat louder into my face, his bony finger threateningly targeting me.

He strides closer until we stand toe to toe. And though I tower over him, he still manages to look down his nose at me as he jabs that same bony finger under my chin, digging into the fleshy area behind my jaw. I swallow, my throat bobs, and I sneer in his direction. My eyes, I'm sure, hold nothing but hostility and hurt from the betrayal by the man I have always called my father. He wants to say something, but the coward balks before confronting me this close.

"Take him to my workspace, please." His voice is demanding yet still pleasant when he addresses the men who forcefully usher me to the heavy door that separates my world from the liminal space that is this man's—the man I addressed as my father.

He turns on his heels, a mockery of a soldier, and marches his way to the solid door, quickly performing the unlocking ritual of painting the three runes with his blood. The hinges creak as the door slowly swings open. My father leads the way, followed by my escort and me; his two loyal followers probably share a single brain cell, considering their blind devotion to whatever fucked-up plan he's trying to accomplish.

The clacking sound of my father's heeled shoes echoes down the dark, empty hallway lit solely by pale-blue light radiating from the occasional sconce. Each step closer to his workspace becomes more foreboding by the eerie atmosphere.

What once piqued my curiosity as a child—my father's workspace—has always been a space deemed off-limits to anyone but him. Like the Window of Cosmos, I was always told—by way of unhinged rambling—that entry to his workspace was earned through knowledge and deeper understanding of the universe, of Spirit, and by truly seeing the bigger picture—a picture I'm not so sure at the moment is worthy of admiring or existing. As I grew older, I believed he was just hiding some weird fetish—or obsession—there, and I most definitely did not want to know about that. Who wants to know what their parents do behind closed doors, anyway?

So as each year passed, I stopped asking to see his workspace, where I once thought he was creating wonders for this world, for the other side, or even for the universe. I stopped imagining and stopped bothering my old man about a room I'd come to think I didn't want to know about to save him—both of us, actually—from awkward embarrassment. I chose ignorant bliss, when I should have kept prodding and asking those hard questions. Maybe this could have all been avoided.

The entrance to this once-secret little shop, where the destruction of the universe as we know it may have been plotted, is at the end of one of the three spiraling hallways that venture off from the main living space at its hub. When we finally reach the study, my gut twists, and my heart sinks at the sight of Mercy's body tossed in the center of the room like a discarded, crumpled-up piece of paper.

Her pale figure is covered by my haphazardly buttoned shirt from last night, which keeps her from complete exposure. Tangled blonde hair, made to appear dull and grey by the light of the room, covers her face and splays all around her head. I release a sigh of relief when I notice a faint rise and fall of her chest, which indicates she's still breathing.

Fury pumps through my veins as I continue to take in the sight of Mercy. I struggle to pull away from the men who hold me hostage, but I'm reminded of the gun to my back by a quick jab. Nausea strikes me when I notice the thin wire binding Mercy's ankles and wrists, cutting deep into porcelain skin, which is given a sickly appearance, thanks to the harsh lighting. Lacerations bright with blood leave marks sure to scar her skin; they must be searingly painful, but still she lies there unconscious.

"Ah, yes. Let's quickly discuss the matter of your female friend, here, before we continue with my plans. Frigg's waited this long; I suppose she can wait a little longer for her son's return."

The last part he mumbles under his breath, and I just barely catch it. *What the fuck does the God of Light have to do with this?* The question slams to the back of my mind as Mercy is dragged to her bound feet by my father's hand fisted in her hair.

A guttural scream of pure agony rushes out from Mercy as her eyes snap open as she is ripped from unconsciousness. Her face is a portrait of pain and suffering as tears stream down her face. Her body bends and twists against the pain inflicted by sharp-wire bindings and the discomfort of my father's hold as he dangles her in front of me like some prize catch.

"LET HER GO!" I bellow, my voice fueled by the fire raging in my soul. "She has nothing to do with this. Whatever the fuck *this* is," I sneer through clenched teeth.

My father shrugs his shoulders and offers me a look of indifference. He releases his hold on Mercy, and she hits the ground hard, knees first. A soft cry escapes her lips, and I pull against the restraining hold of my captors. They again remind me about the gun they have pointed at my back. I will be of no help to Mercy if I'm paralyzed.

At a loss, I remain standing a few feet away from the woman whom I've loved in every lifetime I have ever lived. The horror show unfolding in front of me causes the final break in a hidden dam unconsciously built in my mind. It cracks and crumbles into a million pieces, revealing a rush of blocked memories that all blur together. The majority involve Mercy.

My heart rages in my chest—as if it were a wild animal who had gone mad—trapped in too small a cage, as the influx of memories overwhelms me. The resurfaced knowledge strikes me—

What Mercy is to Hel, I am to Baldur. I am he, and he is me.

It hits me then that the recent dreams and random visions were simply memories buried deep in my subconscious. Memories trying to grab my attention to remind me of who and what I am in my entirety.

My father's laugh is nausea-inducing as he responds, "Oh, but she very much has *a lot* to do with this. But how could you even know, anyway? I had any memories of her wiped from your brain during every cycle you've been through since making my deal with Frigg."

I look at him in disgust and confusion, wondering what he even means by that, but then a soft moan of discomfort and pain refocuses my attention.

"Mercy. Mercy, look at me." My voice lowers, and I do my best to try and comfort her, despite the impossibility of that in her current predicament. Her chin lifts just enough for our eyes to meet, and I feel my heart skip a beat before shattering in my chest. I see that will she fought so hard to find again start draining as the light in her eyes dims.

No.

"Don't give up, Mercy. Not now. You continue that fight. You are strong, Mercy. Don't let go." Each word is said in a more demanding way than the last.

My father stands beside Mercy and shoves his fist into her hair once more, forcing her to look at him. As much as I hate him for it, that forceful show of manipulative power ignites a spark in her eyes. Proof I haven't lost her yet.

"Hello, Mercy," the bastard croons, causing both Mercy and me to thrash against our restraints in revulsion. "Shh. Shh. Shh. Now, let's not make this any harder than it already is. Son, I think you've had enough time with your plaything for this lifetime. I can't have her interfering with your ascension. It's time to get rid of her once and for all."

I jerk against the tight hold on me, struggling to watch him manhandle Mercy. "How exactly would she interfere with my ascension?" My face contorts into a mixture of confusion, shock, and disbelief. "For fuck's sake, Dad. You sure as shit shouldn't be interfering with the timeline, either! We don't interfere with the cycle. *You* were the one to teach me that. I'll ascend when my time has come and I stop reincarnating. We don't mess with the balance of things, remember? We certainly don't mess with things when it involves a timekeeper! Never mind *two* timekeepers, for that matter!" I'm yelling at this point, trying to shake some sort of sanity back into the man. It seems that my father has interfered with my fate so many times that I have forgotten who I truly am—what my vessel's purpose has always been—until now. I take a quick glance at Mercy after this realization.

"Oh, Aiden. If only you knew. Knew how, each life, she would have tried to come back to you if it weren't for me. Would have tried to keep you away from us, to manipulate you and tell you sweet lies. But I have refused to let that happen, time and time again. Each time hoping you would ascend before inconveniently succumbing to your death, only to be reincarnated to go through the whole fucking process again." He paces in angered annoyance just behind Mercy.

"I am tired. Tired of this constant struggle of making sure *everything* is perfectly aligned for you to ascend without this bitch interfering. Tired of having to keep your soul from resting in Helheim between each cycle, to keep Hel from finding Baldur and interfering with the plan. Both my and Frigg's patience—*especially* Frigg's—won't last much longer. She wants her son back, and I intend to deliver." His words are spat from his mouth as if he were an angered venomous snake.

"I'm the vessel for Baldur in this realm, aren't I? He chose me. He is who I'm lost to whenever I go back to Helheim. He is who makes up my whole self, isn't he? Why hide that from me?"

My father nods. "No matter the lifetime, you have always been smart. To think it took this long for you to figure this out is a bit disappointing, to say the least." He claps his hands together in cheerful satisfaction. "But we are here now! Frigg gets her son back with no worries of ever losing him to this cunt again," he crudely remarks while shaking Mercy, his fingers fisted in her hair once again. "And for all this trouble, in return, I get a wealth of knowledge only worthy of gods."

My eyes widen, and I shake my head in unrelenting disbelief. "So that has been your plan this whole time? To keep Mercy and me apart so that...what? Baldur no longer feels tied to Hel somehow? No longer has a reason to return to Helheim to be with his other half because you've erased the memories of her, of us? Tried to erase Mercy, erase Hel from my life...from Baldur's?" Each rhetorical question I ask is emphasized by a look of crazed disbelief plastered on my face.

"Frigg pleaded and begged, so long ago, for Hel to release you from her hold, in hopes of never having to lose you to the responsibilities of being a timekeeper and all that being one entails. Her goal is for you—well, Baldur—to forever reside with her, where he is believed to belong, so that he can eventually create a galaxy and life of his own. A *real* legacy." Leo takes his free hand and gestures to the space around us. "Not slumming it here, or Helheim, assisting lost souls on their journey to enlightenment. She believes you to be above all that. For Baldur to be above all of that." He shrugs. "But, of course, Hel would only entertain her request on one condition."

I can't help the agitated laugh that comes with his insinuation that Baldur never had a choice in the matter. That Hel was simply a greedy puppeteer and Baldur her favorite puppet. In fact, it's too hard to believe; this path must have been chosen of his own volition.

I know it was his choice. My choice—now that I remember everything. Know that it always has been and always will be. I know it was a path he chose and will choose every time because it's the path I will choose…again and again without question. Not because *of*, but *for* Mercy. For Hel.

"From what I'm remembering…finally"—my knowing glare settles on him as if to lock on the target, my words meant to be the dagger that wounds the man I hold responsible for repressed memories and lost time—"I don't think Baldur is too upset about being a timekeeper or having Hel as his company." I begin to see red as anger continues to boil within me. "So…what? You saw an opportunity to obtain undeserved knowledge and took advantage of an overbearing mother whose selfishness kept her from letting her son make his own choices and follow his own path? All for your own benefit of bottomless knowledge? To do what with?"

"Don't forget what comes with such knowledge." He grins with a glint in his eye.

"The last thing you deserve is any sort of power." My eyes narrow, and my jaw clenches tight. The muscles in my neck spasm from the strain of my outrage.

"That's not up for you to decide, son."

"I am not your son. Maybe by blood, but not—" I'm unable to finish spitting my thoughts at him before he interrupts.

"No, actually you're right. You indeed aren't my son. That's the other thing I can't wait to stop having to do. Kidnapping has gotten so much more difficult as time passes, and technology gets better."

Leo groans and sighs as if the act is as monotonous and annoying as taking out the trash. He examines his nails on the hand not attached to Mercy, as if bothered with having to explain himself. "It was truly getting exhausting. But, thankfully, this recent time required no kidnapping at all, with you being reborn to two addicts. They voluntarily handed you over to me, thinking I could better provide for you. Fools."

I try again to pull away from the man who won't take his grubby hands off me, but I stop when I hear the click of the gun's safety release.

"Any last words to your friend here? Be grateful you're getting this moment. Had my original plan of having these fumbling idiots take her out in the shiny red sports car I bought them worked, you would never have had to cross paths with her again." He shoves a thumb in Mercy's direction. "You can blame them for the break of your human heart. I was going to have it spared," he says as if that makes up for everything.

"Just let her go, and I'll do whatever you want me to do," I plead. "Frigg wants Baldur, so give her Baldur. Give her me. I'm not sure how you plan on going about that, but whatever it is that you need to do, just do it. But spare Mercy. Spare Hel. Just take me."

My plea is dismissed with a wave of Leo's hand. We both know, deep down, that I will always find my way back to

Mercy, to Hel. Time has yet to prove otherwise, despite this false father's incessant convictions.

"Oh, Aiden. You know I can't do that. You know what she is. Who she is. The damning obstacle she becomes if I let her go this time. That's what these are for." He pulls dark, jagged stones from his pocket.

I look at Mercy's perplexed expression when Leo suggests this has happened before. Then my heart sinks at the fear in her eyes as she wonders what he intends to do with those stones of crystallized minerals, which are uncharacteristically vibrating with soul-sucking energy.

"If she's free, Baldur will be trapped down there, as he has been before, subject to her mercy." Leo can't help but smirk at the reference.

"I don't know why you think I was trapped down there with her. Why *he* was trapped down there with her," I correct myself.

"You can't tell me Baldur truly wanted to be there. Hel would never let him go, even if he ever came to his senses! She brainwashed him the second she had the chance to do so. Frigg wants back what she claims is hers, and I'm just helping her accomplish what she can't do on her own because she is not able to be here." The bastard puffs out his chest and lifts his chin to look down on me, his features twisting into an unnerving grin. "Which is where I come in, and becoming omniscient is my reward for doing so."

"And what about me? What happens to my soul when you destroy my vessel? Won't I just come back? After all, it's just a meat suit, as you like to call it. There is no way for you to separate Baldur from me. We are one and the same. You can kill me, but you'll kill him, too. Just to have the cycle start again. We cannot be separated without complete annihilation of both of us, which not only is impossible, but it wouldn't accomplish what Frigg wants from you," I snap, my eyes wild and challenging. I jut out my chin, jaw clenched and brows angled, staring down the man I once called my father, and sickened by that thought.

"Well, I did say you would finally stop reincarnating. I just didn't mention that your soul would return to its original state once I force one of these restructured stones down your throat. It's taken time, but I've finally figured out how to rework the chemical and molecular structure of these stones so that their newly manipulated vibrations will sever any connection between your energy and Baldur's," he gloats, grossly impressed with himself. "Why do you think I've kept this room off-limits to you all this time? I couldn't risk you screwing with my experiments." He deviously smiles, and I respond with a scoff.

"No longer will Baldur be bound to your soul, and what then what's left of yours will be left up to the universe. Considering all that rage burning inside you right now, I expect you'll just become an impressive addition to our galaxy. Perhaps, I'll have the chance to name you once you're amongst the other stars."

Leo shifts his gaze to look beyond me, at nothing. His lips are set in a tight line, as if he's pondering what he will name me once I'm nothing more than a fiery ball of gas. He quickly gives up and swats at the empty air in disregard. "I'll come up with something later."

I chance a quick glance at Mercy, whose eyes are fixed on me. Her panic seems to be changing to a state of numbness as I watch her lose the fight to keep from disassociating.

"And Mercy? Is that your plan for her, too? Shove those stupid rocks down her throat to separate her from Hel?"

I chance another glance to check on Mercy, and the sight of her terrifies me. It's not the blood that trickles from the gashes in her wrists and ankles, the scattered bruising all over her porcelain skin, or the labored breathing I can see from the shallow rise and fall of her chest that rattles me. No. It's the look in her eyes. A look of hopelessness and exhaustion from a continuous fight for life steadily dulls the vibrant blue of her eyes.

Stay with me, Mercy, I plead with my eyes. I need her to show me a sign that she has some drive left to fight, but all I find is emptiness in her gaze, as if even the thought of what those stones can do is enough to affect her.

"No, no, no, no. First off, these aren't just rocks. I made something special for her because I don't just intend to get rid of Mercy." A calculated smile deforms Leo's features into something of nightmares as he continues to explain his plan. "Once her and Hel's energies are separated, Mercy will die, and Hel will be trapped here, unable to return home to Helheim. Her energy will be forced to transform into nothing but a cloud of dark matter and dark energy, left to float in an unconscious state of existence for eternity."

Fuck that.

"Mercy, look at me," I beg her.

"I believe she is," my father chides. I ignore his ignorant remark.

"No. Mercy, I need you to truly look at me." My heart pounds faster as her chin lifts, and her distant gaze feebly begins to focus on me.

"Mercy, this might hurt. This might throw you for a bit of a mental loop, but I need you to trust me. I see your strength. I know you can do this." I put all my faith in an idea that is, without a doubt, risky. But I know that all I can do now is have faith that she is strong enough to come back to me without utterly losing that other part of herself.

Please. We need this to work. I'm going to need to rely on her to be strong enough to find that balance within herself again, to regain control of who she is as Mercy, after what I'm about to ask of her to do as Hel.

Mercy's eyes finally begin to show a bit of focus, and all I can do is hope she understands. "There you are. I see you. Nod if you are here with me—mind, body, and soul. I need to know, Mercy." I try to hide the urgency in my voice.

She blinks once and then nods. "Aiden?" My name on her lips just about breaks me.

"Do you trust me?" I would do anything to touch her right now, to comfort her, but I can't risk moving with the gun still at my back.

"Aiden, say your goodbyes, and let's get this show on the road," Leo barks, clearly suspicious.

"I trust you," Mercy says, her voice hoarse from tortured screams.

Tears well up in my eyes as my heart holds on to hope. But that hope is threatened by Leo, who has had enough of our back-and-forth.

He grabs Mercy by the upper arm in an effort to drag her back to her feet. "Enough is enough." He jolts Mercy upward in one harsh yank of her arm.

Her head snaps in my direction, eyes desperate for help. "Aiden!" Her scream is a raspy whisper. She fights against Leo's hold, writhing in his hands.

"Say goodbye!" Leo demands, holding Mercy in front of me, just out of reach.

I hold on to her with my stare and throw my trust to the universe. I speak the words I hope will save us, my eyes locked with hers, "You have shown me Mercy. It's time to give me Hel."

Mercy's look of complete confusion pierces my chest like a knife. *This has to work.*

"ENOUGH!" My father begins dragging Mercy away.

"Give me Hel, Mercy!" I yell and demand again before it's too late.

I can see panic start to take over her body and mind as she realizes what I'm asking her to do. "I don't know how." She weeps, and her distress is something I can no longer bear.

"GIVE. ME. HEL!" I roar at the top of my lungs, filled with fear and the doubt that begins to take over hope.

Suddenly, the temperature in the room drops a few degrees, and the dim lights begin to flicker. My breath catches in my throat, and my heart feels as if it stops briefly before it threatens to beat out of my chest.

CHAPTER 45
MERCY

The entire time Aiden and Leo argue with each other, I'm lost in my own head. Disassociation tries its best to settle in to protect me from this traumatic predicament in which I find myself. So while Aiden fights with Leo, I fight with myself. Fight with the voice in my head that seems to be conscious again. I fight with Hel.

What do I do?

Ha! This is exhausting. Finally asking for my advice now? After all these years. After denying me time and time again? Unbelievable.

What do you mean? I thought we were connecting. I—

You know. It started first with something small—as small and simple as taste buds aching for a taste of something salty, something sweet. You sought control, and so you found it by denying me that simple pleasure. That want...that need. You started by denying me—denying you—the right to eat.

I'm...sorry.

That denial kept transforming, and it grew stronger by the day. By denying me the right to eat, you discovered the key to a box of tools you used to manipulate and control every aspect of this life. Again and again, you denied me, acting as if this side of you—me—is worthy of nothing *but shame.*

I only ever wanted to be better. Be good enough. That's all it was. That's all it ever is. I swear.

You denied. Denied. Denied. Denied. Telling me to stop thinking I was worthy of anything. Telling me I wasn't capable of anything special—jack-of-all-trades and master of none. Convincing me to settle for what I had, to expect nothing more. Telling me to listen to those who "knew better" and to let them *tell* me *who I am.*

I needed help. I still need help. I'm sorry if I went about it the wrong way.

You denied. Denied. Denied. Denied. To a point I thought beyond repair. I've always been part of you, yet you pushed me away. Every time you looked in the mirror and caught a glimpse of me, you only saw me as some sort of nightmare. Continuously refused to see that I am a part of you.

It was easier that way. Expecting the worst. Thinking the worst. Fearful of failure. Full of doubt. My despair became too familiar—so familiar that I made it my home. I cared too much about the things I felt weren't fair. Couldn't help but focus on the details about myself that I hated. Gave my love to everyone but me, every piece of me scattered and spread thin. I focused only on loving others, leaving none for me…for you…for us. I see that now. Help me fix this.

You denied. Denied. Denied. Denied. Until I finally broke. I came to realize I would never be enough, and even then, I still tried.

I am here. I am here now. I see you now. I finally understand you better. Understand us *better. Understand* me.

You burned me from the inside out with all the words of self-hatred that you spoke—words you continue to use against me, even to this day, even when I do help.

My intentions weren't to—

When I burned from fatigue, you told me to run farther, push harder, suck it up, and try again. When my voice became too tired to fight, you scolded me for not speaking, but then hushed me if I did find the energy to speak if I had anything to say.

I—

You denied. Denied. Denied. Denied. My own fire used against me. That fire kept burning hotter, and ignorantly you let it consume me. Let it rage, let it burn, careless and not knowing I might turn to ash. What were you going to do with me? I always wondered but was too afraid to ask.

I was just looking for help. I've always been looking for some sort of relief. I swear I did accept you—that side of me. At least I thought I did…but I also thought—

So I stayed quiet and decided to finally play along and live solely by every negative feeling you shoved down my throat. Shame became my only source of motivation. I realized, in order to save myself from me—from you—I had to choose to bend and break. And instead of disappearing as I feared I would, I felt myself slowly go insane.

I never wanted you to disappear.

You burned me in search of perfection in everything I did. And though I kept on trying, in the end, you convinced me it was never good enough.

I reached out a hand, I swear! I begged for relief, for help—

Don't you remember, though? This game and dance we still seem to share? You may have reached out a hand, but you trained me to deny help. You trained me to ignore help. You trained me not to care. You allowed the pills to numb me—first, a pill to swallow and then one to place under the tongue. You tried and tried and tried until you tried every single fucking one.*

I'm sorry!

It's beyond apologies now. I'm exhausted. Instead of feeling sorry for yourself, how about we end this game today? Play one last round before coming to an end. This time, however, I'm not the one who will be silenced. This time, I call the shots. Let's see if you can handle all those thoughts you drowned me in—those negative thoughts you let plague this head.

Okay, I deserve that. Just…please. Please forgive me. Forgive me for everything I've ever done and everything I've said. I never meant to hurt you…hurt us…hurt me.

I will if you do as I ask. I'll help you so long as you—

I do! I allow you to take the lead.

Aiden and Leo's arguing continues as silence washes over me, and I feel as if I'm falling, even though I can feel the floor beneath my tortured body.

Okay, but first…I need you to get up.

I'm in and out of consciousness. The voice within my head is the only thing that's keeping me from completely giving up. Still, I feel weak and powerless—Leo's grip tightening with each second that passes certainly does not help. My knees continue to give beneath me, and the wires binding me cut deeper, both of which only further empower the doubt in my head.

I can't—

Get. Up.

I choke on the breath that keeps getting caught in my throat with each sob that rattles through my chest. Each sob that connects to past lies about myself that I personally concocted and convinced myself were true. Lies influenced by everyone else's truths, validating the warped versions of my own.

How could I have done this to myself?

Pathetic.

I squirm, trying to get up and fight against the bindings and Leo's hold. My shrill cry pierces the air as he grips tighter, forcing a searing pain to lash through me.

Ignore the physical pain. Get. Up.

I'm trying.

Not hard enough.

I try again, my breath coming out staggered. Then I hear his plea. Hear Aiden beg for me to look at him, to show him I'm still here—not physically, but mentally.

I am here.

I rally everything I can inside me. *This will not be how it ends. Not now. Not ever.*

Get up.

How? When you won't stop yelling at me when I'm down. How is that supposed to help?

How does it feel? Now, get up.

I'm trying.

Try harder.

I need actual *help.*

Don't you remember, though? You never wanted to be a burden; you always felt ashamed when asking for help. So show me. Show me what it is to try harder when you think you have nothing left to give. Show me you're not a burden.

I—

I won't listen to any more excuses. Now. Get. Up.

Dammit, I'm trying!

How does it feel when I lean in harder instead of supporting you? How does the weight feel in your chest when I tell you you're not doing enough, trying enough, being enough? You could just give up, and this will all finally end. Or for once…fucking fight it instead of accepting the poison that seeps its way through your head. Push back. Now. Get. UP!

I. AM. TRYING.

This battle between the two versions of me—Mercy and Hel—continues in my head. The voices rage in a final battle of this long, drawn-out war I've created within myself. It's exhausting and has me wondering if giving up would be in the best interest of everyone…including me.

And then something snaps within my soul.

I don't think you're hearing me. I said…get up! Get up! Get up! GET! UP!

Something stirs inside of me. I'm unsure of what it is, but I hold on to it blindly, in the belief it's what will save me in this final battle I fight inside my head.

Fuck this.

Warmth rushes through me first, and then an icy wave pursues it. There's a tingling in my limbs, as if an electrical current were running through me.

There you go. Now embrace me. Embrace us. Embrace yourself in all your entirety.

I…I do. I…I accept you. I…I accept us.

With conviction this time.

I accept me.

Finally. Good girl.

I'm rewarded with a comforting silence within my head to let it all sink in. But the silence is brief as the threat of what's to happen next weighs heavily in the moment.

Now, know that when you have doubt, you can call on me for confidence. When you feel weak, rely on me for strength. When you find yourself speechless, let me be the one to speak. I am you.

And you are me.

Let's take this fight outside this head.

"Give me Hel, Mercy!" Aiden's voice is both pained and demanding.

I listen to him. I listen to Hel. I stop denying myself and finally listen to me. I call on my confidence. I rally my built-up anger, anxieties, frustrations, and despair. Molding, bending, and twisting them into something that resembles a newfound inner strength. I feel myself become whole and at peace with who I am.

And I could cry for how good it feels.

That moment of peace stays for only three heartbeats, though, vanishing with a guttural scream that could rival that of a banshee as it erupts from the depths of my diaphragm. A sensation takes over my body as if lightning struck me and carved something deep in my bones.

There's a shift in balance within me as the side of me that is Hel completely takes control. I realize then that I've denied that side of myself for so long now that this new balancing act is clearly something I will need to work on in the future.

Because there *will* be a future for me. For all of me.

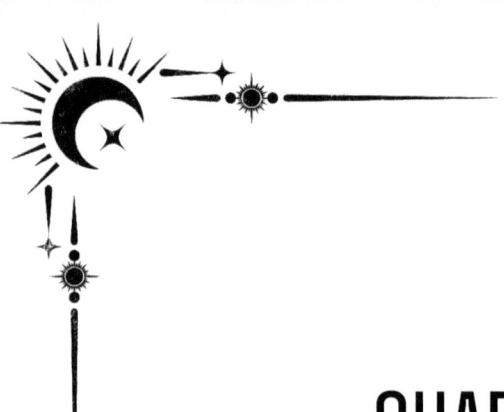

CHAPTER 46
AIDEN

"Take your filthy fucking hand off of me." Her voice is strong and clear, showing no signs of the pain and suffering she has been put through. When she turns to stare down at Leo, I release the breath caught in my lungs as I take in the vision before me.

Most of Mercy's face remains the same, but a hint of bone starts emerging on one side of it. Her skin starts to dissipate, exposing pieces of cheek and jawbone that appear to be engraved with intricately detailed sigils. Her eye on that same side flares silver, the black of her pupil muted to a barely visible grey.

Leo's face drains of all its color as panic and fear start to contort and dull his features. But as quickly as Mercy's transformation begins, it just as quickly starts to recede. Leo's ugly smirk replaces any sign of that brief terrified doubt that came with Hel's attempted appearance.

"You had me worried for a second," Leo says, forcing a rush of hot air through loose lips. "Then I remembered how weak you are in a vessel here, as opposed to when you're in Helheim," he spats at Hel before she's lost to Mercy again.

The insult ignites a fire in Mercy's soul, offering Hel the foothold needed to hold on a little longer. The price of maintaining Hel in the forefront is the loss of a significant amount of energy I watch drain from an already-pale face. But it helps her break free from Leo's hold and the binds that saw into her skin.

Once free, I watch in terrified awe as the goddess takes full control. The other half that is the physical Mercy is unable to come through at all; it is consumed by the side of her that has always been Hel. The consequences of unchecked balance—losing one side to the other.

Mercy—I mean, Hel—stands tall between Leo and me, her body at an angle so that she can glance at both Leo and me. When she does flash a glance at me, dark-blonde tendrils of hair whip across her face, appearing black in comparison to the rest of her hair that has taken on a silvery-white sheen—far lighter than it appeared when she made her grand entrance at the art exhibit.

Two different eyes—one, the iciest of blues; the other, now fully clouded by milky opalescence—fixate on me, paralyzing me in the spot where I stand. The only movements I'm capable of are the panicked rise and fall of my chest and the roaming of my eyes as I search for any sign that Mercy is still there.

"Mercy?" I'm barely able to speak. Her name is just a raspy whisper on my lips.

I don't see her, and my stomach plummets.

Hel refocuses on Leo and begins to speak. The sound of her voice remains the same, but unlike the sweet, meditative tone I'm used to—that's warm, a bit tentative, and inviting—her words march from her lips with a sense of power and defiance, commanding authority and demanding respect.

"*You.*" Hel cocks her head at a predatory angle, eyes glaring and an invisible string tugging at the corner of her lips. "You really think Frigg would gift you the knowledge your power-hungry ass is after in exchange for her son?" She lets loose a heartless laugh. "You don't think, the second she gets what she wants from you, she will discard you like the piece of trash you are?" With a single step, she closes the distance between herself and Leo. "You truly believe she would risk the consequences of fucking with the balance of things, more than she already has, by trying to control the outcome of her son's life?" She stands nose to nose with Leo now. "For *you*?"

I fight the urge to stand between the two, separate them, and simply trust that Hel has everything under control. Have to believe that she will not put herself—and therefore Mercy—at risk of attack.

Leo's only response to Hel's menacing stance is a failed attempt at hiding his fear. But I see it in every clench of his shaking fists. He tries to look down at her—his glasses balancing on the tip of his nose—in a poor attempt to rattle the goddess who stands before him.

Though she be but little, she is fierce, I think to myself, and my racing heart calms just a bit.

"I'm honestly surprised you were able to come through," Leo tells Hel, trying his best to hide the shakiness in his voice.

I catch a flicker of movement in his line of sight, behind Hel. It has my pulse racing again, having lost all trust I ever had in Leo. *What does he have up his sleeve?*

"Why? Because you thought Mercy was weak? Broken?" Hel chuckles. "Broken doesn't always equal weak. For some, it's an opportunity for transformation. For change. For growth." Her chin held high, she looks Leo up and down with repugnance. "Not that you would know anything about that."

A haunting silence fills the air between them. Horror strikes when the silence is broken by a devilish grin that creeps across Leo's face as he snaps his fingers for the two lackeys I had momentarily forgotten about.

"Always be prepared," he says, his smile widening. "It's something I've learned throughout my many lifetimes." He takes a step back, creating room between Hel and him.

I watch as Hel doesn't hide the confusion that contorts her face. Then, out of the corner of my eye, I see what Leo is referring to before she does. In the grips of the two bastards who have been handling Leo's dirty work this whole time hangs a limp Henry and a dazed Tess.

No...

CHAPTER 47
MERCY

The nearly impenetrable strength with which Hel holds the forefront of my mind does not matter. The deal I made—to let her, and only her, come through in exchange for her confidence and power so that I can fight against Leo's hold and free myself from the biting bindings—is completely forgotten.

My body jolts, as it does when in a deep sleep I dream I am falling. Air rushes into my lungs with a panicked inhale and gasp that bursts from my spent body. And when I finally come to, a choked sob constricts the muscles in my chest, and my heart pounds wildly against its bodily cage. I collapse to my knees, hands pressing firmly into the hard floor beneath them. I drop my chin in surrender, fully aware of what I'm about to do. What I'm about to give up.

At the sight of Tess. At the sight of Henry. I have no choice. I do not hesitate. "I'll do it!" My voice does not falter, and it does not waver. For once, even with this physical side of me at the helm, I am confident in my decision about what

I must do. "Whatever it is you need of me, I accept my fate. I accept. I won't fight. Just let them go. *Please*," I grovel and beg, forcing down and ignoring the wild rage with which Hel bellows, demanding I fight back.

I can hear Aiden start to protest. I hear the fear in his voice. The urgency with which he begs me to take back what I just said. With the ogre and gremlin's hands full—holding up Tess and Henry—Aiden begins to close the distance between us, lunging to my side, no longer restrained by our captors.

Leo sucks a sharp breath through his teeth, shaking his head at me in pity. "Well, this is a bit of a shame. I really thought you were going to put up more of a fight. I was expecting I would have to do more convincing, so I—"

Leo's words are cut short as Aiden drops to a knee beside me and bends over my battered body, reaching to place his hands on my shoulders. But just as soon as his hands make contact with my bruised skin, I bolt to my feet and stumble to catch Tess before she hits the ground.

Everything happens so quickly.

Aiden snaps his attention back to Leo in disbelief and horror, his hands still reaching for me but claiming nothing but air. "What did you do?" His voice is both guttural and threatening.

"Like I was saying, I was expecting more of a fight. So I figured I'd be preemptive with my plan to force her hand." He sighs in a pathetic attempt to act as if he cares. "It's too bad. Looks like I poisoned her for nothing."

Poisoned? He poisoned Tess?

I'm on the floor, Tess collapsed in my arms, her failing body draped over my lap, her breathing shallow, her eyes finding mine. A waterfall of tears flows heavily from my bloodshot eyes, dripping onto Tess's face, mixing with the fresh blood that begins to trickle out of her nostrils and seep out of the corners of her mouth.

No.

No.

No.

No.

No.

"*No!*" I scream as her brows pinch together in a terrible combination of confusion, distress, and pain.

Time slows around me. Around us. And though I see life still in her eyes, I know it's faint. Her body becomes heavier in my arms with each shallow inhale she manages.

"Tess," I whisper, my voice cracking, "Tess, stay with me. Stay with me, please."

Everyone in the room remains silent. I feel Aiden beside me and can sense he is unsure of what to do. Leo stands just a few feet in front of us, his energy thrumming with toxicity while he observes what he has done, delighted that he's upheaved everyone's fate. The ogre and gremlin reposition themselves so that they now stand guarding the only exit, having left a knocked-out Henry in a heap on the cold, hard floor.

Tess blinks slowly, trying her best to focus her vision on me. "Mercy?" she calls out quietly, her voice gurgling on the blood that runs rivers of red from her mouth, staining her lips and pooling on my lap and the floor below her.

"I'm here, Tess. I am here." I rock both our bodies back and forth, my cheek pressing against hers. Her blood and my tears create a slippery mess that feels sticky when I finally pull my face away from hers to look at her again.

The confusion and distress that was on Tess's face mere moments ago are gone; they're replaced, first, by a brief moment of shock, and then they quickly transform into something I can only describe as complete serenity. Her hazel eyes look over my shoulder instead of at me, and the corners of her bloodied lips lift slightly with the little energy she has left.

"Mom?" A joyful tear falls from her eyes. "Daddy?" she whispers, her voice hitching.

In my arms, she is both the woman I know she is today as well as the little girl who used to leap into her father's arms when he came home from work all those years ago. Her body is almost lifeless in my arms, causing my strained muscles to cramp and shake, but I refuse to let go.

"Tess?" My voice is barely a squeak as I scan my friend's face for any sign of hope that she can pull through this. I hold my breath as I see the faintest bit of light start to return to her eyes and feel the slightest amount of warmth return to her cold skin.

"Mercy…it's…o…kay," she begins to speak, each word a struggle for her. "My parents are here. I get to be with them now."

I fight back the sob that wants to purge itself from my system. "Tess, I—"

The little bit of light and warmth that had returned to her, I understand now, is just one last rush of adrenaline so she could say her goodbye.

"I'm going to be okay, Mercy," she says in a voice quiet enough that I would be surprised if anyone else in the room can hear her. "I promise," she reassures me with a smile and another glance over my shoulder.

My only response is salty tears that continue to drip down my face, mixed with soft whimpers as her body becomes limp and even heavier in my arms.

"Pr…promise…me some…something?"

"Anything, Tess. What do you need from me?" My grip tightens around her as I try somehow to squeeze the life back into her.

"Don't give up on yourself. Don't give up on your happiness."

I squeeze her tighter, unable to stop myself from rocking our bodies back and forth in a hopeless attempt to find comfort.

"You're...You're more than enough." I think I feel her smile weakly, but I don't see it because my face is buried in her mass of black curls. "You always have been."

No. Take me instead. This should be my *life taken, not Tess's.*

My fingers dig into her skin as if by holding on and not letting go, she can't slip away from me. Can't slip away from this world. Can't leave.

"I love you," I whisper, finally finding my voice, and weep.

"I love you, too. 'Til death..." Tess speaks her final words before letting loose a death rattle while lying in my arms, held tightly against my chest.

"And through eternity," I whisper into her hair, finishing the last bit of our promise to one another.

There is a subtle feeling of weightlessness that I at first imagine to be Tess's soul leaving her body, but then notice a cooling sensation that wraps its way around my arms. An ethereal calmness washes over me as I understand the feeling to be the phantom touch of another's arms supporting Tess in mine. Arms belonging to someone only Tess could see in her final moments.

With their support, I lower her lifeless frame to the floor in front of me, close her eyes, and mourn the thought that I'll never see their hazel color again. I lean over her, push back her crown of curls with trembling fingers, and place my lips on the cooling skin of her forehead. A final kiss goodbye.

"Well"—Leo claps his hands together in disrespect and complete disregard to the tragedy that just took place—"I suppose we should get this show on the road before you change your mind, and I'm forced to threaten the fate of your other friend over there." He jabs a thumb in the direction of a heavily sedated Henry, barely standing, held up solely by the support of Aiden, who carries most of Henry's weight on his shoulder.

"Don't you dare lay a single finger on—"

There is no time for Aiden to finish his threat. I give him none. I don't think twice before I completely hand myself over.

To Hel.

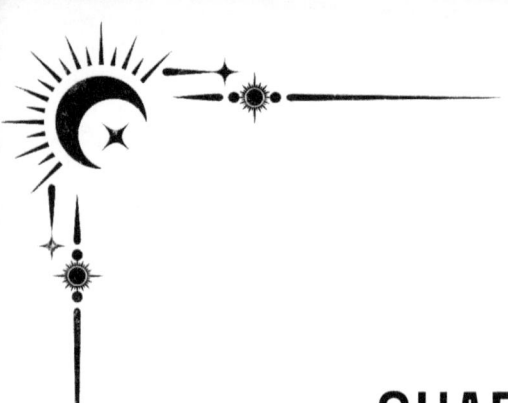

CHAPTER 48
MERCY

Numb. I don't want to feel a single thing. The part of me that feels sorrow, doubt, and worry. The part of me that has ruled my life since before I can even remember—for so long that I forgot there is more to me. More that makes me who I am. A whole other side of me I held prisoner in my own mind until recently. So I block a part of me completely—the part that had control for too long.

That innocent prisoner now roams free as I force that other side of me to take a seat. Stay silent. Breathe. And be happy to observe and hand over the reins. There is that feeling of being struck by lightning again, but this time it doesn't come as a surprise. If anything, I welcome it. Embrace it even.

"You're dead."

I feel my body bolt, eyes narrowing on the target just in front of me. One second, I'm on the floor by Tess's lifeless body. The next, my long fingers find themselves wrapped around Leo's neck. His frail skin, sagging with age and lack of fresh outside air, feels dry to my cold touch. I dig my nails deep into his paper-thin flesh, forcing him to stumble backward, ramming him into the wall made of concrete.

His head smacks into the concrete, bouncing from the impact. Glasses tumble off his nose to the floor, where the heel of my bare foot finds them. The shattered glass embeds itself in my heel, but it feels like nothing but a tickle. I marvel for a brief moment at my rage-driven strength, but snap out of it the second Leo spits blood and chuckles.

"That's fine, Hel. Do what you wish with me. Be the monster that the stories say you are. Why fight it at this point?"

My fingers dig deeper into his flesh, and I push him harder into the wall.

"Frigg will still fight to get what she wants, which means even if you kill me, I will come back again in the next life—better equipped this time—to find you again. To stop you from finding Aiden. From finding Baldur. To finally accomplish the task Frigg has given me. And, most importantly, to finally gain the knowledge and power I deserve."

My hand pushes into his throat, not to completely cut off his airway, but just enough so that the next words that come from his mouth are choked.

"Do it," he rasps. "The cycle will just begin again, as it always does." He chokes against the pressure I have on his windpipe. "So what if a delay to the plans is inconvenient?" He struggles to let out a breathy laugh. "It's just a delay, after all," he says grinning. "You know...a 'to be continued' type of scenario."

Rage consumes me, and I've had enough of his rambling. I blink twice to focus myself before opening my mouth to speak, "For so long, I have dealt with the consequences of stories told about me. Stories that have been twisted and manipulated over time to strip me of my true identity, my true self. Stories that have invoked fear in others. Stories that eventually turned me into a fictional character that took the form of an evil monster who wants nothing but to inflict pain and misery on those who reside in the realm I rule over. A monster who holds souls prisoner in a land of darkness and death. A place where only the wretched belong."

Leo squirms under the vise grip my fingers have around his neck.

"But *you* know the truth. *I* know the truth. Know that man corrupted the truth for selfish reasons. For power. Created the idea of heaven and hell, a good place and a bad place, to manipulate the narrative. Manipulate the truth."

Heartless laughter escapes me. "After all, fuck balance when you can have power. Right?" My head angles, tilting to the side just as a hawk would when targeting a threat. "Fuck balance and what that might do to the truth. How it might taint it. Ruin it. Disrupt the balance of existence as we know it."

"Everything in life has consequences," Leo snaps. "Everything comes with risks. How can we know what they are without challenging them? How do we progress without shaking things up a bit?"

"So that's how you justify this? I agree that challenging beliefs, challenging the balance of things, is needed for progress. But there is a line you do not cross. A line that, when crossed, threatens the destruction of everything. A line that, when crossed, forces the universe to right itself and enforce the consequences." A smile spreads across my face. "The universe always finds a way of restoring itself…of finding its balance again."

My chin lifts, and my neck extends forward so that my lips are only a breath away from Leo's ear. He then hears the last words he'll ever hear spoken sweetly from my mouth—Hel's mouth. "For you, Leo, and all that you represent...the universe sends me as your consequence."

With a tight smile, I shove into his mouth one of the stones he planned to use on me. He fights back, struggling against my hold on him, using his tongue to try to keep the smooth stone from being shoved down his throat. He manages to spit it out, but I catch it.

Adrenaline continues to flood through my system, and I use every ounce of it to pull him by the neck just far enough to ram his skull back into the wall to disorient him. With the force being almost enough to knock him out cold, I take advantage of his delirium and shove the stone into his mouth one more time. Then, with two fingers, I jam it into the back of his throat. I let him struggle to breathe for a few seconds before my hands find purchase on either side of his jaw and twist until I hear the fatal snap.

Deadweight drops to the floor as Leo's soul leaves the vessel as nothing but a cloud of dark energy left to float in an unconscious state of existence for eternity.

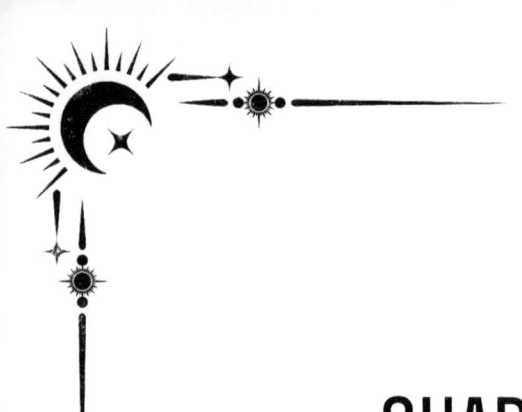

CHAPTER 49
AIDEN

While Hel has her way with Leo, I take advantage of the chaos and the paralyzing effect it has on Dumb and Dumber. They stand by the door to keep anyone from escaping, but they freeze in panic when their boss is thrown against the wall by Hel. The two idiots—fearing the wrath of the goddess—lose any ability to think straight, which gives me a chance to swipe the gun they had held at my back.

After forcing them to help prop Henry up against Leo's worktable in the corner of the room, I make one tie the other up with Mercy's bloodied bindings she discarded on the floor. Once satisfied that the bigger of the two isn't capable of going anywhere, I have the pleasure of taking the butt of the gun and striking the smaller one in the back of the head as he did me earlier. Then, I proceed to tie him up with his buddy.

The thud of Leo's body hitting the floor stops me from inflicting any more damage on the two. No one speaks, and all I can hear is the pounding of my heart and the heavy breathing coming from both Hel and me.

Slowly, the woman in front of me turns around to face me. One eye a vibrant blue, the other translucent and milky. No bone peeks through her skin, but a dark splattering of red is smeared across one side of her face. That smeared blood continues to darken the scattered golden tendrils that already appear black against the nearly white hair that flows freely down her back and over her shoulders.

"Mercy? Are you there? Are you okay?" Each question, I ask with caution.

She takes a few steps closer to me and stops, shoulders back but chin slightly dipped. "All I have ever been is Mercy…and it's exhausting." She sighs. "All he wanted was Mercy, and I was willing to give him exactly what he wanted. But"—she shifts her eyes to Tess's body on the floor and lingers there, refusing to look away—"there was no more left of Mercy for me to give."

Knowing there is nothing I can say at this moment to make things better, I motion for her to come to me, not wanting to leave the only way out unguarded—even though the two soon-to-be convicts lie immobile and bound by razor wire on the floor.

Behind her, with every other step, she leaves a trail of bloody footprints before finally collapsing into my arms. I hold her as she shakes, the impact of everything overwhelming her. I remain silent with her pressed against me, both arms wrapped around her, the gun still in my hand, pointing at the bound men.

I want to tell her everything will be okay, but with one look at Tess and another at Henry, who is still unconscious but breathing, I know that it would be a lie. So I say nothing and hold her while trying to wrap my mind around what we are going to do next.

We manage to get everyone up into the main area of the house—except for Leo, whom we decide to burn in the incinerator he conveniently happened to have for reasons I don't ever want to know. The fact that he lived off-the-grid—his entire life, as far as I know, in the liminal space—takes care of any need to make note of his existence and demise to the police. The whole process takes some time and plenty of breaks so that Mercy can catch her breath, but we manage.

While Hel is still in the forefront of her mind, we take advantage of the fear she instilled in the two bastards whom we refuse to name, referring to them still as the ogre and the gremlin, and threaten them both with the same fate as Leo were they not to confess to everything that has transpired—from that first attack on Mercy to the abduction of Tess and Henry, as well as the senseless murder of Tess.

Hours later, the police come, sirens wailing, and I swear John is trying to hide being upset that I indeed am not the one he is taking away in handcuffs. Two ambulances arrive quickly after the police pull into the driveway, hurrying an unconscious Henry off to the ICU on a stretcher, an oxygen mask strapped to his face. Tess's body is removed shortly after on a stretcher, but unlike Henry, inside a black body bag.

Mercy and I refuse the trip to the hospital, settling on being examined by medics at the house and cleared of any injuries that would require a hospital stay. We answer any questions the police have for us—giving as much detail as we can—and agree to speak more and answer further questions the following day at the station. Once satisfied with what we have to offer, the police ask us to pack a bag after informing us we are not able to stay in the house until all the evidence they can find is collected. We comply, and I pack a bag while Mercy loads Orthus and Void into Henry's car, which we end up taking back to her house.

That's where we are now, until given the okay to return to the home that has been turned into a crime scene. As soon as Mercy is certain that Void and Orthus are comfortable in her home, she takes one look at herself in the hallway mirror and asks if I want to take a shower. I follow her upstairs to her bathroom, with the intent of waiting for my turn to wash away the dried blood and trauma of everything that happened, only to be silently asked to join her under the water, by way of her tugging me along. The understanding is that she does not want to be alone—to be fair, neither do I.

With nothing but the sound of running water, we silently help each other scrub away any remnants of blood until the water is clear as it flows down the drain. When on our bodies nothing is left to scrub away physically, we slump down onto the shower floor, Mercy cradled in my lap with her head resting in the crook of my neck. The only words shared between us are when I ask if the water is too hot after I see her skin turn bright red as the water pelts us from above. Her response is just a subtle shake of the head.

We stay until the water runs cold.

Everything seems to have happened in the blink of an eye. But looking back now as I sprawl out on Mercy's couch, her fighting sleep in my arms, while everything was unfolding, it felt as if it lasted the span of an entire lifetime. Felt as if we were stuck in slow motion while the world around us zoomed by.

Mercy fidgets while on top of me, almost as if trying to burrow into me for warmth or comfort—probably both.

Her body shivers slightly, and I'm not sure if it's from her hair still being damp or from shock, so I reach for the blanket draped over the back of the couch and pull it over us.

"I don't know what to do," I hear her mutter against my chest. "I don't know how to feel." Tears fall from her eyes and drip onto my skin.

"I know," is the only answer I can come up with. What else can I say that would make things better? Nothing. And the fact of the matter is that I feel the same way.

"One day at a time. We will take it one day at a time. Together." The only truth I can offer her at this moment.

After a bit of time passes, I notice Mercy's breathing is steady. I crane my neck and see that her eyes are closed. I look over at Orthus and Void, who—very uncharacteristically—are curled up together on the love seat across from us, both exhausted from the day's traumatic events.

I figure I should take us up to bed, not caring and unsure of what time it might be, knowing whatever sleep either of us can manage will be helpful. I try to lift Mercy without waking her but fail. She stirs and lets out a quiet groan.

"I was going to carry you to bed."

"Thank you, strong man, but I can walk," she teases, catching me slightly off guard.

When she lifts her gaze to look at me, I wince. Reaching out to cup her face, I hover my thumb over the exposed cheekbone and stare into one eye of color and another…without.

"Hel?"

"I think…I think I'm stuck." Worry pinches her brows together.

"What do you mean?" Panic rises in my chest.

"I have no control over myself. Mercy spent so long denying the side of her that is me, that when I finally was accepted by her and called forth—"

I close my eyes and sigh out, "It was too much at once."

"I can't be at the forefront of our mind too long when I'm here, just as Mercy can't be at the forefront of our mind when in Helheim. It messes with the balance of everything both here and on the other side." Hel pauses and then adds quietly, "Threatens not just the continuation of existence, but the continuation of me…of us…that final sacrifice."

"What the fuck does that mean? I thought your sacrifice was becoming a timekeeper and binding your divine soul to someone whom you can share a vessel with to walk the Earth now and again when shit hits the ceiling?" My heartbeat quickens, and I can't help the bitterness in my rambling question.

"Yes, but there's more to it than just that. You and Baldur will go through the same thing…" Hel pauses, and a realization comes to her mid-thought. "Actually, you almost have done so already."

My eyes narrow as I tilt my head, trying to decipher what she means by that, but she continues before I can ask for any clarification.

"As you know, it's a choice we make when becoming timekeepers. And with that choice comes the first sacrifice of relinquishing the ability that allows us to return to our place of origin…as you know already. Which in turn denies us the ability to create a galaxy of our own one day. But we accept the fate of reincarnating for eternity when we permanently tie ourselves to another soul. We are happy becoming bound to the responsibility of maintaining the balance of the universe in whatever galaxy our shared soul resides."

She smiles. "There is no reward for our choice, as there does not need to be. But we know that going into it. Some of us are meant to create life, while some of us are meant to sustain it. Protect it."

"I don't understand, though. If Baldur and I are like you and Mercy, why doesn't he come through to me on occasion like you do?"

Hel sits up and places a cold hand on my face. "Because you do not war with each other as Mercy did with me. *You* accepted who you were from day one. Why else do you think you know the things that you do? Remember the lives that you've lived? Leo suppressed your memories to try and hide Baldur from you, but deep down your subconscious knew all along. Finding Mercy encouraged those memories to resurface...in your dreams and in those moments when you found yourself lost in thought."

My brain hurts from how complicated this all sounds, even though most of what she tells me isn't new to me. Hel notices and reacts with an airy laugh.

"That voice inside your head? Your intuition? You've accepted it so completely that you can't tell the difference between the voice that is one part of you and the voice that is the other—Baldur. By embracing that voice, embracing him, the two of you became seamless long ago. The only thing that has been holding you back—holding Baldur back—from making that final sacrifice...has been the absence of me, of Mercy."

She sighs and then adds with an eye roll, "Thanks to Leo and Frigg manipulating our lives throughout each lifetime, somehow, keeping our souls from the other side, and fast-tracking the next karmic cycle." Then with a bit more sadness laced in with her words, she whispers, "I can't remember the last time I saw Helheim...or Tarini."

I wonder for a second if Mercy's and my souls' lack of rest between cycles—and therefore Baldur's and Hel's lack of attendance in Helheim—has anything to do with my memory loss, or if that is what gave Leo the ability to infiltrate my mind with memory blocks to keep me from remembering Mercy. Thankfully, whatever the case is, it didn't seem to have that great of an effect on the divine sides of us. I can't imagine how frustrating that must have been for both Baldur and Hel. How lonely. Draining. Crushing.

"Wait... Are you going to just skip over the part where you explain to me what this mysterious final sacrifice is?"

"Like I said before. It's a sacrifice of self, Aiden. You don't experience Baldur in the way Mercy experiences me because your souls are already so intertwined. Had it not been for Leo suppressing your memories and constantly getting in between you and Mercy—and in turn, me—you would have already ascended by now."

"How is that a sacrifice, though?" I ask, not able to make complete sense of it all.

"You know this already. The sacrifice, if anything, has more to do with the divine's soul or energy. Once ascended, the divine has made the soul connection permanent. The two souls that share a vessel become so entwined that they will never be whole without the other. It's why I tell Mercy all the time that she and I are one and the same. I am her, and she is me. It's a level of vulnerability that's unsettling to even the strongest of us, knowing that we can't connect to another soul to save our own should anything catastrophic transpire."

"But our souls, they are energy. They cannot be destroyed, just transferred. So how would—" I begin to make an argument, but Hel stops me before I can finish, holding up a hand to stop me from spiraling.

"Don't forget about dark matter and dark energy. How it's created. It's not always just our emotions and thoughts that create them, but also damaged souls as well as corrupted ones."

I cringe at the idea of becoming what I believe to be the closest thing to what some people believe is the concept of death without an afterlife. The idea that once it's over, it's truly over. No reincarnating. No more chances at life. A fade to black…to nothingness.

"How do I help Mercy? How do I help you? How do I—" My hands drag down my face in mental exhaustion and frustration.

"Be there for her. It's as simple as that. Encourage her to accept herself. The person she is. Continue to reach out your hand, even when she's hesitant to take it. Walk beside her as she finds her own way, restores her inner balance, accepts the side of her that is me."

"What if that's not enough?"

"It has to be…or else."

I don't miss the flicker of fear in her features. "Or else… what?" I raise my brow at her.

"That catastrophic thing I just mentioned could happen. Would happen."

I look at her, eyes wide in impatience and the need for her to just spit out whatever it is she speaks of.

"The stronger of the two sides takes over completely, and with that, goes any sense of sanity. Unchecked balance is just as dangerous as unchecked power—both lead to a damaged soul."

CHAPTER 50
MERCY

I feel myself wake when Aiden moves beneath me, and I'm desperate to slip back to a state of unconsciousness in which I don't have to think or feel anything. The physical part of me has reached a limit beyond burnout.

Too much worrying. Too much caring about things I shouldn't. Too much dealing with emotions that for as long as I can remember overwhelm me and tear me down. Too much feeling I'm never enough. All those lies and negative thoughts have not only broken me, but they've officially exhausted me. And instead of healing at this point, all I want to do is feel numb.

As Mercy, I burned my entire life down. Burned myself out completely. Led myself to the person I am now, the one who is unable to find even the smallest flicker of a flame to fix the pain or even try. I need a break from being that side of me after all these years of struggling. As Mercy, I want to feel nothing, do nothing, be nothing.

I blink my eyes and decide it's time I lean more into who I am as Hel. Maybe not just lean…but give myself over to it entirely. And hope I will feel and be better as solely Hel for a while. It's time I let her take control. Not just embrace that part of me that is she, but actually be only Hel.

I was only ever a detriment to myself anyway.

For a brief moment, there is complete silence within my head. Neither voice speaks. Then a flicker of disappointment mixed with anger pulses through me, as one last thought is heard in my head before I numb the side of me that is hurting.

When will you learn?

XVI

THE TOWER

STAY CONNECTED

f C.B. O'Malley

◉ @cbomalley_author

♪ @c.b.omalley

FOR MORE INSIGHT & UPDATES ON THE NEXT BOOK IN THIS SERIES VISIT:

cbomalley.com